BACH'S
WORLD

Portrait of Johann Sebastian Bach (1746).
Painting by E. G. Hausmann. The Bettmann Archive, Inc.

BACH'S

WORLD

JAN CHIAPUSSO

GREENWOOD PRESS, PUBLISHERS
WESTPORT, CONNECTICUT

Library of Congress Cataloging in Publication Data

Chiapusso, Jan.
  Bach's world.

    Reprint of the ed. published by Indiana University
  Press, Bloomington.
    Bibliography: p.
    Includes index.
    1. Bach, Johann Sebastian, 1685-1750. I. Title.
  [ML410.B1C43 1980]   780'.92'4 [B]   79-20813
  ISBN 0-313-22139-1

All illustrations except the frontis, the reproduction from Buno's *Historia
Universalis*, and the list of ornaments are reproduced from *Auf den
Lebenswegen Johann Sebastian Bachs* by Werner Neumann (Berlin, 1953),
with the kind permission of the publisher Verlag der Nation.

Reprinted with the permission of Indiana University Press.

Reprinted in 1980 by Greenwood Press
A division of Congressional Information Service, Inc.
88 Post Road West, Westport, Connecticut 06881

Printed in the United States of America

10 9 8 7 6 5 4 3 2

To my wife Beulah and my pupil Rosalyn Tureck

CONTENTS

ILLUSTRATIONS

PREFACE

WERE the profusely explicit titles of former days still fashionable, this book might have been called "Bach's Education, Culture, and Philosophy as an Elucidation to his Art and its Problematic Place in the History of Music and of Culture in General." But the title I chose alludes to more than this. By "Bach's World" I mean first of all the metaphysical realm in which the master's mind chiefly dwelt. The title also suggests his social environment, in which he often found himself—knowingly or unknowingly—going against the currents of popular world views. Naturally Bach's musical composition occupies the most important place in his world, but all great art is a manifestation of the underlying world view of the artist, and so Bach's art will reflect and be nourished by his philosophy.

This book was not intended as a biography, but for an orderly and coherent presentation of the various phases of Bach's art and culture I chose to build the book around a biographical framework. At times, however, I have found it necessary to break the historical sequence to bring in pertinent general topics, as for instance, Bach's knowledge of history and the influence of Pietism.

The first endeavor of this book is to portray the mind of the master, his peculiarly anachronistic culture in an epoch moving rapidly from the Age of Faith to an era of science. The second, but not the least important aim has been to trace Bach's application of ancient philosophies—musical and theological—to musical equipment technically so much in advance of his time.

For many years scholars have been at variance about such "Bach problems" as his attitude toward instruments, his ornamentation, his symbolism, his use of secular music in church, and his borrowing of ecclesiastical music for secular purposes. I have tried to elucidate these various aspects of his art through examinations of ideologies implanted in Bach's mind during his formal education, of the theology that influenced every aspect of his life, of his general erudition, and of his philosophy of music.

I extend my expressions of gratitude to the University of Kansas, which has supported my endeavors in so many ways, with its skillful librarians, and its kind administrators, who have made it possible for me to spend much time at other great libraries in the United States. Among various scholars I feel indebted to are Mr. Austin Ledwith of the University of Kansas, who was the first to read and criticize my work helpfully. Mr. Paul Henry Lang read part of my manuscript and published my chapter on Bach's knowledge of history in *Musical Quarterly*. My friend, the naturalist Donald Culross Peattie, gave me his profound insight as a modern scientist into the historical significance of my subject. He also gave me valuable advice in choosing the proper person as an editor—of which almost any author today is in need. To Mr. Ross Robertson of Indiana University I owe the discovery of that rare person, Mrs. Eleanor McConnell. I also wish to thank Mrs. Lou Ann Brower, an editor at Indiana University Press, for her work.

JAN CHIAPUSSO

January, 1968
Vienna

BACH'S
WORLD

Introduction

A WORLD WITHOUT CHANGE: LUTHER TO BACH

MEN of many ages and temperaments have responded to the music of Bach. This lasting and universal quality of his music is due to its spiritual content and deep meaning as much as to its technical genius. Even twentieth-century man, with his scientific and rationalistic predisposition, has felt spiritual communion with the music of this artistic giant, although he can find no satisfactory modern explanation for his emotional response. In our particular intellectual culture we take delight in reading the passionate iconoclasms of Nietzsche or the witty sobriety of Bertrand Russell. Yet the voice of Bach's music seems to remind us that great art works contain more permanent substance than any form of discursive thinking. Upon listening to his greatest works—the *Magnificat*, the *Passacaglia*, or *The Art of the Fugue*, to name but a few—we surrender reverently to this voice of spiritual reality that speaks from strata of thought deeper and more immutable than any intellectual forms of communication.

The modern conflict between the intellect and this emotional response of total acceptance arises in part from the uneven flow of our culture. During the time of Bach man broke away from the Age of Faith and entered the Age of Reason with its accompanying rise of science. But many moderns have not quite recovered from the wounds of this cleavage, nor even completely achieved the divorce. The religious existentialism of modern thinkers—Unamuno, Jacques Maritain, Tillich, Niebuhr, and others—points to the uncertain relationship between our rational thinking and our spiritual intuition.

Bach lived during an epoch in which a new philosophy of rationalism

1

gained great popularity. In Leipzig he came into painful contact with the
new movement of the Enlightenment—painful, because his education
had not prepared him to evaluate it philosophically.

At the close of the seventeenth century, the dawn of the Enlightenment, young Johann Sebastian Bach was educated in a world view inherited from the Middle Ages. He lived in a period when the tides of
modernity seemed about to engulf the last areas of traditional culture;
nevertheless the postmedieval world of Martin Luther formed his pattern of life, thought, and work. Rationalist deism in all its fashionable
forms was foreign to him; the discoveries in the natural sciences did not
weaken his acceptance of traditional supernaturalism. Bach remained
untouched by the emancipation associated with the name of Frederick
the Great—though three years before his death he played before Frederick. Nor was Bach familiar with the writings of Voltaire (a sometime
guest of Frederick), nor with the revolutionary theories of Isaac Newton, who died one year before Bach created the St. Matthew Passion.

A study of Bach's education reveals the continuation and persistence
of Luther's conception of knowledge. Bach's cultural aims, his ignorance of science, and his historical perspective came from Luther himself. Traditional Lutheran views were the views of Bach. Although the
interim of two centuries between Luther and Bach had seen great scientific and philosophic innovations, which would eventually emancipate
man from the medieval view of himself as the center of the universe into
an uncertain new orientation, Bach was educated and inspired by the
same "unscientific" views that had fired the religious passion of Luther.
Bach was at least acquainted with the scientific contributions of Coper-
nicus and Kepler—as we learn from the contents of certain musicological books that he read. But he knew mostly the philosophical aspect of
their science, in which they appeared as traditional minds in the Age
of Faith. Though these thinkers gave a first momentum to the fall of the
geocentric doctrine, they were still in many respects traditional or even
medieval. They believed in astrology and in the Pythagorean harmony
of the spheres, in the biblical story of the Creation, in witchcraft and
other superstitions. During Bach's youth contemporary European scientific thinking had but slight influence in Germany. Very little of the
"new" science had yet penetrated the universities, much less the *Gymnasia*, the only schools that Bach attended.

In different eras education has had different objectives. In ancient
Greece, for example, its goal was to produce ideal citizens. Modern aims
in education have varied in emphasis: certainly great stress is now

placed on the acquisition of factual information for practical pursuits. In Bach's time, the aim of education was the same as it had been throughout the preceding Christian era; theology was its focal point. Bach's education laid the permanent foundation for his spiritual world view. It was therefore the strongest factor contributing to the formation of that art which he exercised (to quote his own words), "only for the Glory of God." To understand his education we must go back two centuries to the educational concepts of Martin Luther.

Knowledge of the classics and the study of history had made remarkable progress during the medieval Scholastic period and the early Renaissance. But Luther, zealous to revive Christianity's original simplicity of spontaneous faith, regarded the intellectualized religion of the Scholastics as an obstruction. The church, he claimed, had wandered far from Christianity's original intent when it embraced humanistic studies and called on the assistance of the "pagan and godless" Aristotle to justify its tenets.

At first Luther had the support of sympathetic humanists in his daring attacks on the church, among them Erasmus, Reuchlin, and von Hutten. Like Luther, they were opposed to scholasticism—but for very different reasons. When it became evident that Luther's antischolasticism was merely an aspect of his general mistrust of the human intellect, Erasmus withdrew his support. He feared that if Luther succeeded in excluding humanistic learning entirely, a return to the Dark Ages would ensue.

Luther soon had to modify his opposition to all humanistic studies. His stand against naturalistic philosophy remained firm, however: for Luther the Gospel was supranaturalistic and contained all truth and necessary knowledge. Pagan ethics he also considered an abomination, an arrogant denial of the Christian doctrine of divine grace. And the sciences, as Erasmus remarked, fell into ruin wherever Lutheranism prevailed.[1]

Luther and his close collaborator Melanchthon soon realized however that the neglect of the classics would inevitably lead to the decline of learning. In 1522 Melanchthon, with Luther's reluctant consent, restored the study of certain classical works, including those of Homer, Sophocles, and Demosthenes, for their linguistic and literary values. They were to remain servants of the all-important study of theology, however. "A thorough theology," wrote Melanchthon, "is impossible without philosophy and philology. If theology is not the beginning, the middle and the end of life, we cease being men; we return to the animal state." Later Melanchthon admitted that other subjects might have disciplinarian value and recommended grammar, dialectic and rhetoric (the medieval *trivium*); and physics, morals, psychology, history, mathematics, and astronomy (remnants of the *quadrivium*). These latter studies, called *Realien* (a term derived from the medieval *artes-reales*, or *quadrivium*), were concerned with the "special knowledge" to be found in the classics.

Luther in his zeal to restore pure Christianity was drawn very close to the culture and spirit of the Middle Ages. Truth meant illumination of the soul, which could be received only directly and mysteriously through the Holy Writ and by spontaneous faith. He regarded all discursive knowledge as a hindrance to revelation.

Luther's passionately antirational position had a destructive effect on German education. German schools of the sixteenth century, instead of advancing like the rest of Western Europe, tended to stagnate or even to regress into the Middle Ages. The only notable change in the university curriculum during the seventeenth century was the introduction of the study of Hebrew as an aid to the study of the Bible. Hitherto it had been studied only by individual scholars. The Greek as taught in the universities was not the classical but that of the New Testament. If a scholar strayed into the alluring world of Homer, he was likely to be reprimanded. Joachim Jungius (1587-1657) maintained that the Greek of the New Testament was not linguistically pure, whereupon the Hamburg clergy protested that this was an insult against the Holy Spirit who had written it.

The devastating Thirty Years' War (1618-1648) contributed markedly to the stagnation of learning in seventeenth-century Germany. It left Germany a disorganized and disunited area ruled over by some 300 independent princes. Not until the reign of Frederick the Great (1740-1786) did Germany begin its slow emergence from the feudal state and from its physical and mental regression. It was almost a century before Germany again had schools on a par with those of its neighboring countries who had fought on German soil. (The peace of Westphalia was concluded only 37 years before Bach's birth.)

The curriculum and the general plan of education in Bach's school differed little from those set up by Melanchthon over a century and a half earlier. Latin grammar was often studied before that of the mother tongue, although in this respect Bach benefited from a recent reform. Classical texts were studied for style and the methods of argument; Aristotle had been replaced by Cicero. The knowledge of physics, mathematics, medicine, geometry, cosmology, and other *realien* (or practical subjects) were still studied only from the ancient authors such as Pythagoras, Euclid, Galen, Ptolemy, or Boethius. Since Bach never attended a university, he was deprived even of this classical conception of science.

Luther's anti-intellectualism is very important to an understanding of Bach and his music. The antirational position, however untenable in itself, seems paradoxically to nurture the creation of great and profound music. Art, and especially music, seems to spring from other, perhaps hidden, strata of the religious and artistic mind than the discursive intellect. The ultimate flowering of German music may have been caused in part by the emphasis in German schools on the inner experience of faith over intellectual pursuits. Bach's music, arising out of his narrow, profoundly religious schooling, has been regarded as the highest artistic realization of the spirit of the Reformation—indeed of Christian culture as a whole.

The scientifically conditioned mind of the twentieth century is likely to see only the negative side of an education centered in theology. The old and the new theories of education do not clash over its purpose— which is gaining knowledge of reality—but in the conception each holds of reality. The positivist of today will say that only experimental and measurable facts lead to truth and reality; the Lutheran transcendentalist uses the spirit and inner illumination to find the true and real. Spiritual experiences were the only real experiences, and were the work of supreme reality, the Godhead, operating through the Holy Spirit. The aim of education in seventeenth-century Germany was to condition man for the cognizance of this all-important knowledge.

Which is the correct view? We are still faced with our inexplicable, moving response to Bach's music. His art is revered even if his philosophy is unacceptable. Can it be that our objections to the Lutheran system are not as valid and firm as we expect them to be? Or is it perhaps that Bach's music speaks so powerfully to us because despite our confident faith in the facts of the world, revealed to us by science, we are still uncertain of life's ultimate meaning? Still, we are living in a vastly different culture from Bach's and in order to begin to obtain a true perspective on the master and his works we must understand his cultural environment and his faith in the metaphysical purpose of life and art —in short we must discover Bach's World.

Nurture of the Spiritual Man

1

EARLY YEARS (1684-1703)

THE house of Bach's birth was an ancient structure in Eisenach. Its medieval interior, with red-brick floors, ceilings and walls ribbed with heavy wooden beams, doors of solid oak, and heavy furniture, is an early material suggestion of Bach's orientation to his life and work. In the room in which Sebastian was born in 1684 a portrait of robust Hans Sachs smiled down with clear blue eyes upon pious generations of *Spielleute*. A picture of Bach's father Ambrosius, doubtless painted in a room of that very house, also hangs there. The steep rock of the Wartburg, with its castle turrets reaching into the clouds, dominates the view from the study window and forms the background of the portrait. Ambrosius' face reveals a sturdy, jovial, healthy-looking burgher of good means; a certain pride of independence is expressed in his decision to be painted with flowing hair, and even a mustache, rather than in the conventional formal attire with wig.

Johann Sebastian grew up in the hospitable congeniality of the Bach clan, that famous family of musicians who for seven generations gave their musical services to towns, courts, and churches of Germany. Carl Philipp Emanuel, Johann Sebastian's famous son, vividly recalls their "happy contentment," their "cheery enjoyment of life," and their "clannish attachment to each other." Once a year the clan gathered from all parts of Germany, generally at Erfurt or Eisenach, and sometimes at Arnstadt. Musical frolics occupied a large part of the day's entertainment. These skillful musicians loved to extemporize a contrapuntal mixture of popular songs, called a *"quodlibet,"* which aroused uproarious laughter in listeners and performers alike. The skill necessary for such

8

polyphonic improvisation seems to have been taken for granted. The children must have been anxious to start creating such amusing combinations of melodies as soon as they could manage a clavier.

Sebastian's first teacher was his father Ambrosius (1645-1695), a musician of the court and town whose main skill, but most likely not his only one, was the violin. Ambrosius probably introduced his son to string instruments first, beginning with the smallest and easiest for a small child to handle, the violino piccolo. The boy later mastered the violin and the instrument he preferred to play as an adult, the viola. The viola player was seated in the middle of an ensemble and could best hear all the parts.

Young Johann Sebastian must have had his first experience of hearing—and perhaps touching—the organ at St. George's church in Eisenach where his second cousin Johann Christoph was organist from 1642 to 1703. (There were three Johann Christoph Bachs in the immediate vicinity, identified by their home city—Eisenach, Arnstadt, and Ohrdruf.) This Johann Christoph was certainly among the greatest of the musical ancestors of Johann Sebastian Bach and in later years he remembered him as *"ein profonder Componist."* One of his compositions, a motet, was long taken for one of Johann Sebastian's.[1]

The Gymnasium at Eisenach

At the age of about eight, in 1692 or 1693, Sebastian was first exposed to the stern discipline of formal schooling. Every day, in the early dawn, Sebastian walked to school to gain the grammatical preparation necessary for a gentleman's education. In midwinter the first class met at seven, and in the summer classes began at six. In those days of candlelight early rising and retiring was necessary, and the school hours did not seem as cruel as they now appear. Morning classes continued for three hours, to be resumed for two more in the afternoon.

A photograph of the *Gymnasium* at Eisenach[2] reveals a severe stone structure, three tall stories high, facing an ancient Dominican cloister-church so that its tall, narrow, Gothic windows opened onto a mass of forbidding walls rather than inviting the sunlight. The term *Gymnasium* then covered three kinds of Latin school,[3] including what we would now call a grade school, an intermediate school, roughly equivalent to our high school, and the more advanced school, similar to our college. Boys from five to 21 years old were enrolled in the same *Gymnasium*; not until the nineteenth century did the three types of school separate and each develop a different program of study and pedagogical approach. The rather flexible system of the seventeenth century had an advantage for a precocious student like Bach—he advanced at his own speed and showed a remarkably profound grasp of subjects at a very young age.

Following the custom of the day, young Sebastian learned to read and write in both German and Latin from the beginning. A recent reform in the teaching method had eased the students' task somewhat by presenting the subjects in a series of short sentences in parallel columns rather than requiring tedious memorization of rules and vocabulary. The subjects described were illustrated at the tops of the pages. With this inductive method the student proceeded from concrete examples to general rules.

Comenius (Johann Amos Komenský, 1592-1671), who instituted this reform, held that "knowledge is true when things are apprehended as they exist in reality."[4] He rejected thoughtless parroting of the classics and agreed with Montaigne and Rabelais that a pupil should be furnishd with knowledge of things rather than with mere words.

But the reform of Comenius affected only the method; his other ideas on education reflect a lingering medievalism. His popular aphorisms pinpoint the predominant philosophy of learning of that time: "universal knowledge, so far as it can be obtained by man, has as its object God, nature, and art;"[5] "The ultimate end of man is beyond this life. There are three stages in the preparation for eternity: to know one's self, and with one's self all things; to rule one's self; and to direct one's self to God."[6] Although physics is included in Bach's curriculum, the science taught Comenius' belief that the world was composed of the three elements of matter, spirit, and light; the "qualities" of all things were "consistence (salt!), oleosity (sulphur!), and aquosity (mercury!)."[7]

Comenius denounced classical literature and its pervasive influence in the world of scholarship and theology: "If we really want Christian schools, we must get rid of the heathen teachers. The principal schools of Christians confess Christ only by name; in truth Terence, Plautus, Cicero, Ovid, Catullus, Tibullus, Venus (sic!) and the Muses form their treasure and have their affection. That is why they are more at home in this world than in that of Christ, and that is why in the midst of Christianity hardly any Christians can be found. . . . our greatest savants, even among theologians, the trustees of Divine Wisdom, carry the mask of Christ, but have the blood and spirit of Aristotle and the rest of the heathenish flock."[8]

The sum total of Comenius' reform then amounts only to a more realistic method of teaching and a more humane attitude toward students. In fact, he was not rigidly followed in Bach's *Gymnasium*; several of the classics that were condemned by Comenius appear in his curriculum. These were carefully selected, of course, to avoid contradictions of theological doctrine. Latin remained the mainstay of study, and the reading material in German for the first year consisted of the Catechism, the Psalms, the Gospels, the Epistles, and Bible history, all of which were also read in Latin.

Sebastian's studies were interrupted after only two years by the deaths of his parents; in May, 1694, he lost his mother, and in January, 1695, his father was buried. The orphan, hardly 10 years old, and his older brother Johann Jacob were taken as apprentices into the house of their eldest brother Johann Christoph (1671-1721), organist in Ohrdruf.

Ohrdruf: Stepping-stone to a Musical Career

Ohrdruf, which derives its name from the shallow river Ohra, lies about 30 miles southeast of Eisenach. The small, walled town with a long feudal history is dominated by a medieval castle which boasts of an eighth-century origin, when Saint Boniface built an altar by a spring that still flows from St. Michael's Church into the river. In Bach's time marks of past cultures were evident in several buildings: a Renaissance *Rathaus*, a castle in Italian style, the gabled houses of the late Middle Ages, and the old *Klosterschule*, where Sebastian was to spend the next four years.

When Johann Christoph became organist at St. Michael's, the principal church in Ohrdruf, in 1690, he was 19 years old and had just completed a three-year apprenticeship under Johann Pachelbel (1653-1706) in Ehrfurt. Pachelbel himself had been influenced 12 years before by Sebastian's revered second cousin, Johann Christoph of Eisenach. These two had worked together from 1677 to 1678, when Pachelbel was 24 and Johann Christoph, at 34, was at his professional peak. Pachelbel's influence is clear in several of young Johann Sebastian's compositions.[9] Along with the music of the church, the young student was probably introduced to the easier movements of clavier suites by Pachelbel, Jakob

Froberger, Ferdinand Fischer, Johann Caspar Kerll, Dietrich Buxtehude, Bruhns, and Georg Böhm. Froberger (1616-1667), a favorite of young Bach, was the most brilliant pupil of the Roman composer Girolamo Frescobaldi, and surpassed his master in the composition of toccatas. We see traces of the freedom and improvisatory imagination of his style —which grew out of Italian, French, and English influences—in Bach's work.[10]

Bach responded with ardor and insatiable curiosity to the manner of musical training of his day. He was spared tiresome keyboard exercises and immediately introduced to the secrets of harmonic structure underlying and carrying the tune. He was able at once to try his own hand at making melodies, and this, combined with the arduous practice of copying the music he played (because of the scarcity of printed music), soon made him aware of his own creative powers. Like most enthusiastic children, Sebastian apparently was anxious to play more difficult music than his conservative master deemed wise. Sebastian succeeded in extracting the desired but forbidden music through the latticed front of the locked bookcase, and for many nights laboriously copied them by moonlight. For his diligence, the stern master did not praise him, but took away the manuscripts.[11] It is possible that the young genius was a rather unmanageable little fellow, with whom Johann Christoph did not quite know how to deal. The persistent stubbornness typical of Bach as an adult may have come out early. In any case, he showed unusual self-reliance for his age.

Sebastian entered the *Klosterschule*, which in medieval times had been an adjunct to the monastery with an inner school and an outer school reserved for laymen. Theology formed its main course of study then, as in Bach's time, and its discipline was notorious. During the Reformation when many of these schools were taken over by Protestants, they retained their ancient name of *Klosterschule* (cloister school). The terms *Gymnasium, lyceum, Klosterschule,* and *Particularschule* were freely interchanged by various writers at that time. Medieval methods of discipline were still condoned there in Bach's time and included all kinds of mental punishment as well as the rod—the use of which was usually delegated to one of the older students. Comenius and Reyer deserve credit for beginning a vigorous protest against these practices.

At first Bach's curriculum did not differ much from the one at Eisenach, but soon arithmetic and natural science, which included geography and history, were added. The instruction of arithmetic given students at the end of the Thirty Years' War had not progressed much beyond the requirements at the beginning of the sixteenth century—they were expected to achieve the ability to count, subtract, add, and calculate fractions in German, Latin, Greek, and Hebrew.[12] Knowledge of physics still came from the classics, unlike the universities where interest in new ideas on the science was growing.

Musical instruction, in conformity with Luther's view, took its place in the curriculum second only to theology. Very often theology and music were taught by the same master—as they were by the cantor in Bach's school—when the music teacher had studied theology at a university. Approximately one-fifth of the study time was taken with singing lessons, an equal amount devoted to theology, and the remainder was grudgingly divided among arithmetic, history, and geography.

At the age of 10 Sebastian began to study the rudiments of Greek. There are no signs, however, that he ever achieved his object of reading the New Testament in the original. Only one Greek textbook is mentioned during his school years in Ohrdruf, a moralistic work entitled the *Poiema Nouthetikon* or "Preceptive Poem" of Phocylides.[13]

Spitta states that in Bach's time in Ohrdruf the study of history "was entirely neglected,"[14] but this opinion, based upon the investigations of Johann Christian Rudloff, covers the curriculum only up to 1660. In 1685 and 1693 some changes were made and the new curricula included history in the plan of studies. Thomas quotes the school law by which "the *Historiae Universalis* of Buno and the geography [of the same author] shall be explained . . . and that furthermore Curtius and Terence shall be treated."[15] The study of history in Bach's time is treated in depth in Chapter 3.

At the age of 12 Sebastian was first introduced to the study of theology. Despite his erratic school attendance due to the death of both his parents, and despite the extreme thoroughness and harsh discipline of the times, this precocious student had progressed so fast that he had covered in four years material that normally took six. Bach's master in theology was the cantor Elias Herder (or Herda), a young man of 24 who had just finished theological work at the University of Jena. These studies completed his musical and theological work begun in Lüneburg, a school famous for its music. According to custom the cantors of the *Gymnasia* were held responsible for the instruction of other subjects, and Herder's inspired combination of music and theology may have been a deciding factor in Bach's career. At the end of his four years' study at the Ohrdruf *Gymnasium*, Bach seemed definitely "drawn, if not already dedicated, to the service of the sanctuary."[16] This kind master had just succeeded a harsh and sadistic cantor, Johann Heinrich Arnold, who is described in the town record of his dismissal as "the pest of the school, the scandal of the church, and the cancer of the State."[17] Had Bach been forced to suffer under this master, his musical talent might have been directed into secular channels.

During these four years Bach became a favorite with Herder,[18] who expressed his genuine and personal interest by obtaining a free scholarship in the famous school of Lüneburg for his student. Herder was well acquainted with the great opportunities of his alma mater: the large library, a flexible school curriculum well suited to a music student, its orthodox tenets, and its proximity to several centers of music such as Celle, Hamburg, and Lübeck, all promised rich rewards for an eager and talented student.

Sebastian's brother Johann Christoph had been married five years now, and his family was increasing with regularity. Sebastian's opportunity in Lüneburg was probably a welcome solution to the crowded conditions in his modest home. Bach's departure was duly explained in the school register: "*Luneburgum ob defectum hospitiorum se contulit die Martii 1700.*"[19] Thus Sebastian, together with another deserving student, Georg Erdmann, undertook the long journey to Lüneburg in March, 1700.

The Knight's Academy in Lüneburg (1700-1703)

The two vigorous and adventurous boys made the entire journey of 200 miles on foot, perhaps occasionally accepting a ride on a passing wagon, or on the stagecoach. Their destination, Lüneburg, was one of the oldest cities, dating from Carolingian times. Its prosperity during Hanseatic times had been undermined during the Thirty Years' War, and yet some of the city's monuments to the worldly and spiritual aspirations of past generations that young Bach came to know have survived to this day. The town hall, with its famous *Fürstensaal*, the Hall of Princes, shows wood carvings and stained glass of the thirteenth century. Its churches enclose Gothic vaults of the fourteenth and fifteenth centuries. A tenth-century chapel was still standing in Bach's time.

The ancient cloister buildings that housed the school where Bach finished his academic studies were attached to St. Michael's Church in a quadrangular cluster. During the Middle Ages the entire establishment had been a Benedictine abbey. In 1655 the *Klosterschule* was changed into a *Ritteracademie* (Knights' Academy), an institution born during the second half of the seventeenth century as a school of practical and fashionable education for young noblemen. There future rulers and military heroes became versed in the worldly *savoir faire* necessary at court, in political life, and on the battle field. Courtly and chivalric exercises in dancing, fencing, and riding, plus some knowledge of modern languages, fitted the requirements of the court. Roman law, state and feudal law, politics, and history that the young gentlemen studied there would later be applied to the serious business of managing their state affairs, while their military abilities were enhanced through the study of practical sciences such as mathematics, physics, optics or the science of sundials, ballistics, and geography. Genealogy and heraldry occupied a part of their historical studies. These mundane studies were supplemented with training in Latin, Greek, Hebrew, history, and theology, for the academy also prepared students for the university. The music school (*die Cantorei*) was famous in all of Germany.

In the academy the students had a certain amount of freedom in the choice of their subjects, and just what academic subjects Bach studied in Lüneburg is not definitely known, beyond the fact that he must have selected subjects pertinent to his chosen musical vocation. He undoubtedly continued his study of theology since in Lüneburg, as in Ohrdruf, the cantor taught both theology and music. Bach, who later collected a large theological library, surely would not have neglected this subject in the academy. Did Bach partake in classes in dancing, fencing, and riding? No one knows. He wrote numerous dances, but they are sublimated art forms rather than serviceable ballroom ditties. The young musician may have learned the steps that went along with the rhythms of his later suites; more likely, however, middle-class choristers did not mix with the sons of noblemen in these social or athletic exercises.

Bach's knowledge of French probably did not extend beyond the few French terms used in his suites. Names of dances, tempo indications (he uses the archaic French term *vîtement*), and the like were written in French, but this usage presupposes no more knowledge of the language than the use of conventional Italian terms does for the average musician today.

Even though Bach's music reveals unmistakable French influences, and he did include a preface to the Brandenburg Concerti written in immaculate French, we can be very certain that he did not study the language in school. He did not select a single French book for his own library. The formal style of the preface mentioned above suggests that one of Leopold's scribes actually composed it. Whatever conversations Bach might have had with Frederick the Great were undoubtedly conducted in German; all of Bach's business correspondence was in German. Anna Magdalena, his second wife, had some rudimentary knowledge of French; grammatical exercises are scribbled on the title page of her music notebook, but the Bachs' stay in Köthen ended shortly after these were written so that efforts to learn the language would soon have been abandoned. Bach never learned the fashionable language of the courts of his day.

Most of Bach's time at the *Ritteracademie* was taken up with musical studies, applied as well as theoretical. The scholarship that Cantor Herder secured for his student was given primarily on the strength of Bach's musical talent—chiefly his beautiful soprano voice and unfailing ability to read any part at first sight. Schools at that time were always eager to enhance the quality of their choirs.

St. Michael's Church choir, the *chorus symphoniacus*, totaled between 23 and 27 singers,[20] a larger number than usual for that time. Within this choir a select group of 13 to 18 boys, the Matins choir, performed the most difficult and the most important music. Especially gifted boys, who were generally given financial assistance in the form of either lodging or free meals, belonged to this group. Most of the choir boys dined at the *"Altfrau,"* the *"Viehmagd,"* or the *"Pförtners,"* established boarding houses in town.[21] Some, who tutored high-born families, had rooms on the top floor of the school building. The singers had ample opportunity to earn extra money by singing for weddings and other occasions.

These rather extensive professional activities (discussed at greater length in Chapter 4), combined with Bach's devoted efforts in his study of the keyboard instruments and composition, obviously left little time for a full program of academic studies. Nevertheless, the courses that Bach took in school had a lasting influence on his life and art. The content of the texts he studied provided an intellectual basis for his faith, and he often turned to them even long after he had left school. When Bach was an old man and an esteemed musician, he returned to the studies of his youth and these protected him from dangerous doubts raised by the increasingly popular rationalists. But perhaps more basic to an understanding of early influences on Bach the artist was the belief among all Bach's teachers that the purpose of all education was religious. This conviction dictated the choice of subjects to be studied and their content. And this belief in the divine purpose of all man's efforts, conveyed to Bach in so many, often subtle ways, transformed the talented schoolboy into a creative genius who accepted and achieved a monumental musical mission.

$$2$$

THEOLOGY IN THE CLASSROOM

THE religious focus of all of Bach's formal education deeply impressed him. Although we cannot be sure of the exact content or manner of presentation of theology in the Ohrdruf *Klosterschule* or the Lüneburg *Ritteracademie*, we do know in general about the nature of religious education in German schools of Bach's time. Theology was the primary emphasis of education in this age of faith, and Bach's attitude toward it holds the key to his religion, his conception of all cultural endeavors, history, and literature, and above all to his music.

Luther: Reformer and Sanctifier

The great authority Wilhelm Gass says of Protestant theology in the eighteenth century that "it is not easy to grasp the spirit, or even to touch upon it, so deep lies it hidden behind its bulwarks of various schools and traditions;"[1] its development seems particularly strange and difficult to the twentieth-century mind. Each of the many variants of the original Creed claimed to be the sole custodian of the true faith. Luther did not seek at the start to break with the spiritual intent of the Catholic faith, only to reform it. He attacked the abuses of the Church and the exclusive authority she had assumed over spiritual as well as secular matters. Essentially there was very little difference between Catholic and Lutheran Christianity. In fact, Luther regarded his revolt not so much as a reform as a restoration of the original faith of the fathers. His translation of the Bible into the German vernacular re-

turned the source of authoritative truth to the people and obviated the
need for any intermediary interpreter. He succeeded in this way in animating a rebirth and a deepening of individual religious experience.

Luther curtailed priestly authority by reducing the seven sacraments
to two—the Lord's Supper and Baptism.[2] The liturgy of the Eucharist
had to be revised since the ordained priest was no longer conceived of
as the sole agent endowed with the power to change the substance of
the bread and wine. In fact, Luther utterly denied the doctrine of transubstantiation, the idea that ordinary matter was changed into divine
spirit. The sacrament of the Holy Supper in Lutheran theology therefore became a ceremony of communion with the Spirit of Christ, which
any member of the fellowship of believers could administer. The importance of the rite lay in the state of mind of the participant, and Holy
Communion was taken only when the believer felt the inner need for it.
(Bach is reputed to have taken Communion, together with some of his
sons, about twice a year.)

All the manifold and subsequently developed tenets of Lutheran theology spring from one germinal idea: the assurance of redemption given
freely, without the mediation of a priest, by the grace of God. Man re-
ceives redemption only through his personal faith in God. He trusts
Christ fully to fulfill His promise of forgiveness because of the sinner's
true faith in Him. Luther quotes especially the Gospel of John and the
Epistles of Paul to support his interpretation.

Catholic doctrine holds that man is born in sin—original sin inherited
from Adam—and that faith alone can save him from damnation. Luther,
who had been an Augustinian monk, differed only in his new trust in
man's individual power, inherent in his faith. The Augustinian concept
of original sin comprehends all human strife, actions, and passions as
regarded by themselves and for their own ends; our very nature is isolated and estranged from God.

Just as the connotations and implications of this view of original sin
are limitless, so the concept of faith is capable of infinite expansion, as
Luther's passionate writings suggest. Luther's notion of faith is more
than just an alternative to doubt; it is a dynamic function of the soul,
"the act of faith," which puts man in touch with God—"just as iron
glows red in its union with fire," and "not only gives faith so much that
the soul becomes united with the divine word, but also with Christ, as
a bride with her bridegroom."[3] The Lutheran believed that the act of

faith would ultimately bring full spiritual revelation and complete freedom of "original sin" in death, conceived as eternal life. What the philosophers of a later period conceived as irrelevant to time and space is
represented by the dynamic imagination of religion in the form of an-
thropomorphic projections of deeper, inexpressible perspectives of truth.

Luther retained many medieval traits. He still believed in demons and
witches. But his superstitions did not form an essential part of his faith,
and however medieval Luther seemed in many respects, he was eman-
cipated from that age's conceptions of spirituality and showed himself
a true man of the Renaissance. Medieval man held that the life of the
spirit was entirely incompatible with human life. He severed himself
from life in order to pursue his faith: he lived in celibacy, withdrew into
a cloistered cell, and sometimes even vowed never to utter a word. Saint
Bernard, when crossing the Alps, covered his head lest he be moved by
the beauty of the earth. Luther, reinterpreting Saint Augustine, brought
about a reconciliation of nature with the spirit, of the finite with the
infinite, of the individual with the universal spirit. Life and nature were
again affirmed and accepted as expressions and manifestations of infin-
ity. Luther rejected celibacy and urged marriage for the clergy.

Above all by granting man the certainty of divine grace by faith,
Luther revived individual self-esteem and freed man from the bonds of
his physical existence. The promise of Christ, the promise of man's
exaltation as a reward for faith, replaces despair with joy. Man gains a
powerful sense of freedom in his identity with the spirit as divine universality, as supreme goodness.

Images of Christian mythology, not some rationalistic philosophy,
reveal the nature of faith to the religious soul, and the longing for death,
notwithstanding a healthier attitude toward life, remained a vital element in the Christian's thought. While to the modern's mind this longing can be seen only as symbolic, the Lutheran quite literally desired
death. The theme of his nostalgia occupies a large number of Bach's
cantatas: "Come Sweet Hour of Death"; "Oh World, I Must Leave
Thee"; "The Terror of the Grave and Death No More I Know"; "Sustain my heart by faith divine, that I in life and death be Thine"; "Give
Thy servants power and light . . . till that day when, through the grave,
death to Thee above shall call them"; and "with joy I see the gate of
death, for when the dreary journey is ended, there I'll find nor woe nor
grief, but joy and peace forever blended."

Luther's Followers: Scholastics and Compromisers

While Bach's simple, poetic utterances echo the essential kernel of Luther's faith, the work of the professional theologians in Bach's time was far from such unsophisticated interpretations. Even during Luther's life his intrinsically nonintellectual faith was fitted with extremely precise theological statements, partly due to the proliferation of sects and dissenters during the early decades of the Lutheran Reformation, and partly for political reasons. The Holy Roman Emperor, Charles V, would have been willing to use coercion against all heresies, but he was faced with opposition from the pope himself, and by rivalries among the Catholic princes in Germany, who might by acts of persecution have effected a strengthening of their enemy, the Hapsburgs. The result was compromise and ultimately recognition of the Lutheran faith. At the diet of Augsburg a peace treaty was drawn up in which Philipp Melanchthon (1497-1560), Luther's enthusiastic supporter and the first theologian of the faith, clearly defined the Lutheran position.

In the Augsburg Confession Melanchthon stressed with fine diplomacy the original accord between Catholicism and Lutheranism, but he stubbornly held to the position that the transubstantiation was a Catholic error, and he courageously defended Luther's idea of justification by faith. Writing under the guidance of Luther, his personal friend and collaborator, Melanchthon brought out the essential elements of Luther's ideas without becoming involved in scholastic jargon and metaphysical discussions of the ontological nature of God, the Trinity, and the existence of Christ before Creation. He considered such speculations futile and beyond man's understanding.

Dissension continued to grow, within Protestant sects in general and even among Lutherans. Theology evolved into a new form of scholasticism, with syllogisms to prove or disprove its various theses, and with divisions and subdivisions of concepts, cataloguing of errors, and so forth. Despite Luther's strong aversion to scholastic Aristotelianism, theological polemics, armed with the philosophical terminology of Descartes, Spinoza, and others, built an ultrarationalistic defense of basically unscientific and subjective religious opinion. This trend reflected the need at that time in history to define, redefine, and defend the state religion. The celebrated theologian Paul Gerhardt was employed by the

Elector of Saxony to settle dogmatic questions at Lutheran conventions during the seventeenth century in an attempt to form a supreme tribunal for the Lutheran state church.

Strife and bloodshed inevitably followed from this use of religion as a political tool. Never have men of God fought more viciously among themselves than did these sanctimonious doctrinaires. Few theologians, preachers, or hymn writers of the period escaped the humiliation of persecution, dismissal, even imprisonment, torture, and execution—always inflicted for clinging to doctrinal "errors" that appear to a non-sectarian observer as the acme of pedantry. Catholics and Protestants alike had Anabaptists drowned for denying the Trinity or for being baptized a second time. In Geneva, any who denied predestination, immortality, or the Trinity, could be burned alive or beheaded. Nikolaus Selnecker (1528-1592) induced the Elector August of Saxony to torture and imprison the Philippists. From this grew the Torgau Articles, a confession of faith in which Selnecker lay down a severely dogmatic and strictly Lutheran conception of the Last Supper. (Selnecker's hymns entered the standard repertoire of the Lutheran church, and many melodies of this zealot appear in Bach's cantatas and chorale-preludes.) Paradoxically, the Syncretists, followers of Calixtus who strove to end theological warfare by uniting all Christians in a common faith, were threatened in Denmark with capital punishment.

Indoctrination in the Classroom

Compared to this world of religious strife the classroom of young Sebastian appears a haven of peace. We can picture the intimate atmosphere of devotion in his theology class where the cantor-theologian taught with deep reverence and with respect for his unusually talented students. It is hard to imagine a more propitious situation for molding the mind of an artist destined to devote his life to the sanctuary. In addition, lessons in rhetoric and classical literature were planned to underline right religious doctrine.

Although educators included the classics in school curriculum for their rhetorical instruction, they could not resist using the material further to sharpen the dialectic wit of future defenders of the faith. The students also profited from the historical, dramatic, and mythological contents of their studies; the ancient historical source works will be discussed further in Chapter 3. The Latin works studied at the *Ritteracad-*

emie included Cicero's *De Inventione, Orations Against Cataline, De Officis,* and *Letters;* Eunuchus of Terence; the *Aeneid* of Virgil, the *Odes* of Horace; and the historical works of Quintus Curtius Rufus. Of the Greek works the students read only Cebes of Thebes and Phocylides' *Perceptive Poem,* which Bach had already studied in Ohrdruf.

Cebes of Thebes reflects in his *Pinax* on the course of human life, drawing on Stoic convictions that usually did not offend the Christian tradition. The poetic philosopher was not a disciple of Socrates, as scholars in Bach's time believed, but contemporary with Epictetus and Marcus Aurelius. Lutheran school teachers were pleased with his Platonic theory of pre-existence of the soul and his emphasis on education's role in character formation, which provided avenues for moral teaching in the rhetoric classroom.

Cicero was the major classical author studied at the *Ritteracademie.* Throughout the Middle Ages Cicero's *De Inventione* had been a main text for teaching the theory of writing and oratory. The involved, unnatural, and pompous prose the German language of Bach's time derived from the examples of Latin grammar and construction. German poetry of the period (and the libretti in quite a few of Bach's secular music-dramas and cantatas) followed the style of rhetorical adornment and mythological imagery of Latin examples. Bach was more likely to have been acquainted with the philosophical rather than the historical writings of Cicero, although we cannot be certain of his particular texts or exact course of study at the *Ritteracademie.* He had begun studying Cicero in Ohrdruf and it would have been out of character for him to leave his work unfinished; also, Luther in his *Table Talks,* which were found in Bach's library in two editions, praised and recommended Cicero, for his philosophy and ethics as well as his exemplary Latin. He far surpassed "that tiresome ass," Aristotle, who to him seemed but a heathen, wallowing "in worldly possessions and lazy days." In Cicero Luther found considerable sympathy for his ideas, and particularly for his strong distrust of reason.

In fact, Cicero appealed to almost every school of thought. Both Saint Augustine and his archenemy Pelagius quote from him for support of their ideas. He commanded the respect of the pagan Romans as well as of the pre-Christian Gnostics. Much of Cicero's philosophy contributed to the formulation of Christian thinking of Lutherans and Jesuits, and then rationalists like Voltaire based much of their enlightened deism on his writings. After the French Revolution Republicans quoted from his *Orations Against Cataline*.[4] The noble reflections in his *De Officis*—the work most likely to have been studied by Bach—on justice, generosity, love of truth, and the human appetite for power would be accepted by any serious school of thought.

The main interest in all these classical writings remained, however, in the rhetorical exercise and examples they offered. Bach gained final confirmation of his unwavering orthodox faith in his theology classes. The prescribed theological text was the *Compendium Locorum Theologicorum ex Scriptoris et Libro Concordiae Collectum*, or "Guide to the theological passages from the Sacred Scriptures and the Book of Concord," by Leonhard Hutter (1563-1616). This text, almost completely free of controversial and argumentative material, indoctrinated the young with Lutheran orthodoxy in the simplest manner, and with imperceptible gradations of difficulty. Hutter intended "to have the young imbibe, as with the mother's milk, the first elements of the purest Christian doctrine."[5] According to Wilhelm Gass, Hutter's *Compendium* actually is the purest and simplest exposition of the orthodox faith[6] but failed to make students aware of the historical evolution that had wrought this crystallization of the faith. So meticulous was Hutter in his search for pure Lutheranism that he even criticized Melanchthon and the Formula of Concord.[7]

In 1610, when controversy raged in Germany among various Protestant sects and the need for unity in the face of the powerful Catholic threat was great, Duke Christian II commissioned Hutter to write the *Compendium* in conformity with the Formula of Concord. The document also contains the official articles of the Lutheran church. In 1536 the first Formula of Concord was drawn up between the Lutherans and the Swiss Protestants, and at the same time a military alliance, the Smalkaldic League, was formed to combat the forces of Charles V. Three other attempts at agreement were made from 1573 to 1576, the last resulting in the Torgau articles of Selnecker. In 1582 the Formula was endorsed by signatures of several princes and by 8,000 ministers. But it was far from universally accepted. In many states it was still forbidden, and in Denmark and Sweden its followers were punished by death.

In Bach's time every educated Lutheran burgher knew the articles in this Formula by heart, thanks to Hutter. When Bach at the age of 38 applied for his post of cantor in Leipzig, he had to prove to his examiners that he knew it well, and he, and all other officials of the community, signed it as a pledge of faith. Following ancient school methods, Hutter demanded that the entire *Compendium* be memorized as a requirement for graduation. A quarto copy of 1855[8] contains 203 closely and finely printed pages; memorization was carefully spread over a number of years, with recitations taking place at regular intervals. Moreover, according to a custom dating from the Middle Ages, the students engaged in monthly disputation of the material covered during that period. Hutter's text presented each doctrine in the form of a thesis followed by an objection and its refutation, and a conclusive demonstration of the truth of the assertion by quotations from the Holy Writ. Thirty-four questions or *loci* comprise the entire Lutheran doctrine. They are arranged in order of their difficulty, from the definition of the Scriptures as the source and matrix of the truth through the Trinity, Christ, Providence, the concept of original sin, predestination, to the subjects of free will, justification, good works, the sacraments (especially the specifically Lutheran conception of the Last Supper), and finally, the conceptions of the Last Judgment and eternal life.

The dominant note, both in the Formula of Concord and in the catechism of Hutter is total surrender to God's will. Man's nature is completely corrupt and depraved when isolated from God's grace. Bach and his schoolmates, as well as generations before and after him, memorized these words from Hutter's *Compendium*: "How do you define the justification of man in relation to God? Justification is the work of God by which He absolves man from sin by grace or mercy, but only if man believes in Christ. Then He gives to him the remission of sins; and thus is the reckoning of Christ's justice that, when man is fully reconciled and received in the Son, he is liberated from the snare and suffering of sin, and enjoys eternal bliss."[9] And, "What are good works? They are the internal and outer actions divinely commanded and contained in the Decalogue (Ten Commandments): thus they may be done by the reborn in faith through the Holy Spirit, for the Glory of God, and for the purpose of declaring both our obedience and our gratitude to God."[10] . . . "It is not through our merits that we accept the grace of God, the remission of sins, justification and eternal life, but through faith."[11]

Throughout his discussion of the Holy Supper, Hutter was clearly more disturbed by the calvinistic tendency toward giving the human intellect supremacy over faith than by the corruption of the Catholic Church. Hence the good Lutheran watchword "*Lieber Katholik als Cal-*

vinistisch" (Better be Catholic than calvinistic).[12] And indeed the spirituality of Bach's music has more affinity to the basic irrationalism of the medieval church than to the rationalism of Calvin, Erasmus, and the eighteenth-century Enlightenment that aligned itself with Calvinism and Pietism. The reasons for the rich development of music on Catholic and Lutheran soil—and its impoverishment in calvinistic, Puritan, and rationalistic countries—are not merely exterior and ritualistic. Certainly music could not flourish either in churches that tolerated only untrained, congregational singing of psalms or sentimental hymns, or where Huldreich Zwingli (1484-1531) had banished music altogether. There was no religious occasion for which to compose music. But more significantly, the spirit of music is stifled in an environment of rationalism or of overly moralistic discipline. Music is mystic and Dionysian and feeds on intuition of divine and human nature rather than on reason—though it may employ reason for exterior tools of the métier. The living soul of music, however, is no more accessible to reason than is faith, love, or the essence of beauty.

Early in his education Bach probably accepted the Lutheran reconciliation of matter and spirit. God, and therefore Christ, became ubiquitous, even in the material world. Augustine's statement, "To enjoy is to cleave fast in the love of a thing for its own sake," was now shorn of its pessimism. The newborn individual, through his faith in the promise of Christ, is now able to remain a spiritual being without denying himself the pleasure of living. While the ultimate fulfillment, the complete identification with the ideal, is achieved in personal and physical resurrection in Heaven, the spirit of the Lutheran God pervades life on earth: morbidity is overcome by health.

This philosophy is the key to the understanding of many phases of Bach's art. His practice of incorporating so much secular music, dance music, and "Epicurean" music, to use Luther's favorite term, into his religious cantatas is perfectly consistent with the Lutheran conception of Christ's presence in nature. We can even relate his use of instruments in religious music to Luther's Augustinianism; while the organ was barely tolerated in Italy, composers from northern Germany frequently designated a variety of instruments for the music of the Mass. His spirituality and his continuous regeneration by faith form the substance of Bach's exalting art, and are the source of the endless stream of metaphysical yet utterly human music that flowed from his pen. He expresses his sincere and very real spiritual experience in his music, which was at all times in the service of his deity. To his pupils he often quoted the words of Erhard Niedt: "The sole purpose of harmony is the Glory of God; all other use is but idle jingling of Satan."

Bach's education avoided at all costs provoking resistance against supernatural conceptions. His theology served its magnificent purpose and Bach accepted it as the embodiment of ultimate truth. Although still significant and even efficacious for some, the old theology has lost its power to inspire the composition of great music. It remains as a philosophical symbol of bygone days while Bach's music lives, the object of universal appreciation, precisely because music is not bound to the intellectual framework, either theological or philosophical, of its creator. These scaffolds are temporal. Music remains alive to intuition, and Bach's art finds international response among those who are sensitive to metaphysical realities whatever their intellectual predispositions may be.

3

A LUTHERAN SENSE OF HISTORY

BACH's understanding of history is perhaps the best example of the theological focus of his intellectual life. Early in his life he accepted the premise that history was divinely guided. From this concept, basic to Bach's life and faith, we may gain an insight into his rather unconventional viewpoint on the philosophy and musical speculation of his time. But we become aware of the implications of this providential view of history only through the process of reconstruction. Bach does not tell us himself; he left no extensive correspondence on these subjects. Still by examining the sources of his knowledge of history—the classroom approach and texts of schools of his time—we can put together the fabric of his philosophy of history.

The study of history suffered more than any other humanistic study under the reactionary rule of Luther and Melanchthon. The scientific approach was totally abandoned. The great Renaissance historians—Guicciardini, Machiavelli, and Vasari, among others—had refused to relate every event solely to biblical history and sought the material and psychological causes as well. But their influence was not felt outside some very limited circles. During Bach's time their works had not been printed or translated from the Italian and they did not become available throughout Europe until the nineteenth century.

The German historians who followed the example of the humanists, relating secular events and rejecting classical fables and ecclesiastic legends—Ulrich von Hutten; Beatus Rhenanus, a disciple of Erasmus; Flacius; and Sleidanus—were all condemned by Luther and Melanchthon. Flacius was involved in a theological controversy that branded

him as an arch heretic. Melanchthon charged Sleidanus with being "unfit to be put into the hands of Protestant youth"[1] and regarded as rank
heresy his daring statement that the Protestant revolt was mainly a
political movement. For the same reasons, works of other historians
such as Seckendorf (a disciple of Sleidanus), Pufendorf, and Martin
Chemnitz (1522-1586), were kept from the students in the *Gymnasia*
through the protective vigilance of theologians, and theologian-
historians like Johannes Buno.

The Lutheran historian could not take seriously suggestions that, for
instance, the invention of printing had helped the spread of revolution,
or that taxation in the form of indulgences had added economic weight
to the success of Protestantism, or that the princes had ulterior motives
in seceding. For Bach and many others like him, history was a revelation of God's wisdom. The institutions of state, church, marriage of the
clergy, and especially the Christian dogma, were static and immutable,
and if mankind had been temporarily diverted from the right path, the
sins of particular individuals had caused the movement.

Article VII of the school regulations of 1685 of Ohrdruf's *Lyceum*
reads: "It would be useful if the *Historia Universalis* of Buno and the
Geography would be explained with it, and that Curtius as well as
Terence were treated."[2] In 1702 another regulation advocated the use
of Buno's text, mentioning the partial title: *Idea Universae historiae
Johannis Bunonis cum sacrae tum profanae idea. . . .* The edition with
this title was printed in Leipzig in 1700 and had been updated to 1694
by Buno.[3] Thomas reports that Buno's text was studied in *prima*, the
highest class, at Ohrdruf. Since Bach entered that class shortly after
July, 1699, and followed the course in general history until March,
1700, when he left for Lüneburg, he must have used an earlier edition,
either 1672 or 1692.[4] At the *Ritteracademie* of Lüneburg the study of
history took a prominent place in the curriculum but because the academy allowed a certain freedom in the choice of subjects, we cannot be
sure that Bach continued his historical studies there.

Buno's History

Johannes Buno, or Bunonus (1617-1697), whose name was really
Bonenberg, began his studies with theology, like most learned men of
his time. After a short period of tutoring sons of nobility, he became the
rector of the famous school of Lüneberg, where he taught history and

geography from 1653 until he crowned his career with the pastorship of
St. Michael's, the church in which Bach participated while a student.
Buno's popular books on history and geography were reprinted in Ger-
many several times between 1662 and 1705.

Historia Universalis is a curious document, biased but representative
of the educational methods of the seventeenth century. In the long title
Buno promises a "short, summary picture of the principal histories of
the world, ecclesiastic and secular, beginning with the creation of the
world, leading to the year 1671, represented in agreeable pictures,
clearly and concisely, so that adults as well as young people, and also
those not well versed in Latin, can easily understand and remember
it."[5] The book, like Hutter's, was meant to be memorized, and Buno invented all kinds of devices to aid the students in this task.

Following visual techniques introduced by Comenius, Buno drew
an ingenious series of pictures to go along with the text. Each of the
four millennia before the birth of Christ is represented by a quasi-
allegorical animal or object chosen by alphabetical order: an eagle
(*Adler*) and planks (*Bretter*) suggest the Ark and the boats that the

The Dragon, symbolizing the fourth millennium, in Johannes Buno's
Historiae Universalis, Lüneburg, 1672.

children of Noah built from it, a camel (C) brought to mind the Jew's mode of travel when they returned to Egypt. The fourth is a dragon (D). The centuries of the Christian era are represented in 17 pictures—including a Cerberus, a Griffin, Janus, and a pope—depicting a main characteristic of the period. Innumerable small pictures of historical personages are crowded into these drawings, and the student discovered an object with or near each of them, intended sometimes to remind him of the famous person's contribution to history, and sometimes merely to provide an amusing, mnemonic device. Ogyges, for instance, holds a fiddle, the German equivalent of which, *Geige*, sounds like his name. Two intertwined eels eating each other form a clever pun in German on Alexander the Great—"De Ahle essen 'nander."

Buno sees history from a narrowly Christian viewpoint, and as the following review of the content of *Historia Universalis* makes clear, he uses his subject to comfort doubters and confirm believers. In the 1672 edition a dedication in Latin assures the reader that the chief benefit drawn from the knowledge of history lies in its many lessons for Christians: History represents nothing but a demonstration of Christian truth (*Historia nihil repraesentat, quod Christianus*). Buno inscribes the title page of his book with the pious letters, I, N, J (*In Nomine Jesu*), a custom followed by many authors and composers including Bach.

Buno presents his material in a series of tales, another means of facilitating memorization. These tales explain historical developments in terms of the capacities of various individuals to act in a Christian way. Ideas and movements go unacknowledged; history gains importance only through its relevance to Christian living. Only Christians receive Buno's praise—praise based solely on the profession of true faith, or rather of the right creed. Despite this unscientific viewpoint, the seventeenth-century student did become thoroughly acquainted with a great number of historical facts, and because of the system of memorizing, monthly recitations, open disputations, and general examinations, probably retained them longer than the modern student.

Buno begins, as he states in his title, with Creation which he places in 4004, the generally accepted date. In the first picture we see Adam, who achieves the age of 930 years; Buno uses Genesis for his source here and the Bible continues to be his primary source throughout the work. Buno is not humble in his opinions; he states categorically that "nothing happened" in the sixth and tenth centuries. In the third millennium some secular history is recorded in a separate column, and from this point on the text is divided into three or more parallel columns: church history, secular history (a separate column given for each country), and an account of ancient authors that forms an excellent bibliography.

Church history is always treated in more detail than secular history. Most of the Church Fathers—Augustine, Saint Basil, Gregory of Nyssa, and Saint Ambrose among others—receive unlimited praise for their "glorious writings" (*herrliche Schriften*). The "errors" of heretics such as the Manicheans, the Montanists, the Pelagians, and the Arians are carefully described as are the blasphemous pretensions of Mohammed and his false theology. Emperor Augustus, however, is remembered solely because Christ was born during his reign, and Julius Caesar is barely mentioned. Cicero, the only "heathen" acceptable to Lutherans, is highly praised.

In spite of such glaring gaps in information, the history of Rome commands more attention than the more recent periods of the Middle Ages and the Renaissance, for German schools and universities of the seventeenth century characteristically based almost their entire body of knowledge upon classical literature and that of the Church Fathers. The discussions of most of the Roman emperors center around their dealings with Christians or Jews. Thus the only mention of Vespasian and his son Titus concerns their carrying the golden and silver vessels from the demolished temple of Jerusalem to the Temple of Peace in Rome. Similarly Emperor Hadrian is remembered because he rebuilt the temple of Jerusalem, and insulted the Jews by placing the image of a swine upon the temple wall.

After the Roman period several new columns appear in the text, but the emphasis remains on the history of the popes. Special columns are devoted to dry enumeration of Spanish, Italian, and English historical figures. Dates are quite inconspicuous, other than the lengths of reign of the various potentates, usually given with some mnemonic witticisms. After the Roman period the bibliography becomes considerably thinner. It is divided into ecclesiastic and secular literature, but secular "men of learning" such as Tacitus, Plutarch, Dion Chrysisthemus, Gellius, Lucian (called *der Spotter*, the Mocker), Suetonius, Athenaeus, Pausanias, and Ptolemy, and "Marcus Aurelius Antonius Philosophus" are merely listed.

A drawing of Janus, with his two faces symbolizing the growing hypocrisy of the church, introduces the ninth century. Church history and accounts of the German emperors now take the most prominent place in the narrative until the twelfth century. Buno does not use the familiar historical concepts such as Middle Ages, the Renaissance, or humanistic literature, since the only rebirth conceivable for a seventeenth-century Christian historian was that of the soul through his true faith in the Resurrection, or of the Church in its liberation from the Babylonian Captivity.

Gradually columns for the histories of Denmark, England, France, Spain, Bohemia, and Hungary are added. Buno treats Urban II extensively but mentions none of the complicated motives and politics surrounding the organizer of the first crusade. He does admit the disastrous results of the conquest.

Portuguese and Sicilian history are gradually brought in, and by the fourteenth century Turkish history begins to take a prominent role. Buno also considers the history of Switzerland now. Bibliographies and lists of learned men are abandoned at this point, and French, Dutch, German, and Turkish history dominate Buno's scene.

Buno's cursory treatment of Luther is more than offset by the excessive attention he gives to the arrogance and "errors" of the popes, particularly Julius II, Leo X, and Hadrian VI. The Thirty Years' War is treated superficially, although at some length. The figure of Louis XIV just enters the panorama before Buno ends his history "leading to the year 1671." He does relate Germany's recent wars with Hungary and the Turks, but neglects to say much about the development of numerous German principalities.

Ancient Josephus: Companion to Buno

Along with the text of Buno, Bach read a substantial amount of historical source material. Although *Orations* of Cicero was presented for its rhetorical example and theological implications, Bach undoubtedly gleaned some first-hand knowledge of Roman history from the writings of the ancient statesman.

Bach also had to read the life of Alexander the Great by Quintus Curtius Rufus. Historians today question the reliability of the author, but his book stands out among the gloomy and bigoted texts that dominated the school literature of Bach's *Gymnasium*. The refreshing tale of adventure and pagan times was favored by Reformation educators for its rhetorical bent and the author's Stoicism, but was undoubtedly enjoyed by students for other reasons. Alexander's romantic courage and reckless bravery, and the many frank tales of Oriental

license, indulgences at banquets with concubines, strange sexual relations and passing affairs of the hero, must have been a welcome diver-
sion for schoolboys, unless of course these passages were cautiously
expunged by a protective authority. With such a lively text, the students were probably not too much bothered by the moralistic ending
in which Alexander emerges as a repentant, ashamed soul. Curtius
pleased teachers and theologians for his rejection of the skepticism of
his god-despising age and his tendency toward a conception of universality in divine government.

The work of one ancient historian epitomized the providential conception of history—Flavius Josephus (c. 37 B.C.-95 A.D.). His writings
were regarded in the baroque era as the greatest historical document in all classical literature; Bach owned his complete works, and
most home libraries contained at least a Bible and a Josephus. Many
passages from his works were incorporated into the sermons of the
Protestant clergy of the day,[6] since the viewpoint made them eminently
suitable as commentaries of biblical passages. In fact, some passages
from Josephus support Christian theology so well that their authenticity has lately been under suspicion.[7] Josephus' very detailed description of the temple of Jerusalem[8] and his dramatic narration of its
destruction[9] were favorite topics for the pulpit, because they provided
an occasion for rereading the New Testament passages in which Jesus
predicted its fall.[10] Josephus' admonition that the Jews had caused their
own downfall by disregarding, among other things, the instructions
received in the Holy Script as to the prescribed architecture of their
temple was another appropriate issue for Lutherans. Daniel's predic-
tion of its destruction[11] affirmed the truth of Josephus' history in the
Lutheran mind.

Another attractive passage for Protestant preachers comes from
Flavius Josephus Against Apion. In an elaborate commentary on the law
of Moses, written in answer to Apion, the fifth-century leader of an
antisemitic movement under the protection of the Roman emperor
Caligula, Josephus says: "[T]hey calumniate Moses as an imposter and
deceiver, and pretend that our laws teach us wickedness but nothing
that is virtuous. . . . Moses did not make religion a part of virtue, but
he saw and he ordained other virtues to be parts of religion . . . for all
our actions and studies, and all our words have a reference to piety
toward God."[12] Heathen laws, in contrast, encourage good behavior
from habit rather than thoughtful obedience.

Along with his Hebrew theology Josephus gives the reader a great deal of detailed historical information, taking for granted extensive knowledge in general history and classical literature on the part of his audience. It seems safe to assume that to understand Josephus' works, Bach either read several other historical works after his school days— works suggested in Buno's text—or obtained some assistance from learned friends. He owned a 1544 German translation of Josephus. Very possibly Johann Matthias Gesner, the theologian, classical scholar, and historian whose company Bach enjoyed in Weimar from 1715 to 1717, and in Leipzig from 1730 to 1734, may have assisted the musician in his study of Josephus.[13]

Although Palestine is the center of interest in Josephus' works, both contemporary writers in the ancient world and modern-day students marvel at his erudition that ranged over a great many international historical facts. From these writings Bach gained a realistic and accurate picture of the Mediterranean world as it related to the history of the Holy Land. *Antiquities* traces the story of his people from the earliest times to the Jewish revolt against the Romans in 66 A.D. *The Wars of the Jews* continues and completes the study with the fall of Jerusalem and the destruction of the temple. The detailed story of Herod the Great, given in books XIV to XVII of *Antiquities* and I and II of *The Wars of the Jews*, tells much of Roman history. In his telling of Herod's visit to Rome Josephus provides a close view of the personality of Octavian Augustus, whom he describes as a wise, tolerant, and magnanimous man. Mark Antony, Julius Caesar, and particularly Cleopatra often enter the story; Cleopatra appears here in some interesting traffic with Herod.

According to his own *Life of Flavius Josephus*, the historian was more than a passive chronicler. He held the office of governor of Galilee in 66-67 A.D., while the purple was worn by Vespasian, whose son Titus was general of the Roman army garrisoned in Judea. In *The Wars of the Jews* Josephus describes a country torn by various factions, some revolutionary, and some, like the group to which he belonged, pacifist. On the basis of his conference in Rome with Nero's wife, Poppea, Josephus had an accurate estimate of Roman power, so tragically underrated by fellow Jews. When the Zealots under John of Gischala attacked the Romans, against Josephus' advice, Josephus was forced to join the patriotic forces and was captured by the Romans. He was generously treated and finally freed. In his history of the war Josephus blames the seditious patriots, and thus incurs the hatred of the Jews, who returned a counter charge of treason. *The Wars of the Jews*, written in his own defense, explains how the Jews brought on their defeat, and the demolition of their temple.

History and Creativity

Josephus, who presented history as a startling, factual realization of biblical prophecies, fully confirmed for Lutherans the truth of Buno's dictum that history is nothing but the demonstration of Christianity. From the standpoint of artistic creation such disregard for any "historical sense" may be regarded as good. Too much knowledge of his own cultural heritage often brings today's artist (either consciously or subconsciously) to a painful awareness of his own transcience. His fragmentary efforts seem doomed to be ephemeral when viewed against the long history of predecessors whose acceptance is constantly subject to critical questioning. For Bach the present was vital, full, sound, and purposeful; eternity was its glorified projection. Like historians, working during the Reformation, who ignored material, psychological, scientific, economic, and political causes and motivations of events in the evolution of human destiny, the musician had no curiosity for what we call the cultural background and conditioning of artistic endeavors. He was free in a way we can never be.

Bach could be completely indifferent to the integrity of past styles. His arrangement of Palestrina's *Missa sine nomine*, for example, is not *a capella* but with orchestration. He changed the Palestrinian tonality by adding sharps and flats, to bring the "old-fashioned" modality up to date and to close phrases with the "proper" cadences. He drastically altered the meter by means of bar lines, and arranged the words so that the accentuation would be as much as possible like that in his own works.[14] Today we would consider such treatment a violation of Palestrina's style. But music for Bach was not a museum of past art, to be kept musicologically and correctly mummified: it was a dynamic activity operating in the present and for the glory of a transcendental eternity.

Similarly Bach's providential conception of history is related to his stand in matters of musical speculation, an interpretation which in turn explains some of his stylistic characteristics. His indifference to the choice of particular instruments for the realization of his musical thought; his peculiar fusion of vocal and instrumental writing; and his fusion of secular and ecclesiastical styles, his occasional symbolism, and his conception of the general purpose of music are all related to his sense of a purposeful past and hopefulness for the future.

Did Bach's ideas evolve with the times? During his later life he witnessed the rejection of "antiquated" writers such as Athanasius Kircher and the innovation of theories under the influence of the Enlightenment. In his music he certainly was sensitive to change in the prevailing taste. In his memorandum of 1730 on well-regulated church music, submitted to the council of the town of Leipzig, he says: "Now the present *status musices* is quite different from what it was, its technique is so much more complex, and the public *gusto* so changed that old-fashioned music sounds strangely in our ears. Greater care must therefore be taken to obtain *subjecta* capable of satisfying the modern *gustum* in music . . ."[15] Although Bach was aware that taste in music was subject to constant fluctuation, he continued to regard philosophical ideas—which in his case were dominated by theological dogma—as static and immutable. From Johann Walther's book[16] Bach had the whole evolution of harmony from Zarlino (1517-1590) to his own time before him. Yet this did not prove to Bach that speculative ideas on music too were subject to change, especially if they were a direct expression of theological truth. The structure and style of music might change but its purpose was unchangeable.

Bach undoubtedly believed in the biblical tradition that the origin of music was Hebrew. How much importance he may have attached to the kind of Pythagorean mysticism found in the works of Niedt, Printz, and especially Werckmeister, is not known, but mystical implications of musical mathematics formed an integral part of his theological *Weltanschauung*. The most acceptable authorities available to Bach—acceptable for their orthodox conception of history—approved of the speculative ideas of Pythagoras. Josephus even asserts that Pythagoras received his knowledge from Jewish wisdom.

Bach thus referred to history even in the most specialized and technical aspects of his art. But his providential view of history, together with his confident theological position, are more important to us for gaining insight into the mind of a great artist than for explaining fully the idiosyncrasies of his compositions. Bach's optimism, buoyancy, and sense of purpose all emanate from the view of history and God taught to him. These personal qualities enabled Bach to endow his work with the profound spiritual tone that surpasses the significance of any unusual musical techniques or innovations he used.

MUSIC IN THE SCHOOLS

ALTHOUGH Bach spent a considerable part of his life at princely courts writing secular music, his heart was drawn irresistibly toward the Lutheran sanctuary, to which he devoted the last 27 years of his life. Music held an essentially spiritual meaning for him; it was a medium for reaching the depths of the soul. The Latin schools instilled this basic attitude toward music, for they still adhered to the Lutheran conceptions of the preceding centuries. During Bach's school years music was treated as one of the most important faculties within education.

Reformation of Church Music

Luther had attributed a semimagical quality to music, the power to convey ideas, to steer the will, to fortify faith. This evaluation of music can be traced back to Pythagoras and especially to Plato, who considered musical training "a more potent instrument than any other, because rhythm and harmony [melody, in the ancient sense] find their way into the inward places of the soul."[1] Luther says in his poem "*Frau Musica,*"

> For the divine Word and Truth
> She [Musica] makes the heart tranquil and receptive
> Thus Eliseus has confessed
> That by harping he found the Holy Spirit.[2]

The art of music was not the work of man, but a "most wonderful and glorious gift of God, which has the power to drive out Satan and to resist temptations and evil thoughts."[3] Medieval man valued music for its intellectual discipline; Luther was drawn to music more for its ability to move men to spiritual disciplines.

"I give, after theology, music the nearest *locum* and highest honor," Luther wrote of his school curriculum. The word *locus* in medieval school language is equivalent to a division in the plan of learning, but Luther used the term in its ancient sense of place, or classroom.[4] The far-reaching influence of this conception upon the subsequent development and the idealistic character of German music can hardly be underestimated. Without this vision of music as a spiritual power the world would never have known the genius of Bach or Beethoven.

This tradition is much older than the teachings of Luther. Even since Charlemagne in 789, at the Synod of Aix-la-Chapelle, established his school laws, the boys in the cloister schools were obliged to learn "the psalms, the chant, the Script, the reckoning of church festivities, and grammar from traditionally well-established manuscripts."[5] In Carolingian days music was regarded as the most important "discipline" in the school curriculum, but even earlier, in the seventh century, Isidore of Seville had said, "Nothing exists without her; for the world herself is composed of the harmony of sounds, and the Heaven moves itself according to the course of harmony,"[6] an observation obviously based on the Pythagorean conception that music is a part of the cosmic *harmonia* or proportion. Alcuin, Charlemagne's secretary and educational adviser, placed music among "the seven columns which carry the divine wisdom," and warned that "no one could reach comprehensive knowledge who does not elevate himself by means of these seven pillars or steps."[7] In the Middle Ages, of course, music was one of the arts, that is, a science, and its function was predominantly intellectual, speculative, and theoretical. In the *Gymnasia* of Bach's time musical practice flourished, and these schools became the laboratories that furnished the churches and court chapels with contrapuntal and figural music of the best and most modern composers of the age.

On the eve of the Reformation the church choirs consisted mainly of professional singers, remote from the populace. When Luther restored the original intimacy between the congregation and its ritual, he also reorganized the school choirs, a reform that along with the new Christian hymn and congregational singing became part of the communal liturgy, and formed the basic elements of the lofty art that found its consummation two centuries later.

Many of Luther's opinions on education have been recorded and preserved in his *Table Talks* and other documents. Luther looked upon persons lacking knowledge and skill in music with suspicion: "I do not feel satisfied with those who scorn music."[8] The teacher especially must know music: "A schoolmaster must be able to sing; otherwise, I won't acknowledge him."[9]

Music Among the Academic Disciplines

The earliest school laws, issued by Luther's disciples, Melanchthon and Johann Bugenhagen, set the pattern for numerous other regulations that followed with dogmatic fidelity in various towns and principalities all over Germany. In Braunschweig, Johann Bugenhagen laid down the basic law in a church ordinance of 1528:

the cantors . . . after the command and the will of your Rector must do school work like the other fellows. Moreover it is your particular duty that you teach singing to all children, old and young, learned or less so, to sing together in German and in Latin, moreover also figural music [concerted music] not only as is customary, but also, prospectively, in an artistic manner, so that the children learn to understand the voices, the clefs, and whatever else belongs to such music, so that they learn to sing dependably, purely in tune, etc. etc.[10]

Small details became universal laws, slavishly copied and obeyed in all the Christian (Protestant) lands. For instance, the hour assigned for singing practice came to be the first of the afternoon, presumably on the advice of German physicians, who believed that singing aided digestion.[11] Whether digestion was a help to singing seems not to have been considered. The boys had been under steady discipline since five o'clock in the morning, but school regulations relentlessly repeated the same law that Melanchthon and the Electorate of Saxony issued in 1538.[12] During the course of the seventeenth, and especially in the eighteenth century, this harsh rule began to be relaxed in many schools. But in Ohrdruf Bach still received his music lessons at the conventional hour,[13] five times a week, a considerable portion out of a total of 30 class hours. There is ample reason to believe, on the basis of Professor Junghans' research, that students met every day for music at Lüneberg also.[14] Although a school for noblemen, this former cloister school cultivated music more arduously than most German institutions of that time.

The singing lessons were designed entirely as a preparation for the elaborate church service, which used the most modern and difficult repertoire. The elaborate coloratura passages of the cantatas and motets designated for performance each week demanded a skill in sight-singing that is rarely found today, except among a few highly trained professionals. It certainly would be impossible today to gather a group of choir boys ranging in age from 11 to 23 who could meet the exacting requirements of the music and a master like Johann Sebastian Bach. Only an unshaken faith in the spiritual purpose of the art and a long tradition of adherence to rigid disciplines could produce such concerted musical dedication on the part of composers, teachers, and students.

Generally the choristers were divided in two groups according to the quality of their musical talent and the beauty of their voices. Those who had passed an examination in choral and figural singing were singled out for the performance of more difficult and important music. At Lüneburg Bach was admitted to the Matins choir, an elite group of 13 to 18 voices from the *chorus symphoniacus*, the entire student body of singers with 23 to 27 members.[15]

Cantors of seventeenth- and eighteenth-century choirs spent considerable time and effort seeking and selecting fine voices and musically gifted boys. Since almost all musical training took place in these *Gymnasia*, school choirs all counted among their graduates such famous musicians as Pachelbel, the numerous relatives and namesakes of Bach, Froberger, Reincken, Böhm, Mattheson, Buxtehude, Sweelinck, Handel, Schütz, and Telemann. The choirs were always small, the best ones numbering as few as two or three sopranos, the same or a smaller number of altos and tenors, and perhaps one or two more—if they were available—for the basses. If basses were lacking, a bass fiddle often was substituted.[16] A decree of 1581 reflects the selectiveness of the groups: "Whosoever is unmusical by nature, and who by his voice and singing proves that he cannot perceive harmonies is excluded from music."[17] These talented groups undoubtedly gave good performances in their weekly services, although they had to read their four-hour programs practically at first sight.

The students were always eager to earn an extra penny and the school authorities themselves aided their efforts by offering their students' services for weddings, funerals, and symposia (luncheons of various social and fraternal organizations). Often the cantor accompanied the students on these trips, and took no small share of the money received. In 1700, Bach's first year at Lüneburg, Junghans tells us that the cantor there got one-sixth of the proceeds,[18] leaving young Bach and each of his 22 fellow singers a little less than 14 marks for a season's effort. The boys became beggar-students on certain holidays, saints' days, and birthdays, and groups serenaded at the doors of prominent burghers. Between Martin's and Candlemas the singing companies even went from door to door, sometimes accompanied by instrumentalists. When they assisted in the performance of plays in public theaters, even the rector took a share of the proceeds.[19]

Music Theory in the *Gymnasia*

The reliable and practical musicianship that these young scholars displayed, whether performing church motets, madrigals, or *"Studentenschmauss"* (as Hermann Schein calls his collection of five-voiced student songs), could not have been acquired without a certain amount of theoretical preparation. Music theory, as taught in the *Gymnasia*, was focused primarily on achievement of the highly developed technique of sight-singing called solfeggio. The students were taught to sing intervals, to recognize all keys and sing all time values correctly and with absolute assurance. Textbooks by Otto Gibelius (1612-1682), Georg Falck (ca. 1630-1689), Nicolaus Lange (1659-1720), and the famous Wolfgang Caspar Printz (1641-1717) used during the period, all warn against yielding to the temptation of memorizing what should be read at sight; for repeated infractions the student might be dropped from the chorus.[20]

Quite systematically during the first half hour they were instructed in the *praecepta* or rules for intervals, clefs, rests, and the like, which they had to memorize. Their textbooks recited the rules and presented exercises, generally prefaced with edifying reflections on the lofty purpose of music or speculations on its origin. But strong emphasis on practical execution led cantors to strive more and more to simplify theoretical instruction, which had long been bound to medieval intellectualism and pedantry. Before Luther's time musical instruction at the universities was treated as a *scientia* or a *doctrina*, closely allied to mathematics, as part of the *quadrivium*. The Lutheran schools followed this approach to some extent, but did not sacrifice teaching musical performance. Gradually the venerable classics of the Middle Ages, Pythagoras and Boethius, were relegated to the classrooms of university lecturers, where true music sunk into oblivion. At least a part of this approach was carried over into the Lutheran *Gymnasia*, which still left instruction in composition entirely to private lessons.

A major contribution toward simplification of music theory was made in 1594 by Sethus Calvisius (1556-1625), the first Protestant cantor at the Thomas School (in Leipzig). *Compendium musicae practicae pro incipiendibus*, or Practical Handbook of Music for Beginners, is the first of a succession of textbooks aimed at improving practical execution. In his *Musicae artis, Praecepta nova et facielima per septem voces musicales* (1602), he replaced the old system that had been used since the eleventh century. Instead of the Guidonian hexichord system, which involved shifts from one six-tone system to another, he introduced a modern scale of seven tones, invented by Hubert Waelrant (1517-1595). Like our present-day system, he used syllables, in this case "bo, ce, di, ga, lo, ma, ni."[21] Instead of characterizing music as a science, he designates it as *ars*, a skill, a distinction which radically freed music from medieval rationalism. Calvisius' task was taken up by many other cantors; during the seventeenth century a new textbook appeared somewhere in Germany almost every other year. Admittedly most of these efforts were redundant and unoriginal, but simplification of musical theory definitely progressed through this process.

Considering its practical orientation, the Lutheran world was remarkably slow to adopt even Calvisius' simpler methods. The conservative school of Lüneburg still used a textbook of Henricus Faber (d. 1552), *Compendiolum Musicae pro Incipiendibus* (Handbook of Music for Beginners) in Bach's time. The students at Lüneburg used an edition of the 1548 text by Melchior Vulpius (ca. 1570-1615), with accompanying columns in the vernacular by M. Christoph Rid, printed in Jena in the year 1620. This book was considered important enough to be reissued several times—in 1624, 1636, and 1665—and furnished with a new translation by Adam Gumpelzhaimer (1559-1625). A typical late Renaissance work, the text deals with the ancient notation of pauses, besides the modes, the hexachords and their mutations; it even contains a picture of the Guidonian hand, a mnemonic device of counting the 19 notes on the joints and tips of the fingers, attributed to Guido of Arrezzo (995-1050). So Faber's music theory, along with Hutter's theology and Buno's history, kept Bach firmly bound within a conservative frame of reference.

The conservatism in music, however, does have some practical explanation, since the choirs often had to read music in the old notation. The library of St. Michael's, undoubtedly one of the most complete in the country,[22] possessed many sixteenth-century compositions for which modern editions were not available.[23] The choir had to sing directly from the outdated notation. The repertoire derived from the *Thesaurus Musicus* of Johann Montanus (d. 1563) and Ulrich Neuber (d. 1571)[24] and probably also from Georg Rhau (1488-1548),[25] and from sixteenth-century composers such as Orlando di Lasso (ca. 1532-1594) and Alexander Utendal (psalms of 1570). Modern notation and modern theory were certainly taught also, for the library kept an abundance of modern works. The music in this library was not kept primarily for reference, but for use in the service, and the students became thoroughly acquainted with those works. Bach must have known them well since, after his voice broke, he was probably employed as *praefect*, as assistant conductor, or at least as accompanist.[26]

Canonic singing, which was often practiced in several parts, presented another practical challenge to school boys. The student's score had only his own part printed on it, and this had to be shared by several boys. The young craftsmen had to be very sure of their pitch and intervals, as well as time values, to make their entrance without error. Faber's textbook contains instructions for singing in canons, which he calls by the Renaissance term, *fugae*. *Canon* then stood for either the sign of entrance or a rule governing the *fuga*. In the words of Johannes Tinctoris (ca. 1435-1511) *canon* is "A prescription which pronounces the will of the composer with a certain obscurity."[27] Hermann Finck (1527-1558) calls it "a prescription through which the unwritten part of a composition is called forth from the written."[28] In the several examples Faber includes in the text little signs that indicate the places for succeeding entrances.

If the sign of entrance is lacking, and the place of entrance is to be found by the singers themselves, a puzzle canon or riddle canon is used, a form which only seasoned contrapuntalists should attempt. When identical parts followed each other, beginning at different points but on the same pitch, the boys read the following instruction in their textbooks: *Fuga in unisono, id est, in eodem tono vel tono.* When the second singer was to repeat the melody a fourth higher, he would read: *Fuga in epidiatessaron vel hyperdiatessaron.* If he was to follow in the fourth below, he read *subdiatessaron*; if his answer was to be sung a fifth higher, he knew this by the term *epidiapente*, a fifth below by the term *subdiapente*. When Bach wrote his *Musical Offering* for Frederick the Great in 1747, he used some of these terms in medieval Greco-Latin for canons.

Vocal Quality in School Choirs

The hours spent studying tedious, obscure textbooks and memorizing endless details seems to have been effective, for this knowledge of music theory combined with rigorous practice produced choirs of young boys capable and skilled in performing the most difficult pieces. A glance at the repertoire of St. Michael's reveals a great number of Italian composers of the middle seventeenth century, including Tarquinio Merula (d. 1680); Claudio Monteverdi (1567-1643); Sabbatini, who flourished about 1665; Giovanni Andrea Bontempi [Angelini] (ca. 1624-1705); Antonio Bertali, the opera composer who lived in Vienna (1605-1669); Giacomo Carissimi (1605-1674); and many of their contemporaries. The style and texture of their music required lightness and ability to sing rapid passages, trills, and similar ornaments. Teachers of voice culture were probably not among the faculties of that period; but the cantors, who supervised and generally taught the choristers and had to cope with Italian style, were advised in various school decrees "gradually to accustom the students to agility."[29] Students and teachers could refer to Italian singing manuals now included in the school libraries for additional help. The library of the Thomas School, for instance, had a manual by Carissimi dated 1696.[30] Although musical taste in Lüneburg remained influenced by a severer style, dominated by the Dutchman Jan Pieterszoon Sweelinck (1562-1621), whose students were found all over north Germany, Italian singing methods for coloratura and ornamentation were gradually adopted all over Germany.

Bach's cantatas strikingly exemplify the full effect of the Italian style upon German singing and upon the texture of German church music; he demands part singing, *bel canto* legato singing, utmost control of the breath, rapid passages, and trills of his performers. But even in Lüneburg during Bach's school years, the repertoire was demanding more and more of these techniques. *Bel canto* (maintenance of an even quality of tone throughout all registers and a singing legato) became an esthetic need. The fullness and intensity of the modern tenor voice was not expected then, but lightness and agility of the voice were constantly being tested by the demands of the all-important baroque trill. Detailed singing manuals by Pier Francesco Tosi (ca. 1653/54-1732) and others leave no doubt that a singer's performance of the lighter, slower trill used during that epoch was a measure of the respect he should be accorded.

The artless candor and dispassionate coolness of the school choir boys suited the motets and Masses that rang from the choir loft. Female voice were not heard in churches until the end of the eighteenth century, and in Leipzig, not until 1800. In the Protestant church castrati were abhorred; men, therefore, often took recourse to falsetto singing—masters of which were called *falsetti* or *fistulanten*.[31] The "mixed quartets" of the day combined normal voices with *falsetti*. Often singers were able to sing both normally and with falsetto. Gesner, the preacher and close friend of Bach, relates Bach's ability to give the pitch to "this one in high, the next in low, and the third in middle register."[32] (Magister Vogel boasts of a similar talent in a written application for a position at Bach's Thomas Church in Leipzig.) Schering remarks that had the *B Minor Mass* been performed at the Catholic court chapel of Dresden, it would have been sung by castrati. In Leipzig, however, *falsetti* would have been used.

Instrumental Instruction

The schools usually owned instruments of various kinds; Junghans tells us that the neighboring *Johannisschule* (St. John's School) in Lüneburg in 1651 acquired a regal (portable organ), in 1653 a violin with six strings (probably a bass fiddle), and in 1659 a positiv (a small stationary organ) which was either a spinet, a virginal, or a harpsichord. The school also bought a lute, a pandura (similar to a guitar), a viola da gamba, a treble violin, a bass violin with five strings, a trombone, a Zinck (a high-sounding brass instrument), and three cymbala (tympani). But since the school followed the general custom of employing the ancient guilds, the Town Pipers and Art Fiddlers (*Stadtpfeiffer und Kunstgeiger*), to assist in church performances, the school probably did not offer lessons on these instruments to its students.

Michaeliskirch (St. Michael's), Bach's school, must have depended on some of the students to accompany the Matins choir in concerted pieces. In Bach's time the school owned strings, flutes, oboes, bassoons, trumpets, tympani, trombones, horns, and a tuba.[33] The instruments, of course, differed considerably from their present descendants.

Along with formal study and performance, Bach certainly took advantage of the rich treasures of the church libraries in Lüneburg; he obviously used many of the pieces studied there as models for his own creation. As *praefect* or accompanist, Bach had to study the works thoroughly and to intabulate them, that is, either spontaneously or in writing put the parts together in score form. He never ceased to study and adapt other men's masterpieces, as his creative work throughout his lifetime amply reveals. The emphasis on modern music performed at St. Michael's led Bach to model his earlier works after living composers like his organ teacher Georg Böhm (1661-1733), Böhm's teacher Johann Adam Reincken (1623-1722), the famous Dietrich Buxtehude of Lübeck (1637-1707), his elder brother Johann Christoph Bach of Eisenach, Christoph's teacher Johann Pachelbel, and Jakob Froberger.

5

THE EDUCATION OF AN ORGANIST

Georg Böhm

JOHANN SEBASTIAN easily excelled in his singing classes, and probably led his fellow pupils as a student conductor. His extant compositions of that period reveal his unusual ability on the keyboard. During his Lüneburg days, he developed a remarkable organ technique, under the guidance of Georg Böhm, the organist of St. John's Church in that city.

Several factors point to Bach's student relationship with Böhm, although we lack definite proof. The scores of Böhm and Bach have several distinctive characteristics in common.[1] The preludes of both incorporate long virtuoso introductions for pedals alone. The patterns of wide intervals in most of Bach's and Böhm's pedal solos demand that alternate footwork be used instead of the more common toe-heel sequence. The older organs were extremely difficult to play when additional stops were combined, but Bach and his mentor used this alternate footwork to overcome the instrument's resistance to the powerful registration that both desired.

Böhm revealed his interest in powerful sound—which Bach shared—in his list of 46 stops for installation on the new organ built under his supervision for St. John's in 1712. The pedals alone had 14 stops, six of which were of trumpet and trombone quality, plus additional 16- and 32-foot subbasses. This gigantic brass choir could indeed achieve the thundering, jovian power Böhm's virtuosic passages for pedal solo demanded. Bach never shared with his teacher the delight of playing on this instrument but knew only the extremely old organ, which dated from 1549. This instrument had only 29 stops, a very small number when compared with the instruments of Hamburg—St. Catherine's with 58 stops and St. Nicholas' with 61—and with St. Lambert's in Lüneburg with 59 stops and Lübeck's 54-stop instrument.

Bach's youthful enthusiasm for this sublimized form of virtuosity gradually subsided as he developed a mature style, and the virtuosic passage work of his later toccatas rises above merely powerful sound and speaks with eloquence of soaring spiritual realms. Other elements of Bach's early work suggest his admiration for Böhm's compositions, and the very texture as well as the form is comparable to Böhm's. In both, the thematic material is made up primarily of motives derived from triads. The form of Böhm's preludes and fugues (and also Bach's) retains a close relationship with the older style for toccata—use of rhapsodic passage work; rhetorical, recitative-like melodies; slow movements; and final fugues in lively tempo, generally ending in virtuoso passages. Böhm condensed this sequence based on the *sonata da chiesa*, or church sonata, into fewer movements than we find in the toccatas of Buxtehude, for instance, and Bach developed this shortened form even further.

The strong influence of French culture and French music extending over the territory of Brunswick from the francophile court of Celle left its mark upon Böhm's music. In fact, Bach probably learned more about French style from Böhm than he ever learned from his visits during the same period to Celle, where he heard an orchestra of French musicians. Böhm must have been well acquainted with French organ works, but features and manners of the style of French harpsichord and orchestral compositions are especially prominent in his own organ work. His recently discovered suites show strong French influence, and Johann Wolgast, the editor of these works,[2] believes that the *D Major Suite* is probably a transcription of parts taken from a French opera, a theory that is compatible with the prevailing custom of Böhm's time.

Tonality in Böhm's art reflects the French style, which was more free of modal residue than others.[3] He also shared the French penchant for abundant, and at times, excessive use of ornaments—*tremblements, pincées, ports de voix*, etc.[4] Böhm's chorale variations on *"Vater Unser im Himmelsreich"* is overladen with French *agrements*; hardly any note is spared the additional adornment of a trill or mordent. Bach's *C Minor Prelude and Fugue*, which dates from this period,[5] incorporates mordents (the French *pincé*) even in the pedal parts and is suggestive of Böhm's preferences. But while French organists did not mind transferring their courtly dances to the organ (as long as the notes instructed the organist to play in a more reverential tempo), for the most part, Böhm avoided this adaptation of worldly forms. Only in the work of Buxtehude, who composed some chorale variations in the form of French dances, does the secular intrude at all into baroque church music of Germany.

The most important musician in Lüneburg besides Böhm was Johann Jakob Loewe (1629-1703), who composed *synfonien, galliarden,* and similar old dance forms, and songs for solo voice—something of a novelty in these northern regions. We might surmise that Bach would have especially wanted to know this pupil of Heinrich Schütz, but instead Bach preferred the most recent and modern compositions, and Loewe at 72 did not inspire the budding 15-year-old musician. The dances of Loewe undoubtedly seemed antiquated to Bach, and their tonality and meter outmoded. Bach's Dance Suites show no affinity to his older style of the pavane and galliard. The young explorer was seeking the latest music, and every opportunity to learn more about organ technique.

Bach and Reincken

Lüneburg was relatively near several famous music centers. Hamburg, with a flourishing opera under Reinhard Keiser and some famous organs, was only 30 miles away. Böhm's former teacher, the venerable Johann Adam Reincken (who was 77 in 1700) was organist on the magnificent instrument at St. Catharine's Church there. Not much farther, in Lübeck, Buxtehude was in command of another of the finest and largest organs in the world. Celle, 60 miles in the opposite direction, was the home of a famous, almost entirely French musical assembly in the service of Duke Georg Wilhelm. Lübeck probably attracted Bach most, but unfortunately his visit there did not materialize until years later.

Bach did visit Hamburg, probably on the basis of an introduction to Reincken through Böhm. Thus the boy, now between 15 and 18 years of age, met a musical master older than Loewe but much more sensitive to the modern tendencies that Bach fervently sought and understood, in spite of his conservatism in all other matters.

No definite traces of Reincken's influence can be found in Bach's work of this early period. Some 20 years later he freely—indeed very freely—transcribed two of Reincken's sonatas, taken from his *"Hortus*

Musicus,"[6] the only work that was printed during Reincken's 99-year life. This group of suites may be performed either in church or in more worldly circles. Some have the character of the Italian *sonata da chiesa,* and the influence of Corelli (1653-1711) is quite apparent in them. Others fit the title of *sonata da camera.* All are written for string ensemble with a continuo part taken by the organ or harpsichord depending on whether or not it was performed for sacred occasions. In comparison to Bach's profoundly human music, the small number of Reincken's works that are extant seem rather cold and formal. His Chorale Variations on *"Wasserflüssen Babilons"* are elaborate and long, and demand great virtuosity from its performers. Although we must regret that too little of the famous musician's work is available today to form a meaningful judgment of his original work, Bach was probably more interested at this time in mastering the organ techniques required in his music than in delving into his compositional style. For the foundations of Bach's prodigious organ technique were laid during this period.

Bach's overriding interest in technique and registration probably meant that the chief attraction for him in Hamburg was not its composers but the 51-register organ of St. Catharine's Church, on which the great master performed his famous improvisations. Hamburg's church of St. Nicholas also boasted one the world's largest organs, with 61 stops. In his entire career Bach was never fortunate enough to have an organ at his disposal that compared with either of the Hamburg organs, or with Buxtehude's in Lübeck; undoubtedly he depended on memories of these early journeys for inspiration.

Journeys to a French Community

Fired with sacred enthusiasm, combined with insatiable curiosity and sure conviction of his purpose, Bach also tramped the rough and then dangerous road to Celle more than once. His way led through an unfriendly landscape of sandy regions and lonely marshes, varied only by tufts of heather and occasional clusters of birch emerging from brackish peat bogs. In the eighteenth century the roads were in such universally weather-beaten condition that traveling on foot, though more dangerous on account of robbers, was really not much slower or less comfortable than being tossed about in the stagecoach. Bizarre as this attire may have seemed on a pious musician, Bach chose to travel in the student's uniform of the *Ritteracademie*, including the traditional—and undoubtedly useful—sword on his side.

His student attire served as his passport into the exclusive court of Celle. As a rule the princely castles were inaccessible to the common man. But Celle distinguished itself as one of the most hospitable courts in Germany, especially to students, artists, and musicians. In a history of this "most Serene House" of Brunswick[7] we read that the "costume of a warrior, a *chasseur* [infantry officer] or a musician" insured easy admittance to its wearer. The predominance of nobility in a *Ritteracademie* contributed to this open attitude. Since Bach's name does not appear in the records as a member of the school orchestra which might have performed at Celle, we assume that this welcome was extended to commoner students as well.

The little court at Celle had a glamorous history. Duke Georg Wilhelm, who presided there, was jovial, generous, adventurous, and a lover of the arts. As a young man he was often criticized for preferring the pleasures of travel to political duties, and he frankly favored the gay spectacle of a Venetian carnival to the dreary landscape of his northern realm.

He enjoyed romantic love as well—Eleonore Desmier d'Olbreuse, one of the most beautiful women of Europe, a member of an exiled and impoverished Huguenot family. She followed the duke to Celle-Lüneburg, where she became his mistress until his brother's death cleared the political obstacles to her rights to succession. On their marriage she became the queen of her court and strongly influenced its character.

At the castle of Celle Bach observed French gallant life. Its population was predominantly French, for Eleonore d'Olbreuse had induced her husband to proclaim a special edict of protection in his territory for her compatriots and Huguenot exiles. She spent large sums for the erection and maintenance of churches in which the refugees could worship in their own creed. The entire entourage of the Duchess was French, including the personnel for the theater and the chapel orchestra. At the time Bach was in Celle only 2 out of the 14 instrumentalists were German. The art of the dance, which Eleonore loved above all, flourished in the Rococo ballroom as well as in ballet.

When Bach visited the court, so famous for its elegant gaiety, the shadow of deep tragedy enveloped the lives of the aged ducal pair. Their daughter Sophie-Dorothea was imprisoned in the dismal castle of Ahlden. The growing power of Eleonore had incurred the hatred of the

Hanoverian branch of the family. Sophie was wed against her will to her Hanoverian cousin, the future king of England. When he proved unfaithful with one mistress after another, her young and passionate heart yielded to the temptation of a true romance. The lovers' plans to elope were discovered, the lover murdered, and Sophie condemned to spend the rest of her life in the gloomy confinement of *Schloss Ahlden*. Only her mother was allowed to visit her throughout her 32 years of suffering. Horric de Beaucaire's history of the unfortunate family[8] relates that "after the affair of Sophie-Dorothea was concluded he [Duke Georg Wilhelm] took up his quiet existence dividing his time between politics, visits to Hanover, his days at Celle near Eleonore, and the chase, which always was his favorite relaxation." The opera troupe was disbanded,[9] and the family had no desire to attend the theater or ballet.

The small orchestra, *die Capelle*, continued its private concerts in this now strangely silent castle, and its members continued to receive salaries until the death of Duke Georg Wilhelm in 1705.[10] What type of music might Bach have heard this group perform? French concert music, independent of opera and ballet, was then still in its infancy, but at this time concerts of the music of Lully, Campra, Colasse, Destouches, and others became quite common. Such programs, usually introduced by an opera overture, marked the birth of the orchestral suite.[11] (The independent keyboard suite was already flourishing and Bach had played those of Böhm, Pachelbel, and Froberger.)[12]

The works of Jean-Baptiste Lully (1665-1743) were played most frequently in these concerts, since he was famous and revered by the French, and was also one of the most recent composers. Overtures from his operas frequently opened these concerts, followed by the music from his ballets, and *ballets comiques*, and possibly by some of his table music *(musique de table)*. Lully composed the latter for *les petits violins* of Louis XIV, a private band of 24 string players, intended for performance at some state occasions of the *Roi Soleil*. The music, now lost, was under the spell of dance forms and dance rhythms, like all French instrumental music. The prevailing custom of improvising melodic and rhythmic variations on the written melodies during these performances probably interested Bach far more than the substance of the music.

Besides these concerts the main function of the *Capelle* was the performance of the concerted Masses and motets for the duke and his wife in the little court-chapel. The ducal family attached great importance to religious exercises, especially in these sorrowful days, and they even

engaged a special organist for Sophie-Dorothea[13] in the castle of Ahlden.
The court-chapel was one of the most precious buildings within the
ducal estates, a happy melding of two religious traditions. Instead of
an empty, whitewashed building of calvinistic taste, that one might
expect in a Huguenot colony, the chapel was "a priceless miniature,"
with "winged altar, pulpit, organ, galleries, and *loges* a blaze of pictorial
decorations set in a golden frame."[14] The duke was still officially a
Lutheran and his place of worship reflects that religion. But Madame
d'Olbreuse must have been consulted during its construction for C. S.
Terry adds that it was "an unsurpassable epitome of the Dutch Renaissance."

The miniature organ, suspended at an angle from the lofty height of
the gallery above, was such "as Ste. Cecilia may have played." It was
fashioned after Italian instruments, with only 8 stops, and probably reflects the musical preference of Georg Wilhelm in his younger and more
carefree days. While the northern French organs of the seventeenth
century already had approached in character those of Germany and
Spain—with the exception of a very weak disposition in the pedals—the
Italian organs still resembled the small positives of the Renaissance.
The largest organs found in Italy, those of San Marco in Venice and of
St. Peter's in Rome, had only one manual and the pedals usually did
not encompass much more than an octave. The pedals, moreover, did
not even control their own sets of pipes, but merely borrowed their tone
from the ones controlled by the manual. In contrast to the German organs with their thundering 16- and 32-foot basses, the Italian organs
had no deeper tones than one single set of 8-foot open pipes, the rest of
the meager array of stops consisting of sweetly warbling octaves of 4-,
2-, and 1-foot tones above that one soft 8-foot diapason. A few pipes
produced high partials faintly reminiscent of the cymbals of the powerful north German organs, but true mixtures did not exist.

The cantor of the ducal chapel was a Frenchman named Louis Gaudon,[15] but little is known of the repertoire Bach might have heard, if he
was allowed to attend services in the chapel. No doubt Cantor Gaudon
chose the classical French repertoire, and possibly directed some Italian
motets. Bach probably did not admire the pompous Masses and motets
of Lully and Marc-Antoine Charpentier (1636?-1704) that were regarded as the best French church music. Largely cantatas composed for
chorus, solos, and an orchestra including strings, trumpets, and kettledrums, they were more suited to the glorification of the *Roi Soleil* than

to the needs of a simple Lutheran congregation. In Lully's motets fragments of the Gregorian chant are transformed by adjusting accidentals to a modern, almost secular setting; its rhythm is as regular and precise as in a court dance or an overture to an opera.

Only outward gestures of piety distinguished the church music of these worldlings from their musical parlor gallantries. They wrote in full and sonorous harmony—often using five voices—but missed the deep tone of spirituality the meaning of the music demands. Others followed Lully in subjecting Gregorian chants to pleasing, well-regulated, but inappropriate rhythms, and most composers intermingled court dances, played in slower tempo, with *Kyries, Offertories, Sancti,* and other parts of the sung Mass. The works of André Raison, for example, include a *Passacaglia in G Minor*[16] (that we shall compare later with Bach's monumental work in C minor using the same theme). Raison's work served only as an interlude between a series of *Kyries* derived from the Gregorian missal, and none of his Passacaille was longer than this pretty one of 27 measures. The little organ in the ducal chapel was perfectly suited to music of this limited scope.

When Bach incorporated secular elements such as dances, overtures, trumpets, and kettledrums in his later church music, he endowed them with the spiritual character of the entire work. Lully seems to do the reverse—interpreting spiritual elements in a secular, courtly, though stately and regal tone. He ornaments the medieval melody of the *Dies Irae,* for instance, with numerous trills and ornaments and transposes its somber modality into a bright major key.

Bach's disdain for the "flimsy contents" of these works did not prevent him from seeing their pedagogical value and using them later in teaching students. But the lasting value of Bach's arduous journeys to Celle lay in his experiences of hearing performances of an authentic French orchestra playing the latest French instrumental music.[17] He obviously felt he had gained from them. Both his son Carl Philipp Emanuel and his pupil Mizler related stories of his impressions of the trips in their memories of their master.[18]

Growth of a Master of Music

6

BEGINNING OF A MUSICAL CAREER (1703-1706)

BACH, now 18 years old, had completed his formal education. Its peculiarly seventeenth-century character was implanted in his soul, never to be changed. The roots of its theological doctrine had grown deep and formed the only key he had to the riddles of the universe. Throughout his life he pursued the objective of a career devoted to church music, a goal finally realized in his cantorship in Leipzig. He frequently wrote music for secular occasions, but even this eventually found its way into one of his church cantatas, or other religious pieces.

A Temporary Residence in Weimar

Bach began to look for his first position. He was already an organist of unprecedented ability and all of his applications aroused the enthusiasm of prospective employers. With the help of the Bach clan, and perhaps through correspondence with friends in Ohrdruf and Eisenach, Bach kept informed of vacancies in his native territory of Thuringia and was particularly interested in the organ that was being built in the New Church of Arnstadt.

The old church of Arnstadt, which was called St. Boniface after the bishop who had converted the Thuringians in the eighth century, had been destroyed by fire 122 years earlier. The pious Thuringians said that the Devil had set the spark when a foolish person had tarred the roof on a broiling summer day, against the advice of an experienced neighbor, but undoubtedly the fire was just one of the many that plagued the narrow streets and closely clustered houses in these towns.

Now, over a century later, the old church had been restored and was reopened with the name of The New Church. But another eight years passed before an organ manufacturer, Wender, was engaged to build a new organ in the edifice. Bach left his school in Lüneburg in the middle of the year expecting to find an organ post and an instrument in Arnstadt with which to open his career. But the instrument was still not finished.

Bach began to look elsewhere and applied for the vacancy in the *Marktkirche* of Sängerhausen created by the death of Grafenhayn, the "Town's Judge and Figural Organist" *(Stadtrichter und Figuralorgan-ist)*.[1] (Thirty-three years later Bach recommended his son Johann Gott-fried Bernhard for that same position, which he referred to as "post organist for the figured music then vacant.")[2] He was rejected for the post although the judges unanimously pronounced him the finest musician of all. Their decision had been overruled by the local potentate, Duke Johann Georg of Sachse-Weissenfels, who had a personal preference for Johann Augustine Kobelius, 11 years Bach's senior. C. S. Terry suggests that the duke chose Kobelius for sentimental reasons—his great-grandfather had been court organist at Weissenfels.[3] Indeed employing princes traditionally seem to have respected the prestige of clans and guilds—which formed the pressure groups and labor unions of older days—over strictly musical considerations.

News of Bach's talent quickly traveled to Weimar, where he found employment in the court of Duke Johann Ernst, younger brother and rival of the reigning duke, Wilhelm Ernst. Spitta suggests that this time Bach benefited from loyalty to a musical clan, for his grandfather once had been organist at that court for Duke Wilhelm IV.[4] Since the position of court organist was already filled, Bach was put to work playing the violin in the chamber orchestra. The musical family of the duke profited from his visit for besides performing he taught the duke's young and talented sons. No doubt he found ample opportunity to display his genius at the organ as well since the official court organist, Johann Effler, was very old.

The youngest son and namesake of Duke Johann Ernst took some kind of musical instruction from Johann Sebastian Bach, and at the time of his premature death at 19, the prince left compositions of such excellence that they were mistaken first for Bach's, then Vivaldi's. Bach certainly initiated him in the quintessence of his creative craft, whatever else he may have been specifically assigned to teach the youth. The lessons must have been marked with stern discipline and mutual deep respect for the serious mission of music to have inspired such outstanding student creations.

The stay with this noble family though short was probably a happy one for Bach. The Dukes of Weimar, unlike most royalty of that time, shunned ostentatious pleasure-seeking in emulation of the glamorous court at Versailles. All were seriously disposed, devoted to music, and lived a simple, frugal life that Bach could admire and enjoy.

Performers and Instruments: Servants to Composition

Many noblemen in eighteenth- and nineteenth-century Germany, like Johann Ernst, possessed impressive musical gifts. The achievements of the duke's youngest son have already been mentioned; his second son, who himself employed Bach in 1717, was an accomplished viola da gambist. The compositions of Frederick the Great occasionally still find a place on our programs today. Beethoven met many gifted composers and performers among the nobility; his friend, the Count von Waldstein, left a large number of excellent sonatas for piano, and his pupil, the Archduke Rudolph, was a pianist whose great talent Beethoven acknowledges in dedicating the famous *Hammerklavier Sonata* to him.

We tend to think of these wealthy amateurs as a species of the amateur of our own day, a person capable of playing some instrument in a commendable manner but without finished technique or sufficient knowledge of harmony and other phases of the métier. But the eighteenth-century musician, whether music was a profession or pasttime for him, had an entirely different attitude toward his art than the vast majority today. He was expected to be first of all a composer, for traditionally and naturally, any musician engaged in a position of responsibility—in court or in church—would perform chiefly his own music. As soon as a student could read music and understand the principles of harmony, he was taught to compose, to write in prescribed forms and for particular occasions. The ability to read at sight and to improvise was always stressed above memorization of music.

In general instruments were mastered with greater ease then than today, and this allowed musicians to play many instruments and at the same time devote most of their time to composition. Bach was not unique in his ability to play the viola, the 'cello, the lute, and the violin, and the violino piccolo[5] as well as the viola pomposa.[6] Violin players, for instance, were never called upon for the virtuosity demanded in a Brahms or Beethoven concerto. The old violin bow with its convex stick was incapable of wide dynamic range, but could produce a sweeter tone with less effort than our long concave stick. Vibrato, an indispensable element of modern violin playing, was used very little.

Double notes and contrapuntal pieces were more successful and also easier when played with the old convex bow. A chord of four notes (as in Bach's *Chaconne*) could be bowed without breaking it up. A violinist's tone then was akin to that of the old viol ensembles of the sixteenth and seventeenth centuries, in which vibrato was entirely ruled out by the design of these instruments. The fingerboards were fretted with gut bands; their convexly-curved bows further eliminated dynamic fluctuations; and all instruments of the viol family were held between the knees, like our 'cello, the bow held palm up, an attitude that precludes all accentuation. A viol ensemble sounded more like an organ, and when in Bach's time violins began to replace viols the basic esthetics of the quality of tone did not suddenly change: convex bows continued to be used. Bach's ideal of serenely quiet sonority for his violin compositions is borne out by the organ versions of his famous violin solos— the *E Major Prelude* and the *G Minor Fugue*. It is not even certain whether Bach transcribed them from the violin to the organ or vice versa.

Clavier technique was also transferred to a number of instruments; treatment of the organ, the harpsichord, the pedal-harpsichord, the spinet, the clavichord, and the lute-clavier,[7] differed very little. Like the violins, the keyboard instruments did not require the physical dexterity and power to control dynamics that the modern instruments demands. On the organ and on all harpsichord varieties (such as the pedal harpsichord, the spinet, and the lute-clavier) dynamics were produced by the drawing of stops. Only the clavichord was capable of spontaneous dynamics by sensitive finger pressure, but its loudest tone was but a whisper.

The attitude of the eighteenth-century musician toward his instruments was that of a master toward his tools. Instruments were merely the media through which his music was made audible. During the first decades of the twentieth century this attitude was almost completely reversed. The virtuoso not only displayed his dexterity on his particular instrument, but projected his own individual insight into the composition of a chosen master. This concept of interpreting music was unknown in the eighteenth century. The musician as well as the listener was concerned with the craft of composition; he admired its construction, its modulations, the manipulation of contrapuntal themes, etc. The amateur of the eighteenth century shared the secrets and technical delights of composition with the professional. Bach's title page to the *Klavierübung* neatly reveals this relation between composer and music lover: "Klavierübung . . . Constructed by Sebastian Bach for music lovers, and particularly for connoisseurs of such works, for the delight of the soul." The eighteenth-century attitude toward music was at once more professional and more naive.

Despite this general versatility it is only natural that various musicians cherished a preference for certain instruments. Bach already preferred the organ, partially because this instrument was capable of realizing the most complex contrapuntal structures. At the organ he was master of an entire orchestra. The polyphonic creations that flowed from his pen could all be brought to sound by one person only. His patience need not be taxed with an unruly choir of boys; nor with His Highness' chamber musicians, whose musical comprehension was considerably slower than his own. Above all, of course, the organ was the core of the musical service in church and fulfilled his primary desire to devote his genius to "the exaltation of God's glory."

Bach in Arnstadt

As soon as the organ was ready, Bach accepted the invitation of the townsmen of Arnstadt to examine it, and on July 13, 1703, he inaugurated the instrument. On August 9 he received a certificate, the equivalent of a contract, on which was recorded the date of the inauguration, the concert that was played, and the sum that Bach received in payment —4 Thalers, a good fee according to the standards of the day.[8]

The certificate of appointment Bach received from the *consistorium*, a body of officers appointed by the reigning sovereign, bore the seal of the chancery of His Lordship, Count Anton Günther, and indicates the high official honor this post bestowed upon him:

Whereas The Highborn our most Gracious Lord Count and Lord, Lord Anthon Gunther of the four Counts of the realm, Count of Schwarzburg, etc. has caused you, Johann Sebastian Bach, to be accepted and appointed as an organist of the New Church, as you shall, above all, be faithful, gracious, and obedient to His High Countly Grace.

The organist was engaged by the state, not the church. Bach had thus attained a higher social position than his class-conscious society afforded him in his semifeudal function of chamber musician at the Weimar court. Although his position was not as high as that of a cantor or *Kappellmeister,* he was freed from the additional duties that inevitably befell lower echelon musicians and took them away from their music. The old organist Effler at the Weimar court, for example, had to spend most of his day penning documents and letters in the secretarial offices of the chancery; Johann Paul Westhoff, an eminent violinist and composer who had toured the courts of Italy, France, and Holland, was kept busy as a *"Cammer-secretarius."* Eilenstein divided his time between teaching the young prince Johann Ernst and serving as gentleman-in-waiting. A bassoonist at the Weimar court had the honorable position of inspector at the court of justice. All musicians except the *Kapellmeister, Vice-Kapellmeister,* and *Concertmeister* had to make time for extra duties.

The minimal demands made of Bach, even of his musical skills, reflect the count's artistic indifference rather than his great consideration for a budding genius. In aristocratic circles Anton Günther was regarded as an upstart. He was elevated under protest to the dignity of a princely rank in 1697, but with the death of Emperor Joseph I in 1711, he lost the imperial protection and Duke Wilhelm Ernst of Weimar, with the consent of the Elector, August the Strong, invaded Arnstadt and dethroned the count.

Bach's certificate of employment admonished him to good conduct as well as subservience to the count, and above all "in particular in your office, profession, practice of your art and your science which is given in charge of you with manifest diligence and fidelity." The organ was under his special charge and "no one but he shall have access; and he is promptly to report any defects that may be detected in the instrument." He was expected to be a model of good behavior as well: in his "daily life . . . practice the fear of God, sobriety, and a peaceful temper in his dealings with people," avoid "bad company and distraction from his profession," and "disport himself faithfully toward God, the High Authority, and his superiors."

The last clause states the yearly salary—50 florins, plus 30 Thaler toward living expenses, board, and home. At this salary, about the same as a field marshal's, Bach was able to acquire a harpsichord and several books. Besides, as one of the most respectable citizens in Arnstadt, Bach had to be well dressed. He often visited the court of Count Günther.

Five days after receiving his contract Bach was ceremoniously inducted into office. The keys to the organ loft were handed over to him, and the contract made legal by a traditional pledge of a handshake in the presence of witnesses. His schedule was indeed light. The Sunday morning service lasted only from 8:00 to 10:00. On Thursday there was an earlier service (7:00-9:00), which required less music. And on Tuesday at a short hour of prayer organ music was interspersed with hymns and Bible readings.

At times Bach may have been summoned by Count Günther to assist as a violinist in performances by his band of musicians, though there is no evidence of it.[9] Countess Augusta Dorothea only a few years earlier had completed a pleasure palace (Lustschloss) where concerts and theatricals were performed. Performance of a secular cantata on a text by Salomo Franck—who later wrote such excellent librettos for Bach's cantatas—entitled "Frolockender Gotterstreit" (Victorious Battle of the Gods),[10] had celebrated its opening. In May, 1705, the public was admitted, "on payment of a certain price," [11] to hear a rather rustic, though pompous Singspiel entitled "Von der Klugheit der Obrigkeit in Anordnung des Bierbrauens" (Of the Sagacity of the Authorities in the Regulations for Beer Brewing). As this farce required a great number of actors, some of the local amateurs were not unwillingly pressed into service. Bach was probably given the trying task of training his church-school choir as well for that occasion.

The music of this "musical comedy" was written, according to all indications, by Johann Philipp Trieber (1675-1727), a man of great musical gifts and universal erudition. He had studied philosophy, theology, jurisprudence, and medicine at the University of Jena, and his unorthodox ideas on religion branded him as an atheist, for which crime he was sentenced to six months' imprisonment in Gotha. When this rustic play was performed, he was living in Arnstadt, but Bach would surely have shunned the company of such a free thinker.

Little information is available about the artistic life at the court of Anton Günther and his wife Augusta Dorothea, but the motivations for their cultural endeavors seem to have sprung from jealous ambition rather than from cultural need. The countess was of the Brunswick family, a daughter of Duke Anton Ulrich von Braunschweig-Wolffenbüttel (1633-1714) who had set a famous example of ostentatious court life for his daughter with a continuous round of festivities, operas, concerts, masquerades, fireworks, illuminations, balls, etc. But Anton Ulrich had also been a true Maecenas of science and art; he founded the University of Helmstedt and surrounded himself with artists, architects, and literati. This talented nobleman was no mean writer himself, and may be counted among the first authors of historical novels. To judge from the few known performances at the Augustenburg, the daughter had neither the talents nor the artistic discrimination of her father.

The town of Arnstadt had little to offer the eager young student seeking knowledge of his art from living example as well as from written scores. Even Arnstadt's libraries—in church, town, and at the castle—were discouragingly poor. Nor could he gain much from personal intercourse with his colleagues; Bach's talent far surpassed that of any of the other organists in Arnstadt. At the main church, the *Oberkirche*, Christoph Herthum was either of lesser talent or his natural gifts were not tapped for he also performed duties at the castle that were "engrossing and laborious."[12] Paul Gleistmann, the most talented man in the community, was an able performer on the violin, the viola da gamba, and the lute. But he too was occupied with extramusical duties, as Groom-of-the-Chambers at the court. Trieber and his father, Johann Friedrich, who was rector of the Lyceum, were connoisseurs of music and displayed interest in music theory; the son published a harmony treatise. But Bach demanded that those he chose as friends and mentors share his religious beliefs as well as his passion for music.

Besides the artistic isolation Bach must have felt, he was on a bad footing with the choir he was given to train, a band of ruffians from the Lyceum. (Bach was perhaps experiencing the universal disillusionment of young graduates in their first teaching positions.) Herthum, the organist, picked the best students and singers for his church choir, leaving the rest to young Bach. Olearius, the local school inspector, was lax in his discipline, and a council member described the boys (in a document dated 1706) in the following manner:

The students behave badly . . . They carry swords, not only in the street, but also in school . . . they play ball during religious service and in the classes . . . they frequent places of ill repute . . . cause disturbance during the night by shouting and carousing . . .[13]

A senior student in this gang bore a special grudge against Bach for being called down as a miserable or mediocre bassoonist—a dumbhead (a rather free translation of *Zippelfagottist*).[14] The invective had aroused

his rancor more than Bach realized, and one day as Bach was strolling
with his cousin Barbara Catharina, he was stopped by the boy brandish-
ing his stick. In spite of the five other belligerent boys who supported
this student, Bach refused to apologize. The young upstart called his
teacher a *Hundsfott*, a dirty dog,[15] and threatened him. Bach kept the
ruffian at a distance with a sword until the other boys intervened and
ended the brawl.

The sword that spared Bach a black eye may have been the same one
that protected him on his long journeys from Lüneburg. It would not
have been unusual for Bach to be wearing the students' uniform of the
Knights' Academy, which he left two years earlier. Or he may have
worn the attire of an Hungarian Hussar or *heyduc*, like members of the
ducal orchestra in Weimar—high boots and tight-fitting breeches, a stiff
jacket, heavily braided with horizontal tresses, a cape on one shoulder,
and a huge cap of cloth or fur.

Bach's victory over his students was short lived. When the council
considered the incident, Bach, after some hesitance, admitted his rash
use of words. The impulsive youths were dismissed with a mere admonition for better behavior, undoubtedly leaving Herr Olearius shaking his
head over such free abandon to youthful passion.

Compositions of the Arnstadt Period

Most of Bach's compositions stemming from the Arnstadt period bear
the mark of immaturity. Some 20 works have been identified as dating
from this time, although in many cases their authenticity cannot be fully
established. The prevalent practice, mentioned above, of apprentices
and young composers transcribing and remodeling other composers'
works in the course of learning their métier makes the task of attribu-
tion extremely complex. The cost and difficulty of music printing in
those days made copying commercially as well as pedagogically practical. Faithful reproduction suffered in the process; very frequently an
imaginative scribe imposed improvements of his own on his model. The
usual lack of dates and signatures on such manuscripts compounds the
difficulties of authentication. Thus many youthful compositions of Bach
have turned out to be his more or less free transcriptions of known or
unknown models.

Among the best of Bach's organ works of this period is the tender and
serene *Pastorale in F Major*, a composition distinguished from other

works by its free flow and logical unfolding of melody, more character-istic of Bach's later works. The authenticity of even this exquisite gem of sustained lyricism is under suspicion, however.[16]

A curious capriccio, composed for the occasion of the departure of Bach's brother Johann Jacob to Sweden, also comes from this period. This adventurous young brother, then 22 years old, had obtained an engagement as oboist in the guard of the King of Sweden, Charles XII (1682-1718), who at that time was waging a war of immediate and sensational, but not permanent success, against Denmark, Russia, and Poland. Before departing to the triumphant court of Sweden Johann Jacob visited his family in Thuringia, and at one of the clan's gatherings, which may have taken place in either Eisenach or Ohrdruf, Johann Sebastian presented his brother with this piece of program music for piano—or rather harpsichord, or pedal harpsichord—bearing the fashion-able Italian title of *"Capriccio sopra la lontananza del suo Fratello dilet-tissimo"* (Capriccio on the Departure of his beloved Brother). The work is an ancient type of quaint program music describing the rather senti-mental joviality of the occasion. Its first movement has a German in-scription that this Adagia "is a coaxing by his friends to dissuade him from his journey." The second, Andante, "is a presentation of various *casuum* (calamities) that might befall him in foreign lands." "A general *Lamento* of the friends" follows. The fourth movement announces "here the friends come, since they see that it cannot be otherwise, and take leave of him." The last is a fugue in imitation of the stagecoach's horn, bearing the Italian title of *Aria di Postilione.*

We find some exquisitely tender touches in this rather childish music. The first piece especially consistently expresses a sweet sentiment that grows in its closing phrases into a youthful melancholy, sadly repeating a little motive suggesting a nodding of farewell into an ever-vanishing distance. Not all the movements are equally poetic. The *Aria di Posti-lione* is a brilliant and difficult fugue, strangely alien to Bach's style, even in works dating only a few years hence. Even the physical feeling one gets when playing it on the keyboard is unlike any other clavier music of Bach, partly due to the fact that Bach probably played it on a pedal harpsichord.[17] The entire capriccio, which might be called a fan-tasy or a suite, is strongly reminiscent of the "Biblical Sonatas" of Johann Kuhnau, and young Bach may well have used these species of descriptive music as his model. And Froberger, a great favorite of young Bach, had a gift for musical representation of stories and personal characters. Both composers gave Italian titles to their "program music." The world probably will never know whether the work is an original composition imitating someone's manner or a free transcription of a lost composition.

Another work of this period, the precise model of which is not so easily assigned, is his church cantata "For Thou wilt not leave my Soul in Hell." Although edited as Number 15, in the *Bach Gesellschaft* edition, the work actually is the first cantata that flowed from Bach's pen. We know it only in a 1735 revision that Bach made for a performance in Leipzig, however, and so cannot use the cantata as a true gauge of Bach's creative powers at this young age.

We can learn something of Bach's early ideas on style and form from the cantata because Bach did not disturb these aspects in revision. Here he had not yet adopted the outer form of the Neapolitan opera, with its separate divisions in recitatives, arias, *da capo* arias, duets, overtures, and closing chorales. Later he commonly used the recitative resembling the *recitative secco* of the opera (literally dry reciting, accompanied only by a keyboard instrument) to narrate biblical events or present doctrinal thought. His succeeding aria or duet would then give lyrical expression to the text. In the older form used in this first cantata a type of continuous melody, the *arioso*, an aria-like musical soliloquy, carried the text of verses from the Bible or hymnal. In the later cantatas Bach used libretti prepared by a poet presenting his own version, often of rather doubtful literary value, of Bible or hymn text.

We may conclude from the quality of Bach's youthful output in Arnstadt that he was not a wonder child like Mozart. And neither Bach nor Mozart displayed the epoch-making originality of Schubert—the "Erlking" at age 16—or Mendelssohn—the music to *Midsummernight's Dream* at 17. Both Bach and Mozart were more bound to the styles of those predecessors and contemporaries from whom they learned their craft. Bach's compositions especially fail to reveal any traits of his powerful genius. He concentrated more on performance than creation. Although composition was a necessary part of any musician's role, originality in composition was not. An organist or cantor did not have to be an innovator to fulfill the duties of his post successfully. Bach's 10 or so chorale arrangements of this period merely follow the general practice and skill of the times: full harmonization and glittering passages linking verses of the hymns.

Schubert and Mendelssohn lived in an age of romantic genius worship; originality and genius had become synonymous. In Bach's time music-making was a craft in the service of either the church or the courtly amateur and connoisseur. Composition followed given themes, folksongs, hymns, as well as more learned material, and was made in given forms and for given occasions, with whatever raw materials—voices or instruments—were at hand. The art of Bach's time was not practiced for art's sake.

7

BACH AND BUXTEHUDE

BACH was fully aware of his immaturity and of his need for close relationships with great living artistic spirits. No one in the provincial town of Arnstadt could provide this inspiration. Even his instrument was mediocre, small and always in need of repair. Bach must have remembered with painful longing the magnificent organs of Lüneburg and Hamburg. His choir was a constant source of irritation and the libraries had only meagre offerings.

Bach asked for and was granted a one-month leave of absence to study with the famous Dietrich Buxtehude in Lübeck, without doubt the greatest organist and organ composer in Germany. Bach's young cousin, Johann Ernst Bach (1683-1738), filled his position in his absence.

I cannot accept the suggestion that personal aspirations, other than refinement of his art, motivated Bach to make this pilgrimage. Some scholars have felt that Bach, like Handel before him, had hopes of becoming Buxtehude's successor. The master was 68 years old and was probably considering relinquishing his post to a young protegé. Aside from implications for Bach's singular devotion to his faith and art, several practical reasons almost certainly would have prevented Bach from entertaining such an ambition.

Two years earlier, 18-year-old Handel, together with his 22-year-old friend Johann Mattheson had visited Lübeck with designs on that enviable position. Armed with entrées to influential and wealthy families of this rich old Hanseatic city, these brilliantly entertaining young worldlings were wined and dined, and invited to try out the famous organ as well as all the harpsichords in fashionable society. But their overwhelming ambitions quickly waned, even in the face of triumphant acceptance, when they learned the conditions for the post. Buxtehude insisted upon abiding by an ancient tradition by which the succeeding organist was obliged to marry his eldest daughter. Anna Margaretha Buxtehude at 34 did not inspire romance in a passionate young man, and custom further demanded that the new organist and his bride live with her parents. Since Bach was probably already enamoured of his cousin Maria Barbara at this time, any thoughts he may have had about seeking this prize position would surely have been quickly smothered by news of the personal sacrifices demanded. Thus it was in genuine modesty that he sought out the old master, with the sole object of "studying his profession," as he told the *Consistorium* of Arnstadt.

Bach would not have undertaken the journey of 200 miles afoot. Thanks to his heritage of middle-class frugality he must have saved enough money in the two preceding years to make at least part of the journey by stagecoach. Only in this way could he have had enough time for study.

Bach chose to make this study journey in the autumn, when Buxtehude conducted the famous Vesper Concerts in the Church of St. Mary, the *Marienkirche*. The *Abendmusiken* was performed after the vesper service on five successive Sundays during Advent, the season in the liturgical year when the faithful are admonished to remember and reflect upon the spiritual significance of the coming of Christ. The "cantatas" were sung in the form of dialogues between soloists and the chorus, somewhat like a Greek tragedy. Two singers set forth the theological tenet of an allegory, paraphrasing a fitting passage from the Bible. The chorus responded in lyrical reflections and interpretations of the sacred words. Aeschylus developed a similar relationship between his characters, who talk together of man's destiny and spiritual orientation, and the chorus that gives lyrical and musical expression to the concepts. The form of these vesper concerts made a significant impression upon Bach, for we find the same basic program in his later cantatas: the exposition of theological tenet in the recitative followed by extended lyrical comment through choruses and arias.

Today the music of Buxtehude's cantatas does not impress us as much as his organ music, and Bach's compositions indicate that he too was more profoundly influenced by the master's deeply stirring organ harmonies. Although Buxtehude's recognition today is generally linked to his *Abendmusiken,* his singular genius does not come into full bloom within the restrictions of this conventional liturgy. Five years after his arrival in Lübeck, Buxtehude, a Swede from Helsingborg, inaugurated the vesper music. The rich burghers of the town were delighted with these concerts and commissioned flattering cantatas for secular occasions—birthdays, weddings, political festivals—as well. But Buxtehude gave his creative energy to these duties only until 1690, and when Bach visited him in 1705 Buxtehude had withdrawn to the private pleasures of composing purely instrumental music. In 1696 some of his trio sonatas appeared, and they are remarkable for their contrapuntal skill; he also wrote suites and variations of keyboard instruments, and Bach was greatly indebted to his violin solo music. His best compositions, however, are conceived for organ. As in all Bach's music, the idiom of Buxtehude's favorite instrument dominates his creations.

Buxtehude's Organ Music

Buxtehude's treatment of the Lutheran chorale particularly interested Bach and the fruits of his prolific composition of chorale-preludes for the organ provided Bach with a lifetime of inspiration. Bach's own chorale-preludes would reach the zenith of a historical development that started before the Reformation, when Gregorian chants, as well as secular songs, were ornamented *(coloriert)* with diminutions (motives with half the time value), augmentations (double time values), modified rhythms, imitations and inversions of fragments taken from the main melody, and other contrapuntal filigrees. The Latin term for such devices was *color*—hence the German *colorieren* and the Italian *coloratura.* In the north Bach had found many forms of chorale treatment: the chorale-fantasies, the chorale-variations, the motet-like treatment of the chorale, and various fusions of these forms, each of which could be written with or without a slow *cantus firmus* in long notes, appearing in any of the voices, and sometimes canonically in two voices. Buxtehude's inspired imagination in this his favorite form of composition, and his application of a free, almost licentious ornamental improvisation on the melody, must have deeply inspired Bach to pursue the further possibilities of this form.

Buxtehude's *Passacaglia in D Minor* is a most striking example of his lasting influence on the young organist who came to him. Its intrinsic beauty, its powerful expressive appeal, its daringly passionate harmonies are notable, but we are most interested here in the work's striking affinity to Bach's famous *Passacaglia,* which he composed 11 or 12 years later. Buxtehude has transformed this dance of barbaric though rather recent origin[1] into a medium of ecstatic contemplation. Its short obligato bass theme (only four measures) is endlessly repeated under an unbroken chain of variations that flow together in continuous musical thought. The melodic theme itself, as well as its treatment, builds up intense emotion in the listener. Instead of a dual construction, consisting of a forephrase as a thesis or subject, followed by an answering phrase or predicate, giving grammatical completion to the idea, the passacaglia and chaconne melodies have only one phrase. This forephrase is perpetually unanswered, or rather postponed indefinitely during a long chain of variations. Bach uses this device to create a feeling of awesome suspense.

No similar mystic effect emanates from André Raison's *Passacaglia,* the other work intimately related to Bach's masterpiece. His variations were strung together for practical expediency, linking the *Kyries* in the service, and easily broken off whenever the priest was ready to begin the next part of the Mass.

Bach combined the two composers' themes, using Raison's identical theme for the first half of his motif and completing it with four measures strongly associated with Buxtehude's masterpiece. Thus he was working with a theme twice as long as either of his predecessors'. Here again we are confronted not with plagiarism, but with an age-old conception of the craft and function of composing. Passacaglia and chaconne themes were borrowed so often, with slight modifications, that they became cadential patterns. Bach's absorption of Raison's and Buxtehude's "ideas" is remarkable not for his use of their obligato skeleton melodies but for both his persistent allusions to Buxtehude's variations—that is, to the composition proper—and his genius for lifting the same inventions to greater heights of sublimity.[2] The same phrases that seem to give way with romantic abandon to personal reveries of a visionary under Bach's masterful treatment call to mind prophetic pronouncements of divine inspiration. Bach's *Passacaglia* is conceived on a larger plan (170 measures as compared to Buxtehude's 119) and a stupendous climactic fugue crowns the masterwork that taken as a piece conveys cosmic import.

Besides Buxtehude's *Passacaglia* and his *Chaconne* in *E Minor,* the work of Lübeck's master bears striking resemblances to Bach's great preludes, toccatas, and fugues. From Buxtehude's *Fugue in F Major*[3] Bach found the idiom and learned the almost rhapsodic treatment of this toccata-like fugue[4] that would later inspire his *Prelude and Fugue in D Major*. Both Buxtehude's work and the Pachelbel piece[5] on which it was based are rarely remembered except in Bach's interpretations of them.

The fruits of Bach's musical pilgrimage to Lübeck did not come immediately, but he gained impressions and ideas during his short association with Buxtehude that remained with him for the rest of his life. His works that show definite influence from Buxtehude, including his great *Passacaglia*, actually date from a later period in his life (about 1709-1711) but confirm the clarity of Bach's memory of the sound of Buxtehude's organ and his music, this master's dazzling virtuosity, and his imaginative *rubato* treatment of his rhapsodic toccatas. Above all the color-fantasies elicited from Buxtehude's famous instrument, so rich in registration, engendered and brought to fruition ideas too sublime for full realization on any of the inferior organs Bach himself had to tolerate most of his life.

Resignation from Arnstadt's *Neue Kirche*

When Bach resumed his duties at the organ in Arnstadt in midwinter of 1706, he had begun to become conscious of his future as a sort of musical apostle of his faith. He knew that years of study and labor lay ahead, but he was possessed with a conviction of his mission. His musical imagination was fired with visions incomprehensible to anyone in Arnstadt. In the liberal and progressive Hansa city, long accustomed to a cosmopolitan outlook of a widely traveled and affluent merchant class, Bach had witnessed the absolute freedom of a church organist at the height of his fame. Buxtehude was in a sense a musical sovereign, free to follow any whims of inspiration no matter how subjective or "romantic," apart from the judgment of nonmusical superiors. Bach had heard modulations, harmonic combinations, chorale variations, and improvisations more daring in their unconventionality and personal expressiveness than could be heard anywhere in Germany.

Bach's position in Arnstadt was totally different, as he was to become painfully aware of shortly after his return. His lack of rapport with the congregation brought up renewed frictions with the church council. After he had resumed his organ-playing in service, Bach was summoned to the castle of Count Günther, where he was subjected to a court hearing by Herr Superintendent Olearius, possibly accompanied by other members of the council, and a servile scribe, who faithfully took the minutes of the hearing, which as though for our instruction and amusement, have been preserved through all the years. The document is in the scribe's official language, mixed with some obscure Latin pedantries that may or may not have been understood correctly by either the pompous council or their faithful *secretarius*.

Thus the *"actum de* February 21, 706" [meaning 1706] reads in part:[6]

Nos [we, the consistory]:

Charge him with having hitherto been in the habit of making [surprising] *variationes* in the chorales, and intermixing strange sounds, so that thereby the congregation were [confused]. If in the future he wishes to introduce some *Tonus Perigrinus* he must keep to it, and not go off directly to something else, or, as he had hitherto done, play quite a *Tonum Contrarium.*

The meaning of this high-sounding jargon is a little vague, as it doubtless was to the scribe and the pedants sitting in judgment of an art so new and strange to them. The term *variationes* probably referred to the type of ornamentation that Bach at that time imitated from Buxtehude. The term *tonus perigrinus* can be interpreted in various ways— but not in the ancient sense as applied on Gregorian psalm tones, that is, as a different reciting tone sung in the two halves of a chant. Bach did not play any Gregorian chants, but harmonized Protestant hymn tunes. *Tonus* can mean melody, mode, tonality, or just tone; *perigrinus* means strange and foreign. *Tonus perigrinus*, some scholars believe, describes a theme against the melody[7] while a *tonus contrarius* would be a theme conflicting with the melody. Mr. Terry quotes from the *Leipziger Kirchenstaat* (church regulations of Leipzig): "Finally the morning service shall be concluded with the song: *Gott sey uns gnädig und barmhertzig,* sung to the *Tonus Perigrinus Meine Seele erhebt den Herren.*" Here *Tonus Perigrinus* appears to mean a borrowed melody, a wandering melody to which different texts may be applied. Others[8] believe that both of these expressions mean some unexpected element in the melody or the harmony such as passing tones, short cadences, chromatic progressions, cross relations, and sudden modulations. Pirro interprets the term as simply sudden caprices of accompaniment.[9]

Whatever the precise meaning of this language, we may be sure that Bach had been presenting his naive and untutored audience with a new and disturbing style. Since they had not had any organ in their New

Church for so many years, they had not been educated to the style of chorale-variations that was practiced in many other parts of Germany— Hamburg, Lüneburg, Lübeck, and Eisenach. Of course, this new style was actually just an imitation of Buxtehude's florid manner.

The protocol of this same court hearing reveals yet another contention. The superintendent Olearius politely, perhaps somewhat sarcastically, stated that "it was rather strange that so far no concerted music had been performed;[10] and that he [Bach] was the cause of such neglect, since he did not choose to get along with the students who formed the choir. Therefore, he should declare himself whether he wished to perform figured [instrumental and vocal] as well as choral music with the students, because a conductor could not be engaged for him. If he did not want to do so, he should say so categorically and openly, so that other arrangements could be made and someone could be engaged who was willing to do this." "Ille [Bach] stubbornly responded to this that he would be willing to play, if he would be provided with a competent conductor." It was then resolved that he should answer these charges within eight days.

Bach was not entirely to blame for his poor relationship with the choir. His *praefect*, or assistant choir director, was not able to keep the necessary discipline among the young rowdies (the protocol admits that his misbehavior even contributed to the disorders in the choir). He is accused of setting a deplorable example when he "entered the wine cellar during last Sunday's sermon,"[11] a misdemeanor for which he was forced to sit in carcer for two hours on each of four successive days. Whether this ridiculous punishment succeeded in pointing up a moral for the snickering choir boys evidently did not occur to Herr Olearius.

In view of these semifeudal relations between employer and employee Bach's resolute refusal to conduct took real courage. His contract did not require him to conduct, and he could have pointed this out to the court. The existence of this contract probably explains why Bach did not comply with the council's demand for a statement in a week. About 10 months went by before he was summoned to appear before the council. Neither Bach nor Olearius had mentioned the matter during the interim. In a protocol of November 11, 1706, Bach is asked again, this time in a more angry tone, "to declare, as he had been instructed already, if he wished to make music with the students or not; for, if he considered it no disgrace to be attached to the church and receive its salary, he must not be ashamed to make music with the students until some other orders were given."[12] Again Bach replies that he will give his answer—this time in writing.

Poor Mr. Olearius must have felt his dignity threatened by this adamant resistance, for now he flung another and extremely petty accusation at Bach: "he recently has invited a strange maiden into the choir loft and allowed her to make music." But again Bach is unperturbed: "Ille [he] has informed Magister Uthe [his clergyman][13] about this." The strange maiden whose singing some righteous gossiper had heard from outside the church probably was Bach's cousin, who soon was to become his wife. Bach apparently did not feel constrained to follow the prejudices of that time against female singers in church choirs.

Throughout the meager outline of historical evidence furnished by these protocols we discern Bach's firm character and personality, fired by his sacred and deeply rooted urge to obey only his genius, which he dedicated entirely to his God. At this early age he seems merely headstrong and unmalleable, but as we compare these actions with his dealings with subsequent church authorities we can find a common thread, total dedication to the qualities of sacred music, a motive incapable of compromise. He considered it a waste of time to attempt the education of such crude material of student singers, even if perhaps "some day they might be usable for music," as the consistory had suggested.[14] Instead, Bach used his time for the development of his organ playing[15] and composing, mainly of organ works.

Bach was aware of personal benefits to be gained from bending all his efforts to the perfection of his extraordinary virtuosity on the organ. His reputation for this unusual gift was spreading, and it was in his capacity of organist that he could best expect to advance his career— a youth of 22 would probably not be engaged in the capacity of a cantor.

On December 2, 1706, his opportunity for an advantageous change came with the death of Johann Georg Ahle, the organist at the Saint Blasius Church in Mühlhausen. The position held some honor, since a number of distinguished musicians had given fame to "Divi Blasii." The title of *poet laureate* had been bestowed on Ahle by Emperor Leopold I "for his virtue and splendid talents, . . . for his admirable proficiency in the noble science of German poetry and for his rare and delightful style in highly commended music, and his elegant compositions."[16] Ahle's father, Johann Rudolph, also had been organist and composer at this church, and had been honored with the office of member of the town council, and later with that of burgomaster. Bestowal of high civic offices on musicians reflects the high esteem in which they were held in Mühlhausen. Other musicians of fame had preceded these men of distinction, among them Johann Eccard, notable pupil of Orlando Lasso. In every respect the Mühlhausen position represented great promise to Bach, especially from the vantage point of his unhappy situation in Arnstadt.

The church also employed both a cantor and a choir director, and the concerted music thus was not so difficult to perform as in Arnstadt. The cantor of St. Blasius does not seem to have had the position of prominence that usually goes with such a post, for his name is not mentioned by any of the biographers. Judging from the bulk of church music that both the Ahles have left and the honors bestowed upon them, we may safely assume that at St. Blasius Church the musical direction was firmly controlled by the organist. According to an ancient tradition in Mühlhausen the organist—not, as elsewhere in Germany, the cantor—was expected to compose a cantata to celebrate every new election of the Town Council.

After other organists had been properly examined, Bach was approached and asked what salary he would demand for the position. He merely asked for the same amount he was drawing in Arnstadt—85 gulden—besides the payments in kind that Ahle had received in addition, amounting to "three measures of corn, two trusses of wood, one of beech, one of oak or aspen, and six trusses of faggots, delivered at his door, in lieu of arable." Small as it seems, this salary amounted to an increase of 20 gulden over Ahle's, and what anyone in a respectable profession could demand.

On June 29 Bach informed the city council of Arnstadt that he had accepted the new post and officially returned the key of the organ. His resignation did not take effect until September 14, when he actually began his duties in Mühlhausen. At the time the city of Arnstadt was in arrears of payment of Bach's salary, but since his cousin Ernst (who had taken his place when Johann Sebastian was studying in Lübeck) succeeded him at the New Church, Bach generously assigned part of the last quarter of his year's salary to his cousin, who was in financial distress. Bach could easily afford this act of generosity because on August 10, through the death of his uncle Tobias Lämmerhirt, Bach had inherited 50 gulden, a sum well exceeding his yearly salary. This solidarity of the Bach clan and their willingness to aid one another in time of need helped to insure Johann Sebastian's artistic independence.

One month after his arrival in Mühlhausen the handsome young genius took Maria Barbara to the nearby town of Dornheim to be married by the local pastor, Johann Lorentz Stauber, who was related by marriage to Bach's bride. She was the granddaughter of Heinrich Bach (1615-1692), who had been an organist in Arnstadt. He in turn was the uncle of Bach's father Ambrosius of Eisenach. Her father, Johann Michael (1648-1695), was an organist and parish clerk near Arnstadt, and a prolific composer. This intermarriage, the only one that ever occurred within the entire clan, produced the great talents of Carl Philipp Emanuel, Wilhelm Friedemann, and Johann Gottfried Bernhard Bach.

ORNAMENTATION

THE *melos* of Bach's works may be described as baroque—if we take the much abused term to mean an over-ornamentative style. In many respects Bach followed the *passagi* style, so popular in Germany especially during his early career, and we need a clear picture of the history and nature of musical ornamentation during this period before analyzing Bach's maturing style of composition further. But we must keep in mind the significant differences between Bach's work within this highly developed art of ornamentation and most of the work of his predecessors and contemporaries. Bach's unique transformations of simple Lutheran chorales, achieved partially through ornamentation, into hallowed meditations are far from the ornate confusions of Buxtehude. Yet, as we have seen, Buxtehude's music remained a source of inspiration to Bach throughout his lifetime.

We must admit that the Arnstadters were somewhat justified in their complaints about the art to which Bach was exposed during his stay in Lübeck. Buxtehude's style of florid ornamentation could distract rather than illuminate the congregation, as a comparison of the unadorned melody of "A Mighty Fortress" (taken from Bach's Cantata No. 80) with Buxtehude's treatment of it clearly illustrates (see example). The composer submerges the melody in a maze of serpentine passages, runs, and turns. Possibly in deference to the Arnstadters' taste, Bach's works of that period did not follow the extravagancies of Buxtehude's style. The few existing examples of Bach's work that do strongly reflect Buxtehude's style come from a much later period; even among these Bach creates such masterful expressions of intimate mystic experience

a) The unadorned chorale melody "A Mighty Fortress." From Bach's Cantata No. 80.

b) Ornamented version from Buxtehude's chorale-prelude based on "A Mighty Fortress."

c) repetition with different ornamentation

as "*Oh Mensch, bewein' dein' Sünden*" (Oh Man, Bewail Thy Sins) and "*Wenn wir in Höchsten Nöthen sein*" (When We Are in Greatest Need). Thus the term baroque as used above does not satisfactorily describe Bach's style. In Buxtehude's work ornament seems to weigh down and dominate, while Bach achieves an integration of ornament and melody into a flow of continuous melody of the most expressive quality.

Buxtehude's rather licentious type of coloratura is closely related to the traditional style of the Italian singers and instrumentalists, especially during the sixteenth and seventeenth centuries. Improvisations of these *gorgie* or throat exercises dated back to the Gregorian chant, and during the height of the *a cappella* singing this kind of improvised elaboration—called *diminutione* (diminution) for the division of long notes into a coloratura of small ones—was expected of a good singer.

At first ornaments were never written out; but as these coloratura began to be applied to contrapuntal compositions, it would have been too much to expect a singer to observe contrapuntal rules as his imagination augmented the text. As early as the beginning of the sixteenth century, Johannes Tinctoris (ca. 1435-1511), a Belgian composer and theorist who spent a great deal of time in Italy, relates that there were two kinds of *diminutus: aut scripto* (written out) and *aut mente* (improvised). A master like Adrian Willeart (ca. 1490-1562), the founder of the Venetian school of San Marco, could no longer trust himself to spontaneously improvised ornamentation as the polyphonic art of his day became more involved.

These Italian practices became known and fashionable in all of Europe, and violinists, gambists, harpsichordists, and organists found great delight in allowing their fingers to ambulate over the keys or strings in arabesques of their own invention. In fact, musicologists today do not agree on whether ornamentation is really vocal or instrumental in origin.

This art of diminution, called division in England, has a spontaneous and unpredictable character, which many theorists, especially in sixteenth-century Italy,[1] tried rather unsuccessfully to refine. Rules of execution were formulated and various types of ornaments—*passagi, cascade, tirate,* with their smaller distinctions such as *cascada doppia, circolo, mezzo circolo, trillo, temolo, tremoletto,* and *groppo*—were classified.

There was no universal agreement among the theorists, however, over these rules and classifications. Giovanni Battista Bovicelli and Lodovico Zacconi (1555-1627), for instance, teach that one must never begin with *passagi,* and that one must refrain from ornamenting quarter notes and reserve the diminutions for long notes. Others, like Riccardo Rognoni, find no fault with such "transgressions."[2] What some called *tremolo,* other called *trillo,* and vice versa. Caspar Printz (1641-1717) calls a *trillo* or *triletto"* a tremor, a quivering of the voice in a note above a large note." He writes out the *Circulus Remittus.*[3] The term *accento* for us means accent; in the terminology of the later sixteenth century, it was equivalent to our *appoggiatura* or grace note. Bach, in his small list of *Manieren*—his term for grace notes—which he wrote out for his 10-year-old son Friedemann, still identifies *appoggiatura* as accent.[4] Marin Mersenne (1588-1648) calls the accent *Port de la Voix*, Rognoni, *Modi di portar la voce*. For Germans Johann Andreas Herbst (1588-1666) and Johann Crüger (1598-1663) the term accent included so many notes that it could easily be confused with the *cascata*, a downward scale encompassing about an octave. What Guilo Caccini (ca. 1550-1610) calls a *cascata*, Herbst calls a *tirata*, a term generally used for an upward surge of an octave run. Wolfgang Caspar Printz distinguishes between the *tirata meza adscendus* (four ascending diatonic notes) and *tirata meza descendus*.[5] The same confusion reigned in the application of these grace notes. In Italy, during the eighteenth century, the single grace note, now called *appoggiatura*, was preferably treated iambically, that is, sung or played before the beat; its value was taken from the preceding note. This is contrary to the teachings of François Couperin (1668-1733) and C. P. E. Bach. The opposite practice, that of treating the grace note trochaically, was also common in Italy.[6] In Italy the trill was started more often with the main note than with its auxiliary, especially in chains of trills and short ones,[7] another practice disputed by the teachings of Couperin.[8]

All this disagreement stems from the very nature of ornamentation, which in its freedom, spontaneity, and improvisation resists codification. Living art has always preceded theory; a work has usually been universally established in the hearts and esteem of connoisseurs long before the arid schoolmaster concocts his arbitrary rules. The artist's work springs from the natural fecundity of his personality and his inspired imagination, and the laws upon which it may be based are recognized probably least of all by the creator.

Johann Andreas Herbst, along with Michael Praetorius (1571?-1621), first introduced Italian ornamentation into Germany in 1658. Buxtehude and Bach had access to their works as well as to the large German literature subsequently written on the subject of improvised ornamentation, including works by Adrianus Petit Colico (1499 or 1500-1562), Hermann Finck, Johann Crüger, and Printz. But Buxtehude's teacher and predecessor, Franz Tunder (1614-1667), who studied with Frescobaldi in Rome, probably influenced his development of the art most. Buxtehude undoubtedly passed on his impressions of his first-hand knowledge to his pupil from the north.

Among the most striking examples of Bach's use of Italian ornamentation are his "transcriptions" of Reincken's sonatas in A minor and C major.[9] Bach so transformed even the slow movements of these into elaborate, ornamented passages that Reincken's original text is difficult to recognize.[10] The first movement of Bach's own *Violin Sonata in A Minor*, which he himself transcribed for harpsichord (or clavier), is written in the same ornate style. In this case, of course, we have no original model with which to compare the final composition.

The Meaning of Ornamentation

Moderns generally cannot respond with sympathy to this ornate style, so remote from our current mode of esthetic perception. What seems strangest to us is the realization that elaborate embellishments were universally regarded by Bach and his contemporaries as a means of intensifying musical expression. Even the serene and mystic *cantilenas* of Palestrina, for example, were not always sung as written: long notes were divided in diminutions of more "expressive," fast moving figures. In the following example Bovicelli[11] shows how a text written by Palestrina (upper line) was actually sung (lower line). The respective ornaments are *ribattuta di gola* (repeating beats of the throat), *groppo* (a kind of turn), and *exclamatio* (emotional outburst).[12]

ribattuta di gola   *groppo*   *exclamatio*

Early experiments with the music-drama temporarily subdued enthusiasm for vocal ornamentation. In order to make the words clearly understood—a matter of paramount importance in a music-drama—composers such as Caccini and Claudio Monteverdi urged their singers to refrain from too much coloratura. Most of their improvised embellishments were confined to cadences, *firmata*, *da capi*, and connecting passages, leaving the words free for more distinct pronunciation and natural expression. But this noble purpose in the early music-drama soon gave way to that hybrid of musico-dramatic staging, the grand opera, in which both music and drama were merely vehicles for displays of vocal pyrotechnics.

French Influence on Bach's Ornamentation

French vocal music took a somewhat different path than its Italian counterpart. Under Lully (1665-1743), the dominant figure in French opera, literary meter and stress were zealously guarded against encroachments and interference from the rhythm and accentuation of their musical setting. Louis XIV and his entourage, whose taste was more literary than musical, heartily supported Lully's restoration of poetic diction to primary importance. Musical ornamentation of the text was reduced to the use of short trills and *agréments* (graces) of single notes (the kind Bach called accents), and more elaborate melismata were again relegated to endings and other safe places.

Passagi, however, were still enlivening the instrumental sections. French overtures abound with *tirate, cascate, accenti* of more than one note, *groppi*, and trills of all varieties. In the scores they were not written out but indicated by a cross (+). (Our modern editions in their passion for authenticity also omit these ornaments, making a performance faithful to the composer's intentions impossible to achieve.) Bach uses all these varieties of Italian ornament in his French Overtures, but writes them out in full. "Every ornament, every grace, everything that one thinks of as belonging to the method of playing, he [Bach] expresses completely in notes," Johann Adolph Scheibe complained in the May 17, 1737, edition of his weekly magazine, *Der Critische Musikus*.[13] The statement, which accurately describes Bach's practice, confirms that strict adherence to the art of improvised ornamentation was by no means a thing of the past. Johann Abraham Birnbaum, a music connoisseur and rhetoric teacher at the University of Leipzig, defended Bach and other composers for taking what he called "a necessary measure of prudence,"[14] since singers and instrumentalists alike do not always show enough discrimination.

Both Bach and Buxtehude clearly rejected the uncertainty and fluctuations in quality that the improvised ornamentation of earlier periods must have harbored. Bach, of course, continued to use the conventional stenographic signs, usually developed by French theorists, for short ornaments. He had easy access to the acceptable interpretation of these symbols through prefaces to the works of several French composers—Jacques Champion de Chambonnières (*Pièces de Clavecin*, 1670), Nicolas Lebègue (1677), Jean-Henri d'Anglebert (1689), Charles Dieupart (between 1700 and 1712)—and François Couperin's famous *L'Art de Toucher le Clavecin* (1716). Johann Caspar Ferdinand Fischer, in his preface to his *Musicalisches Blumen-Büschlein* (1698), deals with almost all the French signs used by these composers.

Passagi or diminutions are never mentioned in these books, unlike the Italian and English instruction books of the previous century. In French clavier music only the short ornaments survived. Fixed symbols such as ∿, ∧, ∨, ∾ covered every variety of trill and grace note, and these ornaments distinguished and established the fashionable French music. Although Georg Muffat mentions a few types of the old, florid Italian ornaments, the *tirata* and the *cascade*, in the preface to his *Florilegium Musicale Secundum*, virtually all of this type of improvised ornamentation had died out in France by the time his work was actually published (1695 and 1698).

Bach and Buxtehude did not wish to follow the French manner of total rejection of extended ornamentation (in Germany and Italy freely improvised *passagi* were still in vogue). They simply refused to leave this art to the caprice of others beside themselves. We find examples of written-out *passagi* in Bach's own variations on his sarabandes, in the *English Suites*, in g minor and a minor, which he entitles "les agréments de la même Sarabande." His works based on Reincken's sonatas and his *A Minor Violin Sonata*, mentioned above, are further examples of his practice of writing out ornaments.

The modern listener and the performer can be thankful that Bach so meticulously set forth his intentions for long coloratura passages, for in our time the correct execution of even short ornaments—designated by conventional French stenographic signs[15]—have become a source of controversy among organists, pianists, and harpsichordists. At issue is Bach's strict adherence to the French instruction books. The small list of ornaments that Bach wrote out for his 10-year-old son Wilhelm Friedemann[16] suggests that he did follow their stiff and stereotyped rules quite literally. But Bach surely meant this simple exposition only as an introduction, indicating the basic usages, to which practical execution might reveal many exceptions. Bach himself used many signs not included in this small list and very often wrote out one part of an ornament in notes and the rest in stenographic signs, a habit that adds considerably to the confusion of present-day performers.

Moreover, the explanation for his young son is not entirely in accord with the elaborate and intricate explanations that another son, Carl Philipp Emanuel, who was thoroughly steeped in his father's understanding of music, presents in his famous *Essay on the True Art of Playing Keyboard Instruments*. Recent writers suggest that Philipp Emanuel's book is not a definitive guide to his father's original desires for short ornaments and is in fact misleading.[17] The brilliant son developed a style quite different from that of his father, and some critics

List of ornaments written out by J. S. Bach for his ten-year-old son Wilhelm Friedemann. Holograph, Yale University, Music Library, New Haven, Conn.

feel that he incorporates a new conception of ornamentation into his explanation of this new style. However, the master-student relationship that Carl Philipp Emanuel enjoyed with his father provides strong evidence for rejecting this view. He revered his father and in his autobiography says, "In composition and keyboard performance I have never had any teacher but my father."[18] Many new styles have developed while remaining faithful to tradition, and Carl Philipp Emanuel could accurately voice his father's desires for ornamentation in the same *Essay* in which he calls for uses of harmony and counterpoint radically different from those of his father. Although Philipp Emanuel introduces some new signs not found in his father's scores—such as composites of different ornaments—and in his own compositions used certain ornaments more frequently than others, we may in general regard his intricate rules, with their numerous exceptions, as an attempt to codify his father's practices.

Johann Sebastian never was a slave to one particular style or method, as Philipp Emanuel's statement about "a certain great man," who said

that "one style may be better than another, yet each may offer something specially good, and neither can be so complete as to forbid addition or improvement" evidences.[19] His independent genius did not bind
itself to the style of any one nationality, least of all to the rigid rules
and all-too-simple precepts of the French. Carl Philipp Emanuel in his
role as theorist takes the free creations of true genius as a norm from
which he derives laws for more pedestrian talents.

Philipp Emanuel's associate at the court of Frederick the Great, the
flutist Johann Joachim Quantz, described the German style in his
autobiography (see *Allgemeine Deutsche Biographie*): "The German
artists endeavored to obtain their education in Paris and in Italy; and
among the German composers thus originated the so-called mixed
style; i.e. one adopted the manners of Lully's ballet music and strove
to unite it with the style of Vivaldi." And again in his *Essay on Flute
Playing* (1752) he says, "If one knows how to choose the best from the
taste of various peoples with proper judgment, a mixed taste flows from
it, which one may very well call the German taste, without surpassing
the limits of modesty" (p. 332). These reflections could apply to the
style of Johann Sebastian Bach.

From Bach's oldest biographer, Forkel, we learn that Johann Sebastian, although he held the French school in esteem, "on the other hand
considered them as too affected in their frequent use of graces, which
goes so far that scarcely a note is free from embellishments." Moreover, Bach considered that "the ideas which they [the French school]
contained were, besides, too flimsy for him."[20]

It seems safe to assume, on the basis of C. P. E. Bach's description
of ornamentation and Bach's own strong reservations about French
style, that he did not intend his stenographically noted ornaments to be
rigidly interpreted according to French rules. The most explicit of the
French textbooks, Couperin's *L'Art de Toucher le Clavecin*, did not appear until 1716, long after Bach had established his own style for ornamentation. Bach adopted no Couperin symbol that differed from those
already in use in Germany at the time,[21] and we must remember that
reading French was probably quite difficult for Bach. Bach's style in
ornamentation, to paraphrase Quantz, represents a synthesis of many
schools. Italian composers influenced Bach more than the French,
whose symbols he used simply because they were already in general
use in Germany and current in the scores of many of the composers who
influenced him.

THE ORGAN

THE organ is eminently suited for religious worship. The great volume of the instrument has practical advantages for leading congregational singing. More significantly, the sound of the baroque organ arouses and instills in men a mood of devotion. Like the soaring arches of the Gothic cathedral, the majestic sonority of the instrument's tone, its powerful sound, its qualities of nobility inspire us in the quest for an intimate relationship with the divine Presence, the communion that was the end of all devotional services in the age of faith. This mystical attraction of old European organs for even our secular age cannot be dismissed as merely sentimental childhood memories. Nor are arguments and theories based on reason adequate explanations for the sensual, spiritual, and emotional responses of man to organ music. The history of the development of conceptions of sound and musical esthetics from the fifteenth century on is important, however, as a framework for discovery of some aspects of the mysterious power of this centuries-old instrument.

During the fifteenth and sixteenth centuries the northern Europeans preferred wind-produced sonority to the vulgar vibrations and nervous accents of bowed strings, especially violins, which were despised as ale-house instruments. The impersonal character of a chorus of trombones and trumpets, its solemnity and seriousness, conveyed the spiritual mood with more dignity than the passionate and sensuous violin. Adam von Fulda, a monk from the heart of Germany who wrote a tract on music in 1490,[1] believed that wind-produced music spoke to a man's character, while violins merely aroused his passions. These musical esthetics reflect the attitude of medieval Christianity, which conceived of spirituality as opposed and inimical to mortal personality; reconciliation of these was not dreamed of, even during the Italian Renaissance. As personal characteristics were erased, musical art approached the sublime, thus freeing the mind of the listener from personal intrusions into contemplation of the divine. The organ was proclaimed the king of instruments, for it was completely depersonalized through its use of bellows and air chambers.

Mechanical sound controls were imposed on many fifteenth-century instruments as well. Reed instruments were fitted with sound caps that deprived them of their exquisite powers of expression. Sound caps placed on such instruments as the *Krummhorn*, the *Rauschpfeiff*, and the *Schreyari*[2] severed direct contact of the lip from the reeds, and thus secured an even flow of breath and a uniformity of force and sound quality. Ensembles of these intruments sounded more organ-like and approached the artistic ideals of music of the period. Viols were provided with gut frets, not only to facilitate the pitch but also to prevent the vulgar vibrato. The construction of viol bows and the accepted manner of holding them reduced accentuation to a minimum and erased any suggestion of dance rhythm.

As humanism developed and began to pervade all aspects of late Renaissance culture, artists and estheticians in southern Europe sought to retrieve individual influence in music. They desired drama in music and cultivated close touch with individual emotions. Conceptions of sonority changed. Performers on solo instruments, both string and wind, began to abandon the impersonal art born of medieval Augustinian ideas. The violin became the favorite instrument in Italy precisely because of its ability to express human passions and natural emotions; in 1725 Alessandro Scarlatti remarked to Johann Adolph Hasse of Dresden, "My son, you should know that I cannot suffer the blowing instruments."[3] Not surprisingly, the development of the Italian organ was considerably stunted under these new standards of taste. The infant state of the tiny organ that Bach found at the court of Celle exemplifies the Italian tendency.

In the north the Reformation did not make a clear break with the transcendentalism of the Middle Ages, and in this cultural environment that held onto much of the tradition of past centuries, the organ matured into the magnificent instrument of the baroque period. The sonorous northern organ was pregnant with symbolism; it lifted the soul from its prison into a sphere of infinitude. It was a veritable *vox dei ex machina*. The underlying stability of tone, effected by mechanical contrivances, called to mind an eternal voice, inspiring steadfast faith and confident reliance. The organ was one of the pre-eminent creations of the Age of Faith.

Master of Sound

Despite the impersonality and mechanical character of the organ its tone was not at all cold; the instrument abounded in overtones. A favorable balance of partials (partial tones) insured this warmth of timbre. Every string or air column vibrated in its entire length as well as in its halves, thirds, fourths, fifths, sixth parts, etc., thereby sounding respectively its octaves, twelfths (that is, octaves plus fifths), double octaves, double octaves plus thirds, and so on. In a vibrating piano a sharp ear can distinguish the second, and even the fourth partial. When a pianist strikes a string with all the dampers released (when the right pedal is depressed), all the partials of the other strings will echo any pitch that equals any partial of the vibrating string. These sympathetic vibrations create a much warmer tone, that is, one richer in overtones. The organ achieves the same multiplication of partials by opening the mixture or furniture stops, a multiple row of pipes, each of which produces one of the partials. By striking one key several of the sympathetic partials are thus artificially produced (on a pianoforte this occurs naturally), each sounded by a separate pipe. The mixture on the great-organ of Lübeck sounded 15 pipes at the stroke of one key. On the second manual, the *Brustwerk*, it had eight ranks of mixtures; on the third, the *Rückpositiv*, five; and on the pedal, six ranks of pipes. In addition to these four sets of mixtures, other sets of particularly high overtones called the cymbals or sharp mixtures (*Scharff*) could be used. Moreover, the timbre of a basic tone could be considerably changed by the so-called mutation stops, which emphasized particular partials such as the fifth and the upper third. Again the organ in Lübeck had a rich variety of such stops, among them the *sesquialtera*, the *quintadena*, the *nasat*, the *Rauschpfeiffe*, and the *Gemshorn*. Solo stops on these northern organs consisted in limited combinations of individual timbre. The basic organ tone as a ground color was seldom abandoned.

To the noble tonal textures called forth by these stops, the makers of the dignified baroque organs imposed the sentimental effects of the

Vox Humana and the tremulants, those tear-jerkers of our provincial churches. Not all spirits moved on the same high plane. Lübeck's *Marianorgel* had a *Vox Humana* and a *Trichter Regal*, another tremulous voice, along with two over-all tremulants that could be applied on several stops. It even included two drums and a *Cimbelstern*, a movable star with bells, displayed at Christmastime. Some organs incorporated bird songs and crowing cocks to illustrate the fateful time of Christ's denial by Peter.

Michael Praetorius wrote in 1618 that the tremulant had been known for 60 years. Andreas Werckmeister, in his *Erweiterte und Verbesserte Orgelprobe* (Enlarged and Improved Examination of Organs) of 1681 gives instructions for the tuning of the tremulant, advising very gentle pulsation but leaving the speed of the "beats" to individual taste. (He suggests that the stop sounds best with the *Höhlflote*.) Praetorius does not mention the *Vox Humana* in his description of Lübeck's organ, and since he knew of the stop we may assume it was left off this instrument. Bach had a *Trichter Regal* in the Thomas church in Leipzig, a slight variation of the *Vox Humana* which he used in the *Saint Matthew Passion*. Bach mentioned another tremulous stop, the *Unda Maris* in his report of the St. Wenceslaus Church in Naumburg; bells and chimes were other favorites of the period. Bach registers a subtle dissent from the popularity of such toys in his 1708 report on the organ of St. Blasius in Mühlhausen, in which he directs the placement of the new chimes "desired by the parishioners."

The main stay of baroque registration was contrast in tone color and the choir of reeds formed a powerful counterpart to the massive organ tone of the open diapasons. "Bach was a great friend of the powerful reeds," relates Johann Friedrich Agricola, who was Bach's pupil from 1738 to 1741.[4] Great power was the most admired quality of organ sound, and Bach brought out the full majesty of an instrument's capacities: he made "the organ resound with such fullness, and so penetrate the ears of those present [in Cassel, 1743] like a thunderbolt, that Frederick, the legitimate hereditary prince of Cassel, admired him with such astonishment that he drew a ring with a precious stone from his finger and gave it to Bach as soon as the sound had died away."[5] The organ at St. Martin's in Cassel had a particularly powerful array of stops,[6] especially in the sub-basses, the trombones, the trumpets that produced these "thundering" tones with reeds instead of the vibration of the lips. (Reeds have long since been replaced by metal tongues.)

The baroque organ was designed chiefly to be heard as an ensemble. The specifications (the list of stops) of these northern instruments show an astonishing number of high-pitched stops and registers of abnormal pitch (fifth, twelfths, etc., marked 3 ft., 2 ft., 1½ ft., etc.). These were almost never played solo but served as complementary coloration and modification of other, more substantial timbres. Names of some instruments, now obsolete, appear on baroque organs, including the Swiss fife, the *Krummhorn*, the traverse flute, the *Rauschpfeiff*, the *Blockflöte* or recorder, the *Violdagamba*.[7] But unlike organ builders today, who provide many stops that imitate contemporary instruments such as the clarinet, oboe, and French horn, baroque organ builders borrowed mainly the names and predominant partials of such instruments. The trumpet, trombone, cornet, and *Zinck* (or cornet) stops[8] are the only examples of true imitation. The builder, in fact, strove to sublimate the sonority of individual stops so that their various timbres became so many colors on the musical palette. Like a painting of Rembrandt, very few raw, unmixed, basic tones remained in the final effect, only the glow of light and life. Painters of music like Buxtehude and Bach drew an ever-varying ensemble of sound from their media to blend a sonority rich in life and warmth of soul.

Bach had astonishing mastery of registration, as a short excerpt from Forkel's biography, based on information from Bach's son Carl Philipp Emanuel, illustrates:

To all this was added the peculiar manner in which he [Bach] combined the different stops of the organ with each other, or his mode of registration. It was so uncommon that many organ builders and organists were frightened when they saw him draw the stops. They believed that such a combination of stops could never sound well, but were much surprised when they afterwards perceived that the organ sounded best just so, and had now something peculiar and uncommon, which never could be produced by their mode of registration.[9]

Evolution of the Baroque Organ

From 1618, when Michael Praetorius' *Syntagma Musicum* appeared, to the time of Gottfried Silbermann, who died three years after Bach, German organs underwent many transformations. The art of organ-building was never static during baroque days. When Jakob Adlung (1699-1762) described organs in his monumental *Musica Mechanica Organoedi*, he found that very few of the 219 instruments he had ex-

amined remained unchanged from their description by Praetorius.[10] The
organs in Hamburg, Lübeck, and Lüneburg had been repaired, modified, and augmented several times since 1618, and the history of Buxtehude's organ (which can be traced from its building in 1518 by Bartold
Hering) is an excellent example of the constant refinement of instruments. In 1561 the instrument was enormously enlarged by the addition
of a *positiv*, and in about 1640 Gottschalk and Borchert built the organ
up to about 40 stops. In 1670 Bergiel restored the organ, under Buxtehude's direction, to include the array of 54 stops that Bach witnessed on
his memorable visit. In the same year a few exterior improvements were
also added, including a more up-to-date console and some wood sculp-
tures of trumpeting angels.[11]

But the conception of organ-building was destined to evolve even
further. The famous manufacturer Gottfried Silbermann (1683-1753)
introduced certain departures from the typical baroque organ. Adlung's
criticism of Silbermann's innovations (written in 1767) is quite revealing
of the changing taste:

Mr. Gottfried Silbermann, born in Frauenstein in Meissen, two miles from
Freyburg, who learned the art of organ building from his brother in Strassburg (Andreas) has built this work [the catholic palace-organ in Dresden,
with 45 stops] (his pupil Zacharias Hildebrand finished it, because Silbermann saw his death approaching). . . . True connoisseurs of the organ find
nothing to censure: except the all too uniform disposition, which stemmed
only from an exaggerated precaution to risk nothing of such registers of
which he was not entirely sure that nothing would go wrong with them. Further the far too obstinate temperature, and finally the far too weak mixtures
and cymbals, by which the organs have not enough pungency [*Schärfe*—shrill,
penetrating quality] and piercing quality [*durchschneidendes Wesen*].[12]

He praises the durability of his instruments, their great simplicity and
magnificent intonation, and also their "light and easily playing keyboards [clavier]."

Bach undoubtedly shared Adlung's dislike of the "all too uniform
disposition," although he had only words of the highest praise for
Silbermann. His deference to fellow composers led him to temper any
criticism with mention of admirable aspects of a man's works, and he
took the same attitude of generosity toward instrument makers. Agricola, however, does not spare words in his criticism of Silbermann's
treatment of the powerful reeds that Bach so loved: "Is the convenience
of some organists and organ makers really reason enough to scorn
such stops, to call them names, and to eliminate them?"[13] Mr. Agricola

exaggerates when he accuses Silbermann of leaving the reeds out altogether, but the number of reeds on his instruments had been markedly reduced from that on the older instruments at Hamburg and Lübeck.

The function of the mixtures underwent a steady refinement from the Middle Ages to the period of Silbermann and his school. Praetorius points out the coarseness of mixtures on the older instruments, which "must have emitted throughout a strong noise and a powerful screaming," and "cannot have been particularly pleasing" on account of the great number of pipes that responded to each key.[14] The older builders arranged as many as 30 to 40 pipes to each key for cymbals or smaller mixtures, while Praetorius recommends 10 to 12. When Bach visited the organ in Lübeck its cymbals numbered only three to five ranks.

This steady decrease of mixture and cymbal pipes reflects a change in their function and esthetic purpose in baroque times. In the Middle Ages, like singers of *organum* who delighted in multiplying every note of a chant with consonances, that is, parallel octaves, fifths, and fourths, the organ typically augmented every note of a song with several consonances.[15] By the Renaissance parallel fifths, octaves, and even fourths were considered barbarous and "Gothic," and disappeared from the scores of fifteenth-century composers. But the northern European organ did not abolish its mixtures; it modified the harsh and screaming tone of voice, thus clarifying the fundamentals. Mixtures accenting the natural partials of the fundamental tone were gradually adopted and used to enhance vibrancy without impairing the basic pitch. These northern organs show a more direct transition from the medieval organ to the baroque than the Italian instruments, which omit mixture stops altogether and use the few stops available as weak mutation stops rather than true mixtures.[16]

Silbermann incorporated an astonishingly small number of pedal stops into his organs. He obviously had a different kind of music in mind than that of Bach, Buxtehude, and the great contrapuntal school of the past. Following French taste in general, he stripped the pedals of their power as an active musical force participating in contrapuntal ensemble, and reformed them into an instrument of accompaniment. Silbermann's organ, with its new treatment of mixtures as well as the reduction of reeds and pedal stops, responded more to the predominantly melodic music of the gallant age than to the mystic profundity of Bach's polyphony. The new music and instruments became a polite art for a secular society instead of a source of inspiration to the spiritual substratum of the mind.

The simple console of the organ in the New Church in Arnstadt.

The splendid organ built by Arp-Schnitger in the Hamburg *Jakobkirche* where Bach inspired the aged Reincken with his artistic organ improvisation on a visit in 1720.

In regard to tuning Silbermann was less modern than Bach; but even this rather old-fashioned attitude stems from his commitment to the new French music. Well-tempered tuning is more desirable in Bach's strongly modulatory harmony than in either the gallant music that was coming into vogue—and that Silbermann was used to hearing in France—or the new style that was capturing German taste. Neither ventured into the rich harmonies of Bach's great *G Minor Fantasy*, for instance. Bach used to tease Silbermann about his antiquated tuning by purposely playing in keys that displayed the "wolf" in his tuning.[17]

We can see that from many viewpoints Bach would not have appreciated the improvements of Silbermann or Johann Adolph Scheibe (1708-1776). Along with Agricola's sharp criticisms, which undoubtedly reflect those of his teacher, we have Bach's lifetime of compositions that ignored the simpler, more melodious modern French style. Surely he preferred, and demanded, an instrument suited to his music. We know that in 1720 he applied for the post of organist at the *Jacobikirche* in Hamburg, which had an organ similar to the one Reincken played, of the same period as that of Lübeck, and particularly rich in reeds, mixtures, and pedal stops—precisely those elements that Silbermann had radically reduced in his organs. Silbermann and Scheibe were of a different culture. Scheibe's son, a man of modern taste and "enlightenment," became one of Bach's severest critics; and Silbermann, who once attempted elopement with a nun, cannot have appealed to Bach's strict Lutheranism. He had also received his training as an apprentice of his older brother Andreas in Strassburg, who was in the employ of French Catholics. These were truly men of the age of rationalism and enlightenment and their art and taste reflected all that turning away from theology entailed. Music lost its contrapuntal dimensions and became shallow, elegant, and superficially melodious, however pleasing. Bach, a product of orthodox religion both by education and inclination, continued to prefer organs like those in Hamburg, Lübeck, Eisenach, and Lüneburg for his art over the more popular and contemporary instruments of Silbermann.

A New Golden Age?

Our present generation has set about to recreate the sonority, sound fantasies, and majesty of baroque organ music. Thanks in large measure to the work of Albert Schweitzer, educated audiences have begun to

react against the gaudy instruments and music of the nineteenth century. With Praetorius' *Syntaga Musicum* as a guide, organ-builders
are attempting to reproduce an instrument that will be as close to the
instruments that Bach played and composed for as humanly possible.
Such efforts however are doomed ultimately to failure. The most punctilious reproduction of a past style does not assure the rebirth of its life-
giving spirit.

There are many reasons that we will never truly know the beauty of
Bach's art. Our over-mechanized organs were not constructed with
baroque music in mind, and congregations raised for the last century
on the sentimentalities of extremely inferior composers are not sympathetic to the lofty music of Bach, Böhm, Pachelbel, and Buxtehude. To
meet the requirements of their decadent taste, organ manufacturers
abandoned the basic organ quality of the rich diapasons almost entirely,
indulging mostly in pretty imitations of modern orchestral instruments.
Some of the larger and more opulent churches displayed their wealth in
organs of mammoth dimensions, impressing their worshippers with
colossal effects. A favorite device on such machines was the so-called
crescendo pedal, which at any desired speed throws open all the available stops without discrimination. The swell pedal was invented to help
eliminate the impersonal quality of the organ so praised in baroque
times; with this device the individual organist may "express himself"
by diminishing or increasing the tone through a set of Venetian blinds.

Furthermore, the organ was deliberately moved out of the church into
the concert hall. Organ virtuosi displayed their prowess at world's
fairs, and entertained the tired businessman on a fantastically garish
instrument in the Wanamaker's store in New York, boasting five
manuals, 232 stops, and 18,000 pipes. This aberration of purpose and
taste developed in Bach's own homeland as well as in America. Had
anyone presented Rembrandt with a thousand more paint tubes of various and exotic shades, would he have represented the human soul
with more penetration?

We are now experiencing a reaction to these ghastly guises for true
art. The new organs, inspired by our desire to use a realistic baroque
instrument for the performance of baroque music, have enormously de-
creased air pressure. The diapasons are restored to their former prominence and the instrument divested of all modern accessories. The motives for attempting these restorations are laudable, and the sound of
these instruments have certainly been a welcome change for Bach

lovers. But completely accurate reproduction is impossible. The choice of the Praetorius organ may be a happy one, but we must remember the constantly changing nature of organs in Bach's time. Bach may never have known even one of the organs in the same stage of development in which Praetorius had found it. So this restoration becomes an art for art's sake, a trait totally foreign to Bach's conception of his art. Bach would not have approved of our treatment of his music as merely an art form. He composed and played his music as a means to a transcendental end, and we completely miss the depth of meaning of his work by removing it from its religious foundations.

10

BACH IN MÜHLHAUSEN:
ENCOUNTER WITH PIETISM

Johann Sebastian began his duties in Mühlhausen in a buoyant mood of joy. He was full of zeal to establish his musical ideals and confident of his powers to achieve them. His newly-won happiness in marriage added to his expectations for a rewarding life in Mühlhausen. His first apprentice, Johann Martin Schubart, and he set about to collect and copy all kinds of music that they expected to perform in the church.

This enthusiasm was somewhat unrealistic, however, in view of the conditions at St. Blasius Church. Bach must have foreseen the opposition he was to encounter there, for the Pietists' domination of the church was well known and of long standing. His numerous relatives in Thuringia surely warned him of the musical situation before he took the post. His predecessor, Johann Georg Ahle, had held his position of organist for 30 years and had openly proclaimed alliance with Pietism and shared its opposition to concerted music.[1] Bach's own church in Arnstadt had earlier vigorously suppressed the unorthodox pietistic music Adam Drese had tried to introduce, and memories of this experience must have forewarned Bach of the effects of Pietism on music. But Bach evidently underestimated these, and overestimated his powers as a musical missionary. He had to learn from bitter firsthand experience the full import of pietistic thinking, its threats to the essence of Lutheran dogma, and its destructive influence in music.

Bach and his apprentice managed to bring together an impressive repertoire but encountered only stubborn opposition from the pietistic clergy in their attempts to perform it. During his stay in Mühlhausen,

Bach wrote a few cantatas but only one of them was ever performed at the church. The cantata (No. 131) *"Aus der Triefe rufe ich, Herr"* (From the Depth I Call, Oh Lord) probably was written in commemoration of a great municipal fire such as the one that ravaged the town the year before Bach arrived, but was not performed at St. Blasius; Georg Christian Eilmar, pastor of the rival church in Mühlhausen, is believed to have written the libretto for this piece. Cantata No. 196, *"Der Herr denket an uns"* (The Lord Thinketh of Us), a wedding cantata, may have been performed in Arnstadt on the occasion of Johann Lorenz Stauber's marriage to Regina Wedemann, but was not heard publicly in Mühlhausen. (Stauber had married Bach and Maria Barbara.)

The only cantata by Bach that St. Blasius allowed to be heard was actually commissioned by the city council to commemorate its yearly election. The cantata—then called *Das Rathsstückchen* (the little council piece)—had a religious title *"Gott ist Mein König"* (God is my King) and Eilmar had chosen and arranged a text based on Bible passages, from the books of Samuel, the Pentateuch of Moses, and the Psalms,[2] appropriately alluding to the retirement of the aged councilors. In a joyous last movement Bach orchestrated the text welcoming the "new regime" with great fanfare of three trumpets, tympani, two flutes, two oboes, a bassoon, a string ensemble, chorus, and the usual organ accompaniment.

On the fourth of February the six burgomasters and 42 councilors— the *Rathsherren*—marched in a long procession from the *Rathhaus* to the Church of St. Mary to hear the *Rathsstückchen*, along with an elaborate program of sermons, hymns, and blessings. The entire town watched from wooden scaffolds erected for the occasion as the gold- and fur-bedecked dignitaries passed by, the retiring council in the lead, followed by their younger replacements and then by all the civil servants clad in their special festive colors. The assembly moved in formation in front of the church to take the oaths of loyalty under the open sky. The bakers' guild presented the councilors with a huge cake and the festivities concluded with the traditional banquets and merriment.[3]

The city went to the expense of printing Bach's cantata, the only one that was printed during Bach's entire lifetime.[4] In this way the city of Mühlhausen openly expressed its pride in the talented young composer residing in their community. But though the *Rathsstückchen* cantata was performed in St. Blasius Church on the Sunday following the great inauguration festival, the congregation who employed Bach was not willing to bestow any further tribute for the achievements of their organist. Instead the church was guilty of thwarting the genius in his endeavors of art and religious conscience.

St. Blasius Church benefited from Bach's guidance in the reconstruction of their organ, an enterprise the new city council approved on February 21, 1708, two weeks after their inauguration. Bach's entire report of the organ has been preserved and is a valuable guide to his conception of his favorite instrument. He used the organ in Eisenach, which was on a par with those in Hamburg and Lübeck,[5] as his standard of comparison. But aside from this contribution to the improvement of music in St. Blasius, the church and its pastor refused Bach's every attempt to use his great musical gifts for their services of worship. Every aspect of religious life in the church was subjected to the test of rigid pietistic thought. The freedom and variety that Bach believed essential to well-regulated church music was beyond the confines of Pietism and usually directly opposed to it.

Mühlhausen: A Center for Religious Controversy

Mühlhausen had never been a stronghold of Lutheran orthodoxy. During the early days of the Reformation the ancient city was one of the main seats of Anabaptism, a close relation of Pietism. Anabaptists boldly demanded separation of church and state, in spite of the inherent threat to the established order of medieval society in this cause. Their main doctrinal dissent involved infant baptism. Anabaptists— and Pietists—also sought subjective means of attaining spirituality, rather than adherence to proper doctrinal dictates. Luther, Zwingli, and the Catholics were united in opposition to the sect, and all joined in the recommendation of the death penalty for practicers of the faith. When one of the more fanatical leaders, Thomas Münzer, instigated the Saxon peasants to revolt he was captured, beheaded, and his head displayed upon a spear as an example to the citizenry.

In Bach's time, a century later, the democratic government of Mühl-hausen[6] reversed this harsh treatment of religious dissidents and took a very tolerant, even benign attitude toward Pietism. The sect, founded by Johann Arndt and Philipp Jakob Spener, was officially regarded by Lutherans as descried heterodoxy if not a heresy. The Pietists, like the Anabaptists, attached more importance to the personal experience of spiritual illumination than to passive submission to a doctrinal code of behavior. Both deviated from the orthodox Lutheran conceptions of good works and justification. Violent controversy raged wherever Lutheranism and Pietism came in contact, the old school claiming that spirituality was too lofty for human judgment and the Pietists maintaining that the orthodox alternative was merely frozen, intellectualized dogmatism.

Bach's church, St. Blasius, was led by a preacher who openly confessed his leaning toward Pietism. Johann Adolph Frohne had inspired his congregation since 1691 with his sincere piety in an environment of religious peace. In 1699 Georg Christian Eilmar took the pulpit at St. Mary's church in Mühlhausen and at once launched a violent attack upon Frohne. The vicious fulminations from the pulpits of both the Pietist and the passionate orthodox compelled the intervention of the magistrates, who called for an end to these impious expressions of strife and hatred.

When Bach arrived in Mühlhausen the disputes between the two preachers had flared up again. Some say that Bach sided with Eilmar, but such conjectures are based on rather flimsy evidence of any formal alliance. Bach's first-born child was baptized by Eilmar, but this only shows that he wanted a recognized orthodox to perform this service. As mentioned above, Eilmar also wrote the libretti for the few cantatas that Bach composed in Mühlhausen. The austerity of these libretti, however, can hardly have had a deep appeal to Bach, who worked with Salamo Franck soon after he left Mühlhausen and all his life deeply admired his poetic texts. We really do not have enough evidence to call Bach's association with Eilmar a friendship.

Pietism and Orthodoxy

Biographers have been puzzled by the contradiction between Bach's confessed orthodoxy and his apparently strong pietistic leanings.[7] The contents of his library included several works by renowned Pietists, and the libretti for his numerous cantatas often show a tendency toward the sentimental effusion typical of pietistic poetry. Even the profound sentiment of his music has been related to a pietistic mode of thought. All of this evidence stands very close to Bach's central commitments to life and work. His library provides a good reflection of Bach's viewpoint since it was collected when printed matter was still scarce. His books obviously were carefully selected to serve as guidance and affirmation of his theological convictions. And Bach's conception of music as a tool of religion demanded that he carefully weigh the meaning and emphasis of the words he used as well as the emotional impact of the music. Scholars were correct in finding Bach close to pietistic thought in vital areas of his life and work, but they neglected to investigate the nature of the relationship between Pietism and orthodox Lutheranism. To what extent do they represent opposing points of view? The following brief examination of works, both pietistic and orthodox, in Bach's library seems to suggest that confusion and haggling over minute points were more typical of this religious controversy than outright contradiction.

The 81 volumes of Bach's library, all dealing with religious subjects, form a distinct unit very much reflective of his thinking. The only historical work, Josephus' *History of the Jews*, supplements a theological viewpoint. All the other books are divided between those of pietistic leaning and standard works on orthodox dogma. Along with Luther's complete works in two editions as the nucleus, the collection as a whole serves as a commentary or reference source to Lutheranism, even the ancient Josephus and the medieval Tauler and Thomas à Kempis.

Most of the pietistic, or allegedly pietistic books (with the possible exception of Arndt's *Vom Wahren Christenthum*) were acquired after the Mühlhausen period, in editions of between 1723 and 1741.[8] Only the volumes by the two most celebrated Pietists and founders of the sects bear earlier dates—1606 to 1609 (Arndt) and 1714 (Spener). Possibly Bach began his study of this divisive controversy with these works and later pursued his investigation with the works of lesser figures in the movement.

The best known of these Pietist authors was Philipp Jakob Spener (1635-1705). Bach owned his *Gerechte Eifer wider das Antichristliche Pabsttum* (Justified Zeal Against the Antichristian Papacy), and was probably acquainted with his main work, the *Pia Desideria*, a sensational book in which he condemns orthodox theologians for their hatred of those who practice any deviation from accepted forms. He writes that what they mistake for faith is "nothing but human imagination and an exercise of the intellect," and that of "the true heavenly light and life of faith they are entirely oblivious."[9] Spener never attacked the orthodox creed, always remaining true to his "dear Luther," but he did warn against endless disputations, which often led to the neglect of true obligations toward the congregations. While theologians imagined themselves godly and blessed when they had proved the damnation of a colleague for a creedal error, the true test of a man's faith must always be his life and conduct.

An earlier protagonist of Pietism, Johann Arndt (1555-1621), had first inspired Spener. We find a copy of his widely read *Vom wahren Christenthum* (Of True Christianity) in Bach's library. In this work he reveals his mysticism and revolts against intellectual polemics. The book, appearing at the beginning of the seventeenth century, already accused the Lutheran clergy of lip service, and advocated a return to a life of true self-denial. He called them by a coarse German word, *Maul-christenthum*, for which there is no adequate translation. Translated literally, it means Christianity of the mouth, but *maul* indicates the mouth of a ferocious animal. This dreamer and ecstatic, who leaned toward the mysticism of medievals like Tauler, Thomas à Kempis, and others, remained an enthusiastic admirer and adherent of Luther and never questioned the orthodox documents of his faith—the Augsburg Confession and the Formula of Concord. Nevertheless, for his attack on the clergy he was subjected to the same calumny as Spener. Both were accused of all the usual heresies—Papism, Calvinism, Flacianism, Enthusiasticism, Pelagianism, Wegelianism, and possibly other off-shoots.

The authors of most of Bach's books are, though strictly orthodox, not primarily polemical. One of the most exemplary dogmaticians of orthodox Lutheran theology, Johann Gerhard (1582-1637), was a life-long enthusiast for Arndt. Gerhard had studied under Leonhard Hutter (whose "purest milk" of orthodoxy Bach had imbibed in school) and was renowned as one of the most solid and safest exponents of the faith. But since mysticism had always been suspect—as too personal and defiant of established orthodoxy—Gerhard was strongly chastised for his association with Arndt. The Protestants had no more love for Spener and Arndt than the Catholic church had for Meister Eckhardt. The book that Bach owned—his *Schola Pietatis oder Uebung der Gottselig-keit* (School of Piety or Exercise in Godliness)—was primarily devotional. His two main theological works, *Loci Theologici* and *Confessio Catholica*, together with Chemnitz' *Examen Concilii Tridentini* (which Bach owned) are regarded as the most important justification of Lutheran dogma.

Bach must have been fully aware of the great difference between the living word of Luther and the intellectual prattle of the theologians.

The fact that he owned two editions of Luther's complete works shows that he valued these most of all. And indeed, Luther and the Bible formed the core of his erudition, constant sources of reference for purity of creed as well as personal inspiration. He must have agreed with the Pietists in their attack upon the cold intellectuality and vicious militancy of the doctrinaires. This pedantic, intellectual school of theologians was not created directly by Luther. Melanchthon began a long line of Lutheran theologians intent on formulation and clarification. In a sense Melanchthon became the corruptor of the faith since he fathered that renewed Scholasticism that Luther despised.

But Bach certainly was aware of the limits and dangers of pietistic subjectivity. He owned four volumes of sermons by one of the most fanatic Pietists of his own time. August Hermann Francke (1663-1727) drew people from distant places with his passionate sermons. He was involved in sensational controversies with the universities of Leipzig and Erfurt and helped to expel the rationalistic philosopher Christian Wolff from the University of Halle. Francke deserves to be cited as the prototype of the Pietists who were fanatical in their insistence on personal experience of rebirth. His puritanical condemnation of all natural enjoyments was also more severe than his predecessors'. From the time of his great "rebirth" in his middle twenties, he held all ambition, honors, respect of the "world," riches, and welfare, and all outer, worldly enjoyment in utter contempt.[10] By these words he betrayed an aspect of Pietism contrary to the healthy ideas of Luther, and even of Spener, and it was here that Bach's sympathy with Pietism must have reached its limits. Bach was surely not a puritan.

Among Francke's large following of disciples is Johann Jacob Rambach, two of whose sermons are found in Bach's library. Rambach studied at the University of Halle under Francke and his friends Lange and Breithaupt. After Francke's death in 1727 Rambach became professor of theology at the University of Halle but was badgered by Pietists for proofs of "penitential experiences." The hypocrisy of this fanaticism disgusted Rambach, and he departed from Halle rather than satisfy them. He was primarily a poet and wrote elegies, cantatas, madrigals, sonnets, and spiritual songs. One of Bach's librettists, Menantes (a pen name of Christian Friedrich Hunold), published a collection of the Pietist's poems, together with his own, and Bach's interest in Rambach may well have been aroused by his poetry.

Three other authors in Bach's library deserve mention. Johann

Mattaeus Meyfart (born in 1590), Heinrich Müller (born in 1631), and Christoph Scheibler (1598-1653), all show the tendency toward a gentle mysticism, together with an inclination to asceticism, so typical of Pietism. Although Scheibler wrote many philosophical works in which he took a stand against rationalism, his *Aurifonia Theologica*, owned by Bach, was free from philosophical and scholastic terminology. Heinrich Müller has been called a forerunner of Pietism.[11] Bach owned his *Geistliche Erquickungsstunden* (Hours of Spiritual Refreshment), which is full of tasteless, sentimental figures of speech found also in pietistic poetry and much of German literature of that time. He advises pastors, "Preachers are wet nurses of the congregation; they must give healthy and sweet milk; they must first taste the aliment of the divine Word, they must masticate, digest, and transform it into life."[12]

We cannot be as sure of Bach's reaction to or acceptance of the mysticism of the Pietists as we are of his agreement with their distrust of dogmatism and his objections to their disdain for worldly pleasures. Bach has been called a mystic. His understanding of the meaning and personal import of mysticism, however, was conditioned more by the words of a medieval Catholic than by the books and lives of Pietists. His possession of the sermons of Johannes Tauler (1300?-1361) is a surprising contrast in the fairly uniform content of the rest of his library.

Bach's understanding of Tauler was conditioned by Luther's conception of him and no one in Bach's time had an objective, historical estimate of Tauler's philosophy. The edition of 1720,[13] which Bach owned, is particularly interesting because the some 2,000 double columns include not only the sermons of Tauler, "written for all Sundays and Festive days throughout the entire year," but also has "comments by Dr. Martin Luther, Philipp Melanchthon, Johann Arndt and the testimony of other blessed teachers . . . ," and a preface by Philipp Spener. Other works by Tauler in this edition are "The Imitation of the Poor Life of Christ" (in two parts, 279 pages), *Medulla Animae* (The Marrow of the Soul), *Teutsche Theologia* (German Theology) with prefaces by Luther and Arndt, a German translation of Thomas à Kempis' *Imitation of Christ*, and two other works by Tauler. His biography and two books by Luther's father confessor, Johannis van Staupitz, complete the contents.

The *Teutsche Theologia*, the most speculative work in the entire tome, was discovered by Luther in 1518 as an anonymous manuscript, which he attributed to Tauler.[14] In a preface Luther says that he "learned more from it and what God, Christ, Man, and all things are, than from any other work he knew, except the Bible and St. Augustine." Spener, although he praised the work, believed it was the work of some writer later than Tauler.

The mysticism of *Teutsche Theologia* is definitely more speculative than that of either Tauler or Thomas à Kempis. The entire book is pregnant with veiled philosophical speculations, probably based on mystic thinkers like Meister Eckhart, who received his training with the Scholastics of Paris. It speaks of the Perfect and the imperfect, of the Uncreated and the creature as the *"Schein,"* the semblance, the mere appearance of the former, having no true being other than in the perfect, being in itself a mere chance.[15] These metaphysical speculations resound with strong Thomistic echoes; they also foreshadow idealistic Hegelianism as well as the existentialism of Tillich.

Bach must have read the work with awe, since it was so highly recommended by Luther, but the musician, entirely untrained in philosophy, probably felt bewilderment more. One wonders how he reacted, for example, to those strange, half Neo-Platonic, half Thomistic speculations on the Fall of Adam as a diffusion of the particular from the universal, as if it were less an historical event within time than a timeless, existential condition of mankind. Though he objected to the instrumentality of that "heathen" Aristotle, Luther had received enough training in the Scholastics' work to grasp the mysticism of Tauler. However, modern scholars[16] feel that Luther misunderstood Tauler, that he saw in him a forerunner of his own evangelism and reform. He read Tauler between 1515 and 1518, while he was still a monk and stood closer to medieval asceticism. Arndt more readily recognizes his weak points: "There are many unknown weeds in the forest; one must pass them by, and let them stand untouched." Spener discovers several "papistic errors," in the medievalist whom Luther believed to be antipapistic at heart.[17] The Pietist forgives and overlooks these because in other places Tauler "often offers at your disposal the most glorious arguments by which they must inevitably be defeated."[18]

In the end Luther rejected more of asceticism than the Pietists were later willing to give up. He was far less a puritan than August Hermann Francke and his Halle school. His asceticism was tempered by a belief in the reconciliation of the world and fruits of nature with the spiritual life. The mysticism of the Pietists retained, at least in its prescriptions for life in the world, much of the coldness of the medieval monk's withdrawal, however much the sect would deny the theology of the monastics. In ideological conflicts like these, Bach undoubtedly turned to Luther. Certainly all we can glean from his personal life and his music points toward his love of rather than contempt for the good things and joy of the world.

Bach, who never totally rejected any musical style and was always ready to give credit to a work of the slightest value, was equally just and sober in evaluating the merits of the Pietists. To say he was a Pietist at heart is equivalent to saying he was a pious, warm-hearted Christian at heart, a good Lutheran. Bach was always more interested in a moving sermon than in a sophisticated defense of the dogma and selected for his library an overwhelming majority of collections of appealing sermons, many of which were by Pietists.

Pietism in Music

When the Pietists allowed their puritan, ascetic, subjective tendencies to encroach on music, Bach could no longer take such a tolerant attitude. He could not suffer their condemning verdict on the use of instrumental chamber (secular) music in church, or their ridicule of coloratura singing, which Spener likens to "outbursts of laughter by Italian sopranists."[19] These Pietists considered such elements "carnal," "worldly," and destructive of spirituality. They were unaware of the sublimizing power of a rare artist, as Bach was, illumined by Luther's transcendental faith, who could transform the secular into the spiritual. The Pietists ignored Luther's reconciliation of spirit and nature, but Bach had learned at the organ benches of Buxtehude and Böhm that worldly elements like dances, ornaments borrowed from secular music, and virtuosic display on manuals and pedals alike, could be wedded to and add depth to spiritual chorales.

Bach was no puritan. He loved fun, wrote many dances, smoked his big pipe, and drank his beer. A menu which has been preserved shows that on occasion he could enjoy a more than hearty meal.[20] And his 21 children were not born from ascetic abstention. His rollicking fun in the Coffee Cantata and the Peasant Cantata are certainly not the products of a puritan. The Peasant Cantata is reminiscent of the rustic ruggedness of Luther's frank, uninhibited language. Francke condemns the demand of "The world" for any *Ergötzung des Gemüths* (amusement, delight, or recreation of the spirit); Bach, for his part, inscribes his partitas with the legend, "The art of clavier playing, consisting of Preludes, Allemands, Courants, Sarabands, Gigues, Menuets, and other Gallantries: composed for lovers of music for the delight of their spirit [zur Gemüths Ergoetzung]. von Joh. Seb. Bach . . ."

Spener, like Luther, judged the morality of worldly enjoyments according to the individual case, and did not condemn enjoyment as such,[21] but the Pietists of the Halle school were fanatical and their stringent puritanism inevitably was as detrimental to art as it was to science. When austerity cuts off the life-stream by shunning the world and its natural enjoyments, art is bound to die. The hymns that Francke and other Pietists did compose are marked by bad taste, and Bach never used them in his services. This is the crux of Bach's objection to Pietism. Instead of using music to enrich their spiritual lives, Pietists betrayed religion by outlawing music.

Their worst offence was to replace the sturdy and classical Lutheran chorale, Bach's musical Bible, with sentimental hymns. Francke, Nicolaus Ludwig, Count of Zinzendorf (1700-1760), Johann Anastasius Freylinghausen (1670-1739), and at times even Spener composed hymns with insipid texts and music of weak rhythmical and melodic texture. They abandoned a musical heritage deeply rooted in Christian history. Many melodies stem from Gregorian music, and several are attributed to St. Ambrose (340-397). The hymn *"Herr Gott, dich loben wir"* (Lord God, We Praise Thee) is held to be Luther's translation of *Te Deum Laudamus*, a hymn ascribed to St. Ambrose and St. Augustine, and probably dating back even further.[22] The early Christian congregations may well have sung it. Countless folksongs have grown out of these venerable melodies, and the Lutheran chorale contains ninth and tenth century tropes and sequences of the monks of St. Gall, and Meistersinger and Minnesinger songs of all kinds.[23]

The Lutheran chorale then is not a creation of a person but of the collective genius of many centuries. Again and again these basic melodies appear in sacred as well as secular music, each generation setting them in their own style and modality, without appreciably changing the original structure of the melodies. Bach set these tunes in the harmonization of his time, which was the major and minor mode as we use it, but he left the melody nearly untouched. We can lift the melodies out of the harmonic frames of all his chorale-preludes and find their age-old modal construction—the Dorian, Phrygian, Lydian, Mixolydian, Ionian, and Aeolean.

Bach's fidelity to these venerable tunes has deeper roots than a personal predeliction or mere conventionality. The hymns were part of a sacred tradition related to the Augustinian doctrine of free will. The entire theology, as Bach learned it from Leonhard Hutter's catechism, is the exposition of this idea that Grace is "not accomplished by our natural forces," not "through our merits," but is a gift of God. In the pietistic attitude toward music Bach saw the divine Will subjectified, deprived of its divine origin and debased to a merely personal, psychological level. Bach interpreted his own supreme technique as a gift of God: "I have had to work hard; anyone who works just as hard will get just as far." His humility had its source in the philosophy that Arndt summarized so well in the *Teutsche Theologia:* "man shall not attribute anything that is good in him to himself, but to God."[24]

Bach's awareness of God in music was one with his perception of God through his faith. Illumination and justification depended on God and not on any emotional state of mind. In essence the Pietist hymn writers were putting themselves above God by elevating their emotional responses and the art inspired by them. Their substitution of inspirations of the moment for the classical chorale seemed a sacrilege to both Bach's religious beliefs and his philosophy of art. This pietistic element of subjectivity in the composition of hymns and the puritanical attitude toward figured music drove Bach from Mühlhausen as soon as other opportunities presented themselves.

Departure for Weimar

Bach's desire to leave Mühlhausen evidently came to the ears of Duke Wilhelm Ernst of Weimar, for the powerful prince and lover of music made an offer to Bach, which he accepted immediately. Bach's letter of resignation, dated June 25, 1709, was addressed to the burgomaster, the town councilors, the "highly learned, the highly and very wise gentlemen" (probably teachers and professional men), and to the "highly gracious patrons and gentlemen." He expresses polite gratitude for their having allowed him to enjoy a better subsistence than before. Then, in one of those interminable, labyrinthine German sentences of that period (this one contains 135 words!) he tells the council that he has not been able to honor God with a well-regulated church music,"[25] an end toward which he has striven all his life.[26] In the same sentence he describes his efforts to promote music in the surrounding villages, where "it often excels what we produce at St. Blasius"; that he has at his own cost acquired a good repertoire of music; that he has done his duty toward the upkeep and repair of the organ; that it has been impossible to accomplish these things without opposition; and that there are no signs of improvement in the future, although some souls in this church would rejoice at a change. He adds still further that however simply he lives he does not earn enough. In the next paragraph he announces his decision to join the court-chapel of His Serene Highness of Saxe-Weimar, where he will be able to "pursue the objective of [his] ultimate aim, [the] rightly well-conceived church music" *(die Wohlzufassenden Kirchen Musik)*.[27]

In requesting his dismissal, he offers the city of Mühlhausen his services, and indeed, he was released on the condition that he would continue to supervise the reconstruction of the organ. Bach kept his word. In 1709 he returned from Weimar to take part in the Reformation Festival and played a prelude to Luther's hymn "A Mighty Fortress Is Our God."[28]

Bach's statement of resignation is valuable for the confession of musical faith it contains. Undoubtedly he had been forming his ideal of a well-organized program for church music for some time. Throughout his life his striving toward this goal influenced his moves and decisions. "Rightly-conceived church music" forms the key to understanding of Bach the man, the musical reformer, the fulfiller of Luther's ideal. Although he had to wait 15 years before he could fully realize his ideal, at Leipzig, he never lost sight of it during his stays at the courts of Weimar and Köthen. Tragically the fulfillment of Luther's musical ideals came too late. Leipzig was the only place where his "rightly-conceived church music" was heard, and with Bach's death his music went into oblivion for an entire century.

11

THE WEIMAR YEARS (1708-1717)

IN July, 1708, Bach joined the entourage of that devoutly orthodox but despotic prince, Wilhelm Ernst (1662-1728), the stern older brother of Johann Ernst (1664-1707) whom Bach had served for a short period five years earlier. The two brothers lived out their lives estranged over a struggle for political power. An imperial law of 1629 had given them equal sovereignty, with the younger bearing the title of *Mitregent* or coregent. Constant and sharp disagreements arose over governing the principality and Johann Ernst was driven to appeal, in vain, for division of the already tiny territory.

The two brothers had exceedingly different temperaments. Wilhelm Ernst was a stern religionist, using his faith to make his barren personal existence bearable. Johann Ernst was a much warmer person, although in historical records he is overshadowed by his stronger older brother, who outlived him by almost 21 years. He loved music and spent long hours playing and composing music. Wilhelm Ernst saw little merit in these pleasant indulgences. At nine o'clock all the lights in his castle had to be extinguished—he did not share the current enthusiasm for court theater. He surrounded himself with the edifying company of preachers and theologians, and occasionally appeared in the pulpit himself. He was ridiculously proud that at the age of nine his ability to pontificate had been recognized.

Wilhelm was a lonely man. He was separated from his wife, had no children, was estranged from his brother and later his nephew. He lived for his conviction only. He withdrew into his religion as a refuge and a means to maintain not his humanity, but his stubborn will. His motto,

Alles mit Gott (Let all be with God), gave him the assurance that his own will and God's were identical. In fact, his belief was primarily in his own righteousness, supported, of course, by God. His ostentatious claims for the doctrinal purity of his own faith justified, to him, a ban on mention of subjects of religious controversy from the pulpit. (His staunch Lutheranism was not disturbed, however, when the question of taking advantage of the services of calvinistic Huguenots, at very low wages, came up.)

The Weimar castle, "Wilhelmsburg," in which Bach worked as court organist and chamber musician.

The castle in which Wilhelm resided, *Wilhelmsburg*, was a vast, very high, square structure in French Renaissance style. Spires that seemed to be striving to outreach each other broke the severity of the style with thin elongated points, one of them strangely mounted upon a huge, round tower. The castle was surrounded by a moat, separated from a nearby stream, the Ilm, by a broad promenade.

Johann Ernst's palace, the *Rotes Schloss* (Red Castle), was a sixteenth-century building connected with the *Wilhelmsburg* by a red corridor, the *Roter Gang*. Many busy personnel passed over this passage daily, carrying out the complicated business affairs of a dual seat of government. Bach too must have often trod the long passage, dressed in the ecclesiastic robe of chapel organist.

Many intellectuals of the day lived in the castle community and contributed importantly to Sebastian's cultural and musical development. Wilhelm Ernst had one laudable virtue, that of promoting the education of his people. He erected new buildings for the schools and engaged competent men for the education of the young and for the training of the teachers and clericals. His interest in history prompted him to assemble public archives, to form a collection of coins, and to establish an excellent library.

Bach's duties at this court are not precisely known, but his main function was organist. In the archives of Weimar he is mentioned as *Hofforganist und Cammer Musicus*, court organist and chamber musician. In his own genealogy his title is *Cammer und Hofforganist in Weimar An. 1708*. Bach thus ranked below the *Kapellmeister* and the *Vice-Kapellmeister* in the hierarchy of musical ranks and petty powers. The *Kapellmeister* presided over the choice of music and was expected to perform the fruits of his own talent on most musical occasions.

When Bach arrived in Weimar the office of *Kapellmeister* was held by Johann Samuel Drese (1644-1716), an old and feeble man who was no longer capable of fulfilling his duties. He had been a pupil of his cousin Adam Drese, who, Bach cannot have forgotten, long ago tried unsuccessfully to introduce pietistic music in Arnstadt. The *Vice-Kapellmeister* was Drese's son Johann Wilhelm, who has gained as little praise as his father for his compositions.

Little social intercourse took place between the ducal potentate and his staff of musicians, and all the musicians were employed at other tasks in the feudal relationship. A memorandum of 1714-1716 noted that a bass singer held the office of court secretary, a trumpeter was also chamber servant,[1] and another trumpeter was also palace stewart (a very lowly position). The court secretary, so the record states, boarded at the palace, while the humble trumpeters "draw table allowance."[2] The *Kapellmeister* was reluctantly allowed to draw "a daily ration of one small loaf of bread and one measure of beer from the cellar" in addition to his salary. A "soprano" (a male falsettist) is mentioned as "going along to the free table." Since Bach's name does not appear on the list, he must not have lived at the castle. This distinction suggests that Bach was held in high regard at the court.

The organ in the ducal chapel was very small, compared to those with 55 to 65 stops that Bach had known in Hamburg, Lübeck, Lüneburg, and Eisenach. The instrument had only two manuals, 25 stops, and was even smaller than the one in Mühlhausen. But Bach's artistic imagination would always transcend the limitations of the physical medium in his charge.

The Fruits of an Inspired Organist

Although Bach himself aspired to a higher rank than organist, we may be grateful that for a few years his duties were limited to this office, for in no other period of his life did he compose so many preludes, toccatas, fantasies, and fugues for this instrument. Thirty-nine major organ compositions are extant for the years 1708-1717. He composed more than three times the number of large organ works produced in the 33 years after he left the duchy. Bach wrote the greatest organ music of all time between his twenty-third and thirty-second year; a dozen works of later years equal this body of works but only his chorale-preludes, composed later, surpass his early achievement.

These organ compositions stand as eternal monuments, profoundly expressive of deep, ecstatic spiritual experience. Yet the models upon which Bach conceived these glorious works are easily discernible. But in them Bach achieved the consummation of the artistic aspirations of his predecessors. In several, like the *Passacaglia* and the *D Major Prelude and Fugue* (*BG*, XV, 88)* the styles of Böhm and especially Buxtehude are evident—in the idioms, the virtuosity, the harmonic counterpoint, and the form. In others we recognize the physiognomy of Pachelbel's music. The famous *A Minor Fugue* (*BG*, XV, 189) uses a theme derived from a similar work of that master. The same theme is transformed once more in a clavier fugue of this period (*BG*, III, 334). But in Bach's hands these works reach a maturity while still burning with his ardent fire of youth.

Conspicuously absent from the list of works of this period are chorale-preludes. Perhaps Duke Wilhelm or *Kapellmeister* Drese wished to shorten the service by omitting these meditative preludes to congregational singing. Bach was dedicated to this traditional art, for all his teachers and his illustrious relatives had cultivated it. As soon as his connection with this court was terminated he began working on a set

* *BG* refers to the *Bach Gesellschaft* edition of Bach's works.

of chorale-preludes for the entire liturgical year, which are discussed in Chapter 18.

Bach's toccatas pose another but related problem. The composer's choice of musical forms was determined by their particular job; musicians always composed with a specific occasion in mind, and these factors dictated the choice of personnel and instruments. At first glance Bach's toccatas do not seem to fit any of the occasions for which he was composing at this time. Today the works are performed exclusively on the piano or the harpsichord, and this practice suggests that the music was not played on the organ in religious services. But at the time Bach wrote these works, no sharp distinction was ever made between organ, harpsichord, or clavichord works—they could be performed on any of these instruments—and in most of the extant manuscripts the titles of the toccatas are given as *Toccata manualiter* or *Toccata clamat manualiter*. Only a few are called *Toccata, Cembalo* (for the harpsichord).[3] They were performed on the organ as well as the harpsichord, and probably in the Lutheran church service as extra music during Communion, which followed the regular main service.

Indeed not long before Bach's time toccatas were part of the service. Bach was fully aware of this custom, for continuing in Weimar his practice of copying numerous Italian compositions, he wrote out the entire *Fiori Musicali* of Girolamo Frescobaldi (1583-1643),[4] the Roman organist of St. Peter's. The toccatas, ricercars,[5] and other pieces found in this collection, served at the Catholic Mass and at other liturgical functions. The rhapsodic parts of the toccatas grew out of the improvisations of the organist during the unpredictable span of time that the priest might take for his various changes of robes and mitres, and swinging of incense. In general these interludes—toccatas connecting the more set ricercars—took the form of a dexterous display and sometimes served as preludes to larger compositions. Some of Bach's more virtuosic preludes, followed by large fugues, bear the title of toccata. Frescobaldi's toccata style was introduced to Thuringia by his pupil Johann Jakob Froberger (1616-1667), who undoubtedly shared his master's ideas on the functions of this musical form. He studied with Frescobaldi from 1637 to 1641. Bach's love for Froberger's art is well known, and his compositions, which were among the first that Bach mastered as a young student in Ohrdruf, impressed this conception of the toccata on Bach.

So when our modern piano virtuosi use these toccatas to introduce the more appealing fare of romantic, impressionist, and other entertainment, the original function and import of this music is missed entirely. Bach may have played the rhapsodic parts of these clavier toccatas as the preacher moved around between the performances of his sacred duties in the Communion service, shortening or extending the section as needed. The quiet ricercars were played during the administering of the bread and wine, and the gigue-like, joyful finale echoed the grateful gladness of the communicants as they walked away from the altar.

Seventeen other compositions of this period, primarily small fugues for other instruments, are extant. Few of them, however, show the maturity of the organ works. Six are of questionable authenticity;[6] six others are modeled upon examples by Tomaso Albinoni (1671-1750), Wilhelm Hieronymus Pachelbel (son of the famous composer), and possibly others. One wonders either if they might be attempts by his students or if they belong to an earlier period. The only composition of this group that unmistakably shows the hand of the master is the *Prelude and Fugue in A Minor* (*BG*, XXXVI, 91). Later Bach worked this piece out as a triple concerto for flute, violin, harpsichord, and orchestra, and again, just a few years before his death, he used the theme in a chorale arrangement. The *"Aris Variata alla Maniera Italiana,"* as the musicologist Ernst Naumann points out (*BG*, XXXVI, lxxxvi), has come to us only in the form of copies by pupils and other contemporaries. If this charming composition is really by Bach, he intended it frankly as *"all 'imitatione Italiana,"* as the manuscript of a copy by Kellner reads.

After 1714 when he was given a higher rank of "concertmaster and organist," he was required to compose and direct cantatas for the service in the ducal chapel. Bach had earlier proven his ability in this form: in the fall of 1713 he had performed his cantata No. 21, *"Ich hatte viel Bekümmernis,"* (I had much Sorrow) in Halle, and five other cantatas date from before 1714.[7] In all, 20 cantatas can be identified in the Weimar period with relative certainty; at least two others presumed to date from the same period were either revised or actually composed at a much later date.[8]

Since Bach had a rather small orchestra at his disposal, the Weimar cantatas do not require a great variety of instruments. There were plenty of trumpeters who served in various capacities—including the chase, the one indulgence the austere duke allowed himself. The list of musical employees does not mention an oboist, so one of the trumpeters, perhaps the bassoonist listed, or occasionally one of the town pipers must have filled in. The total number of singers in these ensembles amount to six boys. Tonal balance was practically unknown at this time.

A Congenial Musical Environment

In sharp contrast to the antimusical atmosphere in Mühlhausen, Bach found, at the palace and in the city, a circle of kindred minds who recognized the spiritual power of music. Johann Christoph Lorbeer, a poet in Wilhelm's entourage who won the laureate's crown from the emperor, wrote an extensive lyrical poem, *"Lob der Edlen Musik"* (The Praise of the Noble Art of Music). He even conducted public polemics against pietistic opposition to music. Lorbeer was 40 years Bach's senior, and age probably interfered with any close relationship between the young composer and him. Bach was closer to Salomo Franck, a younger poet who had a decisive influence upon Bach's new stylistic achievements in the composition of the church cantata. Franck, like almost all writers in Germany at that time, followed the cantata reforms of Erdmann Neumeister (1671-1756), who used operatic devices such as the recitative and the *da capo* aria composed upon free poems paraphrasing Bible and hymn texts. This new treatment (discussed at greater length in Chapter 19) called for a new kind of poet—the librettist, an able manipulator of rhyme and meter willing to submit his art to the more powerful claims of music.

Salomo Franck loved and respected music deeply and was willing to collaborate with the composer. In addition to his sympathetic attitude, Franck stands out among all the librettists that Bach employed as the most poetic. Even in his later years in Leipzig, Bach would refer his librettist Picander to Salomo Franck as a model. Bach must have found this happy collaboration exhilarating; the new style and this master of its written form encouraged him in his pursuit of a purely musical expression of his faith, unfettered by binding literary restrictions. His enthusiasm for Neumeister's innovation was fanned by the antipietistic zeal behind it. Neumeister's passionate and violent attacks upon Pietism —widely read all over Germany—must have supported the convictions of the young master that the new style moved in the right direction.

Bach's circle of friends included another ardent admirer, Johann Matthias Gesner (1691-1761), the great classicist, historian, ecclesiastic, and educator. As an enthusiastic music-lover, Gesner was in complete sympathy with Bach's conceptions of the role of music as an integral part of the Lutheran service. Seventeen years later, when he again became Bach's associate as rector of the Thomas school at Leipzig, he gave him the staunch support that Bach so needed. He has described his impression of Bach's musicianship in action in his edition of Quintillian's *Institutiones Oratoriae*, where he says that Bach is "worth any number of Orpheuses and twenty singers like Arion."[9] Johann Christoph Kiesewetter, Bach's former master at the Ohrdruf *Gymnasium*, and Georg Theodor Reineccius, able cantor at the Weimar *Gymnasium*, contributed to Bach's rich social and intellectual life in Weimar.

His cousin Johann Gottfried Walther (1684-1748) was Bach's most stimulating companion, because of their mutual interest in musical theory, the history of this science, and the erudition in philosophical speculations on the divine nature and the spiritual import of this art. Walther's father, Valentine Lämmerhirt, was a half-brother of Bach's mother, Elisabeth Lämmerhirt, and Bach and Walther were fast friends; the report that has found its way into most of their biographies that their friendship later cooled has been proved false.[10] Had Walther's friendship for Bach cooled, he surely would not have copied Bach's entire *Well-Tempered Clavier* and 29 chorale-preludes many years after Bach had left Weimar.[11]

The two friends spent many profitable and pleasant hours together. Walther was only one year older than Bach, and an anecdote from Forkel confirms their jovial comradeship. Bach's continued boasting that he could play anything at first sight inspired Walther to compose a musical trap for his friend. When at a breakfast party Bach found himself stumbling over the little composition, he laughingly admitted defeat to the triumphant Walther. The two composers also exchanged musical riddles, and the solutions to these puzzle canons were mutually challenging and stimulating. Walther's expertise in the art of counterpoint led to one of his chorale-preludes being mistaken for Bach's (in the highly respected Peters edition).

Walther: Guiding Spirit in Musical Study

Walther was an ardent collector of musical manuscripts and books dealing with philosophical speculation on the nature of music and harmonic and contrapuntal theory. Together with his apprentices and pupils—Johann Martin Schubart, Johann Caspar Vogler, Johann Tobias

Krebs, Johann Gotthilf Ziegler, and his nephew Johann Bernhard from Ohrdruf—he copied much music of Vivaldi, Corelli, Benedetto Marcello, Bononcini, Bontempi, Legrenzi, and Frescobaldi. Through this large collection Bach received an education in Italian music. He based numerous concerti on models of Vivaldi, both in almost literal transcriptions and as points of departure for his own development.

The year that Bach arrived in Weimar Walther completed an instruction book on the art of composition in which he discussed the entire history of harmony and counterpoint from Gioseffo Zarlino (1517-1590) to his own time. The work has received lavish praise from his contemporaries[12] as well as from musicologists of our time,[13] who say that its scientific accuracy and thoroughness surpasses any work of contemporaries such as Printz, Werckmeister, Heinichen, and Mattheson. For some unknown reason the work has never been printed, but its manuscript was preserved until very recent times.[14] Bach was certainly well acquainted with it.

Walther's manuscript—which indirectly reveals much about the scope of Bach's knowledge—reviews the history of all music theories of the seventeenth and the latter half of the sixteenth centuries, concentrating on the severe disciplines of composition technique. The work deals principally with changes in the conception of dissonances, the changing relation between melodic and harmonic considerations in the writing of counterpoint, the new role of the bass since the introduction of figured basses, modes and their modern transpositions, and ancient notation. Ornamentation is also considered; all this historical knowledge is directed toward attaining a sound understanding of practical technique in counterpoint. The book contributed to Bach's towering contrapuntal skill, which has roots reaching deeper than the teaching and the examples of Böhm, Buxtehude, or his brother Johann Christoph, and suggests that he studied the science of counterpoint from the works of the older masters and from their instruction books.

It is easy to reconstruct the general content of Walther's library from the erudition displayed in his work. Walther spent a great deal of money on books,[15] and the authors he selected—and discussed in his own work—included Cyriakus Snegasius, Zarlino, Sethus Calvisius, Lippius Baryphonus, Johannes Crüger, Thomas Balthasar Janowska, Adam Gumpelzhaimer, Christoph Thomas Walliser, Christoph Bernhard, Giovanni Bononcini, Johann Georg Ahle, Friedrich Erhard Niedt, Printz, Athanasius Kircher, Andreas Werckmeister, Reishius Kaspar

Schott, D. Angelo Berardi, Marcus Meibom, Johann Andreas Herbst, and Michael Praetorius. Walther's knowledge grew to be encyclopedic. In 1732 he published the *Musical Lexicon*, the first work in the German language of such comprehensive scope. Short biographies as well as musical information on many subjects are given. Even today it is an indispensable source.

Bach's own library once included a collection of books dealing with musical matters, according to the English music historian Charles Burney. (None of these appears in the inventory of his library.) During a visit with Carl Philipp Emanuel, Burney stated, "He presented me with several of his own pieces, and three or four curious ancient books and treatises on music, out of his father's collection, promising, at any distant time, to furnish me with others, if I would only acquaint him, by letter, with my wants."[16] Since hardly any of the older works on musical subjects (before the first decades of the eighteenth century) neglects philosophical speculation, Burney's report confirms Bach's interest in the theoretical aspects of music, ideas which Walther helped shape into permanent formulation. These speculative thoughts undoubtedly strengthened and were integrated with his faith in the divine function of music.

12

MUSICAL SPECULATION: KIRCHER AND WERCKMEISTER

As Walther pursued his study of musical philosophy, he shared his understanding and insights with his friend Bach. His writings on the subject were guided by a long line of musical philosophers of the past, Catholic and Protestant, who based their empyrean flights to Parnassus upon Pythagorean mathematics. In neomedieval fashion, they mixed learned calculations of intervallic musical proportions with allegories and strange astrological and alchemistic formulae. True to the ancient tradition of all these writers, Walther introduced his own treatise on composition with metaphysical speculations about the divine nature of music, quoting from the Bible, St. Augustine, Pythagoras, Kircher, Printz, Baryphonus, and his revered friend and teacher, Andreas Werckmeister.

Neither Walther nor Bach read this literature with a purely historical interest; both looked for practical information and for philosophical support for their commitment to the divine nature and purposes of music. They were interested in discovering what forms of melody and counterpoint resulted from application of the different ancient theories. In the realm of musical practice, religion formed no barrier to the acquisition of knowledge, even for staunch Lutherans, and these searching craftsmen gained from both Protestant and Catholic composers. Bach made a profound study of the works of Romans Palestrina, Giacomo Carissimi (1605-1674) and Girolamo Frescobaldi, whose contrapuntal craft he utilized and transformed into his own style. His concerti and

sonatas had their origin in similar compositions by the Catholic composers Arcangelo Corelli (1653-1713), Antonio Vivaldi, Benedetto Marcello, and numerous others.

Bach often spoke of changing *gustum*, and his understanding of the
steadily changing nature of taste was gained in part by delving deeply
into the works and theories of earlier days. Intervals, regarded as dissonances in the days of Zarlino, later became consonances; though
Palestrina and his school considered it bad taste to leap into a dissonance, later composers did not. Bach and Walther noticed preferences
of certain periods for carrying the melody in the tenor instead of in the
soprano. They could recognize the appearance of the new technique of
laying a bass as an harmonic framework, a practice unknown before
the advent of the figured bass. These vicissitudes of tastes, however, did
not change Bach's conviction that the basic technique and skill of
counterpoint were of unchanging value.

Bach's liberal attitude toward musical craft did not extend to speculative ideas on music when they conflicted with his Lutheran thinking.
Philosophical conceptions, like history, did not evolve but were immut-
ably correct or incorrect in a Christian sense, that is, in conformity with
biblical thinking. A deviation from the truth was due to sin or error.
Bach and Walther then would naturally strongly favor the speculations of an ardent Lutheran author like Andreas Werckmeister—and
Walther had a special attachment for Werckmeister's point of view
since he had studied under him. But since the Jesuit Athanasius Kircher
was universally esteemed as the leading musicologist of that period,
the two friends carefully studied and discussed his major work as
well.

The works of both authors provide insight into Bach's speculative
thinking at this period of his life. Kircher reflects the state of scientific
ideas of the seventeenth century, a curious mingling of Cartesian attempts to give rational explanations to natural phenomena with antiquated medieval analogies and magic formulas. Werckmeister fuses his
neomedieval Pythagoreanism with the evangelical mysticism of Luther
and Tauler. Neither writer recognized the coming Enlightenment. Not
until Johann Mattheson (1681-1764)—a man well acquainted with this
new thinking in England and France and one whom Bach always regarded with suspicion—did musicological writers turn away from
Kircher.

Athanasius Kircher: Genius or Charlatan?

Athanasius Kircher (1601-1680) was born in the small town of Geisa, not far from Bach's own birthplace. For a century all Europe was held spellbound by this intellectual whose scientific mind helped bridge the gulf between the Middle Ages and the modern era. Renowned primarily as a scholar and mathematician, he wrote in a highly entertaining and frankly sensational manner on many subjects, ranging from very questionable and downright fraudulent linguistic interpretations to very real contributions in optics and acoustics. His famous book on music, the *Musurgia Universalis* (The Universal Craft of Music), was a classic for almost a hundred years after its appearance in 1648.

Kircher received his schooling at the Jesuit *Gymnasium* of Fulda, then a great center of learning. For a number of years he was professor of mathematics, philosophy, and oriental languages at the Jesuit College of Würzburg, but in 1631 the tumult of the Thirty Years' War drove him from Germany. He found refuge with the Jesuits of Avignon, where he was allowed to devote full time to study and research. By this time he had already written several scientific works, including his *Ars Magnesia* (1631). In 1635 he was called to Rome, where he remained for the rest of his life, teaching and finally concentrating all his time on the study of hieroglyphics and archaeology.

A true Renaissance man, he wrote on the heavens, the planets, the earth, on subterranean and submarine explorations, on magnetism, on optics, acoustics, and geography.[1] He was also an inventor. He made improvements on telescopes and microscopes, as well as on thermometers, air pumps, pendulum clocks, and marine instruments. He invented an early calculating machine. His most lasting contribution was the invention of the "magic lantern," the ancestor of our picture projector. Kircher knew Greek and Hebrew, as well as Latin, and translated from the Arabic, Syrian, Coptic, and Chinese. He published translations from Egyptian hieroglyphics, which he claimed revealed the secret wisdom of the Egyptian priests but were later exposed as totally fraudulent. Even this did not dim his great prestige throughout Europe, and the Emperor continued his support of the talented rascal. Leibniz himself pursued with Kircher the matter of devising a universal language.[2]

Actually Kircher's unscientific methods were followed by most of the
early scientists. Johannes Kepler willingly provided horoscopes for
wealthy clients. The famous Paracelsus was an astrologer and al-
chemist. He followed magical signs and even joined in the search for the
legendary philosopher's stone. William Harvey, the founder of modern
medicine, believed in witches. Nontheological studies were not taken
very seriously, except by other scientists, and theology, the queen of
the medieval sciences, still reigned supreme.

In the field of music the Bible, along with the classics, was still the
criteria of knowledge, and Kircher's interpretations of their meaning for
music was unquestioned until the spread of the Enlightenment through
Germany.[3] One reason for such prolonged popularity may lie in his
entertaining manner of presentation. Compared with most of the books
in Bach's library, Kircher's writing is nothing short of sensational,
something akin to present-day popular-science magazines. Kircher continually regales his reader with accounts of astonishing curiosities and
near-miracles, although he discredits many of them as spurious or scientifically unsound. He tells of self-sounding bells, echoes that answer in
different languages, subterranean prisons built in the form of a human
ear in such a way that every whisper of the prisoner can be heard in
the castle above (a story which Kircher himself seems to believe), and
he describes the invention of a demented nobleman, the "cat-clavier,"
the keys of which are made to pinch cats' tails. These stories are skill-
fully interwoven with the serious matter of the book.

It is highly probable that Bach studied *Musurgia Universalis*, although
we have no actual proof. The work may have been among those books
in Bach's library that were sold or lost after his death. Bach probably
first read the book in Lüneburg where the library of St. Michael's
Church owned a copy.[4] In the *Gymnasium* as elsewhere Kircher's work
was regarded as the key to all hidden wisdom on musical and musico-
philosophical subjects; it was thought to be possessed with some almost
occult insight into the divine machinery of the world. We can at least
be sure that Bach was familiar with the general content of the book
through his discussions with Walther.

Book One of the *Musurgia Universalis*, entitled *Physiologus*, discusses the anatomy of the human ear, and propounds some valid theories of air vibrations, backed up by Kircher's experiments with airless
tubes and submerged bells. He describes the anatomy of the larynges of
animals as well as humans, also based on actual experiments. He often

marvels at the protective and efficient devices that Nature has made for living creatures.

Book Two, entitled *Philologicus*, deals with the origin and the invention of music. According to Kircher, the word music is derived from an Egyptian word *moys*, meaning water. (Johann Walther is not content with this philological fancy and offers alternative derivations.)[5] Kircher's theories, however, based on biblical accounts, were respected until the first decades of the eighteenth century.

The next two books deal with the Pythagorean proportions, a subject encountered *ad nauseam* in musical treatises over several centuries. The meaning of certain observed correspondences between proportions of string lengths and their resulting pitches had been speculated on for centuries. Kircher uses the traditional monochord, a laboratory instrument with one string and a movable bridge that could be placed at measured points under the string, to demonstrate the correspondence. He treats this phase of neomedieval speculation more fully in a later chapter.

The fifth book contains a complete description of Hebrew instruments, as reconstructed by Kircher's vivid imagination with a minimum of historical evidence. Kircher shares the common belief that music in ancient Jewish times was highly developed and similar to that of his own day, but that it had later been corrupted by the heathens. In his attempt to reconstruct the ancient Hebrew music, Kircher catalogued all the rhythms and figures of speech in the Psalms, and concludes that musical rhythm was originally derived from poetic meter, although the precise character of Hebrew music must remain unknown since it lacked notation. Certain followers of Kircher did not thus restrain themselves. Caspar Printz[6] concludes, on the basis of Kircher's "information" that classical Hebrew music could not have been much different from music of his own time. He flies into a rage at the heretical notion that our music may have originated with heathens like the Greeks.

Kircher also offers an account of Greek music, based on his studies of Boethius and Nichomachus, Plato, Homer, Theocritus, and the Romans Virgil and Pliny. He evidently was also familiar with the works of Gaudentius and Alypios. He assumes that the Greeks used the word *harmonia* in the modern sense of several tones simultaneously sounding; actually of course the Greek *harmonia* denoted a well-sounding and well-proportioned succession of tones in a melody. Parts of Kircher's quotation of an Ode of Pindar, giving its "original" notation and his own modern transcription, correspond to what we know of the surviving fragment, but most of it is as spurious as his translations of Egyptian hieroglyphics.

In Book Six, the *Melotheticus*, Kircher discusses an endless variety of song types, which he classifies and catalogues impressively. In Book Seven he critically compares ancient to modern music, and studies the "affections" of these various types of music, and their physiological effects on the inner organs, the "vapors" and the "heat" they cause in the gall, the liver, and so on. He attempts to give naturalistic explanations of his phenomena, but the results are neomedieval fantasies reminiscent of Paracelsus. The reader is also entertained with tales of cures through music, great catches of fish made as a result of a right choice of tunes, and other musical marvels.

Book Nine, the *Phonocamptica*, deals particularly with the theory of echoes, spiced with legends of talking Egyptian statues, echoes that answer in different languages, and echoes that are locked up in closed chambers only to resound several days later. One passage in his description of many famous ancient buildings designed with special acoustics has a particular interest for us, since Bach seems to have read it. He describes "a room or hall, built with a parabolic surface, prepared in such a way that one standing in a certain and specific place can understand everything that is said." Philipp Emanuel's description of his father's reaction to the Berlin opera house recalls this passage:

I showed him the great dining hall. He looked at the ceiling, and without further investigation made the statement that the architect had here accomplished a remarkable feat, without intending to do so, and without anyone's knowing about it: namely, that if someone went to one corner of the oblong hall and whispered a few words very softly upward against the wall, a person standing in the corner diagonally opposite, with his face to the wall, would hear quite distinctly what he said, while between them, and in the other parts of the room, no one would hear a sound. A feat of architecture hitherto very rare and much admired! This effect was brought about by the arches in the vaulted ceiling, which he saw at once.[7]

Bach could hardly have gathered this information from any other source than Kircher. Père Mersenne dealt with such acoustical problems in his *Harmonie Universelle*, but since he wrote in French Bach would not have known of the passage.

The mighty tome of *Musurgia Universalis* ends with *Analogus*, a most significant chapter in the history of scientific thought and one that may have had a special fascination for Bach. Kircher here presents an elaborate chart, the *enneachordon,* or group of nine tones that function as the occult causes of all phases of existence—spiritual and material. The absurdity of primitive superstition and indulgence in nonsensical occultism that are displayed in such interpretations seem incredible until we remember that the work of the great medieval scientists, including Kepler, was steeped in the same mysticism.

Johannes Kepler (1571-1630) directly influenced Kircher and Werckmeister, the other major figure shaping Bach's ideas on musical speculation. Kepler's philosophy still hinged on medieval metaphysics, which led him into speculations about the "harmony of the spheres," along Pythagorean lines. Kircher, in turn, leaned heavily on Kepler's Pythagoreanism for his own theories of musical harmony. Pythagoras—as Kepler could learn from Plato's *Timaeus*—had discovered certain mathematical proportions in musical intervals. He found that a string half as long (two times as short) as another of the same thickness, and under the same tension, will sound a tone that is an octave higher than that of the first. Thus a ratio of 1:2 is established. Similarly, the octave and the fifth above it are in the relation 2:3; the fifth and the fourth above it are in the relation 3:4; the fourth and the major third above it 4:5; and the major third and the minor third above it 5:5.

Kepler, over two thousand years later, discovered that his calculations of the distances between the orbits of the six planets then known corresponded roughly in the same proportions to those of the Pythagorean musical intervals. This seemed to Kepler to substantiate Pythagoras' "harmony of the spheres" as the law of the universe. Each of the nine musical tones had a corresponding heavenly body, in its sphere, in the heavens. Tones, and these planets, responded to the laws of harmony of the spheres.

Kircher shared a popular misunderstanding of Kepler's idea that the planets produced music. Actually Kepler used harmony to mean a unified and concordant cause, a common cause. But this underlying harmony of musico-mathematical proportions then began to be interpreted as a primary cause of existence. Kircher's own favorite motto, in agreement with both Pythagoras and Kepler, was "Music is nothing other than the knowledge of the order of all things" (*Musica nihil aliud est quam omnium ordinem scire*).

In his *Analogus,* or Analogies, Kircher extends the harmony Kepler found in the heavens and in music to other realms of nature. Kircher uses the term analogy in its ancient sense of proportion and congruence, a correspondence between appearance and reality. His chart of "analogies" presents musical proportions governing some 90 varieties of "entities," ranging from God through archangels, angels, virtues, powers, down to quadrupeds, birds, fishes, plants, trees, stones, and colors. His accompanying text explains the chart in astrological terms. The nine musical tones, which correspond to the nine heavenly bodies, correspond also to certain precious stones, because Kircher observes that these stones shine best at the time when certain constellations are at their height. Similarly, certain flowers turn their heads toward the sun, the moon, or the stars. He cites as authority for these assertions the mythical singer Orpheus—for did he not achieve power over all manner of creatures through the music of his lyre? "Upon the sound of a certain string," Kircher says, mentioning which note it is, "on account of its hidden sympathy . . . everything in the universe is analogous to [corresponds to] Saturn: particularly, the cherubim, lead, topaz, helleborus, cypress, certain fishes, birds, animals, and colors . . . because all these entities are endowed with Saturnal qualities." Kircher then advises a composer to choose the right time and constellation under which to compose appropriate music.

As far as we know Bach never concerned himself about the right astrological time for composing, and probably did not go along with Kircher's ventures into the occult. But it is possible that Bach believed the Keplerian premise that the Pythagorean proportions were of a primary and causal nature, the divine tool of the Creator. Werckmeister presents the same idea—only with more sincerity and reserve.

It is highly probable that Bach was convinced that music was a sacred science, or the wisdom of the *magus*, that the arts of harmony and counterpoint were divine in nature, that they dealt with primary causes, and that they represented the spontaneous impulse and the wisdom of the divine Mind. The musical symbolism and analogies in his chorale-preludes (discussed in Chapter 18) may indeed have a mystic significance, similar to that of Kircher's analogies, for him. It cannot be attributed to accident or mere witticism that Bach fashioned the canon of his chorale-prelude "These Are the Holy Ten Commandments" so that the first note repeated exactly ten times and the *dux* entered ten times in the fugal treatment.

We cannot measure the influence of *Musurgia Universalis* on Bach, but whatever Bach's early response was, he came finally to reject, or at least disregard much of Kircher's neomedievalism. He was not led to this position because he had gained more enlightened scientific information but through his study of the writings of Werckmeister. A staunch Lutheran and of an evangelical nature, Werckmeister related the Pythagorean-Keplerian speculations more closely to experiential spirituality than to the fantastic and magical. His practical work also concerned Bach more vitally—the scientific basis for a well-tempered tuning and his knowledge of the organ formed the background in which Bach did much of his work. Bach's great friend and mentor, Johann Walther, reveals this movement away from Kircher in his remark in the *Lexicon* that he was really no musician—although Walther never specifically rejected or ridiculed the Jesuit. So while Kircher's fabulous work probably influenced Bach early in his career—certainly its contents fascinated him—he found in Werckmeister the source for his lifelong convictions on musical theory.

Andreas Werckmeister: A Kindred Spirit

Andreas Werckmeister (1645-1706) grew up within the same orbit of ideas that was so close to the hearts and minds of Bach and Walther. Born in the same region as Bach, in the town of Bennickenstein in northern Thuringia, Werckmeister received the same type of education as Bach. The solid Lutheranism and providential conception of history that characterized Bach's formal learning dominated Werckmeister's education, one generation earlier.

While a student in the nearby town of Quedlinburg, Werckmeister was possessed with a mystic enthusiasm for the organ, and immediately after his last school examinations he found a position as court organist there. His early success as an organist diverted him from his aspirations to study at a university, but he was always more inclined toward speculation and discourse than art. Today we know him solely for his writing. Only one composition of his has survived—a collection of violin pieces with figured bass accompaniment, entitled *Musikalische Privat-Lust* (Musical Delight for Private Use). Since his interest in all his writings is chiefly centered on keyboard music, it seems strange that none of his works for these instruments has been preserved.

Johann Walther studied with Werckmeister in 1704. The two, drawn together by common ideas and musical erudition, became close friends and pursued a lively correspondence. Walther later reports[8] having read

Werckmeister's *Nucleus Musicus* in manuscript, the author's only work in Latin. The work was never published. The celebrated Buxtehude was also a personal friend and admirer of Werckmeister and sent him a letter of congratulation on the publication of *Harmonologica Musica*.[9]

His literary output falls within four subjects: the modernized tuning of keyboard instruments, organ-building and all that pertains to this art, musical composition and theory, and proper use of music in church. All but the one unpublished Latin work mentioned above are written in German. His writing style is very poor; he was overly fond of long sentences and slanting dashes haphazardly inserted to give the reader an occasional breathing spell. He is no better at giving any sort of logical order to his subject-matter. Mystical reflections often abruptly interrupt some technical discussion on the tuning of instruments or the theory of harmony.

Werckmeister's fame today is based almost entirely on his contribution to the well-tempered tuning of keyboard instruments (which formed the basis for Bach's modern system of tuning), but Bach and Walther also deeply respected his work in musical philosophy. His contribution to the scientific approach to tuning has actually been grossly exaggerated for, although he made minute and excellent calculations of string-length proportions, his actual tuning methods are of a purely practical nature. It is a mistake to think that he ever arrived at the equal temperament as Bach knew it, and as we use it today.

Werckmeister was even less scientific than Kircher, although certainly more honest. Like Kircher, whom he greatly admired, he intersperses in his writing mystical, semi-philosophical reflections, drawing from medieval concepts, Pythagorean number-magic, and astrology, which he manages to fuse with ideas of Luther and touches of Thomist and Taulerian attitudes. Platonic overtones are blended with quotes from Kepler's *Harmonices Mundi* (1619).[10] The rapidly approaching Enlightenment of France and England seem to have affected him not one whit.

In music, where his practical applications were relatively modern, his speculative ideas place him along side Sethus Calvisius (1556-1625) of Leipzig, and Johannes Lippius (1585-1612), whose ideas are even more medieval than Kircher's. He calls upon ancient authorities, and occasionally medieval scholars like Kepler, Scaliger, Zarlino, and Steffani.[11] The ultimate support for his speculative theses comes from the Bible. He labors long to defend music as a science—not art—a subject that probably still interested Bach but had long since disappeared from writings from other countries. This preoccupation and the rigidly traditional approach in his writing reflected the intellectual stagnation in the German *Gymnasium*, an institution that also molded Bach's mind.

Werckmeister on Tuning

Traditional as his philosophical thinking may have been, Werckmeister was progressive in seeking the means of realization of his art, i.e., harmony, modulation, form, and particularly the tuning of instruments. He freed himself from the traditional purity of the Pythagorean proportions in tuning and sought to adjust tuning to the demands of the new musical styles.

During the sixteenth and seventeenth centuries, harmonic combinations grew steadily more complicated; sharps and flats were constantly being added, the church modes became transposed in more remote keys, and modulations within a piece began to venture farther away from their base. When performed on keyboard instruments, these new adventures in music quickly made clear the inadequacy of Pythagorean tuning for harmonies in a wide range of keys.

We have seen that the intervals of the octave, the fifth, the fourth, the major third, the minor third correspond to the proportions: 1:2, 2:3, 3:4, 4:5, and 5:6. The monochord had long been used as a laboratory instrument for tuning on this mathematical basis. Long before Werckmeister, a discrepancy in pitch was observed when the monochord is used to find the fifth partial of a note by piling up five fifths upon each other instead of subdividing the string in two, three, four, and five parts. Thus, instead of sounding C, c, g, c', e' by subdivision of one string, now five strings are tuned in series of perfect fifths, C, G, d, a, e'; the e' of the second series is slightly sharper than the first e'.

The Greeks called this discrepancy a comma or cut and calculated its size accurately. Since the Greeks did not use harmony in our sense and accompanied their singing chiefly with single notes (the strumming of the kythara or lyre being the only possible approximation of what might be called harmony in our sense), the comma offered no practical difficulties. With the complex harmony of Werckmeister's and Bach's time certain compromises had to be made to avoid using thirds that made chords sound badly out of tune. The writings of Gioseffo Zarlino (*Institutioni armonichi*, 1558), Arnolt Schlick (*Spiegel der Orgelmacher*, 1511), and others had suggested adjustments of the ancient tuning over the past century.

If one continues this series of fifths, starting from C, notes like G sharp, A sharp, or A flat eventually pose an even more difficult problem in tuning. When B sharp is reached on the circle of fifths, assuming we start with C, it is considerably higher than C.[12] If a piano were tuned with all the fifths in perfect tune, all chords would sound out of tune.

Two rather haphazard solutions for this are suggested by Werckmeister in *Hypomnemata Musica*. One method is to tune the fifths slightly flat, the thirds sharp, and consequently the sixths flat. Certain "old philosophers," he says, have admitted the feasibility of this procedure.[13] Certain thirds should be tuned sharper than others: "C sharp-F (sic), F sharp-B flat, and G sharp-C may fluctuate [*shweben*] a full comma . . . in case of extreme need."[14] His alternative suggestion is even more arbitrary and intuitive. All fifths may be tuned a little low, according to the desire of the musician, who is to be guided by the divisions of the monochord. The thirds must be tuned a little high, if they will be used in the piece to be played; since in those days the black keys were used less often than the white, the thirds on the white keys will be tuned a little sharper. Individual notes then were tuned according to the artist's choice or need.[15]

These methods are surely far from scientific. They depend mostly upon the natural ear, although Werckmeister's mathematical calculations of the proportions confound a nonmathematical reader. In spite of demonstrations on a monochord with a string of four feet, divided in 900 minute fractions, his advice for actual tuning is really one of trial and error and individual judgment. On the monochord he is able to demonstrate his comma, which he knows as the relation 81:80.[16] But how in practice would one accurately hear half or a fourth of a comma, a minute interval of either a quarter, an eighth, or a sixteenth of a tone? "Beats," the result of interference between two sound waves of different frequencies, can be distinctly heard, and Werckmeister recognizes this in his books on thoroughbass[17] and on the care of organs.[18] He tells his reader that these tremors, shiverings, or hoverings (*Schwebungen*) originate when two strings are tuned almost together. The more closely in tune they are, he observes, the slower they beat (*schlagen*). But nowhere does he suggest counting the number per second, as modern tuners do; for a test of certainty he still consults his monochord. Bach apparently rejected this slow method, since Forkel states that he tuned his harpsichord in 15 minutes. Moreover, there is no indication that Bach ever owned a monochord.

Werckmeister admits that his work only approached the modern system of equal temperament: "... some people think that the temperament in which all consonances have equal value would finally carry off the prize, and in the future ... it would be indifferent whether one would play in C or in C sharp."[19] Bach was the first to fulfill that dream. He was indeed the first to write his preludes and fugues in all 24 keys. An earlier series of preludes and fugures by Caspar Fischer, which he entitled *Ariadna Musica* (1702 and 1715), omitted the keys of C Sharp Major, e flat minor, F Sharp Major, b flat minor, and g sharp minor, indicating Fischer was still stumped in tuning for these keys.

An uneasy conscience may have contributed to Werckmeister's failure to carry out his tempered tuning over the entire circle of fifths; deep down he feared that he was tampering with divine law when he modified the mathematical proportions of Pythagoras. Although he invokes Kepler[20] to demonstrate that the same deviations from the exact Pythagorean proportions are found in the *Scala Planetarum*, and "that therefore God has shown us how wisely we can temper them in order to protect us creatures from evil,"[21] he adds that the same authority warns against modifying the divine laws for man's own use. Werckmeister attributes the evolution of taste to astrological influences: since the constellations never appear exactly in the same positions, artists are driven to discover ever new inventions.[22]

Werckmeister's Philosophy of Music

Werckmeister's more philosophical works deal with the proper use of music—specifically, sacred music, since he believes that the source and end of all music is the Creator. Bach's own thoughts on the use of music for the churches are reflected in these works.

In a curious little book entitled "The Use and the Abuse of the Noble Art of Music" (*Der Edlen Musikkunst Würde, gebrauch, und Missbrauch*, 1691), Werckmeister presents the idea that music is a metaphysical being, a living reality, like a creature of God, which has its existence in the mind of the Creator. Through it, he says, we get a foretaste of heavenly harmony. The German term for this veritable being, *ein ordentliches Wesen*, is pregnant with philosophical implications, *ordentlich* referring to the unequivocal and positive reality of its spiritual existence, as well as to its inherent well-regulated nature. In developing his proof of this order he takes recourse again to the time-worn

cosmology of Pythagoras. Only a true mystic, however, could pronounce the art of music a clear and explicit Being, *ein deutliches
Wesen.*[23]

Without mentioning Plato Werckmeister has elevated the art of
music—or rather the science of music—to the stature of the Platonic idea
with metaphysical and intrinsic reality, fused, of course, with orthodox
Lutheran theology. By responding in our hearts to this metaphysical
being, music, we experience a promise of future complete wisdom: "By
means of music we receive a mental presentation of God's wisdom."[24]
"Wicked souls, therefore, do not respect music very much,"[25] for they
are not endowed with that natural response to the divine.

These reflections may have been inspired by Tauler's *Teutsche Theologia,* in which the nature of reality is attributed to essence (*das
Wesen*) as revealed through sensuous appearance (*Schein*). The word
Schein is there used—in almost Hegelian manner—in the double meaning of shining, as a light, and seeming, as to be appearance only. The
shining forth of the world of appearance, the created things, i.e. music
as it sounds on our ears, is the imperfect manifestation of its true Being
—uncreated, perfect, and existing purely in the matrix of the Creator's
mind. As proof of such divine universality he again falls back upon the
arithmetical proportions of Pythagoras, demonstrating that God created
them in the measurements of various biblical objects such as the ark of
Noah, the temple with its furniture, and other sacred objects. (The proportions of the ark, with a length of 300 yars, a breadth of 50, and a
height of 30, applied to the monochord, would yield a major chord.)[26]

His *Musikalische Paradoxal Discourse* also betrays the Platonic origin
of his dialectics. The world and its audible music is the ectype of the
archetype, that is, as the imitation of the ideational original. The earthy,
known music, he says, flows forth from the harmony which is in God
Himself.[27] He shared Luther's disdain for the unmusical man, for whoever does not carry the image of God's harmony in his soul cannot be
capable of feeling the unity and wisdom of God, qualities that have
been placed in us at the time of our creation by God in the form of
musical consonances.

Bach's Understanding of Werckmeister and Kircher

Bach was untutored in philosophy to judge from his formal education,
and Walther, the devoted pupil and correspondent of Werckmeister,

contributed most in the long discussions the friends shared to an intellectual understanding of his mentor's profound reflections. But both revered this science of musical speculation for its service to theology. Neither could take an objective critical approach to the works. As long as the writers used their philosophical, dialectical discourses of the imagination as revelatory of religious consciousness, their rather naive speculations were beyond reproach. Philosophy was still the handmaid of theology—Pythagoras played the same role in the musical scholasticism of Werckmeister that Aristotle did in Thomism—and neither Walther nor Werckmeister recognized the naturalism and Cartesian rationalism lurking in Kircher's work.

Since Bach did not pursue any philosophical studies beyond the few mystics found in his library, and the sparse bits of speculation found in all music books of his epoch, he may have found the musical scholasticism of Werckmeister and others illuminating and edifying. But his calling was for the manifestation of Being through music. Knowledge of these works undoubtedly deepened his fervor in the mission of his art, but subjects that had practical application remained his primary concern.

Werckmeister did, however, provide Bach with a rationale and support for his musical purpose as opposed to the platitudinous sentimentalities that Pietists fought for in music. Werckmeister also supported Bach's conviction of the need for instrumental music in church, another point of contention with the Pietists. He discovered that in Psalm 150 the Lord commanded the use of strings and violins (although almost no violins existed in the pre-Christian era). Trumpets and tympani were among the ancient Hebrew instruments, and the trumpet's superb display of Pythagorean proportions gave added sanction for the use of these instruments. Bach must have found real solace and reassurance in Werckmeister's justification for the use of joyful music in church. For Werckmeister devotes considerable space to passionate denunciations of those sects that insist on playing "only those slow, sleepy, and mournful songs with their dragging and putrid harmonies."[28] He accuses these antimusical souls of inability to discriminate between truly joyful music and mere beer-fiddling. Only Satan he exclaims, would place the two species on the same level.[29] (The problem of distinguishing between spiritual and secular music is not so easily dismissed, of course, and we will discuss it in more detail in Chapter 14.)

At this time of Bach's life and musical development, he was deeply

imbued, under Walther's guidance, with the musical speculation of
Kircher and especially Werckmeister. His natural bent was, as we have
said, toward the creation and performance of music, not toward developing elaborate justifications for the art. But to the extent that he did
seek philosophical grounding for his work, he relied primarily on
Kircher and Werckmeister. Later in his life, when his faith and art were
being severely tested by the rising spirit of Enlightenment, we will be
confronted by the question of whether he was ever freed from the influence of these two neomedievalists.

13

BACH IN KÖTHEN (1717-1723)

BACH's attachment to the court of Weimar was destined to end. The years there had been fruitful, but Bach had not achieved his "final goal," the full realization of a "well-conceived" and "well-organized church music." In the environment of firmly guarded orthodoxy Bach was encouraged to exercise and expand his powers as a performer and composer for church as well as chamber, and the solid Lutheran foundations at the court permitted performance of instrumental music and the classical hymn, both elements that Bach had spent so much time fighting for in Mühlhausen. But Bach was only the organist, not *Kapellmeister* with authority to direct the entire musical service. Even with his promotion to the higher office of concertmaster (while retaining the office of organist), he was under the aged Drese, and his son, Johann Wilhelm, who had been named *Vice-Kapellmeister* four years before Bach's arrival. In spite of the mediocre talent of both, the duke remained stubbornly loyal to the established order of musical hierarchies. His refusal to recognize genius over existing rank led finally to Bach's resignation.

Growing Fame

Bach's reputation as an organist of unprecedented skill rapidly spread among connoisseurs all over Germany, and he was often invited to examine new or newly repaired organs in various towns, and to judge applicants for the position of organist. Following his completion

of these services, Bach often gave long concerts for the other notables
and musicians.

In 1713 he received an offer from the elders of the Church of Our
Lady in Halle to accept the post of organist. The prospect at first seemed
attractive, especially because the Halle organ, with 63 registers, was one
of the finest in Germany. But Bach hesitated. His musical aspirations
reached far beyond the aural, sensuous gratification that a particular instrument would give him. In spite of his deep love and fabulous talent
for this instrument, the organ was only one part of that greater art
work, the complete musical service. He wanted complete control over
the musical administration, and the elders at Halle did not offer him
this opportunity at first.

His stated reasons for not immediately accepting the offer were the
loss in salary the new job would mean and his failure to receive permission to leave the duke's court. This offended the elders, who suspected
Bach of using their offer to obtain an increase in his present salary at
Weimar, a common practice in those days. Indeed his promotion to concertmaster and court organist did come shortly after the offer from
Halle. Bach, however, hastened to clarify his reservations about the job
in a later letter to the elders: "I would like to have one or two things
changed [in the contract] in the matter of salaries as well as in that of
my services . . ."[1] These services (Dienste) or duties related to the musical obligations that accompanied his rank, and he promised to come in
person to sign the agreement, if beforehand they could agree on these
matters.

In other words, Bach wanted to know more definitely what his
sphere of duties was to be. He did not want a repetition of the situation
in Mühlhausen, where instrumental music was almost entirely banned,
nor did he want to be subordinate to a cantor or other superior official,
whose compositions almost certainly would be inferior to his own. He
could only accomplish the re-creation of the entire service musically if
he were in complete control of all musical activity, and had the cooperation of a sympathetic minister. Bach had known only one composer,
Buxtehude, as devoted as he to this gigantic mission, and he could not
afford to trust to chance any longer in finding an environment con-
ducive to it.

He half expected this situation to develop in Weimar, if he fell heir
to the rank of Kapellmeister upon the death or retirement of Drese. He

could count on the support and cooperation of Franck, one of the modern librettists of the period, if he undertook this task in Weimar. At present, although some of his cantatas were occasionally performed at Weimar, his total output of cantatas amounted to only about 20 (according to Schmieder's catalogue), an average of only two or three a year. And for some reason, as we mentioned earlier, he did not compose any chorale-preludes during this period.

Bach's fame continued to spread through Germany from court to court after his offer at Halle; all musicians spoke of him with unbounded admiration. Mattheson praised him as "the celebrated organist, the celebrated Bach."[2] In 1714 Bach displayed his virtuosity at a new organ in Cassel, where he played for the crown prince Friedrick of Hesse-Cassel, later King of Sweden, who gave Bach a ring from his own finger as a token of his admiration.[3]

By 1716 the authorities of the Church of Our Lady in Halle had forgotten their former differences with the master and they invited him to inspect the now-completed organ, an honor which Bach now graciously accepted. Other musicians from distant places came to Halle, and all were received and entertained as royal princes: servants and coaches were put at their disposal and sumptuous banquets were prepared. The menu of one mentioned among the meats alone, veal, smoked ham, sausages, fish, and a roasted quarter of mutton, all accompanied by the proper wines. Bach met Johann Kuhnau (1660-1722), the cantor at the Thomas Church in Leipzig, during the Halle celebrations. (Seven years hence Bach would take up his position.) If his wit in conversation was as entertaining as his satirical writings, Kuhnau must have added a lively note to the parties.[4]

Another incident that established Bach's fame involves the oft-related meeting with the famous French organist Louis Marchand (1669-1732), at the Dresden court of Elector August II of Saxony, who became King of Poland. Contests between artists were often arranged at the courts, and competition was based on the musicians' ability to improvise variations on given themes. The story goes that, upon secretly listening to Bach's practicing, Marchand left Dresden to avoid the humiliation of defeat. This triumph over France's foremost organist elevated Bach's reputation to that of the greatest organist of Europe.[5]

This crowning success came during the most irritating last months of his stay in Weimar. On December 1, 1716, the old *Kapellmeister*

Drese had died; instead of Bach, the duke appointed Drese's son Johann Wilhelm to succeed him. His hopes suddenly dashed, Bach decided to leave Weimar at the first suitable opportunity.

Move to Köthen

A few months later this opportunity came, from the rival ducal family in Weimar. Duke Wilhelm Ernst's nephew, Ernst August, who occupied the Red Castle, was married to the sister of Prince Leopold of Anhalt-Köthen. Leopold was not only a great enthusiast for music, but an able musician as well. He had probably met Bach at the Red Castle[6] and had recognized his genius at the harpsichord or the violin. Since Bach was on very friendly footing with the family at the Red Castle, they soon learned of his discontent with his present situation and passed this news on to Prince Leopold, who offered Bach the office of *Kapellmeister* at his court in Köthen. Bach accepted the offer, and on August 5, 1717, received his formal appointment. This time Bach did not wait for his demission from Duke Wilhelm Ernst before accepting. He even tendered his resignation, a bold move in a country and a court that was still clinging to the vestiges of feudalism. Wilhelm, ever ready to assert his dictatorial power, refused to release his valuable organist and concertmaster. Since Wilhelm Ernst had forbidden all communication between the two castles on penalty of a fine, Bach's offer from Duchess Eleonore's own brother seemed like open defiance and the duke was all the more obstinately opposed to Bach's resignation. Four months went by, and Bach made a second, more insistent request for release. Thereupon, on November 6, he was submitted to the humiliation of an arrest. He was kept in the justice room of the palace till December 2, when the duke, by issuing a dishonorable discharge, relented in a battle of wills to Bach's stubborn devotion to his musical goals.[7]

Bach often recalled his happiness during his stay in Köthen. Except for the sudden, tragic death of his wife, his life in the employ of the young prince Leopold was peaceful. For the first time in his professional career, there were no frictions or struggles over his ideal in art and the role of art in his spiritual world. In Arnstadt Bach had been criticized for his strange manner of preludizing the chorales and for his lack of interest in a recalcitrant choir. In Mühlhausen his instrumental music was barred from performance. In Weimar he was forced to work with the uninspiring compositions of a mediocre director of music.

The courtyard in Köthen as Bach probably knew it.

Later, in Leipzig, he was to combat new animosities and threats to the sanctity of his art and its function in public worship. But the six years in Köthen may be regarded as a period of further preparation for his life's task, the complete creation of a reorganized church music.

He enjoyed the pleasant friendship of an amiable young prince with unusual musical talent and skill who could appreciate the superior art of his *Kapellmeister*. Bach now had attained the highest rank in musical hierarchies. His salary was on a par with that of a court marshal, one of the highest officials in the little realm. His duties were extremely light and not demanding, consisting mainly of directing and playing in the small band of musicians, and composing chamber music for such occasions without having to meet pressing deadlines. He had several pupils, among them possibly Prince Leopold himself.

In his true vocation, church music, Bach had an enforced vacation. He was not officially connected with any church; there was not a single good organ in town. The little palace organ resembled the miniature one in Celle. With a total of 13 stops, ten for the two manuals and three for the pedals,[8] it was designed merely as an accompaniment to the deadly Calvinistic psalms sung as an official duty by the small congre-

gation of court attendants. The two other churches in Köthen, the
Lutheran and the Reformed, had equally mediocre instruments.

Prince Leopold, a handsome youth of 23, welcomed to his court his
illustrious *Kapellmeister*, who was only 32. He had become the happy
and benign sovereign of his little realm only two years earlier—during
his minority the principality of Anhalt-Köthen had been governed by
his mother, Gisela Agnes. His father, Emanuel Leberecht, had died
when Leopold was ten years old. Both father and son were Calvinists,
but a life of affluence, creature comfort, extensive travel, and artistic
pleasures had rendered them immune to the type of theological enthusiasm that bound Wilhelm Ernst.

Gisela Agnes, a devout Lutheran, had deeper convictions about religion. She had persuaded her husband to build a Lutheran church, St.
Agnes', and a school for Lutheran children. Bach sent his three sons,
Wilhelm Friedemann (born in 1710), Carl Philipp Emanuel (1714), and
Johann Gottfried Bernhard (1715) to this school. Besides these two
institutions Gisela Agnes gave the town a school and home for women
and girls. These religious communities were, as a rule, inclined toward
harmonious and Christian fellowship; one of the young prince's first
official acts was to issue an edict of tolerance. The prince and his mother
seem to have enjoyed a cordial relationship. He named his first-born
child for her.

The art of music drew a twofold benefit from this atmosphere of religious tolerance. At times figural music resounded in the Calvinist
chapel, and cantatas from Bach's pen, composed for festal occasions
like New Year's Day and princely birthdays, and also church cantatas
were heard there. In the Lutheran churches the strict ban against female voices was relaxed, in part just to enlarge the reservoirs of talent—
the Lutheran church and adjoining school were quite small.[9]

Leopold had studied at the *Ritteracademie* in Berlin, where he met
many noblemen and probably received considerable training in music.
His education was completed in the usual manner of young noblemen,
by extensive travel on the Continent. In Italy Leopold developed an
enthusiasm for great paintings; and he engaged artists to copy his
favorite masterpieces. Bach must have seen the prince's marble copy
of Michelangelo's Moses, a rare opportunity for a former Thuringian
burgher.

Prince Leopold also took music lessons with the famous German
composer Johann David Heinichen (1683-1729),[10] whom he met in

Rome. The composer's secular and revolutionary spirit and his uninhibited and powerful personality attracted the bright young prince and
they traveled to Venice together. At this time Leopold offered Heinichen the position of *Kapellmeister* at his court in Köthen. But Heinichen
declined the offer, and remained in Venice, where several of his operas
were subsequently performed with success. Leopold sponsored the performance of three of them in Köthen, but his revenues were not sufficient to maintain a regular theater.

Bach and Theater Composers

Bach undoubtedly gained a thorough knowledge of Heinichen's music
and his rather startling ideas from his former patron, but he probably
received his prince's attempts to enlighten him with only polite interest
and patient tolerance. Although Bach may well have made a fleeting
acquaintance with Heinichen during his recent visit at the court in
Dresden (in 1716 Heinichen was engaged by August II there), he now
had more leisure to evaluate Heinichen's art and writings. A glance at
this man's books assures us of Bach's reaction to his ideas.

Heinichen was one of the chief protagonists of that new movement
that sought chiefly to gain rapport between artist and audience. The
criterion for this rapport was expressed in the French term *goût*, which,
precisely defined, means good taste but in this sense implied fashionable taste as well. France and Italy, where theatrical music was predominant, developed this standard, and the esthetic was beginning to
invade Germany at this time. Heinichen's literary style is spiced with a
generous sprinkling of French expressions—*tendresse, brillant, goût,*
and *touchant* are used with the force of indisputable finality in esthetic
judgment.

Heinichen sharply attacked two aspects of the art and ideals most
dear to Bach and cherished throughout his life: counterpoint and metaphysical speculations on music. Counterpoint seemed to Heinichen a
"seemingly learned and speculative jugglery of notes," the odious practice of a pedant, who "as on the torture table . . . would stretch and pull
the innocent notes . . . by augmentation, inversion, repetition, and
mixings, until finally from this would evolve a practice of countless,
superfluous eye-counterpoints."[11] He suspects contrapuntalists of finding pleasure with the way such learned figurations appear on paper,
and ignoring their actual sound. In contempt of the ignorant church

audiences this fearless iconoclast suggested that only in church can "the contrapuntalist peddle his acquired school wisdom."[12]

This abusive harangue must have struck a sensitive nerve in Bach, for he stood at the opposite pole of these mundane esthetics based upon the fickle judgment of mere mortals, the lay theater audiences. Bach would instead have applauded Augustine's clear distinction between the professional theater musician and the true artist, the latter seeking truth through musical discipline.[13]

But Bach still was willing to borrow whatever laudable material he could find in the textbooks of these worldlings. He copied a great deal from another friend of the theater, Friedrich Erhard Niedt (1674-1708), whose little book, *Musikalische Handleitung* (Musical Manual), uses coarse and offensive language to ridicule the "double, inverted, salted, pickled, roasted, and fatted counterpoint," which "passes among musical ignoramuses for a great musical monster."[14] He makes up obscene puns for the special objects of his contempt—the canon and the fugue.[15] Despite these tasteless diatribes Bach used his text on the thoroughbass for the instruction of his pupils.

Niedt, unlike Heinichen, remained a German provincial, and he continued to praise and recommend Kircher and Werckmeister and pad his little book with a rehash of their ideas, although he lacked their philosophical acumen. It is from Niedt's *Musikalische Handleitung* that Bach in 1738 copied a phrase that gave such precise expression to his musical creed: "The purpose and Primary Cause of the thoroughbass should be none other than the Praise of God and the allowable recreation of the soul. Whenever this is not taken into consideration there is no veritable music, but only a devilish blathering and trifling."

Heinichen expressed a strong distaste for all metaphysical speculation on music, but he offered no polemics. It seems unlikely that his flat statement of disapproval bothered Bach much, or that he would ever have discussed it with young Leopold. If, however, they discussed Heinichen's doctrine of the affections, Bach could have heartily agreed that the object of music should be to move the hearts with "the tenor of the words." Heinichen's method of translating literary thoughts into musical sentiment is essentially the same as Bach's matching of text and musical expression, discussed in detail in Chapter 18. The technique corresponded to Bach's *Loci topici*, descriptive motives or concise little clauses (*kurtzgefasste Clauselgen*), that Bach used with far more freedom and imagination than Heinichen ever dreamed of. He applied *Loci topici* to the canon and other forms of counterpoint, which Heinichen, of course, completely ignored.

Bach did not need the theater for ideas for these *Loci topici*. The tradition had a richer history than Heinichen realized. During his lifetime Bach saw few operas for wherever he settled, the theater had been either disbanded or never allowed. The Celle theater was permanently discontinued on account of tragedy; he visited Hamburg when the theater was closed for the summer. At the court of Count Günther in Arnstadt the few operas performed were so insignificant that Bach only reluctantly lent his cooperation. The Weimar court was too puritanical and frugal to indulge in such worldly frivolity, and Köthen's prince could afford only an occasional opera performance. Just before Bach arrived in Leipzig, the theater there was closed (1720). But Bach drew on religious symbolism instead of theatrical techniques to reach his audience.

Artistic Recognition and Personal Tragedy

Hardly had Bach become established in this new environment when he was again called to give his famous expert opinion of an organ, this time in Leipzig. The organ of St. Paul's Church had been rebuilt by Johann Scheibe, the father of Johann Adolph Scheibe who in 1737 wrote a scathing criticism of Bach's style.[16] Bach's report, which fortunately has been preserved, gives eloquent testimony to his thorough and minute knowledge of organ construction and of the mechanics of the instrument. Bach is scrupulously just in his criticism, and protects Scheibe against blame for defects due to causes beyond his control—and about ten such shortcomings are methodically listed.

During his week's stay in Leipzig, which fell in Advent, Bach was also invited to perform one of his own cantatas. He chose *"Jesus nahm zu sich die Zwölf"* (Jesus Took to Himself the Twelve), a work first heard in 1714 at the Weimar castle chapel; it was performed in one of Leipzig's churches, either St. Thomas or St. Nicholas.[17] This piece (*Stück*, as Bach usually called works of this type) retained some aspects of the earlier cantata style but pointed to new directions in cantata writing, especially in his use of Neumeister's text. He still used arioso and an unaltered text, from St. John's Revelation, but the *da capo* aria and recitative are innovations borrowed from the opera. The music to the opening words, "Come, O Saviour of the Nation," reveals a curiously baroque mixture of styles. The choir boys sing one of the oldest hymns,

St. Ambrose's *"Veni Redemptor Genitum"* from the fifth century, to a Lullian overture with regal and martial rhythms of dotted notes. Bach even marked the conventional fugal section of this overture with the French term *gai* instead of the usual *allegro*. Thus the spirituality of the fifth century is innocently wedded to the essentially mundane pomposity of the French royal court.

At this period in his life the former Thuringian burgher often viewed the social life of the German nobility first hand. Only recently he had been at the royal court of August II of Saxony and Poland; in May, 1718, his young prince took him to Carlsbad, the Monte Carlo of Germany where pleasure-seeking nobility of all parts of the land gathered to take the baths and drink the medicinal waters. Bach and five musicians of the establishment accompanied the prince—including the famous viola da gamba player Christian Ferdinand Abel, whose even more famous son Carl Friedrich Abel later in the century entertained London society with Bach's son Christian. Three servants were put in special charge of Bach's harpsichord, and we may assume that the noble guests in this luxury resort often heard the master play, either in the group or solo.The prince obviously counted his *Kapellmeister* as an artistic asset and was proud of displaying through him his musical *bon goût* to the high society gathering in Carlsbad.

Although any close personal relationship between people of as widely distant social status as Bach and his prince was unthinkable, each obviously enjoyed the other's company. The following November the prince became godfather to Bach's latest son, Leopold Augustus, named after Prince Leopold and his younger brother August Ludwig. Eleanore Wilhelmine of Weimar was godmother to the child, and several illustrious personalities of the aristocracy witnessed the baptism. Unhappily the infant received into this world with such regal honors did not reach the age of one year.

A few days after the arrival of this little son, Bach celebrated Leopold's birthday with a cantata, for which he also wrote the text. His Highness himself sang the bass part in this work, *"Durchlauchtester Leopold"* (His Serene Highness Leopold). Later we will see how this same work was transformed into a church cantata, with the two minuet movements kept perfectly intact.

In December, 1719, Bach learned that George Frederick Handel was in his vicinity, recruiting singers for the new academy in London. These negotiations brought him to the flourishing opera centers of Düsseldorf and Dresden. (Handel's old mother was living in Halle, counting the days until she might embrace her famous son.) C. S. Terry suggests that Count Flemming, who staged Bach's contest with Marchand in Dresden, might have been anxious to arrange a similar competition between Handel and Bach.[19] Perhaps this is the reason that Handel seemed to avoid Bach. Flemming wrote a pupil of Bach that Handel was always out or ill, and he found these excuses somewhat suspect. Even Spitta, who is painfully fair, admits that it is strange that Handel did not once seek Bach out in the eight months he spent in his vicinity in 1719.[20] When Bach heard that Handel was 20 miles away, in Halle, Prince Leopold at once lent him a horse for the journey. Upon his arrival he was informed that Handel had left for England.

Spitta also notes Handel's lack of interest in Bach's compositions, in contrast to Bach's obvious admiration for Handel's work. Bach with the help of his wife, copied in his own hand Handel's *Passion Music* to Brock's text, and one of his *concerti grossi*.[21] Bach also owned an original manuscript of a solo cantata by Handel. This picture of the busy man of the world forms a glaring contrast to Bach, whose incorruptible modesty and never-ceasing eagerness for new music and new techniques guided his creation of spiritual art.

In the spring of 1720 Prince Leopold again visited Carlsbad with his *Kapellmeister* and his staff of musicians. The company enjoyed the relaxed life of the resort from May to well into July. Upon their return to Köthen Bach was met by a tragedy possible only in those strangely primitive days. He found his wife Maria Barbara dead and already buried. Why did no one send a message to Carlsbad? Bach's children were only five, six, ten, and twelve years old, but his several pupils were certainly old enough to undertake the mission. Leopold was too loyal to Bach and too warm-hearted to have withheld this news from Bach. The blame must fall upon a seemingly heartless palace staff.

An Offer at Hamburg

Five months later, in November, 1720, Bach was taking steps to return to the service of the sanctuary. He had heard of a vacancy at the St. James Church in Hamburg. Bach's friend Erdmann Neumeister was pastor there and would be an ideal collaborator in Bach's reorganization of his "well-conceived" musical service. Neumeister urgently recommended Bach. Seven other organists applied for the post, most of them inferior musicians. Perhaps because of Bach's great fame the elders of the church avoided vain competitions among the candidates, but they had a sinister reason as well: they expected the chosen candidate to "express his gratitude with a substantial donation to the church." Such transactions, naturally, are always conducted under careful cover, and we do not know whether Bach knew of this shady arrangement.[22] The elders may even have purposely fixed the date of the hearing too late for Bach to attend, knowing that he never would consent to a bribe. But, quite indicatively, Bach withdrew his application, stating that he was expected back at Köthen to attend the birthday celebrations of Prince Leopold on November 29.

After the other able candidates withdrew, the remaining four were tested. Reincken was one of the judges and saw to it that the fugue subject on which the applicants were expected to improvise was exceedingly difficult.[23] All of the candidates failed and Bach was asked to reconsider. Bach emphatically declined the offer, and after weighing spiritual value of lofty art against gold, the committee decided in favor of Johann Joachim Heitman, the son of a wealthy artisan, who acknowledged his "gratitude" two weeks later with a payment of 4,000 marks. Erdmann Neumeister pronounced his bitter disappointment and indignation from the pulpit: "If angels of Bethlehem had descended from Heaven with the desire to become organists at St. James' church, they would have to fly away again, if they had not brought any money with them."[24]

Before Bach left Hamburg he called upon the old master Reincken, whom he had visited almost 20 years earlier. Johann Adam Reincken reached the venerable age of 99 and his lifetime spanned a period of rapidly changing music style—from Monteverdi to Haydn. Bach extemporized for Reincken on a Lutheran chorale "An Wasserflüssen Babilons" (Upon the Great Streams of Babylon), probably chosen because Reincken himself had written a well-known elaborate set of variations on the same melody. When Bach had exhausted all the possibilities of theme variations—a process that usually took him twice as long as it took others—and after he had displayed all the musical illustrations of the text, Reincken in amazement observed: "I thought this art was dead, but I see it still lives in you."

Reincken then submitted a theme for fugal treatment.[25] Bach remodeled the well-known Dutch tune slightly in order to give it a stronger and more unified character. As a fugue theme contains within itself all its contrapuntal possibilities in embryo, Bach devoted a few moments to this development, and invoking the help of his Creator in a short prayer, he proceeded to unfold without the slightest hesitation one of the most monumental fugues of all history. He afterwards wrote out the fugue—the great *G Minor Fugue*—in memory of the honorable occasion.

Anna Magdalena Bach

Bach was now a widower with a household of four young children. Such a lively family might well have become a heavy burden but fortune sent Bach a talented musical companion, who became his deeply devoted wife and an excellent mother to his children. Anna Magdalena Wilcken came from a long ancestry of professional musicians in Thuringia. At the time she met Bach she held a position as "princely singer" (*fürstliche Sängerin*) at the little court of Anhalt-Zerbst, which at times lent the service of its musicians to their neighboring prince in Köthen. She continued to hold that position, and drew the salary amounting to half that of her husband, after her marriage in December, 1721. At the time of her marriage she was just 20 years old, and Bach later praised the "excellent clarity" of her voice.

She undoubtedly sang at the festive wedding of Prince Leopold,[26] only a week after she married Bach. The undogmatic disposition of Prince Leopold and his great love of music did, as mentioned earlier, lead him to overlook Calvinistic prejudices against figural music in his chapel.[27] Bach wrote several cantatas, with secular as well as religious texts, during this period, and Anna Magdalena often sang the soprano part, to the delight of her happy bridegroom. Since there was no choir available, and only a small orchestra, these cantatas were written for solo voices; Anna Magdalena was assisted by an alto singer, or possibly by the prince himself singing a bass part. She may also have sung at the Lutheran church of St. Agnes.

The duties of her position as "princely singer" at the neighboring court of Anhalt-Zerbst must have been very light since she managed a family of four children as well. Bach too was not hard pressed in his duties. No wonder Bach in later life referred to this period as a happy one. He was surrounded with love and warm friendship. He had devoted pupils, among them his three gifted sons, Friedemann, Emanuel, and Gottfried Bernhard, and his young wife, whom he taught to play the clavichord and harpsichord.

Bach wrote the little notebook for Wilhelm Friedemann, mentioned earlier, during this period. He also made up one for Anna Magdalena about 1722 (see Chapter 15). The instructions for Wilhelm Friedemann indicate that he was then in the initial stages of clavier playing. Anna Magdalena's pieces can have been played only by an advanced musician and the pieces written out only three years later in a notebook can be played only by a pianist of high proficiency. He included some brilliant and difficult partitas in it that challenge concert pianists today.

These precious little notebooks indicate Bach's approach to the art of teaching, but also reflect the happy atmosphere that must have prevailed in this household. The majority of the pieces are gay, even frivolous little dances. Occasionally, a chorale melody is inserted, as "Wer nur den lieben Gott lässt walten" (Whoever Trusts God to Reign) used in Friedemann's book to illustrate the art of ornamenting such a melody. In Anna Magdalena's little book we find an elaborate treatment of the melody "Jesus meine Zuversicht" (Jesus, My Reliance), which exemplifies ornament used for lyrical expansion and abandon to overflowing sentiment. There is a jolly poem about his tobacco pipe that gives the smoker pleasure, drives his time away, and leads to some naive allegorical allusions of a biblical but humorous imagination. A tender love poem that appears is evidently by Bach himself:

> Your slave I am, sweet maiden bride,
> God give you joy this morning!
> The wedding flowers your tresses hide,
> The dress your form's adorning,
> O how with joy my heart is filled
> To see your beauty blooming,
> Till all my soul with music's thrilled,
> My heart's with joy o'erflowing.[28]

In the later notebook we find another song expressing profound conjugal happiness and peace with the world. A spiritual tone is given to the tender expression of love here, and the object of adoration can be interpreted as either human or divine.

> When Thou art with me
> I walk in Joy
> To meet eternal peace.
> Oh, how cheerfully content
> Were thus my end
> When my loyal eyes
> Be closed by Thy fair hand.[29]

14

WORLDLY MUSIC OF THE SPIRIT

PURELY instrumental music dominates Bach's creative work during his six years' residence in Köthen. He wrote relatively few church cantatas[1] (although more than had hitherto been believed);[2] religious compositions are conspicuously absent from the list. The great *G Minor Fantasy and Fugue* that Bach played for Reincken on his visit to Hamburg was his only organ work. The two or three ornamental chorale improvisations were composed for his immediate family, together with a very few songs in this mood. Since Bach's chief occupation was to furnish the music for Prince Leopold's musical soirées, we find a fair, but not unusually great number of sonatas, suites, and concerti for various groupings of violin and harpsichord; viola de gamba, violoncello, flute, either with harpsichord or unaccompanied; as well as for larger orchestral ensembles and for harpsichord or clavichord alone. This comparatively small amount of chamber music can hardly have filled concert programs for five years of weekly (or perhaps more frequent) performances. Works by many other composers must have supplemented the repertoire—probably by various members of the assembly as well as those whose scores could be found in the rather meagre library of the young prince.[3]

How many works of Bach's pen may have passed through the music room into oblivion shall never be known. He must have entertained Leopold and his guests often with his famed improvisations on various keyboard instruments and perhaps also on the violin. Our ignorance of this spontaneous art, an essential element of Bach's music, prevents us from gaining a full understanding of his art. In his improvisations he seems to have combined the greatest intensity of divine inspiration with the finest clarity of exposition reached during that century—and, it is safe to say, on the basis of all accounts of the astonished witnesses to these rare experiences, at any time in history.

Bach's art of accompanying is also irretrievably lost. The keyboard parts to the violin, cello, gamba, or flute sonatas were not played as written. In those days, a second harpsichordist customarily supplied the harmonies indicated by the scores for figured basses, translating the figures into full harmonies. But Bach undoubtedly served as his own thoroughbass player, developing the harmonies with phenomenal ability. He filled in the parts not only with blocks of harmony but with inner counter melodies.[5]

This fuller harmonization of the sonatas seems to have been facilitated by a pedal harpsichord. A set of pedals like the common accessory of the organ could plunk a separate set, or sets, of strings, and could be placed under either a harpsichord or a clavichord.[6] In spite of this, purists today, jealously safeguarding what they take for an unpolluted, uncorrupted style, give us only the bare bones of a once living organism when they play the work with empty basses. In the concerti and orchestral suites (which Bach called *ouvertures* because they are introduced by a symphonic piece in that style), *Kapellmeister* Bach followed the prevailing custom of conducting the ensemble from the harpsichord. He probably confined himself to more simple harmonies, through which the rhythm could be more firmly marked, rather than to development of a florid contrapuntal treatment.

A Musical Reconciliation of the Sacred and Secular

In 1718 or 1719 Bach received a commission from the Margrave of Brandenburg to compose the six concerti now known as the *Brandenburg Concerti*. Bach composed these works at leisure and with utmost care, and they were not delivered until the twenty-fourth of March, 1721. The *Brandenburg Concerti* represent the fruits of Bach's earlier profound study of the concerto form and constitute the first large-scale instrumental works for orchestra in this form. In Weimar Bach had copied numerous concerti by Vivaldi, Corelli, Marcello, Bontempi, Bononcini, and Legrenzi, but in this culmination of his study, he far surpassed his models in scope and import.

Originally the concerto played a ritual role in the sixteenth-century

Italian church service, and Bach did not entirely forsake this religious heritage. In spite of his use of such secular elements as French court dances, in the style of the *sonata da camera* (sonatas for the music room), the music itself is not secular in spirit. In fact, a very large part of all Bach's "secular" music eventually found its way into church cantatas, Masses, and oratorios. Thus later in Leipzig, the first movement of the first *Brandenburg Concerto* is used in place of the introductory symphony *(Symphonia)* to the cantata "*Falsche Welt, dir trau ich nicht*" (Treacherous World, I Trust Thee Not),[7] sung on the twenty-third Sunday after Trinity. Bach recast the first movement of the third *Brandenburg Concerto* in a similar role in the cantata "*Ich liebe den Höchsten vom gantzen Gemute*" (I Love the Highest with All My Heart).[8] And again, the famous *Preambulum in E Major* for unaccompanied violin,[9] which may have been played more than once by either Bach himself or one of the violin virtuosi on the staff in Köthen, became the *Symphonia* of the cantata "*Wir danken dir, Gott*" (We Thank Thee, God).[10] Sung in Leipzig on the occasion of the election of City Councils in 1731, the piece was transposed to D and scored for three trumpets, two oboes, two violins, one viola, an obligato organ part, and a continuo, probably taken by double basses or celli. The organ assumes the virtuoso role taken by the violin in the Köthen version. (Pianists need have no qualms about playing this piece on the pianoforte, even with underlying harmonies; Bach himself arranged it thus for the harpsichord and even for the lute.)

The happiness, inner strength and exuberance, and warmth that emanate from these pieces is not of ordinary dance music. The strong dance element, instead of calling up superficial gaiety, is sublimated through the sturdy, unrelenting rhythm into a symbolic pronouncement of firmness of faith that to Bach was the source of true joy. Bach's transformation of the dance was one realization of the Lutheran-Augustinian philosophy of reconciliation and merging of the human with the divine.

Bach also adapted several harpsichord concerti for church cantatas. The cantata "*Geist und Seele wird verwirret*" (Spirit and Soul Become Confused When They Contemplate Thee, God)[11] borrows an entire movement of a harpsichord concerto (only a fragment of which remains today)[12] for its introduction, with the organ taking the part of the solo harpsichord. All seven parts of this cantata are sung to concertizing obligato parts for organ that may well have their origin in solo pieces first used outside the church. The alto aria on the words

"spirit and soul become confused" is sung to the slow movement of
another harpsichord concerto. Again, in Cantata 49, *"Ich gehe und suche
mit Verlangen"* (I Walk and Seek with Longing), a harpsichord concerto with orchestral accompaniment, transferred to the organ, introduces the cantata, while obligato organ parts continue the accompaniments of the arias in the same concertizing style.

One of the most striking examples of these invasions of secular harpsichord concerti into the church is the appearance of the famous *D
Minor Concerto*. The entire first and second movements are taken
over in the cantata *"Wir müssen durch viel Trübsal"* (We Must Bear
Much Sorrow to Enter Into God's Kingdom).[13] The first, as usual, is
given to the organ, accompanied by the orchestra. On the second
movement Bach superimposed a chorale-like, four-voiced chorus. The
original obligato bass is preserved and sung by the bass voices and
double basses. The harpsichord solo, transferred to the organ, is also
kept perfectly intact. The chorus now sings the text of the title of the
cantata to this melody. The entire work is a most interesting example
of the evolution of an art work finding its final destination in a deeply
religious contemplation. Originally Bach had written the work as a violin concerto, the features of which we can clearly recognize even though
its model is lost. This violin concerto in turn derived its style from its
prototype, the Italian concerto, and especially that of Vivaldi. Thus,
what seems today to be a triple plagiarism is really a continual rebirth
until the final form with its spiritual text reached its true destination.
Bach's concerto was born in the church of San Marco in Venice and
wandered over the earth in worldly garb before finding its home, in
the Lutheran sanctuary.

Bach adapted four other harpsichord concerti to church cantatas.
The moving, universally appealing melody of the famous slow movement of the *F Minor Concerto*[14] introduces Cantata 156, *"Ich stehe
mit einem Fuss im Grabe."*[15] As the harpsichord, and even the pianoforte, seem the most unsuitable of all instruments for the full realization
of this moving melody, in the cantata Bach gives the melody to the
solo oboe, the instrument most able to express the long, sustained notes
that cry for a crescendo. But before he found its ultimate fulfillment,
Bach scored the melody for violin.[16] Cantata 169, *"Gott soll allein
mein Herze haben"* (Only God Shall Possess My Heart),[17] incorporated two movements of the *E Major Piano Concerto*.[18] The gentle,
rocking rhythm of the second movement, reminiscent of a sicilienne,

now accompanies the words "Die in me, world, and all your love, that my heart may develop the love of God." A soprano aria[19] in Cantata 120, "*Gott, man lobet dich in der Stille*" (God, Man Praises Thee in Stillness)[20] is accompanied by an elaborate obligato for the *violino concertanto*, which turns out to be the slow movement of a sonata for violin and harpsichord composed in Köthen.[21] The soprano sings the melody of the violin solo but with simpler figuration.

Of the 43 extant cantatas classified as "secular," only two are thoroughly worldly—the Coffee Cantata and, most obvious, the Peasant Cantata.[22] The majority of secular cantatas, written for inaugurations of notables, for weddings, and for birthdays of princes and kings, have a vestigial religious character, and Bach used music from most of them at some time or other in church cantatas, Masses, and oratorios. But the Peasant Cantata has a pungently earthy quality. The dialect in which the text was written is almost untranslatable.[23] The uninhibited frankness of its language may surprise those who think of Bach as a severe and gloomy churchman. The thoroughly rustic tunes and ditties, some of which are folk or street songs, could never be transformed into a spiritual context. The Coffee Cantata is a jolly little comedy, ridiculing the prejudices of the time against the new vice of coffee drinking. Bach's broadminded attitude toward these harmless fads comes out nicely in this delightful musical farce.

Bach tried his hand at one other type of secular cantata, the *Drama per Musica*. This classical opera on a very small scale generally presents classical characters—Hercules, Diana, Endymion, or Pan—allegorical figures—Fortune, Fame, Diligence, Gratitude, Zephyr, Aeolus, or German Rivers—or other conventional vehicles of edification. The works were performed in the open air, generally in the gardens of notables, where nature provided the only scenery. Costumes were omitted, and action was limited to the musicians entering the scene to a musical march. Bach seems to have stepped outside his realm when he wrote these.

The Dance

In music of the Catholic church, folk and dance tunes were sometimes merged with religious music, but only after they had been so completely changed and dismembered by altered rhythms and by such wide distribution of musical motifs that the original tunes were no longer recognizable. Bach, however, left the dances completely intact in his cantatas. They remain dances: only the words have been changed, and the organ instead of the harpsichord is used for the accompaniment. The dance plays an exalted role in Bach's religious music, as a sublime expression of the human spirit endowed with transcendental possibilities. All his dance suites were composed for our *Gemüthsergötzung*, the delight of our spirit, as he expressly inscribed their title pages.

The dance was very dear to Bach. He composed and taught numerous dances and many of his compositions are related to dance forms. At Köthen and on his visit to Cassel he can hardly have missed observing numerous balls, and although he would never have danced with the ladies of society, he enjoyed this pleasure within his own circle. He wrote many dances for his friends and, graced by his wife whose "form" he so admired in his poem to her, joined them in steps to his own charming music. To the creative musician, however, the music of the dance, not the actual dance experience, would always be its essential element.

In Köthen Bach wrote a cantata for his friend and sovereign Prince Leopold. *"Durchlauchter Leopold"* is a gay, graceful musical eulogy to his youthful master, which contains two minuets. The first, a duet-aria for soprano and bass, shows a remarkable resemblance to that of the first *Brandenburg Concerto*, in the opening motif and in the manner the bass imitates the melody of the violin. The second, for four voices, recalls the *C Minor Minuet* in the *French Suite* of that key for clavichord. The entire six movements of the cantata, minuets and all, were transferred at a later period to the church as *"Erhötes Fleisch und Blut"* (Exalted Flesh and Blood).[24] The first minuet sings the words *"So hat Gott die Welt geliebet"* (Thus God has loved the world), the second, *"Rühre, Höchster, unsern Geist, dass des höchsten Geistes Gaben ihre Wirkung in uns haben"* (Move, Highest, our spirit, that the highest gifts of the spirit may have their effect upon us). Bach seems purposely to have chosen dance rhythms here to express the Lutheran philosophy of reconciliation of life on earth with life of the spirit.

Bach recognized the universal power of the dance to lift man's spirit to extravagant and apparently irrational realms of self-identity. The primitive savage, hypnotized by his dance, imagines himself possessed of demoniac forces through which he can cure, kill, bring rain, or lead his tribe to victory. The Dionysian orgiastic dancer also was transported into a realm where he could call forth fertility, rebirth, sometimes aided by human sacrifice. In the Orphic mysteries the intoxication of the dance could stir emotions that the mind had prepared and refined through ages of civilization. During Bach's time in the unique atmosphere of French court life, the dance was more than a mere etiquette: it portrayed the most refined graces of the soul, expressing devotion and reverence for the *Roi Soleil*, the highest embodiment of idealism.

The noble idealism inherent in the dance music of French culture proved to be perfectly compatible with Lutheran humanism in Germany. In the eighteenth century the sentiment of adoration for an almost deified king was almost the same as that bestowed upon divinity. The delights and tender transports of these highly refined dances were quite acceptable, just as, for Luther, conjugal, sexual love was reconcilable with a divine life. Only the puritan Calvinist saw in dance music an antithesis to holiness. Werckmeister justified the use of dance music in the liturgy with the words: "To the pure, all is pure." Buxtehude, the exemplary Lutheran composer, had composed a dance suite on a hymn theme with the words *"Auf meinen lieben Gott trau ich"* (On My Dear God I trust in Fear and in Need).

Ironically, much of Bach's dance music originated in Köthen, and little of it in Weimar. Prince Leopold, although ostensibly a Calvinist, was more tolerant and more human than Duke Wilhelm Ernst of Weimar. Thus, despite the calvinistic environment, Bach's Lutheran spirit was more free here and his sojourn in Köthen was indeed the happiest time in his life. Although he must have regretted not having a musical post in a Lutheran church, he did not forsake his religious mission in music, even while he was composing secular music. As we can see, much of his music from this period had qualities of depth not usually found in court and chamber music, and eventually these compositions were transformed into music for church service. Especially in his treatment of the music for the dance we can see the master's ability to perceive sacred elements in everyday life and to endow the secular with eternal significance.

15

COMPOSITIONS FOR THE KEYBOARD

Even excluding his organ music, Bach's keyboard music presents a
bewildering complex. The works may be divided into three classes:
pieces for the instruction of his pupils, pieces that may actually have
been used in church (and in that case transferred to the organ), and
Hausmusik, music for private use that Bach wrote for "the delight of
the soul" and "the allowable recreation of the spirit." This classification
is not a rigid division, but rather a means of distinguishing Bach's
purposes and motivations for composing various types of music. In
this chapter we will concentrate primarily on Bach's pedagogical works.
He was a great teacher, and his philosophy and method of education determined to a great extent his composition of musical exercises for his
pupils.

Bach the Teacher

Many of Bach's little pieces which he intended for a specific purpose are often dished up to suffering and reluctant students today who
swallow this fare as unwillingly as they do their spinach. They are told
that they are in the presence of the immortal Bach, whom they are
expected to revere through these—to them—utterly meaningless and
frustrating little atrocities. This ill-chosen teaching material generally
instills in novices a life-long distaste for any and all music of Bach.

Bach did not intend most of these little preludes[1] as finger exercises,
but even less as musical creations. They were illustrations of harmonic
progressions, for Bach first taught his pupils the inner construction of

harmony and then its application on the keyboard. It was unthinkable in Bach's time to teach children merely to play an instrument without making them aware of the harmonic foundations of music and preparing them to compose their own pieces as soon as possible. In view of this custom, it is possible that many compositions ascribed to Bach are actually the products of his pupils.

A simple prelude, such as the first in the *Well-Tempered Clavier,* consists of chords only, ambling through a few modulations and using certain broken-chord formations. Similarly the notebook of Friedemann presents several pieces of this type, only here Bach calls them *preambulum.* They serve a double purpose: first to acquaint the pupil, through practical experience, with the stringing together of a beautiful succession of chords (sometimes enlivened with sparkling figurations, as in the D major, d minor, and c minor preludes of the *Well-Tempered Clavier*); and second, in the *Well-Tempered Clavier,* as an introduction to the main work, often a fugue. In Friedemann's little notebook these fugues do not appear. Many of the preludes *(preambulum)* are in a somewhat rudimentary form, and some may well have been composed by Friedemann himself. Since most were written in Bach's own handwriting, he probably helped to bring the little pieces to their finished form.

The famous *C Major Prelude* of the *Well-Tempered Clavier,* Book I, which appears in the notebook in a handwriting that is not Bach's, may have been conceived as a lesson in harmonic progressions. The figuration of broken chords is written out only in the first six measures; after that block chords are written. In an earlier draft for the *C Sharp Major Prelude* of the second book (written in C major instead of C sharp) the word *arpeggio* has been written between the lines of solid chords.

The *E Minor Prelude* of the first book shows an interesting evolution. The first draft, as it stands in Friedemann's notebook, shows the left-hand figure of this prelude, but instead of the delicate melody for the right hand found in the final form of the *Well-Tempered Clavier,* there are merely chords. Instead of the 41 measures, the original exercise omits the entire presto section and occupies only 22 measures. The entire "presto" part is lacking. Bach evidently recreated his prelude from Friedemann's exercise in ornamented thoroughbass, and used it as the accompaniment to the tenderly mystic melody of the final form. By this example we can observe the organic growth of one of the most inspired melodies.

Forkel explains that Bach taught his pupils first of all the thorough-bass in four parts.[2] The basses of these preludes in the notebook reveal a certain uniformity. For the first five (corresponding to the *Well-Tempered Clavier* preludes, Book I, in C Major, c minor, d minor, D major, and e minor) after an opening cadence that establishes the key, the bass consists of descending scales. In the *E Minor Prelude* the descent continues over more than two octaves, until at the very end, it progresses chromatically. The teaching of a thoroughbass began by establishing a bass. The harmonies were then laid over this, and in the third stage, as is evident from this *E Minor Prelude*, a melody is added. The saraband that Anna Magdalena wrote into her notebook in 1725[3] —the same piece that served as the air upon which Bach later composed his variations for his pupil Goldberg[4]—was undoubtedly composed by the same three-step process: first the bass, then the harmony, and finally, the melody. In the 30 variations built on the same bass, there is no trace of the melody of the air,[5] for here Bach uses the bass as the substance and backbone of the composition.

We will never know whether many of the pieces in these notebooks are the result of the combined efforts of master and pupil, or whether the pupil had merely copied them from the master's manuscript. But since Friedemann grew to be an eminent composer while Anna Magdalena did not, it seems plausible that at least parts of some of the pieces from Friedemann's book were his own compositions. One little minuet in the notebook is marked "Menuet Trio di J. S. Bach," suggesting that while this specific piece is by the father the other ones may be the combined product of father and son, but we will probably never be able to firmly establish authorship.

The first drafts of all the two-part "Inventions" (here entitled *preambulum*) appear in Friedemann's notebook. These differ only slightly from the final form in which Bach published them in 1723, so we may assume that they are essentially composed by J. S. Bach. They were included in the notebook as models for the art of composition rather than as part of his introduction into the mysteries of harmony. Bach gives a good summary of the guiding purpose behind his teaching method in an inscription on the title page:

A candid primer, in which the lovers of the clavier, but especially those eager to learn, are shown a distinct way, not only (1) to learn to play cleanly with two voices, but also, after further advancement, (2) to deal correctly and ably with three *obligato* voices; and at the same time also not only to acquire good *inventiones,* but also to develop them well; and above all, however, to attain a *cantabile* manner in his playing, and besides to acquire a strong foretaste for composition. . . .[6]

Bach obviously uses the Latin word *inventiones* here in the sense of idea, theme, or motive, and not with the medieval and Renaissance connotation of craft or skill as opposed to creation of something entirely new. But as we have seen, for Bach the value of the *inventiones* lay not in their originality or expression of a mood; first and foremost, a musician must have the ability to develop and combine given material artfully. Self-expression was only an accompaniment to this. He himself has left very few completely original melodies in spite of being the most powerfully individual composer of all time.

Bach relied not on his own human talents but on his faith in God for musical inspiration, and he passed on his convictions about the religious basis of the art he taught to his pupils. Above the composition and performing exercises for little Friedemann we find the inscription "I N J," *In Nomine Jesu.* Bach also always began lessons with a prayer.

Although the little notebook is entitled *Klavierbüchlein,* it is not devoted entirely to the keyboard. The very first entry shows six scales (all without accidentals) written out in various clefs—the violin clef, the soprano, mezzo soprano, alto, tenor, and the three movable F clefs (or bass clefs.).[7] Friedemann must have already mastered considerable clavier technique; his father believed he was now ready for instruction in reading all these clefs as they appear in vocal scores. Bach himself never wrote in movable F clefs but taught all eight clefs as a means of reading chorales in open score, and possibly some ancient chorale-motets, arranged for that purpose. The student probably was first taught to read each clef separately, the two together, then three, until several could be read at once. This process most likely progressed at the same pace as agility on the keyboard.

Forkel tells us that Bach played a great deal for his students, and that his example inspired them to approach their teacher's skill at the keyboard. Bach kept his beginning pupils "for months on end" on "nothing but isolated finger exercises in both hands, with constant regard to clear and clean touch." He did not feel it necessary to write these exercises out, and the notebook begins after the student has advanced considerably from this arduous practice. Along with these exercises in finger dexterity Bach must have given rudimentary information on the principles of harmony, scale construction, and thoroughbass to prepare the student for his more advanced presentations in the notebooks.

The art of reading various clefs was also taught in the Lutheran schools, as we have seen in Chapter 4, but Bach did not feel that this was adequate preparation for his sons' achievement of one of the chief marks of musicianship—the ability to read anything at first sight. In school the students had to learn only to sing single lines—all that was needed to sing the Lutheran service. This choir training in Gisela Agnes' Lutheran school was not enough for Bach's children. Bach wanted his sons to become complete musicians, like all other Bachs (there have been 54 of them). Sight-reading, composition, and improvisation were all abilities demanded of musicians of his day. Later, in Beethoven's time, thanks to the flourishing music publishers, many composers no longer needed to perform their compositions in order to make a living by their art. In Bach's time very little printed music was in circulation, and composers were required to perform and conduct their works either at a court or in church.

Hence the master was responsible for teaching his students more than how to work out contrapuntal problems on paper. His student would one day have to prove himself as an unfailing sight-reader of any full score, an improvisor on given themes and in any given form, and a composer skilled as a performer. Bach taught his students not merely to play a keyboard instrument but to fulfill the manifold needs of the professional musician of his epoch, and many of his pupils, including his four sons, went on to fill positions as church composers and organists, or as directors of music at royal or princely courts.

Anna Magdalena did not receive as broad an education from her husband, however, since she worked primarily on singing, harpsichord or clavichord playing, and copying music for her husband. But we know she must have had considerable knowledge of music beyond mere keyboard playing to have copied his enormous orchestral and choral scores. Although her notebook of 1722 includes one fantasia for organ, and she may have occasionally played on one of the organs in Köthen, most of the pieces in both her notebooks consists of songs and dances for either harpsichord or clavichord.

Hausmusik and Religious Toccatas and Sonatas

Bach's keyboard suites and partitas, often referred to as *Hausmusik*, were composed for sheer pleasure and relaxation, to both listeners and performers. They were obviously intended for his own family's enjoyment: the notebooks, two complete suites—known as the French—and two complete partitas, along with numerous minuets and other dances. Almost any of this so-called *Hausmusik*, however, might have found its way into a church service.

Another type of Bach's keyboard music now in the repertoire of pianists is the toccatas and sonatas conceived for the communion service in the Lutheran church. Most of these works did not originate in the Köthen period since Bach had no affiliation with any church there, except possibly for an occasional small after-service performance at St. Agnes'.[8] Two toccatas and three sonatas, two of which are ornamental transcriptions of Reincken's sonatas and one a transcription of Bach's own violin sonata, served this religious function. It may not be too far-fetched to presume that the *Chromatic Fantasy and Fugue* also belongs in this category.

Bach uses "fantasy" in this case as just another name for toccata. Historically a fantasy was a type of ricercar, a musical form which itself sprang from the motet[9] and anticipated the fugue. The fugato themes of a motet were derived from a worldly or liturgical song, and originally the ricercar was nothing more than a motet transferred to a keyboard instrument. When its themes were freely invented rather than derived from song, the piece was called a fantasy, and Bach merged this ancient form with the rhapsodic and recitative elements of the toccata. Gradually the toccata elements came to dominate his works. His *Chromatic Fantasy and Fugue* consists of the same recitative passages found in the piano toccatas; it is interspersed with similar improvisatory passage work. Instead of the two ricercars this work concludes with one fugue, and thus could be classified as a prelude. Because Bach often combined forms in one work, he also often used different titles for the same piece when he transcribed it for another instrument or incorporated it into a larger composition. (Thus he freely interchanges the terms *symphonia* and *fantasia*, *preambulum* and *invention*, *praeludium*, *toccata*, and *fantasia*, *ouverture*, *suite*, and *partita* in the same types of, often identical works.) Bach may have chosen the term fantasy in this case because of the length of the work and the absence of ricercars in it, but it is folly to attempt to guess Bach's reasoning in giving titles to his works.

The declamatory tone of the entire *Chromatic Fantasy* relates the work to the *G Minor Fantasy* that precedes the fugue in that key. Also, like the g minor work, it obviously is not a piece motivated by the gay spirit of his suites, but was meant for deep contemplation of a great mystery, possibly during the Holy Communion. Here again we can see that when Bach meditated musically, he did not give in to the vague reveries of a Romantic, but focused on a particular religious symbol or thought. In both the *Chromatic Fantasy* and the *G Minor Fantasy*, he calls forth the gigantic, superhuman forces of the chaos before creation. Like Michaelangelo's painting of the Creator stretching out His omni- potent arms in a light-giving gesture, these musical fantasies are filled with biblical representations and images from a deeply religious soul too mysterious and profound for verbal translation. But in listening to these mighty recitatives, arioso-like cantilenas, and virtuoso passages we feel instinctively in touch with a mind struggling with the tragic and eternal relation of mortals to divinity.

Bach's Attitude Toward Instruments

In our discussions of Bach's keyboard compositions we cannot ignore the controversy that continues today over their proper, authentic per- formance. The argument has already been touched upon when our present-day attempts at reconstruction of a true baroque organ were described in Chapter 9. There we could conclude that although Bach revered the organ above all other instruments as the means of trans- mitting the religious depth of his music, he was not bound to one par- ticular version of the baroque organ. Our attempts to search out his preference and recreate it are in vain and in fact ignore the guiding inspiration that gave purpose to his creative work.

In the same way, modern musicologists err when they claim that proper interpretation of Bach's style depends on correct choice of in- struments. Bach's selection of instruments for his compositions was based on their availability in the place in which he was composing and on other purely practical considerations much more than on timbre and expressibility. Bach conceived his music independently of any physical manifestation or realization and his art can be incarnated through various media, even the modern pianoforte, if the spiritual im- port is retained.

Bach's attitude toward instruments had its philosophical foundations in medieval, north European conceptions of the art of music. In 1490 Adam von Fulda, and later Kircher and Werckmeister in the sixteenth and seventeenth centuries, described music as a mirror of divine order.[10]

Accordingly, the musical proportions existed prior to creation. Adam von Fulda resented the Italian, humanistic suggestion that music should have a physical instead of an ideal and metaphysical origin. He observes with indignation that in southern countries, in France, Italy, and their neighboring regions, musical art is derived from the sounds coming from particular instruments.[11] This kind of music lacks the power to penetrate into the true essence of music. Sensuous experience with instruments, actual sound produced by handling instruments, cannot inspire true musical thought; this must spring from the consideration of intervallic relations, from the contemplation of consonances and dissonances, from *speculatio*. Music is prior to its sound. Corporal, actual, sounding music, according to von Fulda and later Werckmeister, moves within the realm of semblance, *Schein*, which is not its true being. True being is ideal, primordial, and divine in nature.

Bach may never have read Adam von Fulda's work—though his compositions were in the library of the Thomas School in Leipzig[12]—but his musical application of Platonism lived on in the minds of generations of pious German musicians, and Bach found it expressed in the works of Tauler (*Teutsche Theologia*) and Werckmeister. Even if he did not embrace these ideas as a philosophical system, he held them as a working principle and a credo underlying his art.

This attitude explains why Bach's vocal parts sound instrumental, and his instrumental compositions sound as if they were meant to be sung. For the same reasons Bach had no reluctance about transcribing compositions from one instrument to another. When Bach inscribes a title to one of his works "for harpsichord with two manuals" or "*Pro cimbalo*," or "*Vor ein clavicymbel mit zweyen Manualen*,"[13] this designation is not necessarily meant as final. We have seen how he transferred harpsichord concertos to the organ when he used them in cantatas, and how he transcribed a violin solo to various other media.

The instrument Bach assigned to his *Chromatic Fantasy* discussed above is not definite. Naumann lists 15 of the most reliable manuscripts for this work, most of them copies made during the life of the master. Only four assign the work to the harpsichord; most do not mention the instrument at all. One—a collection that belonged to Bach's pupil Johann Christian Kittel—lists the work with a "collection of great preludes and fugues for the organ by J. Sebast. Bach." It may be that rather than having been used like a toccata as I suggest above, the work was performed as a prelude or postlude to the main service, like the famous St. Ann's Fugue, which Bach himself designated for this use. The essence of musical thought in art works such as the *Chromatic Fantasy* can be expressed as well by the harpsichord as the modern pianoforte, although the organ is, in some respects, most suitable.

When Bach gave the title *Klavierübung* to the four volumes of keyboard music he published between 1726 and 1742, he revealed something of his own general attitude toward instruments. The word *Übung* may best be translated by cultivation or pursuit, but Bach's choice of the word was prompted by its ancient religious connotation of "religious exercise." The word *Klavier* in Bach's time was the generic name for all keyboard instruments, including the organ.[15]

While Bach indicates in his choice of this general title for the collection his concern for an entire class of instruments, rather than specific ones, he designates a specific instrument for each composition. He based these particular choices on the performance requirements of the individual works, however. C. F. Becker aptly points out that "it might not be superfluous to observe that Bach, like most clavier players of his time, served himself for the execution with a double keyboard plus an additional set of pedals."[16] He assigns a set of chorale-preludes and the famous *St. Ann's Fugue* to the *organo pleno*, and another to the *manualiter*. The *Partita with a French Overture* and the *Goldberg Variations* are marked "for a harpsichord with two manuals." Forkel confirms that Bach, in order to be able to combine a reading of three or four separate parts (which he laid side by side), selected "two clavichords and the pedal, or a harpsichord with two sets of keys, provided with a pedal."[17] Bach probably owned one or two *Pedalklaviere* of this second type, with plucked strings. The clavichord type was more common.[18]

Bach's choice of instrument, whether harpsichord, pedal clavier, clavichord, spinet, lute-clavier, full organ, or the mere use of manuals on a small organ, did not depend upon the particular timbre or expressibility of the instrument, but upon its playability and function. The texture of the music determined whether one or two manuals were needed to execute the polyphony. If the voices crossed a great deal, two manuals would facilitate their realization; if not, as in the *French Suites,* a one-manual clavichord would suffice. Both the harpsichord and the clavichord could be combined with a set of pedals to make more complicated combinations easily playable. (The clavichord was especially recommended to beginners and girls, whose fingers were as yet too weak for the more resistant plucking action of the harpsichord.)

Anyone who has played the *Well-Tempered Clavier* on either the harpsichord or the clavichord knows that some of its fugues cannot be played on manuals only. Many others present formidable problems of fingering when played on manuals alone.[19] The modern pianist can overcome these difficulties by the use of the sustaining pedal—a device that did not exist in Bach's time—and can avoid the risk of striking undesirable neighboring keys when playing some of the unusually large stretches, while the single-manual harpsichord or clavichord is very prone to speak upon the slightest touch. (The manual parts in Bach's organ works offer none of the fingering puzzles of the *Well-Tempered Clavier*, and never is a stretch greater than the octave required.)

Why did Bach not write out the pedal parts for his clavier works if he played the basses (and sometimes the middle parts) on the pedals? The only answer is that any musician in that day would know when to use a pedal board. Many of the fugues in the *Well-Tempered Clavier* obviously can easily be played on manuals alone. It was only during Bach's lifetime that pedal parts began to be written out even for the organ; the organ works of Froberger, Pachelbel, and Buxtehude were still written on two staffs only. The organist had to decide where to apply the pedals, which were by no means used in the bass only. Even Bach did not consistently use a third staff on his pedal parts.[20]

Bach's choice of keyboard instruments was thus determined mainly by the capacity of the instrument to exhibit the polyphonic structure and other features of the composition. When Bach played the *Well-Tempered Clavier* for his pupil Heinrich Nikolaus Gerber, he probably used a clavichord with an additional *Pedalklavier*, furnished with clavichord tangents. In the light of this interpretation, all problems of registration and fingering in the work become much clearer and simpler. While present-day harpsichords always have a 16-foot stop on the lower manual, this stop was rare on harpsichords of the eighteenth century, although it was always found in the pedals.[21] The clavichord also, when the dynamic variations provided by the 16-foot pedal tones are added, can answer the expressive demands of certain works in the collection—for example, the wonderfully sustained *C Sharp Minor Fugue* in Book I with its subtle *chiaroscuro* and *Bebung* (vibration). Another interpretation might be that the pedal-harpsichord would realize more fully the plasticity and clarity of the contrapuntal structure. This keyboard instrument could augment the treble voices with its four-foot stop, while the middle voices remained unthickened, in mere eight-foot pitch. The pedals then could expand the pitch downward into the lower octave. The registration then approaches more closely that of the baroque organ, and the orchestration of Bach.

Function too played a role in Bach's selection of instruments. If a composition was destined for the church, the organ was his natural choice. Of course, this does not mean that he did not play and rehearse some organ works on the pedal clavier. Both Albert Schweitzer and C. F. Becker cite examples of this.[22] While composing, however, Bach did not make his musical thought dependent upon a particular instrument. He never composed *for* an instrument: he assigned his compositions *to* an instrument. Forkel tells us that "he rigorously kept his pupils to compose entirely from the mind, without an instrument. Those who wished to do otherwise he called, in ridicule, 'knights of the keyboard' (Klavier-Ritter, or Klavier Hussaren)."[23]

Expressive Capabilities of Bach's Instruments

Bach's basic detachment from instruments does not imply indifference to the delights of varying sonority. He once asked the famous instrument maker, Zacharias Hildebrandt, to manufacture for him a lute-clavier—a keyboard instrument with gut strings.[24] According to Spitta Bach acquired this instrument "because the tone of the clavier [meaning the harpsichord] was felt to be so hard and expressionless." Though its less metallic tone probably appealed to Bach, the instrument's power to control louds and softs was no greater than the harpsichord's since both were operated by a plectra. The lute-clavier was coming into vogue at this time and Bach liked to invite his friends to listen to this instrument from outside his room and tell him whether he was playing the theorbo (a large lute with extra bass strings) or his new lute-clavier. His friends' inability to distinguish between the sonority of the two was a source of great merriment. Nevertheless, he never that we know of wrote a composition specifically for the lute-clavier.

Forkel tells us that, according to C. P. E. Bach, of all keyboard instruments (except the organ) Bach preferred the clavichord.[25] Modern harpsichord enthusiasts insist that the statement only indicates his son's own bias, as a child of a new era of "style of sensitivity" (*Empfinsamkeit*) for the more expressive clavichord. Undeniably Emanuel did not accept his father's beliefs, founded in Adam von Fulda and others, in the metaphysical relations of his art, but I cannot accept this as proof that the son was more sensitive to the expressive qualities of an instrument than his teacher-father. I am convinced that these arguments are just as prejudiced as C. P. E. Bach's may have been, except that practical considerations rather than questions of taste determine the position of modern-day concertizing harpsichordists.

It would certainly be impossible for these performers to play before large audiences on a miniature clavichord. Even the Pleyel harpsichord used by Wanda Landowska had to be built with the thick strings of a modern pianoforte—thus making necessary extra (piano) dampers and a steel frame—in order to be audible in a fair-sized concert hall. In Bach's and Emanuel's time the clavichord was just as unsuitable for public performance. Since Emanuel was more interested in sensitive articulation of his own music than in the art of composition, he preferred the clavichord. Moreover Emanuel had the reputation of a clavier player while his father was known as an organist. So Emanuel's statement of his father's favor for the clavichord may reflect some of the personal preference the harpsichordists charge him with. But the entire controversy does not provide any fruitful perspective on Bach's art, for he himself was most concerned with the creation of music, not its performance.

I feel it is very likely that Bach shared his son's feelings about the clavichord, and he unquestionably preferred it for special purposes of expressing lyrical and intimate sentiments. Bach's imagination was, of course, not limited in any way to home music.

While his musical mind soared beyond all instruments, conceiving his creations prior to any instrumental realizations, it is nevertheless helpful in understanding Bach's attitude toward and treatment of instruments to compare the expressive capacities of various instruments of his time, particularly keyboard instruments. These may be divided according to their capacity of declamatory expression, that is, the use of dynamic as well as agogic accentuation and of crescendo and decrescendo within a phrase. The organ, the harpsichord, the spinet and its derivative, the pedal harpsichord (the set of keys played by the feet like an organ), and the lute-clavier are relatively incapable of dynamic accents. All the stringed instruments, the lute, the flutes and woodwind instruments (especially the oboe and its related double reed instruments), and among the keyboard instruments, the clavichord with the pedal clavichord, the fortepiano, and the cembal d'amour, are capable of a wide variety of declamatory expressions for which the human voice has always been the supreme model.

Although Bach shared this age-old reverence for the voice—in his preface to the "Inventiones" he points out that they are to develop a *cantabile* style of playing—the expressive elements, accentuation, dynamic and agogic, and changes in volume, so natural to the voice, are completely impossible on either the organ or the harpsichord, the keyboard instruments most often used by Bach and his contemporaries. The clavichord, as we have said, is somewhat more expressive, but its diminutive scale sharply limits its use. In fact, during Bach's time, composers did not even want to elicit such humanistic elements from these instruments. As we discussed in Chapter 9, the organ reigned supreme among the instruments, and its metaphysical esthetics to some extent suppressed the use of the full expressive powers of even the voice; guileless and less expressive boys' voices were preferred.

We have already spoken of the comparative expressive capacities of the harpsichord and clavichord. Because the clavichord is struck with a brass tangent, instead of the leather plectrum of the harpsichord, and attains the desired pitch like a violin,[26] the clavichordist can produce crescendi and decrescendi, as well as dynamic accents. Vibration of tones in a vertical direction, like the violin and voice, adds to the expressive powers of the instrument. But the volume of the clavichord limited its use, and Bach could never have used the instrument for compositions intended for the palace or any public place.

Ultimately the fortepiano satisfied the desire for an instrument capable of a wide range of expressions. Although interest in an instrument with this quality was growing even during Bach's lifetime, the pianoforte was not satisfactorily perfected until the nineteenth century. Bach first became acquainted with the fortepiano in 1726, through an instrument built by the famous German organ builder, Gottfried Silbermann. Silbermann was not the inventor, but followed the principles developed by the Florentian, Bartolomeo Cristofori, who in 1709 completed a harpsichord on which loud and soft tones could be produced by finger pressure.[27]

Bach's pupil Johann Friedrich Agricola, in his addenda to the *Musica Mechanica Organoedi* by Jakob Adlung (Berlin, 1768) gives this account of Bach's reaction to the instrument:

... of these instruments Mr. Gottfried Silbermann had at first manufactured two. One of these the late Capelmeister Johann Sebastian Bach has seen and has played upon. He has praised the sonority of the same, yes, even admired it; but he found fault with the treble which sounded weak, and the instrument was too difficult to play. Mr. Silbermann, who could not suffer any criticism of his endeavor, has taken this extremely amiss. He therefore was for a long time on bad terms with Mr. Bach. And yet, his conscience told him that Mr. Bach was right. He therefore judged—and this must be said to his fame—that the best course was not to issue his instruments any longer; but on the contrary, all the more diligently to think about the faults discovered by Mr. J. S. Bach. On this he worked many years. And that this was the true reason of his delay I doubt all the less because I have heard Mr. Silbermann himself confess it to me. Finally, as Mr. Silbermann really had found many improvements, especially in regard to the manner of playing it [*sonderlich in Ansehung des Tractaments*][28] he again sold one to the princely court of Rudolstadt. Shortly after that His Majesty the King of Prussia ordered one of these instruments; and as this found great success, still several more. Those who had heard the old instrument, and among them myself, could very easily see how diligently Mr. Silbermann must have worked on them. Mr. Silbermann has also had the praiseworthy pride to show one of these instruments to the late Mr. Bach, and to have him examine it; and he received full approval of it.[29]

Nevertheless Bach never acquired one of Silbermann's fortepianos. And by the time he played on Frederick the Great's pianofortes, in 1747, three years before his death, he was less than ever interested in the interpretive phase of music-making but was devoting all his efforts to the mystic cult of contrapuntal discipline. The alternating vigorous and tender, graceful and fervent human affections found in the suites of the Köthen period, the expression of which would have been enhanced by the pianoforte, were very remote from the art of his last decade. The six-voiced ricercar that he improvised for Frederick the Great displayed Bach's astounding contrapuntal art but not the particular potentialities of the pianoforte.

In fact his later sparing use of ornaments, so abundant in the Köthen suites, points up an inadequacy in the instrument that Bach must have recognized. Philipp Emanuel admits: "I doubt that the most intensive practice can lead to complete control of the volume of the short trill at the pianoforte." And elsewhere, "The more recent pianoforte, when it is sturdy and well built, has many fine qualities, although its touch must be carefully worked out, a task which is not without difficulties."[30] Today the ornament presents infinitely greater difficulties even on our perfected pianos than on either the harpsichord or the clavichord.

In the period of more than a century that elapsed between the invention of the instrument and realization of its full potentialities, entirely different styles of compositions had evolved. The extended compass in both bass and treble and the addition of pedals—both improvements on Silbermann's original instrument—allowed an infinitely wider range of volume than could be imagined on the early version of the instrument that Bach knew.

A few other instruments used during Bach's time, which are now museum pieces, deserve mention. Bach seemed particularly attracted to the lute-clavier, as we have said, undoubtedly because of its timbre since the dynamic capabilities of the popular instrument were no greater than those of the harpsichord. The violo pomposa—violoncello piccolo—had practical advantages that must have appealed to Bach. The instrument had five strings (tuned C, G, d, a, e') and thus could be played by either a violinist or violist. Bach's purchase of one of these was certainly for the advantage of this exchangeability, not for any special timbre or expressibility. The rare cembal d'amour belongs to the clavichord family, but was reported to be superior in three respects: its tone was louder and could be held longer, and more pronounced louds and softs could be achieved by varying the touch.[31] However, since the dynamics of even the early pianoforte were much superior, the cembal d'amour rapidly died out and no example of it has survived.[32] Bach probably never knew this instrument.

Accentuation in Bach's Music

These limitations on expression of the instruments at Bach's disposal present problems of composition, of course, and one of the most obvious of these is accentuation. When Bach combined the human voice and the austere organ in his cantata choruses, such problems were bound to arise. The verbal text introduces an additional demand on accent. By examining a few specific passages in Bach's works in which he had to deal with this problem, we may gain some insight into Bach's method of composition, which in turn further reflects his attitude toward instruments.

In Cantata 50 (*BG*, X, 343) the musical accent in the opening chorus falls precisely upon the accented syllables: "NUN ist das HEIL, und die KRAFT, und das REICH, und die MACHT, unsres GOTtes SEInes CHRIStus WORden" (Now shall the grace and the strength and the rule and the might of our God and His Christ be declared). In the German text the words form a three-fourths time with a hemiola,[33] beginning on the word "Gottes." The music demands that the singer give the accented syllable a sharp and forceful emphasis, further enhanced by the higher pitch of these accents. This treatment gives the music strongly dynamic accents with an irrepressible agogic element, which was Bach's intention.

A parallel passage in a work without the problem of verbal accent, the prelude of the g minor *English Suite* for harpsichord, reveals a similar rhythm. Since accents on a harpsichord cannot be affected dynamically, Bach produces this slightly agogical accent by slurring the third beat to the following first. (Of course, on a modern pianoforte, with its powers of dynamic emphasis, the accent can be enlivened beyond its agogic. For this reason also a hemiola in measures 31 and 32 can be brought out more clearly on the pianoforte.)

The first movement of the fifth partita (in G major) offers another intriguing problem of accentuation. It is impossible, when the piece is performed on the harpsichord, to hear whether the opening sixteenth notes form an upbeat or fall upon the first beat, and the listener is left uncertain until the eighth bar, when the low bass notes unmistakably emphasize the beats. Here again dynamic accents on a pianoforte can make this rhythm apparent and although some have argued that Bach intended to keep his listeners in suspense, such speculations, based upon the limitations and defects of Bach's instrument, seem entirely inadequate to me. The *D Major Fugue* of the *Well-Tempered Clavier* (Book II), unlike these previous examples, is intended for purely musical contemplation, and Bach completely disregards accent in it. The bar line is no guide for accentuation.[34] Busoni's suggestion that the words *Kirie Eleison, Christi Eleison* are a fitting accompaniment to the theme led to the unhappy accentuation of the second, weak syllable in the word *Christi*. This indicates that Bach clearly did not desire verbal embellishment in this work; in addition, its complete disregard of accent, the terse and telling harmonic suspensions, make it eminently suited for the organ.

. As we mentioned briefly in the preceding chapter, the rhythm and tempo of the *C Minor Minuet* of the *French Suite* in that key is related to arias in two cantatas for which Bach used identical music but different words. In the first, a secular cantata, *"Durchlauchter Leopold"* (*BG*, XXXIV, 13), the verbal accentuation follows the gently graceful swing of the minuet rhythm, and in fact gives us the clue to the musical rhythm. The same rhythm is kept in the church cantata *"Erhöhtes*

Fleisch und Blut" (No. 173, *BG*, XXXV, 83), although the inscription *Tempo di Menuetto* is omitted. The verbal accentuation similarly coincides with the rhythm of the minuet. The *C Minor Minuet* has the same melodic structure, although considerably lengthened in the cantatas. The work was composed, like the cantatas, during the Köthen period and the correct interpretation of the tempo and rhythm of the piece can be found in the syllabic accentuation of these two corresponding cantatas. The ideal realization of the *Tempo di Menuetto* lies in the cantatas, however. The harpsichord is too mechanically incisive for this gently flowing rhythm of one strong and agogically prolonged beat, followed by two weaker ones. The clavichord would be more suitable, and our modern pianoforte certainly is the most successful.

The above discussion makes obvious the intellectual ramifications and technical difficulties of interpreting Bach's works. As he left much to the performer's discretion and did not elaborate on aspects of his works that followed prevailing musical customs of notation and performance, many questions about his works will remain unanswered. But it is most vital to realize the importance of recreating the authentic spirit of Bach's music over and above concerns of authentic performance. Bach's primary concern was never with instruments, but with the spiritual substance of his compositions, and this latter element can be, indeed has been, experienced in every age since Bach's death. Thus in spite of the differences in instrumental realization the Romantic and the man of the atomic age can share with eighteenth-century contemporaries of Bach the experience of music that sings of eternal truth.

16

CALL TO LEIPZIG

ON the fifth of June, 1722, Bach finally was given the opportunity to enter the career to which he had pledged himself as a young man. When Johann Kuhnau died, one of the most famous and ancient cantorships in Germany—Leipzig—was left vacant. The city council of Leipzig once more began a search for a director for all musical activities in its four churches, and Bach's long cherished hope of improving the music of the sanctuary could now become reality.

The dignity of this office was enhanced by a long history of distinguished musicians, including Johann Hermann Schein and Sethus Calvisius. The office of the cantor dates from before the Reformation, for as early as the thirteenth century a cantor was selecting students for the choirs of the St. Thomas and St. Nicholas Churches at Leipzig. The Thomas cantor Georg Rhau (1488-1548) composed and directed a Mass for the famous debate between Martin Luther and Johann Eck. Sethus Calvisius, the astronomer-musician, proposed reforms both in the field of calendar computation and musical solmisation which, although never permanently adopted, were recognized for their soundness. The romantic poet-musician Hermann Schein, inspired by Italian humanism, sent fresh southern breezes through the dull and chilly northern music of his days. Bach was well acquainted with the musical contributions of these predecessors and appreciated the new vitality they had brought to the music of church and school.

Despite this glorious history—and the promise this post held for a young musician who dreamed of reforming the music of the Lutheran service—Bach hesitated a long time before even applying for the office.

The St. Thomas Church and the Thomas School in Leipzig.

He was reluctant to give up his peaceful association with his amiable friend and sovereign in Köthen and to have to meet the several demands of a city council, church consistory, and rector. He was certain to have to sacrifice the virtual independence in musical matters he enjoyed as *Kapellmeister* in Köthen. Bach's superiors in Leipzig would look upon his musical performances and compositions only as one of his duties and not with respect for the musician and for the sanctity of his art, as the sensitive prince in Köthen did. Bach was clearly aware of the strong provincialism and mediocrity of the church councilors, traits which are strikingly represented by their utter failure to recognize that Bach's genius placed him far above the other applicants for the cantorship.

Eight years after Bach had taken up the Leipzig cantorship he wrote Georg Erdmann, his old friend from school in Lüneburg, that "it was the Will of God that I should be called to be *Director Musices. . . .* I ventured in the name of the Highest and betook myself to Leipzig."[1] Bach had tasted the bitterness of enforced submission to men of artistic ignorance and insensibility, and it seems natural that he should scrutinize the situation most cautiously. He waited four months before applying for the post. When he finally decided, Bach bowed to Divine Providence, as he told Erdmann. But Bach had other motivations for his decision to leave Köthen than faithful obedience to what he believed to be God's will. He seems in his distress over immediate troubles to have forgotten these when he wrote Erdmann. Despondent, physically fatigued, and irritated by frictions with church authorities, Bach even considered resigning from Leipzig cantorship and wrote to his old friend that he had once intended to devote the rest of his life to his "gracious prince, who both loved and knew music." Surely when Bach first learned of the opening at Leipzig he was excited by such an opportunity to broaden and ennoble his musical career; Bach knew the limitations of his Köthen position, which hardly helped him toward his musical mission in life. At Leipzig he could finally fulfill his pledge to devote his talent to God and His church.

Along with the promising prospects and honor the Leipzig cantorship held, there were personal reasons for Bach's decision to move. It was only natural for a staunch Lutheran to want a Lutheran education for his children. Besides, as he tells Erdmann in the same letter, his "sons were inclined toward academic studies." In Köthen their only opportunity to pursue these interests was the calvinist *Stadschule*, and Bach was already noticeably uneasy about his family living in a strongly calvinist environment.

On the title page of Anna Magdalena's notebook of 1722[2] (the year in which he decided to move), Bach noted titles of two books by a Lutheran theologian August Pfeiffer, for his wife's edification and protection. One of the books, *Anticalvinismus, Evangelische Christenschule*, a defense of orthodoxy, called the Calvinist faith damnable and prayed for divine protection from union with these infidels. The other, *Antimelancholicus oder Melancholeyvertreiber* (Antimelancholicus or Expeller of Melancholy),[3] extols simple piety and is addressed to the uneducated, of which the middle-class German woman formed a conspicuous part. A fine copper engraving in the book vividly illustrates the author's attitude. A melancholy person is seated in a large armchair holding his head in his hands. On his right are a devil with long claws, a woman with her breast nearly bare, and a warrior with drawn sword; on his left stands a humble Christ enshrined with a large halo. Obviously Bach felt these dreary tomes would help his wife to stand firm in her faith and to bring up their sons in strict Lutheran orthodoxy. Surely the religious climate of Leipzig would help her succeed in this task.

Perhaps the family deliberated together about the move, weighing the advantages of court life and Anna Magdalena's professional opportunities in Köthen against correct theological education for the children. In any case, family and religious considerations helped draw Bach to Leipzig.

While Bach deliberated, he watched the developments in Leipzig. "Fatalities" is the expression he used in his letter to Erdmann to describe the course of his life.[4] After Kuhnau's death the civic council in Leipzig discussed for 11 months the merits of six candidates for the position of *Director Musices Lipsiensis*, cantor of the Thomas School and general director of music of the city of Leipzig.

Meanwhile the services were donated by the organists and choir directors that were available in the four churches of the city, among them, Görner, the organist who was to work—and disagree—with Bach at the Thomas church for many years, and Georg Baltasar Schott, organist of the New Church. Guest musicians were occasionally commissioned to write and perform music for festival occasions. Christoph Graupner (1683-1760), *Kapellmeister* to Count Ludwig of Hesse-Darmstadt, was invited to deliver a Magnificat on Christmas Day, and Bach was asked to perform an original Passion on Good Friday. On March 26, 1723, his *St. John Passion* was heard here for the first time.[5] Bach was known to Leipzig before this; in 1717, when he inspected the university organ, he had presented his cantata *"Nun kommt der Heiden Heiland"* (Now Comes the Gentiles' Savior), No. 61, either at the Thomas or the Nicholas Church.[6]

The discussions among the eldermen and the three rotating mayors of the city, preserved in the minutes of the town clerk, show that Bach was not considered one of the most desirable candidates. Despite his fame his name was not mentioned as a candidate until December 21, 1722. Of all those mentioned, only Georg Philipp Telemann (1681-1767) is remembered today as a distinguished composer. Very few compositions by the other candidates are even in print. Most of them were quite proficient on the organ and on other instruments, and all enjoyed good reputations in their day. The music of these competitors—Telemann, Graupner, and certain of their contemporaries—represent the taste and spirit of a new era totally foreign to Bach's religious soul.

Seventeen cantatas of Graupner, published in 1926,[7] resemble Bach's in outward form but Graupner does not rise above the essentially secular character of his art, and the works remain formal and perfunctory. Courtly entertainment was the true element of these musicians, all of whom were good craftsmen, able to deliver any type of piece—music suitable for any religious ceremony, concertos, garden music, table music, and operas of classical or lighter bent. The extant concertos of Graupner, Johann Friedrich Fasch, Heinichen, and Telemann,[8] modeled after the Corelli-Vivaldi example which by this time had been reduced to a fixed formula, are strikingly similar and lack any outstanding individuality. Theirs is a reasoned, shallow, formalistic clarity of construction, with conventional thematic statements—fugal subjects that one hears *ad nauseam* in the Italian repertoire, empty sequences forming the necessary links in the skeletons that fail to come to life. There is good harmonic counterpoint, too, sober in its simplicity, correct, clean, immaculate, but lifeless, transparent as glass but revealing nothing. Their work merely echoes the true sentiments that inspired the straightforward and naive strokes of Vivaldi and Corelli. Once expressions of metaphysical ecstasy, the style had been reduced to stock ideas, easily followed and easily taught. Since music was rarely printed and the *Kapellmeisters* were expected to compose their own music for every required occasion, this perpetual and perfunctory reproduction for an accepted and fashionable style was an easy substitute for living musical art. But this shallow musical style apparently pleased the Leipzig council, for they interviewed several of its followers before finally consenting to hear the truly individual style of Bach.

Among the strong competitors for the Leipzig post was Johann Friedrich Fasch (1688-1758), *Kapellmeister* at the court of Zerbst. His high official rank in a reputable court impressed the council; he also was an alumnus of the Thomas School, where he had studied law, and music under the late Kuhnau. Christian Friedrich Rolle (1681-1751), a lesser figure, enjoyed an excellent reputation as an organist, but his compositions are insignificant: neither Johann Gottfried Walther nor our contemporary Robert Eitner mention him in their exhaustive lexica.[9] He must have devoted much of his time to composing, however, since he applied for the post of cantor, whose chief duty is composing.

Telemann, the most famous musician in Germany at that time, was the councilors' first choice, but did not consider the position seriously. He used the Leipzig offer as a means of exacting a large raise in his salary as cantor of the Hamburg Johanneum and musical director of the principal church.

The city council then commissioned Graupner and Bach to compose church music in the interim but did not invite either to apply for the position until a month later. The two candidates they did consider were Georg Friedrich Kauffmann, *Kapellmeister* at Merseburg, and Andreas Christoph Tufen of Brunswick. Schott, Johann Martin Steindorff (cantor in Rossleben, Graitz, and Zwickau), and Lembke submitted applications; neither of the last two left any compositions.

After Telemann, Graupner was the favorite. Heinichen, then *Kapellmeister* to the King of Saxony, had strongly recommended his fellow classmate and student of Kuhnau. But Graupner also used Leipzig's offer as a lever to better his own financial status and guarantee a generous pension for his wife, and children until they reached majority. Then he refused the offer.

Only one man, Herr Baumeister Wagner, supported by Herr Chamber Councilor Jocher, suggested that the council might consider Bach and Rolle. Councilor Holzel added that he had heard that Rolle surpassed even Telemann.[10] Rolle subsequently was examined, on February 2, 1723, and Bach was invited to perform a cantata—No. 22, "*Jesus nahm zu sich die Zwölfe*" (Jesus Took Unto Himself the Twelve)—which he directed on February 7.

The council was willing by April ninth to consider Bach of Köthen, Kauffmann of Merseburg, and Schott of their own New Church. Some time was spent discussing the cantor's obligation to teach Latin, including the Catechism. Telemann and some others had flatly refused this chore, and in the case of the celebrated Telemann, the council had agreed. The three remaining candidates, they decided, should not be exempted from this traditional duty. Appellate Court Councilor Herr Plaz observed that "Since one cannot get the best for this position of cantor one must be contented with the mediocre."[11] With this testimony to its total incompetence to judge the relative merits of its applicants the council closed its meeting.

On April 22 the council met again and unanimously voted Bach as their final choice. Although one would like to praise this faint glimmer that the dull judges could recognize quality, their choice actually was based on Bach's greater fame. Council member Dr. Steger was so satisfied with the decision that he pronounced Bach to be "as much of a person as Graupner." The latter, from his high perch at the court of Hesse-Darmstadt, recommended Bach as "a musician just as strong on the organ as he is expert in church works and capelle pieces," and who "will honestly and properly perform the functions entrusted to him." Steger insisted on a special stipulation that Bach should refrain from making "compositions of theatrical character." Presiding councilor Dr. Lange best expressed the prevailing concern: "It was necessary to get a famous man in order to inspire" (meaning, of course, to impress the students).

Move to Leipzig

After Bach was informed of the council's decision, he asked Prince Leopold to release him. The Prince granted his request with regret and reluctance, although the formal letter presented to him was written in the cold language of a clerk. Bach now filed his formal application to the "Noble and Most Wise Council of the Town of Leipzig" for his "candidacy for the vacant post of Cantor to the Thomas School in that place." In it Bach acknowledged the many specific duties of the post and agreed to:

instruct the boys admitted in the school not only in the regular classes established for that purpose, but also, without special compensation, in private singing lessons. I will also faithfully attend to whatever else is incumbent upon me, and furthermore, but not without the previous knowledge and consent of A Noble and Most Wise Council, in case someone should be needed to assist me in the instruction in the Latin language, will faithfully and without ado compensate the said person out of my own pocket, without desiring anything from A Noble and Most Wise Council or otherwise.[12]

These Latin lessons alone required five hours a week to both the third and fourth classes, besides the time spent correcting written exercises.[13] Spitta thinks that Bach could have gotten the position at once without this extra teaching burden, but that at the time he was willing to accept this condition. Bernard F. Richter, on the other hand, believed Bach had to do all in his power to obtain this cantorship.[14] As we shall see, however, Bach was soon relieved of this burden, as well as of his singing instruction.

On May 5 Bach signed an agreement in duplicate in which he pledged to the "Honorable and Most Wise Council" of Leipzig that he would behave like an exemplary schoolmaster. The conduct expected of him is set forth in 14 points, most of which relate to his obedient submission to the authority of the council: he is forbidden to go out of town without the special permission of the Honorable Burgomaster; he is ordered always, so far as possible, to walk with the boys at funerals, according to custom; and he is pledged to preserve the good order in the churches and to arrange the music that it shall not last too long[15] and shall be of such a nature as not to make an operatic (theatrical) impression, but rather incite the listeners to devotion.

But even this solemn and written promise by Bach was not sufficient for the officials—one more investigation had to be made. Bach still had to be examined on his acquaintance with Lutheran dogma. Thus on May 8 Dr. Johann Schmid questioned Bach and pronounced him theologically sound. His approval was officially recorded in a Latin document signed by this theologian and by the superintendent Deyling.[16] Five days later Bach fulfilled the final requirement by subscribing to the Formula of Concord.[17]

A grand convocation on June 1 celebrated Bach's formal installation. All the town officials and the staff and student body of the Thomas School marched into the large assembly hall, in the order of their rank and station, their colorful costumes, robes, tresses, chains, and barrets in full display. Behind the doors the students sang a motet, and then filed in to their assigned places. The Chief Town Clerk introduced the new cantor "in the name of the Holy Trinity," and admonished him publicly to fulfill his duties faithfully and industriously, to show respect to his authorities and superiors, to endeavor to be on good terms with his colleagues, conscientiously to instruct the youth in the fear of God and other useful studies, and to keep the school in good repute. Little did anyone present suspect that the reputation of this school for centuries to come would rest solely upon the greatness of its new cantor.

The *Director Musices* was expected to compose or select the music for the four Leipzig churches that had sufficient facilities for musical performances. The most elaborate services were held in the Thomas Church. Next in importance was the Nicholas Church. Learned persons, the aristocracy, and rich burghers made up the majority of the congregation at the Thomas Church, while the Nicholas Church, attended by the poorer classes, was known as the *Schola pauperum*.[18] Bach directed his music in these two churches, on alternate Sundays with 12 to 17 of the best singers[19] and a leader *(praefect)*, all of whom he trained and selected from the boys of the Thomas School. We can identify the cantatas performed at the Nicholas Church by their organ parts, for they had to be transposed; the pitch of the organ at the Nicholas Church differed by a minor third.[20] Bach had no personal duties except to supply a chorus *(kantorei)*, of secondary quality, at what was known in Bach's day as the New Church (now called Matthew Church). Bach merely appointed one of his *praefects* to train the chorus for all occasions—from music for the main service to songs the boys sang in their *Currenden*.

For the smaller *Peterskirche* and the *Johanniskirche*, Bach had only to select eight of the lesser singers, and these were led by four *praefects*. These churches had no figured music nor any organs of magnitude, so that their music was limited largely to congregational singing of hymns. The boys were used for the intonation of the few chants used during the service. As we shall see, Bach's responsibilities for the University Chapel, the *Paulinerkirche*, soon became a matter of dispute, but after much bitter controversy, Bach was also charged with furnishing this church with singers from his *Kantorei*.

As the *Director Musices* Bach composed cantatas for civic festal occasions, such as the visit of King August of Saxony, or the birthdays of great notables. He was paid extra to lead the chorus at weddings, funerals, and other ceremonies, but these were still viewed as part of his responsibilities. Although the prospect of a genius of Bach's stature leading his black-garbed mercenaries through the motions of gloomy processions in all kinds of weather seems incredible to us today, Bach did not fret at this duty but rather at the scarcity of such opportunities to earn extra money.

When Bach was in a complaining mood he often referred to himself as a cantor, that office being only one role of the *Director Musices*. Of course, when he wanted to impress, he used his more imposing title, but he obviously resented some of the burdensome duties expected of him as cantor. They made him feel like a mere schoolmaster. First among these was the irksome job of teaching Latin, but he did not continue this time-absorbing work for very long. After a year he exercised the option he had had the foresight to insist upon in his formal application. He merely hired a substitute.

Still other of the duties listed in the 83-page book of regulations for the Thomas School (printed in revised form on November 4, 1723)[21] must have weighed heavily on Bach. This little booklet gives an intimate picture of the narrow and restricted lives of the schoolmasters, but even more so of the pitiable, overworked and overdisciplined schoolboys. The cantor had to act as inspector, that is, he had to call the schoolboys for the opening of the classes at six in the morning, and the best among his very proficient choir boys at five. The cantor had to say prayers again at eight o'clock, and to see that no lights were smuggled into the dormitories. Further, he had to assure that there was no carousing, that the Bible or a historical book (probably Josephus) was read during the meals, and that the boys (whose ages ranged from 12 to 20) did not return drunk after funerals, weddings, and especially the winter *Currenden*. On Sundays the cantor had to march the first *kantorei* in formation to the main church, the *conrector* led the second to the other principal church, and the sextus took the third to the New Church. The inspector on duty (cantor) also had to visit the sick in the school hospital adjoining the church. Since absence from these duties was fined with only four to six *Groschen*, however, the master may occasionally have shirked these cumbersome responsibilities.

The students had to bear severe and cruel punishments for behavior that to us today would be accepted as normal for young boys. The ignorant schoolmasters did not seem to suspect that the youngsters' misconduct was the inevitable result of the tensions and unrelenting disciplines they had to endure. For instance, leaving the religious service before the end—it lasted from seven to noon—was punished with a birching. When severe cold in the unheated church became unbearable youngsters were excused to go to the school building, but then were read the sermon, and had to prove by written examination that the pious words had not fallen upon sleepy, deaf ears.

Bach was not a rigid disciplinarian and based on what we know of his first experience with choir boys in Arnstadt, we can surmise that he was not overly conscientious about administering the regulations. There is no biographical information on Bach's relationship with his choir boys in Leipzig.

Bach's life centered around the Thomas School. His house was attached to the school, he trained his choir boys in the assembly hall and kept all the music he needed for major and minor performances here. During the summers he worked diligently in the school library. The music hall where the cantor held daily singing lessons and rehearsals was on the same level as his living quarters. From here he could enter directly into the bedrooms of his children.

Despite its proximity to the school and its lack of external charm[22] Bach's home was very cheerful, with spacious rooms and large windows that looked out upon Leipzig's city moat and surrounding meadows. It had ample room for his continually growing family. On the first floor were five large rooms, a parlor with four windows, a dining room, two bedrooms, and his study, in which his immortal work was penned through the hours, and often through the entire night. Within the house the tinkling of harpsichords and clavichords or the clear voice of young

Anna Magdalena could be heard all day; over 20 instruments were kept in the three-story dwelling.[23] The solid walls of the building and the subdued tone of the instruments allowed the whole family to practice without disturbing each other.

Several beautiful parks and promenades through which the river Pleisse peacefully flowed were within easy walking distance. The old town was still walled in, and the Thomas Church and School were just at the outskirts of the town. Outside the old town many large homes were built, surrounded by lavish gardens. In the summer the Collegium Musicum under Bach's direction met in the garden of the rich burgher Gottfried Zimmerman; the Peasant Cantata was performed in the garden of Carl Heinrich von Diskau, exchequer, *Kammer-Junker*, and district-lieutenant.

The life of the city's boulevards, frescoed inns, and coffee houses was gay: "Little Paris" and "Little Paradise," it was called. The promenade abounded in the gallant life and gained the nickname of *Lästerallee*, alley of vice. Goethe was so astonished when he visited Leipzig that "he thought at first he had entered the Elysian fields."[24]

The famous university made Leipzig a center of intellectual activity, and many distinguished residents visited the home of the city's famous composer. Anna Magdalena, who was already versed in the amenities of court life, must have made a gracious hostess to those paying homage to her cultured husband. They entertained colleagues at the Thomas School and professors as well as poets, many of whom collaborated with the production of Bach's vocal compositions. And Leipzig was already the hub of the printing business—as it remained until World War II. The famous printing house Breitkopf and Hartel was founded there in 1719. The same firm 100 years after Bach's death began the edition of the master's complete works.

Many of Bach's works were conceived of in Leipzig; many were transformed here from an earlier setting to a form rich in spiritual meaning. In the gay, sophisticated, and stimulating environment of Leipzig Bach began to devote his creative genius entirely to music for the Lutheran service. Later the winds of cultural change would disturb the faithful composer to the point that he retreated into a more private form of art. But when he first arrived in Leipzig Bach brought with him the goal he had set for himself long ago, inspired by his Lutheran education—to dedicate himself and his art to the greater glory of God.

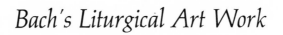

Bach's Liturgical Art Work

17

FULFILLMENT OF LUTHERAN REFORM

At last, in Leipzig, Bach would realize his final object: "well-conceived and well-regulated church music to the glory of God."[1] He was master of the musical service; he could elevate the musical liturgy to the loftiest heights of his imagination. In previous situations he had been active in parts of the service only. In Weimar he had furnished only the organ music that the service required. Inspired by Erdmann Neumeister and Salomo Franck, he conceived a new form of the cantata, but his subordinate rank prevented him from making full use of the form. Now, finally, he took up the gigantic task of composing complete yearly cycles of the liturgy—the musical part of the service that Luther had sketched out and suggested 200 years before.

The Lutheran Liturgy

The general program of the Catholic Mass was largely preserved in the Lutheran liturgy. Luther had changed only those parts that conflicted with the essential ideas of his reform. Otherwise he had kept its construction intact for he loved the sacred ritual and revered its significance—the commemoration of the Incarnation and the Crucifixion. His reform was essentially one of emphasis, but because of these changes one function of the music of the liturgy came to dominate the service.

The sermon, not the acting out of the mystery of Holy Communion, was the climax of the Lutheran service. Instead of a priest performing the drama of the Eucharist alone, with the congregation as observers, a minister taught and interpreted the gospel. The music before and after the sermon gained in significance because it was sung to a text related to the preacher's topic. This topic was determined by the liturgical calendar. The appropriate Bible passage was usually read in the early part of the service; in Leipzig, in Bach's time, it was chanted in plainsong by the minister at the altar. Before the reading from the gospels a hymn, corresponding to the gradual in the Catholic Mass, was sung, called the *Detemporalied*, the song for the proper time. The liturgical rules of the *Leipziger Kirchenstaat* required that "a song were sung according to the nature of the gospel."[2]

For example, on Advent Sunday the cantor might choose the hymn "Now Comes the Gentiles' Savior" as an introduction to the corresponding passage in one of the four gospels. A chorale-prelude that Bach wrote to precede this congregational hymn contains graphic illustrations of the text, as well as the deep, often tender, sometimes exalted and jubilant musical representation of Bach's personal reaction to the sacred drama of the text. The same hymn formed the musical motive for the cantata: and its poetic text would expound the topic of the day. It is easy to see why this coherence of gospel passage, sermon topic, *detempora* hymn, and cantata, inspired Lutheran composers to spend their greatest creative energy and imagination on this part of the musical service, which achieved central importance in the liturgy.

The other parts of the service—the *Kyrie*, the *Gloria*, the *Credo*, the *Sanctus*, the *Benedictus*, and the *Agnus Dei*—were less important. The first two were designated as "Missa," the Mass. Bach did not necessarily compose music of his own for these parts, but usually used music of other composers, Protestant and Catholic alike. Sometimes the texts of these selections would coordinate with the topic of the day. Thus, on Christmas Day the motet before the Kyrie would be *"Jerusalem Gaudio Gaudio Magna."* Bach had access to motet collections of Erhard Bodenschatz (ca. 1576-1636), Melchior Vulpius (ca. 1570-1615), and the *Neu Leipziger Gesangbuch* (1682) by Gottfried Vopelius (1645-1715),[3] all in the Thomas School library. He seems to have had a preference for the collection of Bodenschatz,[4] which included, among others, works by Hans Leo Hassler (1564-1612), Andrea Gabrieli (d. 1586), Sethus Calvisius, Hieronymus Praetorius (1560-1629), Christoph Demantius (1567-1643), Melchior Vulpius, Giovanni Gabriele (1557-1612), Melchior Franck (ca. 1579-1639), and Benedetto Pallavicino (?-1601).

Bach had envisioned his "well-regulated" church music as completely coordinated with the liturgy. Since the cantor—not the preacher—

chooses the *detempora* hymn, Bach could integrate the music according to his own judgment. He could work at these compositions sufficiently in advance to give them all the care and attention such significant art-works needed. It has been estimated that the composition of a cantata took Bach about a month, and many of these works were conceived and composed long before they were performed.

The *B Minor Mass*

Although Luther loved the beauty of the Latin Mass, he realized that because of language the uneducated classes of the population were ex-cluded from the instruction of the liturgy. Reluctantly at first, he published a German Mass in 1526. The Greek words *Kyrie Eleison* (Lord, have mercy upon us), were retained, but only as a refrain in a German incantation hymn, *Kyrie Gott Vater in Ewigkeit! Gross ist dein Barm-herzigkeit* (Kyrie God, Father in Eternity, Great is Thy Mercy).[5] Simi-larly, the *Gloria in excelsis Deo* became a hymn *Allein Gott in der Höhe sei Ehr* (Only God On High Be Honored). But, as Luther himself wrote:

On festival days, like Christmas, Michaelis, Purification, etc. it must go as hitherto, in Latin, until we have enough German songs because this work is in its early beginnings; therefore everything that belongs to it is not yet ready.[6]

Faithful to this pronouncement, Leipzig conducted the liturgy in both languages, especially in the Thomas and University churches, which the educated upper classes attended. Here many chants were alternately sung in Latin and German. On many festal days the entire service was in Latin.

Luther's love of the traditional language of the church was probably Bach's motivation for writing one magnificent Mass entirely in Latin—the *B Minor Mass*. Bach's respect for Latin, shared with Luther, inspired his departure from the common German text, and does not, as many scholars have tried to prove, betray a leaning toward Catholicism. He did send parts of the Mass to the Catholic Elector of Saxony, August III. Admittedly, any part of the Mass could be used in the Catholic service, even the solo arias and duets, since similar songs appear in the Masses of Bach's Catholic contemporaries like Johann Adolf Hasse (1699-1783), a pupil of Nicolas Porpora and Alessandro Scarlatti.[7] On the other hand, Bach wrote five yearly sets of German cantatas, comprising

the staggering amount of 295 (according to his son Carl Philipp
Emanuel as related by Forkel), as compared with a very small number
of Latin works. He even composed German works for festal days, although Luther had recommended Latin; there are 56 German cantatas,
among those extant, composed for such feasts as John the Baptist (Nos.
7, 30, and 167), Mary's Visitation (10 and 147), Christ's Ascension (11,
37, 43, and 128).[8] Cantatas in Latin are rare; Cantata 191, in Latin, was
performed during the festivities of Christmas.

Ten parts of the *B Minor Mass* consist of partial transcriptions from
other works, six of which are cantatas.[9] Recitatives were excluded from
these Latin services, but Bach borrowed the great choral introductions
and symphonies, as well as a duet and an aria for alto solo. The aria
Ach bleibe doch, mein liebstes Leben from Cantata 11 ("*Lobet Gott in
seinen Richen*"), became the *Agnus Dei* of the Mass, and the duet from
the Latin Cantata 191, which became the *Gloria in Excelsis Deo*, was
also derived from a German work, now lost. The *Gloria in Excelsis Deo*
of 191 is identical with the *Gloria* of the great Mass; the *Gloria Patri*
of this cantata, which was sung *Post Orationem*, appears in the *B Minor
Mass* as part seven, *Domine Deus, Rex Coelestis*; and part three of this
cantata, *Sicut erat in Principio*, emerges in the *B Minor Mass* with the
words "*Cum sancto Spirito in Gloria Dei Patris*."

The *B Minor Mass* was never performed in its entirety, nor did Bach
intend this when he wrote the work. This, along with Bach's overriding
concern with the German cantata form, should dispel any doubts about
his possible tendency toward Catholicism. Only parts of the *B Minor
Mass* were performed for special festal occasions. Spitta is of the opinion that the *Sanctus* was used as a Christmas piece, even that it was
composed for that purpose.[10] Moreover, the rules of the Leipzig liturgy
demanded that the *Sanctus* be sung at that time, at the end of the main
service, before Communion. The *Kyrie* of the *B Minor Mass*, because of
its unusual length, may have been sung on the Sunday before Lent. The
Credo would fit in on saints' days, when it was customary to sing the
entire Nicene Creed.[11] (In Bach's time no independent services for
saints' days were observed, for they were merged with the nearest Sunday.) Bach's son Philipp Emanuel, who possessed the vocal and orchestral parts of the *Credo*, performed just this section of the Mass in
Hamburg when he was musical director there.

The absurdity of the supposition that Bach's Masses were written
with the Catholic service in mind is most evident in the *Kyrie* of the *F*

Major Mass,[12] which would never have been tolerated in the Catholic church. The *Kyrie*, a contrapuntal gem, has a Protestant chorale melody, played by two horns and two oboes, which form an obligato above the fugal quartet of voices. Together with this four-part fugue on the words *Kyrie Eleison*, and the hymn tune for the horns and oboes, the bass voice and the bassoon sing a *cantus firmus* which is clearly derived from the Litany, a chant that was intoned in the Leipzig churches on the first Sunday of Advent and Lent.[13] Similar interweaving of the Catholic with Lutheran music appear in the *Credo* and in the *Confiteor* of the *B Minor Mass*. For the fugue of the *Credo* Bach used the theme of the ancient Georgian plain chant *Credo in unum Deum*, which was sung by the Lutheran choir after the gospel reading. In measure 73 of the *Confiteor* the bass sings another church intonation, *Confiteor unum baptisma in remissionem peccatorum* (I acknowledge baptism for the remission of sins). Luther discarded most of the sacraments, but not baptism, and this ancient chant could be used in Catholic and Lutheran churches alike.

Bach's four Masses, in F major, A major, g minor, and G major (also derived from cantatas)[14] contain only one *Kyrie* and a *Gloria* in four movements. Only the *B Minor Mass* is complete, including the *Credo*, the *Sanctus*, the *Benedictus*, and the *Agnus Dei*, as well as the *Kyrie* in three movements and the *Gloria* in eight. In the Protestant liturgy the erm *Missa*, or Mass, referred to only those parts of the ancient Mass that were used in the Lutheran service, in particular the *Kyrie* and the *Gloria*. The Thomas Church prescribes:

MISSA: (Choir): Kyrie eleison, etc. or the hymn "Kyrie Gott Vater in Ewigkeit," followed by the Gloria, sung by the choir either in Latin—in that case the entire text, which in the B minor Mass comprises eight movements, and in the four shorter Masses four—or in German. In the latter case the hymn "*Allein Gott in der Höhe sei Ehr*" is suggested.

Besides these *Kyries* and *Glorias* five short *Sancti* and one *Christe Eleison* in g minor have been ascribed to Bach.[15] One more major Latin work remains to be mentioned—the glorious *Magnificat*.

Bach's *Magnificat*

The *Magnificat* is the gospel canticle that the Blessed Virgin Mary sang in ecstacy when she knew she was to give birth to the Savior. Its text comes directly from Luke 2:46-55. Following tradition, and

Luther's admonition, Bach used the Latin of the Vulgate[16] for this festal performance.

Since the fifteenth century composers have set this text to music, and have performed it at Vespers during Christmas. True to tradition, Bach's *Magnificat* was performed on the first day of Christmas, in the afternoon. Since the bells began tolling at 1:15 p.m. and the sermon began at 3:00[17]—after the organ voluntary, the motet on either *"Cum natus esset Jesus," "Hodie Christus natus est,"* or *"Surgite pastores,"*[18] a cantata, and the pulpit hymn *"Ein Kindelein so löbelich"*—one may assume that the service began at between 2:00 and 2:30, and that the *Magnificat* was sung around 5:00, which brings it *ad vesperam*, at sunset. This work, which lasts about 35 minutes, is Bach's only Latin work that can be performed in its entirety without violating the composer's original design.

Not long before Bach came to Leipzig some ancient theatrical customs still prevailed. The churches continued to display the manger and to rock the Infant Jesus until 1702. Another custom, that of singing antiphonal hymns between the movements of the *Magnificat* canticle was followed in the early days of Bach's cantorship: for in an earlier version of his *Magnificat* (in E flat)[19] Bach had written out two chorales, a *Gloria*, and part of a Latin hymn *Virga Jesse*, which were sung by a small choir in the gallery opposite the main one, following the custom in Leipzig of singing antiphonal hymns, accompanied by a smaller organ on that gallery,[20] between movements. But Bach abandoned even this last remnant of a theatrical effect in the definitive version (in D major).

Indeed, Bach needed no theatricals to communicate the content of this poem; his music portrayed the Virgin's state of mind much more graphically and penetratingly than any visual display. Indescribable is the ecstatic joy in the music to the first verse *Magnificat anima mea dominum* (My soul doth magnify the Lord). Only by sharing grateful ecstacy with his own bride at her first pregnancy can Bach have absorbed so completely Mary's feeling at this heavenly event. The austere text of the Vulgate and of the King James version does not adequately reflect Mary's exalted state of mind. Just how Bach experienced it becomes clear upon reading the free paraphrase on this text in Cantata 189, *"Meine Seele rühmt und preist."* Instead of "My soul doth magnify the Lord" it reads, "My soul glorifies and praises God's kindness and goodness, and my spirit, heart, and senses, and my entire being is filled with joy in my God." (*Meine Seele rühmt und preist Gottes Huld und reiche Güte, und mein Geist, Herz, Sinn, und ganz' Gemüte ist in meinem Gott erfreut.*)[21]

The work was performed on Christmas Day, 1723, the year that the Bachs came to Leipzig. Since Bach first composed another version of this work, he must have conceived the work in Köthen. The first and last movements have the distinct character of a concerto grosso, the idiom which in Köthen so filled his mind. The other movements picture the text with surety and directness that call to mind the powerful brush of Michaelangelo, as in Luke 1:52, *Deposuit potentes de sede et exaltavit humiles* (He has put down the mighty from their seats, and exalted them of low degree), or the natural simplicity of a Giotto, as in verse 53, *Esurientes implevit bonis et divites dimisit inanes* (He has filled the hungry with good things; and the rich he has sent empty away).

The *Magnificat* lies close to the hearts of all Christians for its basic humanity from which the spirit soars to divine heights, while the *B Minor Mass*, though no less lofty, is not only more formal but more austere as well. No borrowings or transformations of former works led to the creation of the *Magnificat*, which ranks among Bach's most inspired creations. His imagination was aroused by palpable human experience, sublimized by his idealistic and mystic conceptions of Virgin worship.

It is not difficult to understand Luther's reluctance to translate the Latin texts when we listen to Bach's *Magnificat* for, though the Latin of the *Magnificat* forms a regrettable barrier between the average listener and the full absorption of this sublime art, an adequate translation would be difficult without injury to its delicate sanctity. But Luther was thoroughly convinced of the desirability of congregational participation. The outgrowth of his reform, the Protestant hymn, became the principle foundation for the new Protestant art work that was to flourish in the next two centuries.

18

THE CHORALE

THE Catholic church had almost entirely abandoned congregational singing, and here lay Luther's third reform. The singing, he believed, should come directly from the hearts of all believers and not be treated as an esoteric art only, although Luther himself was sensitive to the beauty of artistically refined and sophisticated music. He loved the contrapuntal compositions of Josquin Deprès, Heinricus Isaac, and Ludwig Senfl, and he wrote a most eloquent and romantic eulogy to polyphonic art. He stated that he did not wish all the arts crushed out of existence, clearly opposing certain religious sects that were inclined toward such barrenness.[1] Thus Luther preserved not only congregational singing but also the infinitely more valuable treasure of Germany's great religious musical art.

The Lutheran chorale kept many ancient hymn tunes alive. Luther, who abhorred the deliriously wandering melismata in which the words evaporated like incense, sought to restore the intelligibility of the text. With the help of Johann Walther and Conrad Rupff, he recast many old tunes to new words of his own, which were German paraphrases on ancient Latin texts. In these sessions, the religious genius would pace the floor, playing his lute (some say it was a flute)[2] experimenting and adjusting old Gregorian and Ambrosian melodies, folksongs, *Minnesinger Lieder*, or ancient tropes and sequences of the ninth century. In the manner of song writers of his day, he fashioned everything after the rhymed and metrical pattern of folksongs.[3] His melodies are stirring, strong, and sincere.

Some salient features of the evolution of the chorale should be men-

tioned here briefly. In Luther's time the congregation sang in unison
without accompaniment, while the professional choir performed the
more sophisticated polyphonic art works of the period. Since these congregations were not accustomed to singing, they were urged to attend
regular practice hours to learn the new devotional songs.[4] The professional choir relied on the Catholic repertoire at first but soon Protestant
polyphonic songs began to increase in number. In 1586 the preacher
Lucas Osiander published "fifty spiritual songs and Psalms, with four
voices in contrapuntal manner . . . so constructed that the entire Christian congregation can join in with them." For this communal purpose
the melody was laid in the soprano, instead of in the tenor, as had been
customary. This new practice coincided with the general change in
style that came to Germany from Italy with those composers that had
spent their years of apprenticeship in that country such as Michael
Praetorius, Hans Leo Hassler, Hermann Schein, and Johannes Eccard.
Osiander's title page shows that the choir attempted to lead the congregation, still in great need of assistance. During the first decade of the
seventeenth century Hans Leo Hassler, with the same purpose in mind,
added instruments to his setting of four-voiced *gemeine Melodien*.

At the same time organ builders moderated their medieval concep-
ions of confused mixture stops with Italian clarity, and these instruments became the permanent guide for congregational singing. By
Bach's time, the full harmony of the organ and the professional choir
were joined by the entire congregation in unison, thoroughly familiar
with the chorales after two centuries of practice. Every burgher with
even the least musical qualification knew his Lutheran chorale as well
as his Bible, for he sang at home as well as in church. Moreover, the
hymns were heard at all occasions. The city pipers (*Stadtpfeiffer*), the
guild of professional wind instrumentalists, played them almost daily
from the towers of churches and from the balconies of public buildings.

Although the harmonization, rhythm, and general setting of the
hymns underwent considerable transformation during the two centuries
between Luther's creation of the Protestant chorale and Bach's acces-
sion to the cantorship, its original melodic texture changed remarkably
little. Especially in the chorale-preludes Bach preserved the original
church modes and the rhythmical malleability of the chorale melodies,
even though his harmonization is in his own contemporary style. He
retained the signature used in the sixteenth and seventeenth centuries:

the flat, in those days, indicated the transposition of one fifth down from the original church mode, and a sharp that of a fifth up from the original. Thus the Dorian mode (roughly equivalent to D), transposed a fifth down, apparently sounds in g minor; yet it shows only one flat in the signature. Even when Bach actually harmonized such a transposed Dorian melody in g minor, he kept only one flat in the signature. Similarly the Mixolydian mode, transposed one fifth up, shows only one sharp, although it sounds in D major. Many modern editions of the chorales have abandoned this ancient manner of writing the signature, but most good editions of the chorale-preludes preserve Bach's original notation.

These melodies would seem quite devoid of character, and tonal as well as rhythmical direction, when heard by themselves. Through Bach's harmonization, however, they gain life and the music evokes feeling for the text. Bach's four-voiced harmonization is of such contrapuntal mastery that each individual voice is actually more melodious than the given chorale melody itself. Yet the whole sounds so simple and natural that Bach's transcendental technique is not apparent at first hearing.

Almost 400 of the chorale harmonizations of Bach have been preserved, gathered together by modern editors who gleaned them from various works in which they were incorporated—cantatas, Passions, oratorios, and motets. But it is estimated that these constitute about one half the amount he actually wrote for organists and choirs that performed regularly in the four churches under his direction.

In his private library Bach had the encyclopedic collection of hymn texts in eight volumes by Paul Wagner. For melodies, he had access to several collections in the Thomas School library, the oldest among them Vopelius' *Neu Leipziger Gesangbuch* of 1682 and a large collection by Paul Gerhardt (1607-1676). The Vopelius collection contained the oldest chorales, which the Leipzig congregation gustily sang them out from memory;[5] Gerhardt had included a much larger number of melodies; but the largest was the collection of 1729, *Das vollständige und vermehrte Leipziger Gesangbuch*, which had 530 pages of hymns and an index of *detempore* hymns.[6]

On the strength of his prerogative as cantor Bach chose the hymns for every service, a task he approached with a staunchly conservative bent. Terry states that more than half of the 76 hymn writers whose verses appear in his cantatas belong to the sixteenth century.[7] Bach preferred the hymns he believed to have been written by Luther himself or his contemporaries.

The Chorale-Preludes

One of the most important duties of the organist was to introduce every hymn, whether sung by the congregation or the choir, with a prelude. This body of almost 200 chorale-preludes, perhaps the choicest treasure among all the works Bach has left us, forms in itself a mine of thoughtful, philosophical, descriptive, and symbolic musical poems, as well as instruction for composers and aspiring organists.

With this musical form Bach traced the entire history of music, as far as he knew it in extant compositions, in an amplitude of infinite variety in musical devices, forms, and techniques. Numerous chorale-preludes are composed in the style of the motets and madrigals of Luther's time. As musical commentaries on the succeeding hymn, these preludes always use the hymn tune as their motive for elaboration, ornamentation, musico-philosophical illustration, or other flight of the imagination. The hymn tune, *cantus firmus*, can be presented either in its original continuity or broken into small episodes that are linked by interludes that can be part of a motet-like or madrigal-like structure, or of a free fantasy of new and possibly unrelated material. In the motet each phrase of the hymn is treated fugally. In the madrigal-like prelude, fragments of the hymn tune are distributed over the entire score of four to six voices in a mosaic of inverted, diminished, or augmented pieces of the original tune. The hymn tune in its original tempo or rhythm may accompany any of these forms; usually it is more unified and slower. The hymn tune is often presented in canon, either in double pedal (in two basses), or in any two other voices. Bach also composed half a dozen chorales in variation form, an antiquated style the old Hamburg master Reincken taught him. But this form was not suitable for preludizing, though it may at times have been used in organ voluntaries. One chorale-prelude is an adumbration of the sonata form.[8]

The extant chorale-preludes fall into six groups: the *Orgelbüchlein*, which Bach began in Weimar, but never finished (46 preludes); the series in the *Klavierübung*, published in 1739 (21 preludes); four canonic variations, published in 1747 by Balthazar Schmidt in Nürnberg (not suitable for liturgical use); and transcriptions of cantata movements published by Schubler in 1747 (six preludes); 18 chorale-preludes that Bach composed shortly before his death; and some 80 more that were collected by his pupil Johann Philipp Kirnberger and others. And this phenomenal production represents only a part of the work of his fluent and speedy pen. How many times did that inexhaustible musical mind improvise for his God and His angels, producing finished though highly artful compositions that amazed the greatest connoisseurs and colleagues for their perfection of form as well as for their profoundly moving humanity. If Bach had finished his *Little Organ Book*, it would have contained, 124 more preludes. He finished the works for principal feast days, and left blank pages, except for the titles, for the remaining Sundays, which would be apt to vary in different towns. (The services in several German towns in Bach's time varied enough that Bach had to write out a reminder to himself of the first Leipzig service he directed.)[9]

Orgelbüchlein

While being detained against his will in the service of the angry Duke Wilhelm Ernst, Bach began working on an important portion of his "well-conceived" and "well-regulated" church music, a complete program of chorale-preludes for the entire liturgical year.[10] The *Little Organ Book*, the *Orgelbüchlein*, was to include preludes introducing and interpreting all the hymns sung by the congregation or choir over a year's span.[11] Bach considered the content of the words of each hymn of foremost importance and he used a great variety of musical motives, rhythmical and ornamental figures, and descriptive intervals to illustrate the text. This highly refined art of musical symbolization, dating back to the Renaissance and earlier, usually falls undetected by the uninitiated, but in Bach's time it was an essential part of the religious music literature. In select circles these devices and their meanings were well known. Fourteenth-century musicians saw all sorts of mystic connections between numbers of tones and corresponding numbers of gospels, apostles, and so on. Some even constructed the entire edifice of musical theory as a replica of the Church with all its ramifications, spiritual as well as secular. This play of intellectual imagination with hidden meanings continued to lure especially northern musicians for several centuries. André Pirro, in his *L'ésthetique de Bach*, detected many of the

descriptive devices that Bach used in works of several of his predecessors and contemporaries, including Johann Wolfgang Franck, Johann
Sebastiani, Johann Theile, Dietrich Buxtehude, Johann Fischer III, Heinrich Schütz, Reinhard Keiser, Heinrich Bach (1615-1692), Giacomo
Carissimi, Philipp Heinrich Erlebach, Giovanni Andrea Bontempi (An-
gelini), Sebastian Anton Scherer, Andreas Hammerschmidt, and Johann
Ahle. Early opera adopted many pictorial figures from the madrigals
of the sixteenth century. Bach's contemporary Heinichen, in his *General Bassschule* of 1711 and 1728, recommends these devices to opera
writers for proper "expression of the word and the emotions in music."
He speaks at length about the "doctrine of affections" (*Affectenlehre*),
this technique of employing certain "musico-rhetorical" (*musikalische-
rhetorische*) and well-conceived, short clauses (*kurtz gefasste Clauseln*)
or *Loci topici*.[12] When applied to church music the art was called *Bibelauslegung*, interpretation of the Bible.

Thus in the chorale-prelude "*Vom Himmel kam der Engel Schar*"
(From Heaven Came the Host of Angels) while the chorale melody is
heard in the soprano, the middle voice pictures the descending movement suggested in the text by sixteenth notes rapidly falling along a
scale two octaves in span; the bass also descends, but in the slower
pace of quarter notes, over an equally wide span. In the fiery, ecstatic
"*Herr Gott, nun Schleuss den Himmel auf*" (Lord God, Now Unlock the
Gates of Heaven) the figures of sixteenth notes depict the twisting
movement of turning keys and then the upward rush of a series of
swift runs, while the bass constantly leaps up in exuberant octaves. A
similar device is found in "*Erstanden ist der Heilig' Geist*" (Arisen Is
the Holy Spirit): figures, rising and marching in various tempi, combine with upward steps in the bass. In "*Herr Jesu Christ, dich zu uns
wend*" (Lord Jesus Christ, Turn Thyself to Us) the accompanying figures again are suggestive of a turning and bending movement.

In "*Durch Adams Fall ist gantz Verderbt*" (Through Adam's Fall is
All Corrupted) the fall is depicted by the gloomy sound of descending
diminished sevenths in the bass, intervals of traditionally fearful and
dreadful connotation. The chromatically winding middle voices cunningly depict the coils of the corrupting serpent. Joy, in "*Der Tag, der
ist so Freudenreich*" (The Day Is So Rich in Joys), is expressed mainly
through a swiftly tripping dance rhythm   , a device that
probably offended any sober Pietists who heard it. Similar dancing
rhythms enliven "*In Dir ist Freude*" (In Thee Is Joy) and in "*Mit*

Fried' und Freud' fahr Ich dahin" (In Peace and Joy Do I Meet Death). In such meditative chorale-preludes as *"Das Alte Jahr vergangen ist"* (The Old Year Has Passed Away), *"O Mensch, bewein' dein' Sünde gross"* (O Man, Weep Over Thy Great Sins), and *"Wenn Wir in höchsten Nöthen seyn"* (Whenever We Are in Deepest Distress) Bach expands the melodies by that highly developed art of ornamentation that, in his hands, has the poetic spontaneity of improvisation. These preludes are deeply moving by virtue of their utmost sensitivity and profound penetration of their literary content.

In this collection eight significant symbolic canons appear in the chorale-preludes: *"Gottes Sohn ist kommen"* (God's Son Has Come); *"Indulci Jubilo"* (a sweet jubilance in contemplation of the infant Jesus); *"O Lamm Gottes"* (Christ, Thou Lamb of God); *"Hilf Gott dass mir's gelinge"* (God May Help that I May Succeed to Sing my Praise in the Name of Thee, Noble Creator); *"Erschienen ist der herrliche Tag"* (The Glorious Day Has Dawned); *"Liebster Jesu, wir sind hier"* (Dearest Jesus, We Are Here); and *"Dies sind die heil'ge zehn Gebot"* (These are the Sacred Ten Commandments). (The "magus" Kircher, and Werckmeister as well, regarded the canon as fraught with scientific meaning, but we prefer to interpret the form as symbolic or emblematic.) All these canons deal with the concept of God and His Son, and whenever the text alludes to an immutable law, Bach is apt to reach for the canon as its symbolization. To make the canon he has had to adjust the original rhythm of the hymn tune so that the intervals would fit, for intervallic relations had important mystic meanings for musicians of the day. Bach may well have felt that in mastering these complex calculations he was actually dealing with a similar mystic power, a musical mathematics similar to that which Kepler believed to have discovered in his *De Harmonice Mundi,* in which he states that "the celestial harmonies depend on the various and varying velocities of the planets, of which the sentient soul animating the Sun was the solitary auditor."[13]

Bach meant the *Little Organ Book* as an instruction for the art and science of writing chorale-preludes, and as a complete yearly series. The hymns follow the Lutheran calendar of Sundays and feast days for Advent, Jesus' birth, His suffering, His Crucifixion, and His Ascension. Bach's unexpected release from incarceration, and his new duties in Köthen, prevented him from finishing the entire series. He also seems to have run short of music paper, for on his last page he wrote out one chorale in an improvised tablature: instead of using notes he jotted down an entire prelude in letters. He inscribed the series with a little rhyme on the title page that summarized his purpose:

> Dem höchsten Gott allein zu Ehren,
> Dem Nächsten, draus sich zu belehren.

> In honor only to the Highest God
> Next to that, from this to gain instruction.

This comparatively small work, containing only 46 chorale-preludes, is only a small example of a number of larger cycles of church music that were to be composed in Leipzig. Bach would have to wait another seven years before he could even begin to realize his goal.

Klavierübung

In the Orgelbüchlein Bach wrote preludes for hymns and motets used during the year and subject to detempore variation. The Klavierübung[14] presents a set of preludes played during one Sunday service, for only those hymns and motets that are not affected by detempore variation. The Leipzig series is composed of the chorale-preludes preceding the hymns that took the place of the three Kyries, the Gloria, the Creed, and the Lord's Prayer in the Lutheran service, and the three hymns in the Communion service, that were never varied, following the main service—the baptismal hymn, "To the Jordan Came Christ Our Lord"; the confession of sin, "Out of the Deep Have I Cried Unto Thee"; and the Holy Communion hymn, "Jesus Christ Our Savior, Who Turned the Wrath of God from Us." In these preludes, like his Ogelbüchlein, Bach placed prime importance on the composition of music that would transmit the deep meaning of the hymn text to the congregation through musical symbolization.

The preludes to the three Kyries do not call for descriptive motives, however, and since the Kyrie hymn[15] is an ancient chant sung as a hymn, the preludes to this hymn are kept in motet style, quite in conformity with its traditional character. That means that every phrase (in the hymn marked by a firmate sign⌒) is treated fugally, with stretti, inversions, and imitations. The cantus firmus (hymn tune) appears as augmentation in any of the four or five voices. In the first Kyrie, "Kyrie Gott Vater in Ewigkeit," the motet-like prelude treats the first five phrases of the Dresden hymn in this fugato fashion. In the second

Kyrie, "*Kyrie, Christe, Aller Welt Trost*," the six phrases of the second section of the same hymn are developed; the *cantus firmus* is consistently taken by the tenor, while the other voices play around this chant as in a motet. The third *Kyrie*, "*Kyrie Gott, Heiliger Geist*," has the *cantus firmus* in similar style, but the third part of the Dresden hymn in the bass now emerges with greater calm, in measured steps of regular half-notes, while the other four voices increase the tempo of their diminutions, inversions, and *stretti* to eighth notes, creating an effect echoing Luther's ecstatic description of polyphonic works of Senfl, Isaac, Josquin, and the like:

One voice taking a simple part and around it sing three, four, or five other voices, leaping, springing round about, marvelously gracing the simple part, like a square dance in Heaven with friendly bows, embracing and hearty swinging of partners.[16]

A certain symbolism may perhaps be read into the successive treatment of these three *Kyries*: the three appearances of the *cantus firmus* may symbolize stages of increasing confidence gained by the believer. In the first *Kyrie* God is invoked as the Creator of all things, hence the *cantus firmus* is woven in with all voices, like Christ's ubiquity. In the second, when Christ is implored to have mercy upon sinners, the *cantus firmus* is separated from the rest of the voices, as men in sin live apart from God. In the third, God the Holy Spirit, is asked to give consolation, strength, and confident faith, therefore the even and more quiet rhythm of the *cantus firmus* appearing in the bass. Other, more lively, voices reflect the hopeful words that we may "blithefully and joyfully be relieved of this sorrow"[17] (Arbitrary as this kind of symbolism may seem, it was directly related to Kircher's conception of analogies, see pages 128-30, in which congruent elements were thought to have a common mathematical cause.)

The next great prelude in this series, Luther's German setting for the *Gloria*, "*Allein Gott in her Höhe sei Ehr*" (Only God on High Be Honored), is one of the most perfectly balanced in structure of all Bach's compositions in this form. Here Bach depends exclusively on thematic material developed contrapuntally. No extraneous matter appears at all. The jubilant counter-subjects to the hymn tune, following each other in two-voiced fugato fashion, are in themselves florid variations on each phrase of the hymn. Even the leaping basses, in the interludes between the phrases of the hymn tune, punctuate the themes, while the fugato variations frolic upside down, like heavenly creatures unfettered by the limitations of gravity. After the first half of the hymn has gone through the usual repetition, except that the voices' positions have been exchanged (triple counterpoint with obligato bass), the second period of the hymn modulates rapidly through D major, e minor, b minor, a minor, d minor, D major, back to G major. This modulating episode is very rare in such short compositions as hymns and chorale-preludes, but here Bach has extended this melody over 117 measures. This modulatory section and its sequential treatment give the composition as a whole the key balance and structure of the classical sonata. Within this form canons appear in the *cantus firmus* without in the least encumbering the joyous dance rhythm that reflects a warm and pure soul abounding with that peace and good will that the *Gloria* sings of.

In the prelude to the hymn of the Ten Commandments, Bach constructed a canon around the *cantus firmus* to symbolize the immutable laws, as he had done earlier in works in the *Orgelbüchlein*; but here the canon is arranged so that the same note sounds, unrelieved, ten times. In the *"Vater unser im Himmelsreich,"* the hymn sung before the Lord's Prayer, the pictorial image of the hymn's first words is symbolized by the usual canon in the *cantus firmus*, while two other voices, in Luther's words, "leap and spring about" in swift staccato arabesques, trills, and graces (all fully written out). This hymn also is an ancient one, dating from 1593.

The last three chorale-preludes belong to the baptism and the Communion service. The flowing passages of the first, originally composed by Johann Walther in 1524, *"Christ unser Herr zum Jordan kam,"* (Christ Our Lord Came to the Jordan), depict the smooth and peaceful movement of waves while the *cantus firmus* moves in even, slow steps in the bass. The second, *"Aus tiefer Noth schrei Ich zu Dir"* (In Direst Need I Cry to Thee), one of the most inspired and intensely felt supplications that Luther put into hymn verse, is not suited to a symbolic setting. Bach treats this ancient (1524) Phrygian melody in motet style with the *cantus firmus* in the tenor, the style that was often used in Luther's time.

The third hymn again calls for powerful pictorial imagination, and *"Jesus Christus, unser Heiland, der von uns den Zorn Gottes wand"* (Jesus Christ our Savior, Who Averted the Wrath of God from Us) has one of the most extravagantly mad fugue themes to be found in all musical literature. Wide intervals leap like bolts of lightning. Organists probably chose the strident and penetrating reed stops to create this frightening effect, heightened by the stern *cantus* singing its Dorian melody in the pedals with thundering 16- and 32-foot trombones.

The entire *Klavierübung* series is introduced by the famous *Prelude in E Flat Major*, originally played before the Introit, between seven and eight in the morning. Other organ voluntaries, the above described chorale-preludes, plus the *detempore* chorales with their chorale-preludes, the motets, and the cantatas followed. The musical service was climaxed toward noon by the *St. Ann's Fugue*, a triple fugue based on the hymn to St. Ann. Today when the series is performed in concert this Prelude comes immediately before the *St. Ann's Fugue*.

Luther included in his German liturgy a catechism for children, and so Bach accompanied all these chorale-preludes of the *Klavierübung* with a set of preludes for the small organ (the Thomas church had a second, smaller organ for just such occasions). These preludes in miniature are marked *"Manualiter,"* that is, to be played on manuals only. Although they display the contrapuntal master touch, they are less interesting because they are devoid of pictorial, symbolic content.

It is not difficult to imagine how much the musically sensitive persons of that epoch were moved by this magnificent music so rich in spiritual symbolism. Bach's musical *Bibelauslegung*, or pictorial explanation of the Bible, combines the creation of a visual image in the mind's eye with the emotional essence of its idea. Bach's friend, the preacher Johann Matthias Gesner, who possessed both a highly cultivated mind and a profound and ardent faith, wrote glowing accounts of Bach's organ playing. Marianne von Ziegler (who wrote such fitting texts for Bach's cantatas), Anna Magdalena, Bach's numerous students, and poets and philosophers of the University all were indebted to Bach for enriching their religious lives in the Leipzig churches.

In our century a new philosophy of symbolic thinking has appeared in the writings of Hans Vaihinger, C. G. Jung, and Susanne K. Langer,[18] who regard symbols as spontaneous and direct means of transmitting thoughts or ideas, bypassing reason, and communicating directly and intuitively, giving rise to meaningful myths, religious rites, and various forms of art, especially music. In the case of music this obscure and subrational function of the mind might perhaps be designated as prerational or superrational. But Bach seems to proceed quite conventionally and consciously in his use of *Bibelauslegung;* his symbolism is not merely emblematic, however—nor as subconsciously dynamic as these modern philosophers describe it. In his case the idea given by the text is translated into music by emotion disciplined by esthetics.

Although the untrained listener of today cannot know spontaneously that a musical canon stands for law, or for the union of the Father and the Son, in Bach's time initiates were versed in this symbolism. In their religious minds profound admiration for the masterful ingenuity of contrapuntal feats merged with feeling of awe that the symbolized idea communicated to them. Both these apparent miracles seemed to them to emerge from the same divine mind. Thought and emotion mutually joined in one esthetic and religious experience.

19

THE CANTATA

As a result of Luther's reform in the liturgy the cantata became the principal music, the *Hauptmusik*. The entire musical service led up to the central point of the liturgy—the sermon. From the opening grand organ prelude through the *Introit* (on the occasions when it was included), the *Kyrie*, the *Gloria*, and the *Credo*, in their full development through motets and hymns with their chorale-preludes, the music is focused on the particular episode of Christ's life that was to be the subject of the sermon: the music introduced, adorned, and illumined its content. *Hauptmusik*, the most important and complete musical and poetic commentary, immediately preceded the sermon and was often called a sermon in music. On festal days a second part of the cantata, or another cantata with a similarly related text, frequently closed the service.

The *Hauptmusik* held Bach's lasting attention and creative energies. According to his son Carl Philipp Emanuel, he composed five entire yearly sets of cantatas. Since the liturgical year calls for 59 cantatas, Bach produced a total of at least 295 cantatas, as compared with his single complete Mass, of which 10 parts are transcriptions of cantatas. Today 190 church cantatas are extant.

Of course the voluminous production of many of the eighteenth-century composers is awesome, and Bach was by no means the only prodigious musician. Telemann is reputed to have written seven yearly series of cantatas; Fasch, if called upon, was capable of penning four cantatas in a week;[1] Graupner produced no less than 1,418 cantatas in 50 years. One cannot help but be impressed by the 95 volumes of

Handel's works in the Breitkopf & Hartel edition; the 153 symphonies, 66 divertimenti, and so forth of Haydn; and the greater production in relatively shorter lives of Mozart and Schubert. Bach's output seems quite normal, if not rather modest, and in fact, Bach worked with more care, more conscience than his contemporaries did. The vast production of others pales, however, in the face of the richness of Bach's polyphonic texture, the depth of the religious feeling he translated into music, and the thought bestowed upon his work. Many of Bach's cantatas borrow or are derived from earlier concerti, overtures, and various other orchestral and vocal forms. Some remained unchanged when Bach transplanted them from one usage to another. Bach then cannot be accused of perfunctory mass production. The choral introductions to 200 extant cantatas and their contrapuntal texture show at once an enormous variety in thematic material and in contrapuntal treatment. Bach's genius, his transcendental technique, and his unfailing penetration of his spiritual subject, realized in musical thought, are truly unequalled.

The Cantata Form

The method of presenting the musical and textual material of the cantata is almost identical with that of the oratorio and the Passion: all work within the framework of recitatives and arias of the opera of that era. There are some differences, however. Many cantatas contain duets, trios, and quartets, but these are not found in the Passions. The cantata, moreover, is introduced by an orchestral and vocal motet or by a symphonic introduction and almost invariably closes with the chorale that is designated for the Sunday or feast day the cantata commemorates.

Some pious devotees viewed the cantatas' resemblance to operatic style with considerable apprehension. Johann Kuhnau, Bach's predecessor, objected to what seemed to him an invasion of worldly practices. And during the first performance of Bach's St. John's Passion a lady in the congregation indignantly proclaimed: "God help us; it's certainly an opera-comedy." At the beginning of the seventeenth century the narratives of both the classical drama and the biblical story were related in a melodious chant or arioso instead of as an aria separated from the recitative. This musical narrative by a single solo voice was the arioso. Monteverdi and his German pupil Schütz excelled in composing expressive musical narratives, some parts of which contain recurring melodic sections of remarkable emotional appeal. The introduction of this representative style had been prompted by a group of enthusiastic Italian poets who wished to restore the lost art of musical representation of the ancient Greek drama, following the esthetic principles of Aristotle and other Greek "art critics" such as Aristoxenus and Plato. Monteverdi wrote, "The text should be the master, not the servant of the music." In the midst of a golden age of contrapuntal masters advocates of *nuove musiche* attempted a revolution of poetry against the supremacy of music. In exclusive circles, musical *literati* no longer used music to enhance the meter and rhythm of the word, nor to reflect the emotion of the drama. They followed what they believed was the model of the classics.

But music had already matured as an independent art, and a subservient role would not be tolerated for long. As long as these experiments were limited to circles of learned men of letters, historians and artists, sponsored by exclusive gatherings of noblemen, the classical idea could be pursued. But when musical theaters were opened to the public, audiences unversed in the refinements of poetic meter, rhythm, and rhymes demanded freer dramatic action and more specifically musical entertainment. Therefore, the elements of narrative and action became concentrated in the recitative, while the lyrical effusions were poured out in the aria. The recitative used prose sentences emphasizing the natural inflections of speech, but in the aria the words, set in strophic verse, became entirely subservient to the melody and the rhythm of the song. Moreover, librettists were engaged to fit their texts to the plan of the composers, instead of musicians offering their talents to the service of poetry. The *da capo* aria—developed mainly by Luigi Rossi (1598-1653), Giacomo Carissimi (1605-1674), Pier Francesco Cavalli (1602-1676), and Alessandro Scarlatti (1660-1725)—is a striking example of the primarily musical appeal of this style, since the first part was repeated in refrain-like manner. The same style was extended to duets, trios, and quartets and proved to be of more lasting favor than the sophisticated literary efforts of poets, historians, and their learned sponsors.

In Germany, during the first part of the eighteenth century, literature was still in its infancy and poets were found chiefly among the clergy. The operatic form of presentation was well suited to the oratorios, Passions, and cantatas of the Lutheran service, where a spontaneous response of faith in the ubiquitous presence of the Spirit could be aroused more immediately by the superrational power of music than by the intellectual appeal of poetry.

This outward form of the eighteenth-century opera was eagerly adopted by cantata writers all over Germany, in spite of its rather stilted character and uneven narrative flow. Action was not of interest in the cantata; contemplation of the theological topic of a particular Sunday formed its main content. The cantata text was prepared by the librettist in the form of an epigrammatic poem—concentrated on one idea related to the sermon—specifically intended for integration in a musical art work. The poem merely suggested the thought, from which the music developed in a metaphysical flight into the regions of religious emotion. In Bach's cantatas music is the master, hence the seemingly senseless repetition of words over dozens of musical measures: the essence of the epigrammatic poem is absorbed by the song, but the words have become a vocal conveyance for the free expanse of melismata.[2] (In the Passions and oratorios, with their greater emphasis on action, one may expect a different relation between word and music.)

The theologian and preacher Erdmann Neumeister was the first to sanction publicly the fusion of secular operatic forms with devotional texts. He wrote an oblique attack on pietistic thinking in his Preface to *Geistliche Cantaten* (1704):

The cantata has the appearance of a piece taken from an opera, and it might almost be supposed that many would be vexed in spirit and ask how sacred music and opera can be reconciled, any more than Christ and Belial, or light and darkness.

Neumeister found that composing cantata texts actually helped him in his own meditations:

When arranging the regular services of the Sunday, I endeavored to render the most important subjects in my sermon in a compact and connected form for my own private devotions, and so to refresh myself after the fatigue of preaching by such pleasing exercises of the mind. Whence arose now an ode, now a poetical oration and with them the present cantatas.[3]

The minister, dedicated to the "reform-cantata,"[4] wrote *Fünffache Kirchenandachten* (Fivefold Church Devotions), a collection drawn upon by Bach and Telemann, among others. Telemann composed three entire yearly sets of Neumeister's work. Bach first became acquainted with the operatic style Neumeister advocated in Weimar. He used five

Rector Erdmann Neumeister, author of cantata texts, who through his bold innovations introduced modern operatic forms into church music.

of his texts in cantatas he wrote there. By the time Bach had moved to Leipzig, the style was well established and Bach found many other librettists who had adopted it. Only two of the cantatas Bach composed while Director of Music there were based on Neumeister's texts. It is interesting that while Bach fully approved of Neumeister's efforts for change, he never used Neumeister's term cantata, but preferred *Hauptmusik, ein Stück* (a piece), *ein Concert*, motet, or some other term.

This reform-cantata, of course, is far removed from the union between text and music later composers sought; from this standpoint the style is open to criticism. Albert Schweitzer expresses regret that Bach did not revolt against "the stilted poetry," and "the empty forms of the

Italian recitative and the *da capo* aria," and return to the "true, simple, and really dramatic church music."[5] These operatic devices can present a very real barrier to a twentieth-century concertgoer's full enjoyment of Bach's cantatas. Musically, the recitative is too formal and stereotyped, and the poetry of the aria is often embarrassingly maudlin. The Passions and oratorios are music dramas full of action and events with ageless appeal, while the cantata contemplates at length a single theological idea. It is understandable that the Passions and oratorios are performed much more frequently, even though the music in Bach's cantatas is often far superior. But before discussing Bach's style in individual works, we should know something of the poets, clergymen, and others who provided the texts—and whose work contributed to the dated character of the cantatas.

Librettists

German poetry was at a very low ebb just before blossoming in the second half of the eighteenth century, and most of the cantata texts Bach had to choose from were hopelessly bad. Preacher-poets unwittingly borrowed the tasteless sentimentality of the Pietist poets and mixed it with dry products of the reasoning theologian, trying to appeal through popular platitudes. But lack of talented poets at the time does not fully explain why Bach used mediocre texts. Clearly there are real difficulties with a collaboration between a musical genius and true poet.

Throughout his life Bach preferred to collaborate with local poets. The quality of these varies greatly but from the time Bach moved to Weimar he selected writers who followed Neumeister. In Mühlhausen, the anti-Pietist Georg Christian Eilmar (presumably), who arranged six cantatas (71, 106, 131, 150, 189, and 196), still used Bible texts, psalms, and hymns. Number 189 is a free translation of the Latin *Magnificat*. In Weimar Bach found a sympathetic preacher-poet in Salomo Franck, whose poetry appealed to him because of its sincerity, depth, and mysticism. Bach returned Franck's texts a few times in Leipzig and regularly included Weimar cantatas in the repertoire of Leipzig.

Bach was not officially a church composer in Köthen, but on certain occasions he wrote religious cantatas for his prince and for the small Lutheran church built by Leopold's mother. Since this small establishment lacked a choir, Bach composed only solo cantatas during this period. He was forced to use nonresident poets here, for none were available in Köthen. For Cantata 47 "*Wer sich selbst erhöhet der soll erniedriget werden"* (He Who Exalts Self Shall Be Humbled) he used a text by Johann Friedrich Helbig,[6] a government secretary in Eisenach, whose series, *Aufmunterung zur Andacht* (Incitement to Devotion), fails notably to incite religious inspiration.

While in Köthen Bach also set to music texts by the notorious Christian Friedrich Hunold (1681-1721),[7] who wrote under the pseudonym Menantes. Hunold is a curious figure to be associated in any way with the pious composer. Early in the century his skill as libretto writer for the Hamburg opera brought him into close contact with the frivolous world of its singers and actors. When he began to describe scandals of Hamburg society he was expelled from this "Second Paris." A man of doubtful integrity, he pirated a manuscript of Erdmann Neumeister,[8] which he published without the consent or knowledge of the author.

Upon arriving in Leipzig, the Bach family developed a cordial relationship with that of Christian Weiss, pastor of St. Thomas. The preacher's daughter was godmother to Bach's son Johann Christoph Friedrich, and five years later, in 1737, the preacher's son Christian, who later was named archdeacon at St. Nicholas, was godfather to Bach's daughter Johanna Caroline. Both father and son lent their literary skill to Bach's libretti. Their free verses wove together Bible quotations and hymn verses intended to correlate the cantata and the sermon.

Another glib insincere librettist like Menantes with whom Bach came in contact, this time in Leipzig, was Christian Friedrich Henrici. Fifteen years Bach's junior, Henrici was a backslider. But Bach must have enjoyed a cordial relation with him: Henrici's wife was godmother to one of Bach's children. Henrici tried to make a living by his satirical poetry, unrestrained imitations of Johann Christian Gunther's songs, but failed and turned to writing devotional songs. In the Preface to his *Collection of Profitable Thoughts for and upon the ordinary Sundays and Holidays* he inadvertently exposes himself in his naive question, "Why should he not then employ this natural gift" of "verse making" that "was easy for him, and took him very little time," "and turn it to account for his living?"[9] Picander, Henrici's pseudonym, soon lost his religious enthusiasm and wrote three farces. When these failed to reap financial rewards he was inspired to write cantata texts again. He finally accepted, in 1736, the profitable job of tax collector, which he retained till his death in 1764. Bach could not have taken too stern an attitude toward Picander's satirical poems, since he set to music this poet's lusty Peasant Cantata.[10]

Bach set one poem of Leipzig's poet Johann Christoph Gottsched to

music: the Mourning Ode for the death of Queen Christina Eberhardine, Electress of Poland and Saxony, the Lutheran wife of the Catholic
King August II. Bach later transferred the music of this cantata to his
Passion of St. Mark—a work now lost—asking Picander to supply a
suitable text.

One other librettist whose poetry Bach used in some of his later
cantatas was Marianne von Ziegler, a wealthy and influential lady in
Leipzig society. She was the first woman in Leipzig to open her home
as a salon for musicians and men of letters, very much in the style of
the *grandes dames* in French literary circles. Bach visited her home
when he lived in Leipzig; she survived him by 10 years. Her personal
life was marked by tragedies. Her father. a mayor of Leipzig, accused
of some unknown state crime, died in prison. She was twice widowed.
But these terrible blows of fate seemed unable to break her spirit. She
made music, and also pursued literary studies under Gottsched's lead-
ership. She was a woman of strong artistic convictions for despite Gottsched's open antipathy to opera she defended her predilection for this
art and its related forms.

Bach used several of her texts in his best cantatas. As a poetess she
surpassed all preceding librettists in sincerity, warmth, clarity, and flu-
ency. She published *Vermischte Schriften in Gebundener und ungebundener Schreibart* (Miscellaneous Writings in Strict and Free Manner),[11] and was honored with the title of Imperial Poetess. In spite of
these recognitions of her literary achievements and her excellent schooling, she was instilled with the humility needed to submit her talents to
the role of librettist for Bach, whose genius she was able to appreciate
and whose art she respected.

We do not know who collaborated with Bach in the construction of
his later chorale-cantatas, which are based on the original hymn texts
used in an earlier period of more naive, less artful, and more direct religious utterance. The "operatic" construction of the Neumeister model,
however, is superimposed even upon these works. Although the texts of
these hymns appear in unadulterated form in the choral movements,
they are often freely paraphrased in the recitatives and arias in madrigal
stanzas. In some cases a recitative by a solo voice sings a short line of
commentary between the stanzas of the original chorales. A few times
only (in Cantatas 100 and 107) Bach uses hymn verses exclusively. In
these cases they are sung by the chorus, using solo voices in arias and in
the closing chorale. Only one stanza in these two cantatas is set to a
recitative.

One wonders with Schweitzer why Bach did not employ better poets. In the city of Leipzig he had easy access to such men as Gottsched (1700-1766), Christian Gellert (1715-1769), Rabener (1715-1771), and Elias Schlegel (d. 1749). The answer lies partly in the natural independence of the true poet; only the verse maker is usually willing to make himself subservient to another art. Bach needed a personality that he could guide, verses he could remodel when necessary. Mature poetry makes its appeal to a different part of the human psyche than music: it reaches the soul through reflection not sheer emotion. And, as Spitta aptly observes, "artistic feeling and emotions in the domain of religion, during Bach's period, found vent almost exclusively in music, and from the moment when sacred poetry made itself felt as a prominent influence, religious music began to decline."[12] A versifier like Picander could be induced to model his texts after those of his favorite librettists, Johann Jacob Rambach and Salomo Franck; or Bach could insert lines of his own into Picander's text without the poet's objecting.

Since a true librettist—and one Bach was prone to choose—is always willing to accommodate the desires of the composer to his own artistic needs, it is not always possible to identify his literary work. In many cases Bach may have written the entire text himself, or made the necessary revisions without consulting a literary expert. C. S. Terry ascribes the texts of 32 cantatas to Bach.[13]

Bach's Cantata Style

The cantatas are still seldom performed and only occasionally, and imperfectly recorded, primarily because the works cannot be heard out of context as naturally as the Passions, oratorios, the *Magnificat*, and even the *Mass*. Their texts sing of specifically Lutheran theology, while Passion drama is equally gripping for Catholic or Protestant, Jew or Gentile. The *Christmas Oratorio*, the *Magnificat*, and the *Mass* also have a universal appeal, unhampered by the subjectivity and bad poetry of the cantata libretti.

It is a great loss, for Bach bestowed his greatest efforts on the cantatas, which contain some of the most superb music of his entire output. Much music of the *Mass*, oratorios, the *Magnificat* had its origin in the cantatas. The cantata constituted the source and end of all Bach's music. He incorporated parts of his work with forms outside the church such as concerti, symphonies, dances (some of which heretofore existed in secular form only), and overtures in imitation of those used by Lully and his disciples for curtain raisers to their operas. Numerous passacaglias can be found in the cantatas such as are found in the music dramas of Monteverdi; there are chaconnes, bourrées, Gavottes, and innumerable other dances of unknown origin as well.

In his earliest cantatas he used mainly Bible texts, psalms, and hymns, often arranged by preachers. Cantata 15 ("*Denn du wirst meine Seele nicht in der Hölle lassen,*" Thou Wilt not Leave My Soul in Hell), dating from his Arnstadt period, constitutes Bach's first attempt at composing a cantata. Even the transformation that is available to us (the original version is lost) shows unique features that distinguish it from the predominant type of later days. Bach's cantata style was constantly growing. The introductory motet is lacking in this early work, and some sections that bear the name of recitative show characteristics of ariosos.

The opening motets alone exhibit an inexhaustible variety of contrapuntal devices and techniques; their architecture is nothing short of awe inspiring. In the opening chorus to No. 80, "A Mighty Fortress is our God" (the basic choral motet of which was composed in Weimar) Bach takes themes of the famous Lutheran hymn and constructs a fugue on each of its six phrases, and weaves them all into a motet. The second phrase appears as the counterpoint to the first. Bach reveals his genius to fashion given themes by slight rhythmic and intervallic adjustments to his ends without appreciably distorting them. He succeeds in leaving the original melody sufficiently intact to recognize it spontaneously while strengthening its original design. In Leipzig he superimposed upon each fugal section a canon in which the trumpet part in the highest register was followed identically by the lowest trombone stops on the organ, a climactic effect so charged with spontaneous symbolism that it inspires awe for the Creator in Heaven as well as for its creator in St. Thomas.

Cantata 14, "*Wär Gott nicht mit uns diese Zeit*" (If God Were not with Us) opens with a hymn by Johann Walther on Luther's free translation of Psalm 124. Bach again treats every phrase of the hymn melody fugally, this time, however, accompanying each theme with its own inversion in canon, while the horns and the oboes sing the original phrases in augmentation (a tempo twice as slow). To carry such treatment throughout all seven phrases of the hymn and resolve all the contrapuntal problems demands a unique skill in which Bach never has been surpassed.

Together with a synthesis of all contrapuntal skills, all instrumental and vocal forms, all secular and ecclesiastical devices, the cantatas are also richest in *Bibelauslegung*, the musical exposition of religious concepts we found in the chorale-preludes. One example not found in the organ works vividly points up the wealth of symbolism in the cantatas. In the soprano aria of Cantata 11 Bach pictures Christ's ascension as He is lifted up toward Heaven and then hidden from sight by a cloud.[14] By means of three high-pitched instruments and a soprano voice, significantly omitting the *terra firma* of the thoroughbass, he gives the illusion of height and imitates the billowing undulations of the cloud. He reenacts the emotional excitement of the Ascension while painting the scene in music. The soprano, in a state of bliss, expresses the essential idea of this age of faith: "Jesus, your love stays with us, that I may now refresh my spirit in the knowledge of Your future reign."

But this intricate symbolism is usually lost on modern audiences. A second reason that the cantatas are rarely performed more is the almost unsurmountable difficulties they present for the soloists. Today a professional concert singer, expected to master all styles of the past centuries, at least four languages, and a full-throated and very substantial tone, cannot possibly accomplish the agility of Bach's choir boys. Trumpeters today are in the same position as the singers. The lip technique required to play music of Bach's era calls for the sacrifice of good lower registers; Bach did not use special trumpets for his high *tessatura*.

Few of Bach's works are as hampered by the limitations of modern large-scale production and undisciplined technique as much as the cantatas. In Leipzig Bach's chorus consisted of about 17 singers: seven basses, five sopranos, three tenors, and two altos. The instrumentalists numbered about 10 to 12, depending on the orchestration needs of the particular text. The organist played the continuo part (Arnold Schering and Arthur Mendel have unquestionably proved that the harpsichord was never used to accompany the cantatas).[15] The organist reinforced the harmonic body of the composition from his figured bass. Bach's pupil Kirnberger reminds us that when Bach accompanied his own compositions he always kept the inner voices moving contrapuntally. The relentless and monotonous beat of a harpsichord plucking stiff blocks of harmony, commonly heard in present-day performances, destroys the expressive beauty of this primarily melodic music. This harmonic time beating with chords is especially offensive when it is done on a harpsichord with its incisive, plucked tonal attack.

The number of wind instruments and strings was not determined on the basis of harmonic balance, as in our modern orchestra. The four-string instruments of Bach's orchestra could not possibly balance their volume with the penetrating *oboe da Caccia* or the high registers of the trumpets; the strings were employed mainly as support and guide for the singers, generally played the same parts, or nearly the same, as the voices. In those days violins sounded much softer than they do today, because they were played with shorter bows, the sticks of which were convex.[16]

Bach's choice of wind instruments depended on the sentiments suggested by the text: the flutes suggested sweetness, quiet contentment, tender lament, or pastoral grace; trumpets appear with jubilant texts; horns were associated with royalty, but at times also accompanied pastoral scenes; and timpani were often used to illustrate force, power, and courage. Bach, however, is not consistent and his choice of obligato instruments resists classification according to emotional content of the text.[17]

Another prejudice against the cantata is the absurd belief that all movements must be performed in strict time; nothing is more deadening than this time beating. The recitatives lend themselves naturally to a *parlando* style. When Bach wished a stricter treatment he specifically instructed the singer (who had only his or her own part before him) with the term *a battuta* (in strict time). In Cantata 38 *"Aus tiefer Noth schrei Ich zu Dir"* (From Deepest Need I Call to Thee) he calls for the recitative to be sung *a battuta* because the accompaniment is the chorale melody upon which the cantata is built. This special warning to keep strict style represents a deviation from the norm, however. Most now accept the idea that recitatives generally should be sung, but the same interpretive freedom in the arias is still frowned upon. Yet, obviously, the most lyrical movement in the cantata should receive the most lyrical treatment, an impossible feat with a relentless, inelastic beat.

Naturally, any many-voiced composition will require a stricter style than a solo, especially when in fugato style. Trios, quartets, and solos with obligato instrumental parts also follow a steady and uniform figuration; still these ensembles are notably poorly performed by today's groups. Bach rarely marked the tempo, and this constitutes one of the major difficulties. The minutest difference in tempo one way may encourage elasticity and facilitate breathing, while a change in the other direction may destroy all freedom of expression.

The profound, varied, exquisite music of the cantatas is almost com-

pletely lost to the general public. Dull, obscure libretti, stringent demands on vocal and instrumental performers, and uncertain tempo instructions all contribute to the absence of cantatas from the concert
stage, but most of all the cantatas suffer more than any of Bach's church
music when they are severed from their liturgical function. They are
much less at home in the concert hall than the *Mass* and the Passions.
The audience who reads their libretti (unless there be some staunch
Lutherans among them) feels ill at ease with their baroque poetry. Only
parts of the cantatas, mostly the opening motets, invite enjoyment of
the music for its own sake. The other movements remain immersed too
deeply in their liturgical context.

20

THE PASSIONS AND ORATORIOS

Evolution of the *Passion*

THE dramatization of Christ's tragedy is one of the oldest traditions of Christendom. Early medieval *historiae* acted out biblical scenes from the story of Christ's birth or resurrection, using the dialogue form later adopted by those writing musical dramatizations of Our Lord's sufferings—the Passions. Some scholars have traced these dramatic presentations back as far as Saint Gregory of Nazianzus (329-389). This poetically and dramatically inclined Church Father patterned theatricals after the chanted dialogue and choruses of Greek tragedy. In 1260 a Passion was performed in the Roman Colosseum. Simple *laudi*, religious songs of praise in the vernacular, made up its music. These ancient sacred theatricals suggest some striking similarities to Bach's Passions. Both strove for close contact with the congregation through vernacular lyrics and the personal dialogue form of dramatization.

One might expect that Luther would have been enthusiastic about these representations of the Lord's suffering, as a form of instruction for the German congregations. But in his book of instruction for the German Mass he gives but little attention to it, saying only, "that the Passion and the *Evangelia* [the gospel readings] that are arranged at the same time [during Holy Week] shall remain . . ." and warning against too many performances and long sermons: "but not so that one . . . will sing four Passions or that one feels one has to preach for eight hours on Good Friday."[1] For the Passions that Luther knew were the highly sophisticated works, composed in motet form only, that the

Catholic church encouraged in his day. Since in his German Mass he is chiefly interested in bringing the gospel to the people, Luther would not have felt these motets in Latin furthered this goal. His musical collaborator Johann Walther copied a motet Passion by Jacob Obrecht (ca. 1450-1505) which abandoned the plain chant setting traditionally used for the words of the Evangelist and Christ. All of the biblical text was woven into the polyphonic web, completely destroying the dramatic appeal of the Passion.[2]

Luther's conception of congregational participation soon inspired a return to the traditional setting of the Passion, simple recitations in the language of the people. In fact, the older type similar to medieval mystery plays had not died out entirely. In 1580 a Passion after St. Matthew was performed in Leipzig on Palm Sunday, following an established custom. Immediately before the work the congregation joined in the singing of Luther's famous hymn *"Aus tiefer Not schrei ich zu Dir"* (From the Depth I Call to Thee), which linked the emotional reaction of the people to the interpretation of Christ's words "My God, why hast Thou forsaken me?" On Good Friday the *St. John's Passion* was introduced by the congregation singing *"Nun freut euch, liebe Christen"* (Now Rejoice, Beloved Christians), a hymn reflecting on the meaning of Christ's sacrifice for the sins of humanity.

The seventeenth century, as we have seen, saw the development of Italian opera and oratorio. When Heinrich Schütz, a pupil of Monteverdi and Giovanni Gabrieli, produced four Passions in 1666, he combined the virtues of the Italian arioso with the liturgical style of the older Passions. The dignity of the Bible words was fully preserved in these most expressive ariosos. The dramatic choruses were sung without instrumental accompaniment, and the opening and closing choruses provided the only elements of subjectivity. No effusive arias disturbed these very dignified works.

In the next generation, however, the text and the music began to be molded by individual interpretations. In the *St. Matthew Passion* by Giovanni Sebastiani (1672) numerous highly lyrical arias are interspersed between the recitations of the biblical narrative. Sebastiani also used a number of chorales, retaining their original texts but usually setting them for soprano solo, accompanied by strings and continuo. New texts had to be written for the arias, of course, and soon the Bible texts too would be paraphrased.

A whole generation of librettists grew up out of this development.

These poets were given almost free rein, without much need to hold closely to the biblical text. This rather unique species of baroque poetry flourished in the theatrical atmosphere of Hamburg where through constant cooperation with opera composers such as Reinhard Keiser, Mattheson, Telemann, and the young Handel these poets became accustomed to writing with theatrical production in mind. Keiser, Mattheson, and Telemann also held positions as cantors of the various churches and were obliged to write church music. The two styles tended to merge and the sacred music took on a decidedly theatrical tone. It was chiefly this quality that branded such librettists as Hunold, Postel, and Brockes as baroque in the most derogatory sense of the word.

Of all these librettists, Barthold Heinrich Brockes was the most successful. A member of the city council and a man of high social standing in Hamburg society, he carried much prestige. His Passion-Oratorium *Der Für die Sünde der Welt Gemarterte und Sterbende Jesus* (Jesus, Who was Tortured and Who Died for the Sins of the World) made a great sensation, and was set to music by the renowned Reinhard Keiser, who directed its first performance in Brockes's spacious mansion. Five hundred members of Hamburg's high society were present, among them "all the foreign nobility [and] all embassadors with their wives."[3] His work was translated into several foreign languages, and Mattheson, Telemann, and Handel (at 19) all composed musical settings for this libretto, which truly represents the culmination of decadence and subjectification of the sacred text. The biblical narrative was now completely versified. Even the words of Christ flow on in a rather saccharine current of iambic rhythms, upon which shocking images arrest our attention. For instance, Christ pronounces His Testament at the Holy Supper:

> This is my blood in the New Testament
> That I want to shed for you and many others
> It will serve those who partake of it
> For the eradication of their sins.

This verse is followed by a contemplation of the allegorical Daughter of Zion and a lyrical chorale of the Christian Church.[4] No less than 29 arias are sung by the Daughter of Zion, Peter, Judas, Mary, and even by the evangelist and Jesus Himself. There are solos, trios, and choruses of the other allegorical person, the "Believing Soul." The Daughter of Zion, representing the people of Israel, and the Believing Soul had been introduced before by the satirist Hunold. These figures form the medium for the congregation's contemplative reflections.

The music of Keiser, Mattheson, Telemann, and the young Handel was as undramatic as any opera of that period, and their Passions are similar to their oratorios and operas, consisting of a series of arias with elaborate coloratura display. Only the absence of acting and costuming distinguished them from the opera. Although the example of the Hamburg Passion was applauded in most German cities, the Council at Leipzig, and especially Kuhnau, Bach's predecessor, refused to allow the introduction of theatricals into church, and ordered a written agreement from Bach to that effect.

Bach's Passions

As Mizler related in the Necrology, Bach composed five Passions, probably to correspond with the five sets of cantatas. Only two have survived—*St. Matthew Passion* and *St. John's*. A third, published by the *Bach Gesellschaft*, is regarded as a copy—in Bach's own handwriting—of an unknown composer. It dates from the Weimar period in which Bach had much trouble with the Council. A text of a Passion according to St. Mark exists, but its music is lost.[5]

Bach adopted Heinrich Brockes' allegorical figures of the Daughter of Zion and the Believing Soul in the *St. John's Passion*, the older of the two existing works, but with some drastic alterations. Even though Bach purges some of Brockes' worst expressions from this work belonging to his Köthen period, the texts do not belong with the best poetry. Bach's Passions restore the original intent and purpose of a Passion performance, effecting a synthesis of many elements of preceding styles. First of all, Bach returned to the pure, unabridged Gospel word. The evangelist relates his story in the *recitative secco* of the contemporary opera, accompanied by only a few chords. The words of Peter and Judas are treated in the same manner.

But in the *St. Matthew Passion* the words of Jesus are supported by sustained chords, played by a quartet of soft string instruments. The effect that Bach desired, especially as it sounded on ancient instruments with short bows, has been interpreted as picturing a halo surrounding the Saviour. When Jesus at the Holy Supper scene lifts the cup and pronounces the Sacrament the music develops into an arioso, and the recitative takes on a more expressive and melodious character.

For the parts in the *St. Matthew Passion* spoken by several persons—
the group of disciples, the Israelite priests, the Roman soldiers, or the
populace—Bach introduces the most dramatic music that was written
in his era. The cries of "Crucify Him, Crucify Him," set to a double
chorus of four voices each, create an overwhelming effect of cruelty and
spiritual chaos of a wild mob. Yet, this very short *fugato*—only eight
measures long—is written in conventional contrapuntal fashion. The
theme also follows the usual style of the *loci topici*, the four principal
notes of the motif forming the design of a cross. A simple motif suffices
to give a strong dramatic effect to the evangelist's narration of how the
temple curtain was rent in two. The work was written for two choruses
and two organs;[6] the first sang the narrative and most of the biblical
personages, and the voices of the False Witnesses resounded from the
second choir, in which the boys of lesser training sang. Lyrical arias
on free poetry and chorales interspersed within the drama reflect the
congregation's reaction, but the worshippers were not invited to take
an active part in the singing, as in earlier days. Although the major
portion of the *St. Matthew Passion* consists of unaltered Bible texts,
for the arias and the hymns Bach relies partly on Brockes and partly
on Picander.[7] But Bach himself modified both poets, and even induced
Picander to model a hymn after an example of Salomo Franck.[8]

The Oratorio

The history of the oratorio parallels that of the Passion. The term
derives from a Roman practice in the latter part of the sixteenth century, when devout souls would meet for prayer in a hall used only for
this purpose. This place was called the *oratorio*. There they sang *laudi*.
The priest Philippo Neri initiated the enactment of biblical scenes
there. Later, influenced by contemporary music dramas, this practice
evolved into what is presently known as the oratorio. The only extra-
liturgical presentation Luther approved, however, was the Passion.

Three of Bach's works have been given the name "oratorio" even
though technically they are not since they were written for the Lutheran
service. One, the so-called *Ascension Oratorio*, is listed among the
cantatas as Number 11, *"Lobet Gott in Seinen Reichen"* (Praise God in
His Realms), though it bears the title *Oratorium*. The others belong
to the two major celebrations of the Christian year—Christmas and
Easter.

There were always several extra services during Christmas week, and since naturally the theme for the sermon and all the musical parts in the liturgy was Jesus' birth, the cantatas were sung on the three Christmas days, on New Year's day, on the first Sunday after New Year, and on Epiphany. This sequence of six is known as the *Christmas Oratorio.* Inasmuch as they followed the narrative of the Bible rather than embarking on a lyrical meditation of a theological idea, these cantatas were given the name oratorio. Nevertheless they contain as many lyrical arias as the usual cantata, and, save for their lack of dramatic treatment, their form resembles that of the Passions. Since the story does not lend itself to particularly stirring dramatic action, the lyrical elements quite naturally predominate. The Evangelist sings the narrative, as in the Passion, but occasionally he deviates from the Bible text and, following cantata style, states the underlying thought for the ensuing aria.

As in the *B Minor Mass,* Bach utilized previously composed cantatas that had served more worldly purposes. The opening chorus of the third part was originally written for the Queen's birthday. Four arias, a duet, and a chorus had been a birthday cantata for the crown prince.[10] One aria came from a cantata at the occasion of the King's visit to Leipzig. Although this practice of transcribing need not lead to the conclusion that Bach was indifferent toward these compositions, he did write special music, completely planned for its sacred purpose,[11] for the *Passion* and the *Magnificat.* These compositions occupied a foremost place of importance in the Lutheran liturgy.

The Easter Oratorio is as long as one cantata. Its subject is John 20:13-17, which tells of the discovery of the open sepulcher. The names of the *dramatis personae,* Mary Magdalene, Simon Peter, and "the other disciple," are not mentioned. The recitatives and the arias are entirely paraphrased. The work is introduced by a jubilant symphony and closed by an aria in which the theological theme of redemption is turned into a song of praise. The work hardly deserves to be called an oratorio. There is no dramatization and its cantata character is more apparent than in any part of the *Christmas Oratorio.*

A Lifework for Eternity

Thus it was during a period of about 17 years that Bach completed the greatest monument of Protestant liturgical music. Many other

Lutheran composers have been as prolific, but without Bach's craftsmanship or his underlying profoundly sincere devotion: Schütz, one
of the great spirits of the Protestant era, did not devote himself exclusively to Lutheran music; Buxtehude, a thorough Lutheran, was of
considerably smaller stature than Bach; the virtuoso Reincken lacked
the mystic spirit in his music; and Froberger vascillated all his life between his Catholic and his Lutheran leanings. Among Bach's contemporaries was a smooth, fleet pen, but the theater was closer to their
hearts than the sanctuary.

Bach fulfilled his mission. Every detail of the elaborate Lutheran
liturgy was now properly introduced, ornamented, illustrated, and
closed with fitting music. The entire service began and ended with the
mighty organ preludes and fugues, never to be surpassed in grandeur
and profundity. All the congregational hymns, the *detempora* hymns,
and pulpit hymns now had their preludes with their musical commentaries. Organ voluntaries were heard at intervals during the long service. For the Communion after the main service all the fitting organ
music was provided. He even composed a complete set of chorale-
preludes for the children's service. During this relatively short period
Bach composed five yearly series of cantatas, with five Passions to follow the Gospels, a complete Mass from which every part could be used
for the proper Sunday. Towering art works were created such as the
Magnificat, the Passions, and the *Christmas Oratorio* for all the festal
days. For such secondary festivities as the Reformation anniversary
Bach also wrote special cantatas. Most of his motets and cantatas
written for state occasions and important weddings and funerals were
ultimately absorbed into the regular service. No composer has integrated the entire yearly service with such absolute devotion and such
a profoundly mystic spirit as Bach.

Did Bach realize the permanence, even the eternity of his accom-
plishments? Naturally, he was aware that the next cantor, according
to custom, was again to provide the church with his own music, and
not with that of his predecessors. And just as Bach considered the
music of those who went before him antiquated, he too was soon considered out of date by his followers. For many years much of his
music remained on the shelves of the Thomas library, for some of it
was used after his death. But it gradually disappeared, to be discovered
in orchards and shops where the manuscripts of musical masterpieces
served as wrapping paper. In time, the religious spirit was dampened

by the rationalism of the next generation, and the service became shorter. Only 16 years after Bach's death performances of the *Passion* were discontinued. In 1740, during Bach's lifetime, the second organ that was needed to accompany the second chorus of the *St. Matthew Passion* was removed from the Thomas church.

Exactly a century after its completion Felix Mendelssohn revived the almost completely forgotten *St. Matthew Passion*. Many cuts and alterations were made in the score to appease the musical taste of a public alien to the spirit of Bach. On March 11, 1829, in the concert hall of the Berlin Singing Academy, a mammoth chorus and orchestra performed the *Passion*, in striking contrast to Bach's original scoring. The continuo parts were even transferred to the piano, played by Mendelssohn himself.

In an age of punctilious historical conscience this stylistic mutilation is seriously criticized, but the fact that Bach's music, written and conceived for the sole purpose of religious worship, is now relegated to the concert hall and phonograph, completely severed from its liturgical function, proves that despite his great enlightenment throughout history modern man still cannot truly identify with Bach's original motivation. Nevertheless, Bach's great spirit and deep faith has reached us through the beauty of his music. For Bach's religious art work, although depending on visions of a particular religion at a particular time, draws its vitality from a higher reality, the universal and absolute spirit, and speaks with great intensity to our age.

In fact, our age has a much deeper appreciation of this transcendental music than did the pillars of the St. Thomas Church. The subsequent chapters tell of how Bach had to fight to protect his prerogative as cantor against the encroachments of deans, deacons, and preachers who were unaware of the presence of such genius in their midst.

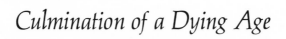

Culmination of a Dying Age

21

SIGNS OF CHANGE

BACH could not have been aware that he was the last composer to give voice to Lutheran philosophy, to construct a gigantic musical architecture in the Lutheran liturgy; he could hardly have recognized his role as the historical climax of an epoch. The idea that he was living at the dawn of a new era, that his art actually belonged to a dying age, was totally inconsistent with his providential conception of history. Bach correctly judged his own talent as a musical craftsman and knew full well that his art surpassed that of all his contemporaries, as well as of the Lutheran composers of the past two centuries. But his art work was not, as he envisaged, one more link in the development of the Lutheran service, but the culmination—and end—of this long evolution of music for the sanctuary. In fulfilling his gigantic task of constructing "well-conceived and well-regulated" church music, he was continually confronted with irritating obstructions by church and school authorities, whose opinions and desires infringed on his domain as musical director of Leipzig. He attributed these interferences to personal ambitions and misplaced officiousness of these "strange folk," as he called them, when in retrospect such personal interferences were surface tremors of deeper historical and cultural displacements.

Bach was always vigilant for any such encroachment upon his authority and his rights as *director musices*. Only invested with the full authority of his office could he accomplish his life work. In the second year of his directorship in an action of remarkable independence and pride he revealed himself as an artist unwilling to compromise his musical standards. According to a custom established in 1721 a Passion was performed on Good Friday, alternating each year between St.

Thomas and St. Nicholas churches. In 1724 the performance was to be in St. Nicholas church, but Bach decided that the choir loft at St. Nicholas was too small for his *St. John's Passion* and besides the harpsichord was in need of repair. He therefore took it upon himself to print programs announcing that the performance would take place at St. Thomas. This unexpected move forced the church council into action: the seating capacity in the choir loft was enlarged, and the harpsichord was repaired. Then new programs were printed.[1]

At the same time Bach was involved in a much more serious controversy, one not as amicably and obligingly concluded, and one that threatened the integrity of his office. Since time immemorial the services at the Leipzig University had been the responsibility of the general Musical Director of the city. In 1710 the University instituted a regular Sunday service in its church, in addition to the traditional five festal services, the Reformation anniversary, and four academic celebrations, all of which were known as the *Alt Gottesdienst*, the Old Service. For the *Neu Gottesdienst* the University appointed its own director, thereby disregarding the traditional prerogative of the general director. No new city laws had been passed to make this new arrangement legal, and Bach's predecessor Kuhnau filed a protest for his right to the directorship. Eventually he was accepted but only after promising not to expect any extra remuneration. When Kuhnau died, Johann Gottlieb Görner (1697-1778) took this position temporarily, receiving the 12 Thalers that really were part of the Director's salary. Thus the University was performing music at the expense of the city and its employed musicians.

The musical equipment of the University—its organ, chorus, and orchestra—was of such excellent quality that the conductors preferred to perform their works there. They also could draw on this superior organization for various secular occasions. Görner, an inferior[2] and scheming musician, profited from this fine musical equipment and the diverted funds.

As soon as Bach arrived in Leipzig he put in a claim for the directorship of the Old Service, and naturally also for its remuneration (12 Thalers was not an inconsiderable sum in days when 5 Thalers could buy a pedal harpsichord). The university council at first tried to ignore him, but Bach stubbornly persisted and after two years the council restored the directorship of the Old Service to him—but still withheld part of his fee.

At last Bach appealed to higher authority. He wrote a letter on Sep-

tember 14, 1725, to the King of Saxony himself. The government in
Dresden, acting with remarkable speed, ordered the university council to present its version of the case. Bach was well acquainted with his
opponent's evasions of the truth and requested a copy of the council's
report from the government. Point by point he refuted the council's
misstatements in a precise, systematic, and complete account of the
facts.

Again, the government acted promptly. The Saxon Solomon, as
C. S. Terry calls the royal arbiter, gave concessions to both parties.
Bach won responsibility for the Old Service and its emoluments, and
Görner was allowed to continue directing the Sunday services. The
matter of the direction of special state occasions, however, was left un-
decided, to be settled less than two years later.

In the spring of 1727 August the Strong visited Leipzig and from
the balcony of one of the gabled houses on the market place listened
to a cantata in honor of his birthday. The university students showed
their discrimination by choosing Bach over Görner for the composition
and conducting of the work. The libretto for Bach's celebration of
August's presence is trite and affected, but typical of the common man's
attitude toward royalty.[3] The dignity of royalty, regardless of the character of the person wearing the crown, was revered, and even a man of
Bach's genius and religious strength paid respect to the rulers. In this
case, August II hardly deserved such tribute; he loved wine, women,
and war and had won the throne of Poland by renouncing the Lutheran
faith and becoming Catholic. The music of Bach's cantata in his honor
is lost, although parts of it may be in some of the known church cantatas, for as we have seen he often recast his secular works.

Four months later the students again sought Bach out, this time to
compose music for the mourning demonstrations for the death of
Queen Christina Eberhardine, wife of August II. She had been estranged from the king ever since he renounced his native faith to gain
the throne. At her death the Lutheran Saxons demonstrated their respect for her loyalty to the state religion by observing a mourning
period of four months.

Hans Carl von Kirchbach, a student of noble birth representing the
student body, wished to deliver a funeral oration in her honor and have
a mourning ode performed on words by Gottsched, the famous poet
and university professor. The old strife between Bach and Görner
stirred again. Görner demanded the right to compose and conduct the

music, or else at least receive part of the fee.[4] Why the faculty sided with him can probably be explained by their feeling of superiority and independence of the city. The students in this case showed finer discrimination than their professors.

Kirchbach informed the *Concilium Professorum* (faculty council) that Bach had already received his fee, and was busy composing the funeral ode, performance of which was only a week away. The council's proposal that Bach's music should be conducted by Görner raised ultimatums from both sides. The final decision awarded Görner the 12 Thaler, but allowed Bach to compose and conduct the music.

Görner had prepared a document for Bach to sign, in which Bach was to pledge never to claim the right to act as director in St. Paul's church or to compose music for any University celebration. The beadle of the University took this document to Bach, but after an hour of futile persuasion he returned with the document unsigned.

Two weeks before its performance Bach finished the score of the Mourning Ode and little time could be spent in rehearsal. This proves the superlative capacity of the university chorus to read such difficult music at sight. Bach conducted from his seat at the harpsichord in the gallery. In the church, where a large catafalque with the emblems of the Queen, a Hohenzollern, was erected, the beadles distributed the printed texts of Gottsched. The programs stated that the music had been "set by Herr Kapellmeister Bach in the Italian style."

Although his victory in this shameful case was obvious, Bach was never again asked to deliver any occasional music for St. Paul's church. The university students did invite him to compose a serenade in 1734 when August III was elected King of Poland. But this performance took place outdoors with torch light and illuminations.[5]

These squabbles may seem trivial and contemptuous, but Bach was determined to protect the dignity of his office—and the integrity of his art. So far his difficulties had been in the defense of his office of general director and his prerogative as composer and performer of its secular functions. His next conflict concerned his broadly conceived integration of the musical service. His choice of hymns was one of the basic elements in his vast musical architecture, but in 1728 the deacon, Gottlieb Gaudlitz, took it upon himself to select the hymns for Sunday Vespers. Bach refused to perform them, and the matter was laid before the council. (In Lutheran state churches a consistory, composed of a body of clerical officers, is appointed by the sovereign of the state.

This body could dictate policies to the council of each particular church, and in the absolute monarchy, could in turn be ordered by the King.) When the council informed Bach that it expected him to comply with the deacon's choice of the hymns, Bach immediately appealed to the consistory.

His letter of September 20, 1728, sets forth his rights, basing them on the "traditional usages" giving him "the exclusive right to select the hymns preceding and following the sermon . . . their selection to correspond with the Gospel, the Dresden tradition, and their places in the season."[6] Bach's arguments based on tradition and the self-contradictory claims of the council ultimately brought victory, but only after the consistory spent a year and a half deliberating. In a letter of February 16, 1730, "The Electoral and Royal Saxon Consistory" wrote that "in the name of His Most Serene Majesty" (followed by 17 other royal titles) no new and untraditional songs should be sung in the church service.[7]

Homage to Köthen

In the meantime, on November 19, 1728, Bach's friend Prince Leopold of Köthen died. On March 23, 1729, his entombment took place in the church of St. Jacob, where Bach performed the funeral music the following day. His wife, his eldest son, and his choir accompanied him to Köthen. Instrumentalists were gathered from Halle, Merseburg, Zerbst, Dessau, and Güsten. There was no time to compose special music, for the performance of the St. Matthew Passion was only three weeks away, and the composition and preparations for it occupied all Bach's time. Bach therefore utilized several parts of the Passion and of the Funeral Ode for Queen Christina Eberhardine—both eminently suited for this sad loss of his dear and highly esteemed friend.

A new text was provided by the facile Picander, who had a convenient talent for hammering out verses in the identical rhythm— word for word and syllable for syllable—of the lyrics in the Passion. His text for this occasion appears in the third volume of his poems of 1732.[8] Smend has discovered a text that was especially printed for the occasion in Köthen. The score, if one ever existed, is presumably lost, but Smend suggests[9] that for that occasion, as for similar ones, the parts were copied separately and perhaps slightly altered here and there.

The death of Bach's dear friend meant great personal sorrow, and loss of professional status; he had to relinquish the title of *Kapellmeister*. It was more than vanity or professional pride that caused Bach to regret the passing of this honor. In the German hierarchical ranking, the loss of a title meant loss of prestige. In Leipzig, where he had been confronted with so much animosity, jealousy, and disrespect, his title had helped greatly, impressing his provincial adversaries. (In his letter to Erdmann he clearly states that "at first [he] found it not altogether agreeable to become a simple cantor after having been a *Kapellmeister*.") He did receive an honorable title of *Kapellmeister* *"von Haus aus"* to the Duke of Sachsen-Weissenfels in 1723,[10] and Bach's visit to that court three months later probably confirms a mutual recognition of the honor. Upon the death of that duke in 1736 this title also expired.

Bach was fully aware that his provincial church authorities regarded the function of cantor mainly as that of an instructor, and not of a composer. Their complaints about him were always based on his indifference toward his job as teacher. They also accused him of too many absences from the town and were annoyed by his persistent failure to ask permission to leave. Bach naturally did not accept this conception of his office as a mere instructor, but saw his role as creator of a great musical monument in the service of his God. The pedestrian church officials were incapable of such visions—the only thing they understood was prestige in the eyes of powerful upper classes.

A Choir of Rogues

Only a few weeks later the council again proved its contempt of the mere cantor, and its total ignorance of a great artist's needs. These first rumblings of cultural conflicts between old and new standards in education were recognized on both sides as merely conflicts of personalities.

During the Easter examinations nine scholarship students graduated and left school, and 23 new candidates applied for the rather remunerative stipends. Bach examined them for musical talent and the quality of their voices, and considered it his duty to examine new students according to Luther's criterion of giving "after theology music the nearest *locum* and highest honor." When he reported his findings to the council, he pronounced ten students "possessed of musical qualifications," eleven completely lacking such, and two of passable quality.[11] The council ignored Bach's verdict, choosing five boys from Bach's approved list, four of those who were rejected, and one whom Bach had not even examined. The arrogance of the council appears all the more insulting in view of the momentous first performance of the *St. Matthew Passion* that had just taken place.

It is surprising that Bach did not appeal at once to authority. The history of the following year is obscured by a lack of precise information. Bach may have been discouraged. Spitta expresses surprise that Bach did not immediately resign from his office, but suggests that Bach hoped to draw better students from the *Collegium Musicum*, an organization initiated long before by Telemann. Every week Bach rehearsed this group, the best singing organization in town, and they performed on several festive occasions. (Like his predecessor Kuhnau, Bach cherished the hope that the Thomas church might pay the singers of the *Collegium* to assist its choir, but the council seemed to expect those boys to give their services free.)

Meanwhile, the conditions of the Thomas choir and of the entire school had deteriorated alarmingly, partly because of the venerable rector Johann Heinrich Ernesti (1652-1729), who was then 77 years old. He had been a worthy scholar of theology and philosophy, but he had no talent for leading and guiding his faculty in their inevitable human frictions, he had no disciplinary influence over the students,[12] and he lacked enterprise to improve the physical equipment. The school buildings under his regime were antiquated and inadequate. Often several classes had to be held in the same room.[13] The bedrooms for the students were cramped and unsanitary, and harbored disease.

Although the reputation of this historical institution had suffered under the long regime of this unrealistic and inert old man, applicants kept coming, lured by the availability of scholarships to musical students. These, however, were seen as valuable positions with little responsibility attached. Gradually, uncouth and undesirable boys began to fill the jobs. They received their board and room, and had opportunity to earn extra as mendicant students, in the traditional *currenden*, the singing groups that went from door to door. This custom had lost some of its earlier romance; now only people of the less fortunate classes had any taste for it.

Moreover, the big city of Leipzig, that gay "second Paris," offered these rowdy bands of boys many activities not compatible with a choir of angels. The more talented and ambitious boys left school, attracted by the nearby operas in Dresden and Weissenfels, where good singers could be used in minor but remunerative capacities. Leipzig also had a short opera season, at fair times, until 1729.

An iron hand was needed to discipline this raw material for heavenly choirs and neither Bach nor old Ernesti possessed it. But the old rector died on October 16, 1729, and Bach's old friend Johann Matthias Gesner, who had been preacher in Weimar when Bach was there, was appointed to the post.

Two months after Gesner's installation Bach had another disagreeable encounter with the church council. On the second of August this parochial body met; "their magnificencies" expressed their displeasure with Bach's neglect of his classes and with his boldness in sending a chorist to the country without their consultation. They complained: "The cantor not only did nothing, would not even explain himself, does not keep the singing hours." They reported "other additional complaints; a change became necessary, because some day things would inevitably break anyway, it therefore [became] necessary to make other arrangements." At first it was suggested that Bach should be admonished. But, as one dignitary remarked, "since . . . the cantor was incorrigible . . . it was resolved [by a majority vote of seven to four] that the cantor's earnings [*Besoldigung*] should be impounded."[14]

The earnings referred to were not his regular salary,[15] but benefit from extra fees that had accrued during the interim between Ernesti's death and Gesner's appointment. The council customarily paid those who took over the extra duties during that time, but since Bach had neglected his classes—using his time to compose the *Saint Matthew Passion* and other works equally unnoticed by Their Magnificencies— he received nothing.

Bach did not argue their charges of neglecting the lessons. Instead, he prepared a detailed statement of the bad conditions of music at the Thomas school, vainly hoping to enlighten the council as to the true causes of the choir's deficiencies. Now Bach, who hitherto "would not explain himself," presented to them "A short but extremely necessary outline of a well-regulated church music with a few unprejudiced reflections on its decline."[16]

The report begins with a simple outline, in layman's terms, of Bach's requirements for the performance of church music. To our modern standards they seem ridiculously modest, as they were even then, in comparison with musical organizations elsewhere in Europe. For the chorus he required at the absolute minimum three sopranos, three altos, three tenors, and three basses, plus some ready substitutes in case of illness; four choirs were needed for the four churches of Leipzig, a total of at least 36 singers. Hitherto, the university students and the Thomas alumni had been called upon, for a small remuneration, to make up for any gaps in the Thomas group. Financial support had gradually been withdrawn, "and with it also their willingness is lost; for who wants to work for nothing?" He complained that the string instruments, played by untalented students, gave little support to the singers, and the choirboys too lacked ability; they cannot even produce the interval of a second. Moreover, to train them would take at least a year.

Since, however, the present state of music is so different from what it was; since artistry has risen so much; taste has so wonderfully changed . . . the more assistance we need. But the little financial support that should be in-creased, has instead been withdrawn. . . . Of our boys more is required than from professional opera singers; for the former have to learn our music at once, read it at first sight, while the professional *virtuosi* have studied it long in advance, so that they almost know it by heart. Besides, they are well paid.

(One may well imagine how this comparison to the opera was received by this stingy and artistically callous group.)

Bach concluded by stating that he leaves to the council the respon-sibility to choose whether music can continue to exist or shall still further decline, and by listing the names and abilities of his students— three assistant conductors and 17 singers are usable, 20 not as yet usable, and 17 are unfit. Significantly, Bach signed the document as *Director Musices*, not as *Cantor St. Thomae*.

Apparently, Bach's effort to enlighten Their Magnificencies accom-plished nothing; no money was raised. History is silent as to Bach's reaction. He did begin a rather active search for another position. A short time later (October 28, 1730) he wrote the letter to Georg Erd-mann referred to in Chapter 16, describing conditions in Leipzig.

1) this situation is not as good as it was represented to be, 2) various *acci-dentia* relative to my *station* have been withdrawn, 3) living is expensive, and 4) my masters are strange folk with very little care for music in them. Consequently, I am subjected to constant annoyance, jealousy, and persecu-tion. It is therefore in my mind, with God's assistance, to seek my fortune elsewhere. If your honor should hear of a *convenable station* in your town, I beg you to let me have your valuable *recommendation*.[17]

No answer is on record from Erdmann or any of the other friends

Bach presumably contacted. It was his ill luck that other positions did not come within his reach at this time.

Gesner: Reformer and Patron

Promise of better conditions came with Gesner's appointment as the new rector for the Thomas School. A great lover of music and an ardent admirer and warm and devoted friend of Bach, he shared with Bach that sacred fire of enthusiasm for the role of music in the Lutheran service. At the same time he was endowed with unusual tact and diplomacy.

It is entirely appropriate that Gesner should be Bach's spokesman in

Johann Matthias Gesner, rector of the Thomas School from 1730-1734, a friend and admirer of Bach.

this age of philosophical upheaval, for he combined conservative ideals in religion and music with progressive ideas in education. Not only did he effect enlargement of the old building which had stood unchanged since Luther's days, but he also improved sanitary conditions. But most important were his new and healthier conceptions of education, through which the students felt again genuine interest in their studies. As a result, discipline was considerably improved.

Gesner's modernized methods of education contrasted remarkably with those Bach knew as a youth. He relaxed the arid discipline and awakened an interest in the contents of the classics rather than in the form. Instead of a minute study of each grammatical turn of phrase, Gesner read authors' entire works through with his students. Moreover, while formerly the authors of the classics were regarded as heathens intent on corrupting the reader, Gesner now revealed their lofty thoughts and elegance of style. He even had the courage to admit that Homer's Greek was superior to that of the New Testament, a statement equated with rank heresy in Bach's time. Much to his regret, he still had to teach New Testament Greek first because beginning students were not ready for Homer. Only a very broad-minded and spiritually secure soul could dare to expose youth to the beauties and true enjoyment of pagan philosophy and culture without diverting them from their Christian education. Gesner lived at the dawn of Goethe's era. He was the first to make German translations of the classics. By the next generation the market was flooded with various translations.[18]

Despite this awakening of interest in the subject of their learning, other disciplines remained as severe as in ancient times. And they were just as naturally resented by adolescents as similar restraints are today. Total lack of recreation drove the older students to drinking and smoking, for which severe punishments were dealt. Attendance at the Sunday services was still enforced by law, although Gesner softened the punishment somewhat. Instead of the birching required by the 1723 regulations,[19] Gesner allowed students to be excused, in extreme cold weather, to be read the sermon when they returned to school.

But even Gesner was not free from a schoolmaster's vindictiveness; he prescribed special punishments for intentional mistakes in singing. The custom of appointing young students from among their own midst as assistant conductors (praefects) did nothing to encourage respectful behavior. The poor students were still subjected to a daily discipline that to us appears as beyond human endurance. From five o'clock in the morning their daily life was a dreary succession of prayers, sermons, lesson, funeral services (for which the scholarship students had to sing), and studies under constant supervision. It seems strange irony that Gesner, who rejoiced in Homer's affirmation of life, should commend to these weary young souls the Pythagorean practice of contemplating their spiritual profits of the day before sinking into that blissful oblivion provided by nature.

Bach spent the four years of Gesner's directorship in profitable and productive work. Gesner's unbounded admiration for him, combined with his tact and generosity, brought about an improvement in the relations between the council and their "incorrigible" cantor. Gesner succeeded in lightening Bach's teaching duties by getting the council to agree to release him from all teaching except musical subjects if Bach would practice more with his singers. Even the fees impounded by the council were now restored to him. With the new building program, Bach's living quarters were enlarged. In June, 1732, the new buildings were inaugurated with the usual procession, speeches, sermons, and festive music set to rhymed eulogies. In his inaugural speech, which emphasized the particular importance of music to the Lutheran service, Gesner showed that he was not unaware of the growing tendency among academicians throughout Germany to shift the weight of their values from musical studies toward academic pursuits. (Gesner's school laws of 1733 also gave music a prominant place, pointing out its spiritual force and its traditional function.)

During Gesner's directorship, Bach composed the *B Minor Mass*, between 40 and 50 church cantatas, overtures for orchestra, and a dozen concerti for one or more harpsichords with orchestral accompaniment. He also undertook the publication of his *Klavierübung*, made up of keyboard compositions written in earlier periods.

Busy as he then was with composing, engraving, rehearsing, teaching, and performing, he was far from idle at the various keyboards, judging from the number of clavier concerti of the period. He had enough instruments and competent musicians in his own household to have performed his multiple harpsichord concerti in his own newly enlarged apartments. As he told his friend Erdmann he could "form an ensemble both *vocaliter* and *instrumentaliter*" within his own family.

Although as cantor he did not play the organ at the Thomas church (the organist was Christian Gräbner, and later the incompetent and unmanageable Görner), Bach's prodigious keyboard technique had not slackened in the least. In September, 1731, he astonished a large audience of notables and connoisseurs in an organ recital at the magnificent Sophia church in Dresden, where the night before he had attended the first performance of the opera "*Cleofide*" by his friend Johann Adolf Hasse. At this occasion the entire staff of royal musicians was present.[20] The next day a local poet with the pseudonym Micrander wrote a poetic tribute to the master in a daily paper, the *Dresdener Merkwürdigkeiten*, relating the amazement of all who had heard him.

One wonders if Their Magnificencies of the Leipzig council ever read this news report and whether, even if they had, they still would have muttered their discontent among each other at Bach's absences without their permission. In any case, during the next year Bach traveled three times for similar occasions. In February, 1732, he was invited to examine an organ at Stöntzsch, and in September he examined the organ at St. Martin's Church at Cassel, where Prince Friedrick royally entertained Bach and Anna Magdalena for a week. They were lodged (at the Prince's expense) at the most fashionable hostelry, where only nobility and royalty could afford the extravagant charge of 84 Thalers. (The King of Sweden had stayed there on a visit in 1714.)[21] "Porteurs" with a sedan chair awaited Bach and his "Bachin" to carry them to their various destinations. Bach gave a public recital on the recently renovated organ on Sunday, September 28. In those days when only the aristocracy was privileged to hear great artists and others heard them only during the religious service or at state festivals like royal birthdays, the burghers must have been bewildered by these mighty toccatas and fugues.

For these services Bach was well paid, and with Anna Magdalena's companionship the trip must have been a refreshing recreation and a source of gratitude and pride for both after the humiliations suffered in Leipzig in the previous year.

The recognition and appreciation accorded Bach by the secular, artistic world contrasted sharply with the opposition he had faced from congregations to whom he humbly submitted his efforts. Perhaps he realized that he had accomplished all he could in creating a complete musical liturgy—surely he knew he had outstayed his welcome in the churches of Leipzig. In 1733 he applied to the Saxon king for the office of Court Composer.

22

ENLIGHTENMENT DARKENS BACH'S HORIZON

Bach's increasing dissatisfaction and discomfort in the Leipzig post were certainly forboding of the future: the university in particular was approaching a period of fundamental change. One member of the university community especially regarded Gesner's respect for the art and discipline of music as a remnant of the past, one that should be discarded. The son of the former rector, conrector Johann August Ernesti (1707-1781), vigorously opposed music as a degrading, rather than ennobling influence. He saw its emotional power not as "linking the soul to the heavenly choirs above," as Gesner has described it in his speech, but as an anti-intellectual indulgence, confusing and obscuring clear thinking. As long as Gesner was the reigning rector of the school, of course, Ernesti kept these new and subversive ideas to himself, for he was a man of tact and diplomacy, knowing when discretion and agreement would profit him. The right moment would come for him to make his views known.

Both Gesner and Ernesti were among the leading forces revolutionizing educational methods. Both broke with the old ways of learning; both were enthusiasts for the classics—their literary, linguistic, cultural, and even philosophical value, breaking with the traditional Lutheran evaluation of pagan writers as inferior to Christian thinkers. Both humanized learning through the Greek culture. The value of the classics went beyond that of disciplinary tools. But sharp differences divided the cultures and the personalities of the two men. Two years later Ernesti assumed the rectorship of the Thomas School, when Gesner left to become professor at the University of Göttingen. Then certain personality traits became apparent and soon led to serious conflicts with Bach. The ensuing struggle involved two opposing cultures, not merely individual differences of opinion and temperament.

This clash would not have occurred had Gesner remained the leading power at St. Thomas. For despite the fact that he shared the enthusiasm for pedagogical emanicipation of his successor, he remained a devoted Lutheran by temperament and schooling. A man of 42 when he set forth his concepts of education in his school laws of 1733, he still attributed spiritual powers to music, linking its psychological function to that of faith. At this time Ernesti was 25. Although he too was inevitably exposed to thorough theological studies, his philosophical training was radically different. When Ernesti developed new school laws (1773), music was not even mentioned in his curriculum.

His indifference to music took root in the barren soil of rationalistic philosophy that was taking the universities by storm. The study of music was looked upon as indolence by enthusiastic rationalists. Luther had regarded unmusical people as wicked souls to be distrusted; Werckmeister integrated this opinion into his metaphysical, Pythagorean construction, presenting the unmusical mind as outcast from the sphere of heavenly harmony, truth, and goodness. Ernesti, however, was not a part of that generation of Pythagorean visionaries and allegorical mystics. He subjected all ideas, including church doctrines, to rational and objective reasoning, like a son of the Enlightenment; but he did take the middle road between orthodoxy and the rationalism of the universities.

In Wittenberg he had studied philosophy with Schlosser, a protagonist of the new philosophy. At the University of Leipzig he had studied theology under Borner and Deyling (the superintendent and chairman of the council that later opposed Bach in the matter of hymns), and philosophy under Gottsched. Here the traditional ties between theology and philosophy had already begun to loosen with the granting of the chair of philosophy to Gottsched, the poet devoted to the rationalistic philosophy developed by Christian Wolff.

Christian Wolff

Until the advent of Christian Wolff (1679-1754), philosophy in the German universities had been a semi-Scholastic subject, completely subservient to theology and treated only as a preparation to this superior and all-important faculty. Just as Catholic theology in the Middle Ages had formed a political bulwark for the Church with the support of philosophy, so Lutheranism under the protection of German potentates had called upon theology—and consequently its accessory discipline, philosophy—to defend national dogma against the numerous heresies. Philosophy was actually providing Protestant theology with Aristotelian weapons originally developed to preserve the Catholic faith.

This arsenal of logic was now enriched with the concepts and terminology of Descartes, Locke, Newton, and Leibniz. Theology professors in the German universities felt a pious horror toward these independent infidels, but German princes, traditionally detached from religion and culturally broader and more international than their parochial subjects, began to favor independent thinkers. Karl Ludwig, the Elector Palatine, offered Spinoza a chair of philosophy at the University of Heidelberg in 1673, but this sensitive and peace-loving thinker firmly but graciously declined the honor, knowing that the trade of lens grinding would assure him more serenity than an honored position in that theological lion's pit. Similarly no German university at that time would have welcomed a philosopher like Leibniz, who strove to unite all creeds and sects into a universal philosophical concept, and who was too much of an international figure among scientists in every branch of inquiry. As a student of international law, a historian, and a man with keen practical judgment in politics of his time, he found ready employment with three powerful princes of Brunswick-Lüneburg.

Christian Wolff was the first philosophy professor in a German university to pronounce the complete autonomy of his branch of learning. He was well versed in the philosophy of Descartes, Spinoza, and Locke, but the strongest influence upon his world outlook came from Isaac Newton. Wolff also was so devoted a disciple of Leibniz that his philosophy, to his own displeasure, was often referred to as the Leibniz-Wolffian school.

In 1706 he was appointed professor of mathematics at the newly established University of Halle. He soon branched out from mathematics, through physics, into all areas of philosophy, after the manner of Leibniz who pervaded his entire polyhistoric learning with philosophical reflections. However, whereas Leibniz had strewed his philosophical ideas about without any attention to organization,[1] Wolff proceeded systematically to expound his own natural—or rational—the-

ology. A variety of deism, his theology could hardly support the orthodoxy of theologians, but instead glorified human intellect and natural
laws that human reason has discovered in the world. Faith had no
place; truth is established only by a chain of logic, which must have
mathematical certainty—that is, subject to proofs that proceed from indisputable axioms and definitions through data given by experience to
logical conclusions. Wolff also vigorously rejected all supernaturalism.
Everything must have its conclusive reason—in philosophical terms its
"sufficient cause" (der zureichende Grund)—and knowledge of the world
is not enhanced by useless speculations about final or original causes,
or a prime mover. Newton, despite his mechanical view of the universe,
remained a deeply religious man, and believed that God was the Creator of His perfect clockwork, the universe. He even accepted the conventionally calculated time of Creation, 4004 B.C., for the idea of
evolution was as yet completely unknown.

It seems as if many ages lie between this new scientific viewpoint
and the Pythagorean mysticism of Kircher, Werckmeister, and his pupil,
Johann Walther, who transmitted their sense of awe to Bach. Yet, at
the time that Werckmeister published his neomedieval reflections on
the nature of music, Newton's *Mathematical Principles of Natural Philosophy* had already begun to revolutionize the traditional European
conception of the cosmos; Wolff was the first to bring this enlightenment into the German universities.

Although this deism did not inevitably lead to skepticism and athe-
ism, it was obviously incompatible with Protestant theology and far
removed from the latent awareness of noncognitive, intuitive knowledge often felt by artists, philosophers, and some scientists. He sought
enlightenment through science and reason, unbounded by adoration for
the Unknowable "that passes human understanding." His natural theology had no place for biblical concepts, and he makes no mention of
Christ or of any of his teachings or of the Old Testament, in his treat-
ments of God and of the human soul. His theology is concerned only
with the problem of the soul and reason *versus* this mechanical universe,
the nature of the mind *versus* that of matter, and eternity *versus* finite
existence.

Most historians of philosophy (for example, Kuno Fischer, Wilhelm
Windelband, and Hegel) do not regard Wolff as a truly speculative philosopher, for although he was a disciple of Leibniz, he failed to penetrate the idea of the pre-established harmony by which Leibniz had

described the metaphysical nature of the Godhead. For Leibniz, this harmony consisted in God's power of perpetually creating the objective world of mental presentation (as it appears for man) and existence (as it issues from God's mind). Leibniz conceived the pre-established harmony as antecedent to existence and preconditioning it, rather than as preceding it within a succession of time. Where Leibniz had attempted to describe nature as an intrinsic part of divine reason (the absolute mind), as the realization of reason, and as the immanent purpose of God's exstence, Wolff, like all deists who thought of God as outside the world, could conceive of thought only as the process of human reasoning. Thus he interpreted Leibniz' immanent purpose of God from the standpoint of human understanding also, stating that God created this wonderful mechanism for the purpose of man's adoration and for his maintenance. (This parochial and vulnerable point was heartily ridiculed by Voltaire, a deist of a different variety.)

So Wolff's philosophy was unsympathetic to the truly speculative philosopher as well as to those of religious temperament, but his rationalism influenced quite a few in Bach's immediate environment. Among them were his colleague, Gottsched; Marianne von Ziegler, who wrote several fine libretti for Bach's cantatas; Johann Adolph Scheibe, the organist who criticized Bach's art after he had been rejected as organist under Bach; Lorenz Mizler, a strange pupil of Bach and the most ardent rationalist of all; and his rector, Ernesti.

Wolff's immediate influence upon literature and art was negative. His vapid sobriety failed to inspire poets and musicians, failed to stir their hearts with spontaneous intuitive ideas. Instead, Gottsched occupied his mind with criticism and the creation of rules for poetry. Mizler tried to discover the "sufficient cause" of musical esthetics, and Ernesti wanted to abolish music altogether as obscuring those "clear and distinct" purposes of factual education.

It is not difficult to see why certain disciples of this "enlightenment" regarded music as an obstruction to clear thinking and understanding. Clarity of understanding—the true object of man's life—required one to distrust emotion as well as all reasoning that cannot be conclusively proven. In disregarding the conception of the soul rising out of Leibniz' idea of the pre-established harmony and the monads—that were conceived as individualized universalities—Wolff harks back to a Cartesian dualism in which the soul consists of the rational and the empirical, and the demands of the empirical determine the process of reasoning.

The theologians were equally justified in their fears of Wolff's effect on religion. His natural theology rejected all miracles as contrary to the mechanical clockwork world created by a rational God. In his *Rational Thoughts about God, the World, and the Soul of Man*, Wolff writes:

The world and all that it contains are the means through which God accomplishes His ends, because they are machines. From which it is clear that they become a work of God's wisdom, because they are machines. Whoever, accordingly, explains everything in this world rationally, as one customarily does with machines, he is led to the wisdom of God.[2]

If in a world everything takes place naturally, it is the work of God's wisdom. On the contrary, when things occur that have no reasonable ground in the essence and nature of things, then they happen supernaturally or through miracles, and thus is such a world . . . a work of power, and not of wisdom.[3]

Wolff is still more daring and to the point when he develops the idea that this intelligent machine is a much greater miracle than any breach of God's own natural laws. It is not possible that God has done natural as well as supernatural wonders, "and therefore are the latter either fictitious or natural phenomena that one takes for supernatural by want of understanding."[4] He exalts that "now we have a criterion by which we distinguish true miracles from fictitious ones. . . ." This iconoclastic idea seriously undermined religion, and when Lutheran theologians began to incorporate Wolffian philosophy into their work it constituted a retreat of orthodoxy. To reconcile orthodoxy with natural theology unbelievable examples of sophism were conjured up, and rationalism emerged victorious.[5]

With the university students this transparent but shallow stream of systematic thought at first found enthusiastic response. Thousands flocked to Wolff's lecture rooms. The theological faculty was in despair over these gullible infidels but was powerless to remove its adversary, who was a royal appointee.

King Frederick William I, the semi-barbarous King of Prussia, father of Frederick the Great, inadvertently relieved them of this troublesome colleague. He had more interest in his tall soldiers than in disputes among his professors, but listened to the cunning advice of his court tutor, who in his clever intrigue played the role of a court jester. This sophistic wit interpreted Wolff's idea of the pre-established harmony to the king as a kind of fatalism, in which man has no free will. He convinced the king that such dangerous ideas, should they spread among the soldiers, might encourage desertion, which they could argue was the pre-established will of God. The enraged king immediately gave orders that Wolff should leave Prussia within two days on penalty of death. The theologians, who had prayed and preached against Wolff's brand of enlightenment, saw in this sudden dismissal the protecting hand of God. Francke, the Pietist, publicly and loudly thanked God on both his knees for this deliverance from evil.

But a professor's chair was immediately found for the rational theologian in Marburg. Moreover, the scandal caused such a stir that the Academies of Science in London, Paris, and Stockholm honored him with membership; and Peter the Great made him vice-president of the Academy in Petersburg. These honors moved the king to withdraw his decree against Wolff and invite him to return, but Wolff stayed safely out of Prussia until the king died. When Frederick the Great took the throne in 1740, one of his first acts was to recall Wolff. This enlightened prince could be trusted, and Wolff returned to Halle.

The era of theological supremacy in the German universities came to a close with Frederick, who himself had absorbed all of French and English Enlightenment, and who received Maupertuis and Voltaire as guests at his court. From these higher strata of society and learning the modern movement spread to the rest of the population, and the new conception of education in the institutions of higher learning soon filtered down to the *Gymnasia*. However little Wolff has contributed to the discipline of philosophy or science, his influence was one of the chief causes that led German education away from the theological purpose of learning to the primary pursuits of the sciences and positive factual information.

Ernesti fervently hoped to accomplish this emancipation at the Thomas School. All over Germany the importance of school music dwindled together with the diminishing prestige of theology. During Bach's last years the hours for musical training in the *Gymnasia* everywhere began to be shortened, and more and more time was assigned to academic studies. By the close of the century the student-singers were replaced by professional outsiders. Even under Ernesti's father, the tradition of awarding scholarships solely on the basis of musicianship had begun to weaken. Outstanding academic students were receiving special favor.

How doggedly Bach fought for the preservation of this musical tradition in the Thomas School shall soon be seen. According to his providential outlook this new academic emphasis reflected only personal sins and errors of arrogant young men. There is no direct evidence of his response to other phases of the Enlightenment but the few data and hints that are available—the contents of his library, statements about his erudition by his contemporaries, and an examination of his intercourse with leading intellectuals in his environment—point toward his persistent orthodoxy. The consistency of his religion and the character of his art also reveal the nature and direction of his attitude toward the new era.

23

WOLFFIAN PHILOSOPHY

THE contents of Bach's library strongly suggest that he had no interest whatever in any but orthodox ideas. Not a single book represented even the most elementary phase of the new movement. Of French literature Bach was singularly ignorant. His knowledge of the language was less than adequate, and German translations had not yet appeared in Germany.

Two men of the younger generation have dropped hints of Bach's utter indifference to the new rational philosophy that they themselves valued highly. One of them was Johann Adolph Scheibe, who in 1738 wrote a spiteful, impertinent pamphlet against Bach, after he had applied in vain for the post of organist at the Thomas church. In a long tirade criticizing Bach's "turgid and confused" style, his excessive ornamentation,[1] and the extreme difficulty of execution, he gives the following reason for this incomprehensible art: "How can a man be faultless as a writer of music who has not sufficiently studied natural philosophy, so as to have investigated and become familiar with the forces of nature and of reason?"[2] Since Bach was not versed in natural theology or deism, he was not a man of sufficient culture to write "with feeling and expression."

Disregarding Scheibe's lack of artistic judgment and his personal rancor, and the asinine philosophic conclusions, we are interested in the remark as another indication of Bach's indifference to the new thought. Most certainly Bach had not "studied natural philosophy"; and it must have been true that Bach had paid no attention to Wolffian rational theology at a time when his mind was filled with the genuinely mystic beauty of the *B Minor Mass*. Whatever rumors about this new "heresy" may have reached his ears, he remained oblivious of them. But Bach's cause was taken up by an able amateur musician and teacher of rhetoric at Leipzig University, Professor Birnbaum, in an article that now serves as a source of valuable information regarding Bach's art of ornamentation,[3] but does not deny the spiritual, nonrational foundation of his art. The article drew forth rebuttals and answers by others and created quite a stir in all of Germany, but throughout it all Bach kept serene silence.

The other remark about Bach's indifference toward the new philosophy is more veiled, and in fact, misleading. It was made by Bach's pupil Lorenz Mizler (1711-1778), who wrote the closing four sentences of the Obituary (Necrology), the oldest biographical document of the master, composed primarily by Carl Philipp Emanuel Bach and another pupil, Johann Friedrich Agricola. Mizler writes, "Our lately departed Bach did not, it is true, occupy himself with deep theoretical speculations on music, but was all the stronger in the practice of the art."[4] Although Mizler may be referring here to the speculations of Kircher and Werckmeister, or to the first volume of Fux' *Gradus ad Parnassum* (which Mizler translated into German "under Bach's very eyes," as Spitta relates), it is most probable that this vainglorious eccentric in music and musical speculation was referring to his own dubious theories on composition, a curious amalgam of Wolffian rationalism.

Lorenz Mizler

It seems especially pertinent, while we are piecing together a picture of Bach's reaction to rationalism, to understand how some of his pupils diverged from his orthodoxy when they embarked on their own careers. Mizler particularly moved drastically away from his master's position. Among the many pupils of Bach, most of whom made excellent and well-deserved careers, Mizler cut a strange and somewhat ludicrous figure. He never reached enough proficiency as a musician to attain a professional position; his 24 odes were ridiculed by Mattheson and Scheibe, who considered them "so bad that they brought disgrace upon the printer for exposing such miserable scribblings to print."[5] According to Scheibe this opinion was shared by Telemann.

Lorenz Christoph Mizler (1711-1778) absorbed the traditional musical and theological program of the *Gymnasium* at Anspach. But

his interest in the new philosophy was aroused early by the persistent
fulminations against Wolff and Leibniz by the theologian Georg Ludwig Oeder, who regarded them as the originators of all modern evil.
From 1731 to 1734 Mizler studied philosophy and mathematics at the
university in Leipzig and music under Bach. There he came under the
influence of the Enlightenment, mainly through Gottsched's lectures on
French literature and the Leibniz-Wolffian philosophy. During Mizler's
years as a student Gottsched published his own resumé of the entire encyclopedic philosophy of Wolff in two volumes, entitled *Weltweisheit*
(World Wisdom). After his studies in Leipzig Mizler studied law and
medicine for two years in Wittenberg, but music, mathematics, and the
new philosophy continued to fascinate him, and he devoted the rest of
his life to "enlightened" speculations on music, and since he was not
free of vanity, to the propagation of his new ideas.

Upon his return to Leipzig in 1736 he published a monthly magazine,
the *"Neu eröffnete musikalische Bibliothek"* (The Newly Inaugurated
Musical Library), and in 1738 he organized a society of the musical sciences *(Societät der Musikalischen Wissenschaften)*. Its aim was to advance the "science" of music. Just as Gottsched had traced the esthetic
appeal of poetry to rational and natural causes grounded in Wolffian
thought, and after the manner of Boileau, from these causes had established rules for future poets, so Mizler challenged the members of his
learned society to find the proven cause of musical esthetics in reason,
mathematics, and natural laws. It should be possible, he was sure, to
calculate the effect of chords and melodies upon the soul, and on the
basis of these mathematical results establish esthetic rules for composition. This blend of French and Wolffian rationalism would thus lift
genius and musical instinct from its dark prison of subjectivity into the
light of reason and make the technique of musical creation common
knowledge. In 1739 he offered a prize to anyone who could demonstrate
scientifically why parallel fifths and octaves are offensive in contrapuntal writing. Many allegedly scientific proofs were offered by theologians, allegorists, and rationalists alike, but none proved satisfactory to
Mizler. He wished his society to be another academy for the foundation
of musical criteria based upon the new philosophy of Enlightenment.
His Wolffian motto was *"Conscia mens recti famae mendica ridet"* (The
mind, conscious of the right vocation, laughs at lies). Such a search for
truth may be laudable in the realm of "enlightened" religion, but how it
can be applied to music is not at all clear.

Mizler wrote a dissertation in which he claims to demonstrate that music is a science, and should be part of philosophy. In the Middle Ages also music was called a science, and even Bach still employed the term often since he regarded it as a branch of learning in the service of religion. But during Bach's lifetime music came to be generally accepted as an art—a practice for its own end. Mizler's endeavor therefore sounds reactionary, a historical retrogression. In fact, he supports some of his views with quotations from Kircher. However, he rejects Kircher's analogies based upon Pythagorean mysticism, and he no longer looks upon mathematics as the cause of phenomena, but attributes a certain symbolical significance to this science. Drawing upon Leibniz for support of this viewpoint, he writes:

According to his [Leibniz'] view it [music] is an unconscious arithmetic exercise of the soul, that does not know that it calculates, because much takes place in indistinct and nonsensous perceptions, . . . Even when the soul is not aware of calculation, be it as pleasure arising from consonances or as displeasure from dissonances.[6]

Mizler often mentioned a project for a book entitled "Uses and Advantages of the Wolffian Philosophy for Music" (Nutzen und Vorteil der Wolffische Philosophie in der Musik). His philosophical prattle echoes Gottsched's Weltweisheit, which in turn resounds with all the pedantry and unimaginative sobriety of Wolff's Rational Thoughts.[7]

Mizler sought fame and immortality as the discoverer of new natural laws of music on a mathematical basis, as Newton had discovered them in cosmology. He was convinced that just as science could reveal the efficiency of the world conceived as a machine, so the mechanical secrets and the natural laws of composition could be discovered by scientific means. He even envisioned a work entitled "The Thoroughbass Machine" (der Generalbassmachine).

Mizler mistrusted all spontaneous creation of the musical mind. His musical mathematics never reached any clarity, however, and his scientific dreams and desires hovered between conceptions of Kircher and the rationality of Wolff, while in Bach's and his own time musicians had already freed themselves from mathematics. Werckmeister, despite his calculations of split commas, was actually depending on his ear for the tuning of his clavier. (And as we have said, Pythagorean calculations had even less practical value for Bach, although in his Weimar days he had been fascinated by Werckmeister's metaphysical and mystical speculations.) Mizler's philosophical speculations were of a very different nature from those of the pious Werckmeister, who dutifully absorbed them into his Lutheran theology and made them an integral part of faith. Mizler attempted to explain the mechanism of the musical soul through the application of the law of sufficient cause upon composition. His speculations, growing out of Wolffian deism, tended to destroy orthodox theology.

For Bach, the genius engaged in the reality of musical creation, Mizler's speculations must certainly have appeared as theoretical shadow plays and futile but dangerous investigations. In a footnote to his translation of Fux' *Gradus ad Parnassum* Mizler says, "According to the reasoning of the immortal Newton the assumptions and teachings of Kepler regarding his *Harmonia Mundi* are false."[8] Bach undoubtedly had read these words, for at the time he commented that the counterpoint in Fux' *Gradus* was too strict and confining; he probably kept silent about the speculative part of this work.[9] For the truth of the speculations of Kepler or Newton, of Werckmeister or Mizler, was secondary to the spiritual truth of Bach's own orthodox faith or to its flowering in his art. Bach dealt in eternal metaphysical (ontological) realities, and could ignore Mizler's intellectual exercises.

Mizler did succeed in attracting some famous musicians, including Bach, to his *Correspondierende Societät der Musikalische Wissenschaften* (The Corresponding Society of Musical Sciences). His vanity was flattered by such members as Telemann, Gottfried Heinrich Stölzel, Carl Heinrich Graun, Sorge, and even Handel. Mattheson was approached, but this fiercely independent critic-composer-author had no patience whatever with Mizler's musico-philosophical endeavors. Bach waited a long time before he condescended to accept an invitation to join. He yielded to Mizler's urging, but C. P. E. Bach later made this comment about it to Forkel:

It would hardly be worthwhile to mention that in 1747 he became a member of the Society of the Musical Sciences, founded by Mizler, did we not owe to this circumstance his admirable chorale *Vom Himmel Hoch komm' ich her* (From Heaven High Do I Descend).

He presented this chorale to the Society on his admission, and had it engraved afterward.[10] Bitter maintains that this work served as a formal test for admission, while Handel and Graun, on account of their fame, were admitted "on their merits" (*aus eigenen Bewegung*). Bach also presented the society with a puzzle canon that the learned members were unable to solve at the time.[11] In a puzzle canon only one voice is written out; the place of entrance for the other voices must be calculated. In the case of a triple canon, it takes an initiate of unusual ability to find its solution. Mizler with all his "science" was not the man for such a task.

Bach's Sons: Modern in Orthodoxy

Several scholars have given evidence suggesting that Bach's sons eventually left the strict orthodoxy of their early home life, but the direction of their lives and work indicates the strong and steady influence of the faith of their father. Bach's son Friedemann is reported to have befriended Mizler, and to have been inspired by his interest in mathematics.[12] Both Friedemann and Carl Philipp Emanuel studied at the Leipzig University—Friedemann in 1729-33, and Emanuel in 1731-34. Both chose to pursue law courses, which Emanuel continued at the University of Frankfort-on-the-Oder. Their program included mathematics, three branches of law, logic (*Vernunftlehre*), and philosophy,[13] which Friedemann studied under Jocher and Ernesti.

The influence of Ernesti was not unduly disturbing to the orthodox Bachs, for at this early period in his career the rector was taking a carefully diplomatic approach to theological matters. A book he wrote in defense of the Lutheran dogma of the Holy Supper dates from that time.[14] Not until 40 years later—in his school regulations of 1773—did he boldly advocate instruction in natural theology. When the two brothers studied in Leipzig their father was still on friendly terms with Ernesti; in 1733 the young rector stood godfather to Sebastian's son Johann Christian, later known as the London Bach.

It is sometimes held that later, when Friedemann lived in Halle, he was influenced by natural theology. This assumption is based only on the lack of religious fervor in his church music. This lack, however, plus his small output of church music, must be ascribed to the animosity to music that was prevalent in the pietistic church of Halle, rather than to Friedemann's inclination toward Wolffian philosophy.[15]

Bach's sons did not cause their father any anxiety over their spiritual corruption. On the contrary, the loving and proud father had reason to rejoice in the harmonious development of these two talented young men. Even the environment of Frederick the Great's court did not divert Emanuel from his parental Lutheranism. After 28 years of service in the sophisticated court he eagerly accepted the vacant post of cantor in Hamburg, where in 20 years he produced an enormous amount of church music, including no less than 20 Passions. Perhaps his setting of Christian Gellert's *Geistliche Oden und Lieder* in 1757 points to a slight leaning toward rationalism. But Gellert, who followed the model of French poetry, was not affected by Wolffian philosophy. He was more of a true poet and a more truly religious man than his colleague, Gottsched.

Johann Christoph Gottsched

One of the strongest protagonists of the Wolffian enlightenment was the university professor Johann Christoph Gottsched, the poet who had provided Bach with the text of the *Mourning Ode for Queen Eberhardine.* He had been Mizler's and Ernesti's philosophy teacher, and he was the author of *Weltweisheit,* a resumé of Wolff's philosophy. Bach occasionally visited his home, but the contact was made chiefly through Mrs. Gottsched, who was an accomplished musician and who took lessons in composition from Bach's talented pupil Krebs. Bach's acquaintance with Gottsched was probably extremely formal and superficial—perhaps even a bit strained. For not only were the two men separated by a wide chasm of two opposing philosophies—of which they must have been painfully aware—but also because Gottsched had written some pointed remarks about the vocal style of cantatas that cannot have pleased Bach. Spitta doubts that Bach could "have had any very warm sympathy with a man who was so emphatically antagonistic to opera"[16] but Bach might well have overlooked Gottsched's criticism of opera[17] for he himself was not a great enthusiast for this form of art. He never wrote an opera (unless one classes the little Coffee Cantata as a miniature comic opera), and although Bach maintained a cordial personal friendship with the Dresden opera composer Hasse and his celebrated wife, the beautiful prima donna Faustina, he seems to have considered his friend's musical works only for light entertainment. At times he would invite his sons to visit Dresden to hear some of the "merry tunes" at its opera.

More likely what offended Bach was the professor's criticism of cantatas in his *Versuch einer Kritischen Dichtkunst* (Essay on a Critical Art of Poetry). In the second chapter he severely criticizes and ridicules the style of musical treatment of the text that today we call baroque. He has

no respect for the librettist who lowered the art of poetry to accommodate composers: "The more the music gained, the more the poetry
thereby lost. . . . If the ear got to hear a lot, reason was offered all the
less to think thereby."[18] The rationalistic attitude in these words is only
too apparent.

He further ridicules the use of recitatives and arias, especially the *da
capo* aria:

As not all poetic lines were easy to set to these twisted ornaments, they let
these lines sing off and pray off mechanically, so that the singers could all
the better prepare themselves for the next more artificial strain. This last
thing they called Aria.[19]

He attacks Menantes (pseudonymn for Bach's librettist Hunold) saying
that he has given:

. . . a mass of rules and made who-knows-what secrets out of them, that no-
body understands, unless he is a great connoisseur of music. All these result
in saying that the poet must be a slave to the composer, and must not think
or say what he wants, but write so that the musician can let his caprices be
heard right well.[20]

When he hints at the foolish adoration of the librettist for the composer, probably referring to Henrici, the adored composer can be no one
but Bach. And no other musician wrote in such style that:

By an extravagantly wasteful musical art the work of poetry becomes invis-
ible, or so hidden that it is not discernible. . . . This happens mainly when
through countless repetitions of a line, half-hours are spent; when single
words are so dragged out and expanded that the singer has to breathe ten
times, and cannot be understood by his audience for the endless trills.[21]

After this tirade he then gives considerable praise to Handel, Graun,
and Hasse, but never even mentions Bach. Clearly he had no love for
Bach's art. He praises the "Critische Musikus" of Hamburg (Mattheson), who had given such "reasonable rules" for vocal writing[22] and
who we remember criticized Bach for the "unreasonable" repetition of
"*Ich, Ich, Ich*" in Cantata 21, "*Ich hatte viel Bekummerniss*" (I Had
Much Sorrow).

Reason and nature shape the musical esthetics of Gottsched, Scheibe,
and Mattheson, and also form the typical criteria in Boileau's judgment
of "good taste." The new esthetics of rationality actually reached Mattheson from France and England (he was connected with the English

legation), more from reading Newton, Locke, and French writers than from his compatriot Wolff. And despite these influences Mattheson adhered to the formal religion of the Lutheran church. Others of the new movement, whose musical ideas must have reached Bach's ears more and more frequently, were not so orthodox in their faith and adopted more of Wolff's philosophy.

Bach met the damaging incursions into his art by these enlightened estheticians with serene composure. He avoided theoretical discussions with them. Although famous musicians were welcome and frequent guests in his home, their conversations must not have centered on the new musical esthetics. Bach took to battle only when the domain of his church music was invaded by irreverent intruders. Then his defense was stubborn, methodical, and implacable. Art was the manifestation of truth and ultimate reality, and needed no polemics. Musical creation merged into one with the act of faith.

24

CONFLICT WITH AN "ENLIGHTENED" RECTOR

At about this point in Bach's life an open clash, lasting more than two years, between two personalities representing the old and new cultures began. It was instigated by the self-admitted enemy of music, August Ernesti, who undertook the rectorship of the Thomas school late in 1734, when Gesner, staunch friend and supporter of Bach's musical ideals, left for a university post at Göttingen. A year earlier he foresaw the danger of Ernesti's cultural leanings and wisely took steps to strengthen his own position.

Bach Courts the King

After King August II died, on February 1, 1733, Bach applied to his son August III for the title of Royal Court Composer, for such an attachment to the head of the state would immeasurably enhance his prestige in the eyes of his employers. As an example of his skill in composition he submitted two movements of the *B Minor Mass*—the *Kyrie* and the *Gloria in Excelsis*. A letter that accompanied this gift clearly shows the object of his application:

At the same time I solicit your Majesty's powerful protection. For some years past I have exercised the directorium of the music in the two principal churches in Leipzig, a situation in which I have constantly been exposed to undeserved affronts, even the confiscation of the *accidentia* due to me, annoyances not likely to recur should your Majesty be pleased to admit me to your *Capelle* and direct a *Praedicat* to be issued to that effect by the proper authority.[1]

The application did not receive immediate attention for the king was involved in the same political difficulties in Poland that had plagued his father. Political affairs and military conflicts kept him much too preoccupied to attend to such minor matters as bestowing a title upon a cantor. But three years after the application had been filed it finally was honored.

Meanwhile Bach found several opportunities to demonstrate his art to the royal family. On August 3, 1733, he performed a cantata for the king's birthday; on September 5, a more elaborate work was performed for the birthday of August's son. For this unhealthy and lame crown prince the ever helpful Picander constructed a eulogistic poem ironically entitled "The Election of Hercules" *(Die Wahl des Hercules)*. The music for this insincere piece of poetry (except for recitatives and final chorus) is that of the *Christmas Oratorio*, which was performed a year later. Which was the original and which the parody poses a difficult question.

Three months later a Bach cantata celebrated another royal birthday. *Tönet ihr Pauken* (Sound ye Tympanies) was performed in honor of the Queen-Electress Maria Josepha. A daughter of Emperor Joseph I, she was the sister of Maria Teresa (the imperial successor to the father), and aunt of Marie Antoinette, the fateful Queen of France. The cantata in honor of this noble lady sings of the triumphs in Poland (triumphs that at the time were still rather problematical and that were finally achieved by Peter the Great rather than by the unwarlike August). This cantata shares four movements with the *Christmas Oratorio*.

In 1734 Bach demonstrated his talents to the royal house on four more occasions: at the crowning of August as Polish king on January 17; at his birthday on August 3; and on the celebration of his "election" to the Polish throne on October 5, when the king himself traveled to Leipzig and heard the cantata *Preise dein Glück, gesegnetes Sachsen* (Praise Thy Fortune, Blessed Saxony). For this occasion the city of Leipzig was illuminated with 600 burning wax torches carried by university students; cannons were fired. In this incongruous setting Bach's *Christmas Cantata* and *B Minor Mass* music was again heard, this time to laudatory rhymes by Christian Clauder.

Praise ye thy fortune, fair Saxony blessed! God doth the throne of thy Prince firm sustain! Happy thy land! Give thanks to Heaven! Now rev'rence the hand by which thy fortune is daily increased And all thy borders in surety remain!

The irony of such exultations is painfully apparent when one remembers how Saxony was being ruined by the former king, the present one, and the corrupt minister Brühl, how part of its territory had been sold to buy soldiers for these ruinous Polish enterprises, and how both kings forsook the Lutheran religion for their greed of power and lust.

That the music of such sacred works as the *Christmas Oratorio* and the *B Minor Mass* should be used to glorify unworthy monarchs would seem the height of insincerity, if the people of Bach's world had the same political consciousness as Westerners of the twentieth century. But the librettist was perfectly in tune with those days of absolutism when he wrote, "Are we not justified . . . to recognize thy glorious doing as God's in thee fulfilled." He simply states the idealistic psychology of his time. This illusionary and sublime relation between the citizen and his government is difficult to understand, today; then, it was not an insincere gesture.

Ernesti Becomes Rector

Meanwhile on November 18, 1734, Ernesti was promoted to the position of rector of the Thomas school. He was 22 years younger than Bach but had none of the respect a more humble young man would have shown to a venerable celebrity. Instead, he was aspiring to further his own ideals of education, which were at sharp variance with those of Bach. He was completely indoctrinated in Wolffian philosophy, which was far removed from Luther's conception of "good works," and had no use for music. In a curriculum written much later for his school laws he prescribes the study of philosophy for the higher classes, specifically "the doctrine of the human soul, which comprises the foundation of the doctrine of reason and morals, as well as the doctrine of concepts in general." The expression is typically Wolffian, but the influence is even more obvious in the following:

In the highest classes thereupon shall be undertaken the doctrine of reason and the natural theology and moral philosophy, whereby its correspondence to revealed religion is to be demonstrated. In reference to moral philosophy Gellert's moral lectures shall be used.[2]

(Although Gellert, a professor of literature at the Leipzig University, was not an avowed Wolffian, he was of the French school of Enlightenment, in which morals were pragmatically defined.) The enmity between

Johann August Ernesti, rector of Thomas School from 1734-1759, whose modern ideas on education resulted in a deterioration of his relationship with Bach

Bach and Ernesti thus went deeper than the open disputes over music in the school and was rooted in the conflicting philosophies of the two men.

The emancipation of education dreamed of by Ernesti would have been impossible in 1734. It would have amounted to a fierce but surely unsuccessful revolution, because the traditional school laws were firmly legalized and backed up by the state machinery of councils, the consistory, and, above both, the supreme power of the sovereign. The Saxon government, with its Catholic kings, tended to be conservative; Bach generally won his disputes by appealing to established regulations and ancient tradition. The Enlightenment movement glided practically unnoticed past their lives of carnal enjoyment and their pastimes of war and the chase.

Ernesti was not a man patiently to bide his time, even though he was forced to postpone some of the major elements of his reform. He took every opportunity to disparage the music students, to infringe upon the cantor's prerogatives in musical matters, and thus to impair the successful performance of the musical service. When he found a student practicing his violin he would snap, "So, you want to become one of those beer-fiddlers." He might have unsaddled a less indomitable opponent with these petty tricks, but Bach proved to be the stronger and the wiser. Still the story of the ensuing two years does not portray merely a struggle for personal authority but the tragic conflict between the last and most mighty musical representative of the age of faith and one of the younger protagonists of the age of reason and science.

During the years 1734-35 Bach's choir suffered a great loss with the graduation of seven excellent singing musicians. Among those who began independent careers were Christian Friedrich Schemelli, who later became cantor of Zeitz; Johann Ludwig Dietel, afterwards cantor at Falkenheim; Johann Ludwig Krebs, one of Bach's best pupils; and three of Bach's sons, who began their careers as organists in Dresden, Hamburg, and Mühlhausen. The seventh graduating student was Gottfried Theodor Krause. A series of troubles began over this talented young man that display both the educator and the artist in the worst personal light. Ernesti, wanting complete authority, irritated and humiliated Bach relentlessly, causing him more than once to lose his usually dignified composure.[3]

Bach had selected Krause, upon graduation, to take the post of head *praefect*, and Ernesti approved the appointment on the basis of the student's excellent academic record. The choirs this young man had to conduct were among the most undisciplined and most unmanageable. As "the evil and indecent behavior of these young students in the churches and at other sacred functions got worse and worse,"[4] Bach advised the use of force for their control, but when Krause applied the stick, the culprit precipitated a crisis by complaining to the rector. Ernesti seized this first opportunity to assert his authority over the cantor, and at the same time, to undermine his prestige with the young singers.

According to Gesner's school law of 1723, the rector was allowed to

punish the *praefect* for exceeding his prerogative.⁵ Ernesti ordered the
praefect to be thrashed in the presence of the entire student body, a
sure way to ruin his prestige when he was so much in need of support.
The ulterior thrust of this cruel punishment was aimed at his superior.
Bach, feeling responsible for the incident, had pleaded for the boy. The
implacable rector had responded cunningly; by ordering public humiliation he reasserted his authority. The unfortunate Krause begged for
permission to leave the school, but Ernesti refused him. Krause then departed secretly, leaving a few of his personal belongings behind. Since
he had been a scholarship student the school laws permitted Ernesti to
confiscate his few pieces of furniture and 30 Thalers in salary due him.

Now Ernesti, feeling confident in his new power over Bach, appointed
a new *praefect*. By a confusing coincidence this man's name also was
Krause: Johann Gottlieb Krause. Bach objected to the nomination of a
man of bad character and told Ernesti that he considered him *ein lieder-
licher Hund*, a dissolute dog. Nevertheless, a compromise was soon
reached; the second Krause was made third *praefect*. When the post of
first *praefect* again became vacant Ernesti wanted to give it to Krause.
This time Bach objected on the basis of his musical deficiency, and presumably also because he felt that Ernesti was infringing upon the cantor's prerogative to choose his own assistant conductors.

The overly detailed school laws, however, specified that the cantor's
choice had to be ratified by the superintendent *(Vorsteher)* of the school.
Bach had overlooked this minor point of law earlier when he appointed
his student Krause, and Ernesti self-righteously reported his neglect to
Deputy Mayor Stieglitz, then acting superintendent. Perhaps overawed
by the order of an official, Bach gave in and promised to reinstate
Krause. He could not fulfill this promise immediately because he suddenly departed on a two-weeks journey. Upon his return, August 11,
1736, Ernesti wrote him that he would reinstate Krause himself unless
Bach did so without delay. This threat aroused Bach, and as on previous
occasions, he chose to present his side of the case in a series of letters,
methodically dispatched first to the council, then to the consistory, and
finally to the king.

The first letter, written on Sunday, August 12, 1736, begged the
council "to instruct Ernesti in the future to act in accordance with the
usages and practices of the school," which he explained had given the
cantor prerogative to select *praefects* on the basis of musical compe-
tence "without interference on the part of the rectors." On this same

Sunday, however, Ernesti had quietly reinstated the incompetent Krause. When Bach ascended the choir loft and saw Krause at his post, he immediately replaced him with Kittler, the more efficient second *praefect*. Ernesti used the interim between the main service and Vesper to reverse Bach's orders under the threat of suspending all the singing money of the choirboys. When Bach returned for the afternoon service and saw the boys at their places, he lost his temper and chased Krause from the gallery "with loud cries and noise," a commotion that did not pass unnoticed by the congregation. Since Ernesti had given the choir-boys strict orders not to sing under anyone but Krause, they were struck with fear and confusion. Bach, however, made them sing under his pupil Krebs. All day Bach remained in a state of uncontrolled wrath over the affront. When he entered the refectory in the evening and saw Kittler there, he drove that poor lad out for having obeyed Ernesti's orders.

The next day he dispatched another letter to the council, in which he related the events of the preceding Sunday, accusing Ernesti of having "seriously weakened, if not wholly undermined my authority over the scholars in the churches under my charge. If high-handed action such as this is repeated, the *sacra* are in danger of interruption."

Meanwhile it had come to Bach's ear that Ernesti insisted upon Krause's competence. Promptly Bach wrote a third letter on Wednesday to supplement Monday's. This document is the chief source for the story. He headed it "The full and authentic history of alumnus Krause, and of the rector's attempt to force him on me as first *praefect*." With great clarity and precision Bach relates the history of the case, including reference to Krause's dissolute character and incompetence, the musical difficulties that a *praefect* has to master, and a detailed description of exactly which aspects of conducting he had so utterly failed.[6]

Two days later the council received a very lengthy letter from Ernesti stating his version of the case. He pointed out Bach's neglect of submit-ting his nomination of Krause to the superintendent, a point which might have tipped the scale of judgment against Bach. When, however, Ernesti directly contradicted Bach's expert judgment of Krause's compe-tence as a musician, he lost his advantage. Then Ernesti brought up the old contention "that he [Bach] might in general fulfill his office with more diligence," for Bach had left his post for a fortnight.

The council, undecided, took no action, but its request for another explanation from Ernesti, following Bach's urgent request that they settle the matter as soon as possible and reprimand the rector,[7] seems to indicate that the members favored Bach's position. Ernesti complied with the council's request. In this letter (September 13, 1736) he begins to lose his restraint. He malignantly questions Bach's veracity and makes some vicious insinuations against his character. There, however, the matter again remained, undecided. At last, on November 19, 1736, the much desired title of Court Composer was bestowed upon Bach. In his new office he drafted a fresh account of his grievances, to be submitted to the Consistory in Dresden, that body of supreme judges appointed by the king himself. He tactfully mentioned only the essential points of the controversy and requested their "Magnificences to protect [him] in his office, and to let Ernesti understand that he must in the future abstain from molesting him, refrain from choosing *praefects* without his consent and knowledge," and so forth.[8]

In April, 1737, the council in Leipzig finally came to a decision, one not wholly satisfactory to Bach, however. It amounted to a compromise, upholding Bach's prerogative of appointing his *praefects* but cautiously avoiding censure of the rector. Moreover, Krause was to retain his post till Easter. Thus the main issues for Bach—restoration of his professional prestige and improvement of the generally weakened position of cantor—had not been resolved. A clause in Gesner's school laws, requiring the approval of the rector for an appointment of a *praefect*, had already lowered the cantor's status. (Gesner had perhaps not foreseen this possible consequence, but the elder Ernesti had opposed this clause.)

Bach tenaciously continued the struggle. He wrote another letter to the Consistory, pointing out that these new school laws had never been ratified by this higher court, and therefore "had never been legally in force." Bach shrewdly commented that the present rector Ernesti had discouraged their publication because of this, but that he nonetheless tried to enforce laws that suited his purposes. He finally requested the Consistory:

. . . that Rector Ernesti be admonished not to interfere with me, that my dignity, which has been lowered, be forthwith restored in the eyes of the scholars, and that I receive your support in my opposition to the new school laws, in so far as they prejudice my office and impede my duties.

But the Consistory continued to delay. After two months it sent the question to the council, who shelved it temporarily. This time Bach did not give his opponents time to realign their forces. He wrote to the king himself, stating that Ernesti wanted to enforce a law that had not been ratified by His Majesty's Consistory—a law that Bach did not "accept as valid." Therefore he appealed to His Majesty:

To direct the council not to molest my prerogative of appointing the prae-fecto chori musici, jure quaesito, but to uphold my prerogative therein . . . to be pleased graciously to order the Consistory here to demand an apology from Rector Ernesti for the indignity put upon me, and to charge Superin-tendent Dr. Deyling to instruct the student-body to show the respect and obedience due to me.[9]

The government took immediate action; the Consistory ordered the council to examine the charges. To all appearances the matter was then settled but we do not know the actual outcome since no record of the council's decision has been found. But the importance of this tedious battle of accusations and counteraccusations lay in its psychological effect on Bach. Soon after this he retreated from the bitter philosophical mêlée at the school and devoted himself entirely to his musical art.

By coincidence the king came to Leipzig during Easter of 1738—about the time Bach had written his appeal to him—for the celebration of Princess Amalia's marriage to Charles IV of Sicily. Bach provided a serenade on a poem by Gottsched, "*Wilkommen, ihr herrschenden Götter der Erde*," (Welcome, Ye Reigning Gods of the Earth). The com-bination of Gottsched's grossly exaggerated homage to mundane power with the metaphysical quality of Bach's music (most probably again in-corporating parts of religious works) created a thoroughly baroque phe-nomenon in the worst sense. Bach's score to this work has not been pre-served, for the same obvious reason that there are no scores for similar musical occasions; they never existed.

Bach's Liturgical Art Work: The Final Chapter

Bach lost his zest for writing church music after this long conflict with Ernesti. A year later, at the approach of Easter, 1739, Bach printed and distributed the libretto for the Good Friday Passion, as he always had done. This time he received an order from the council to withdraw it, on the petty grounds that he had not submitted its publication for official approval. Bach immediately expressed contempt for any further duties as church composer, an attitude he would not have taken had his rela-tions with church authorities been fully restored to mutual respect and cooperation. Bach replied that he had acted according to previous cus-tom, but that he did not care whether the performance of the Passion took place at all, for it was nothing but a burden—*ein Onus*—to him anyway.[10] He treated the annual Ratswahl cantata with similar indifference by using a work, *"Wir danken Dir,"* performed 8 years before.

From this time on no liturgical music flowed from his pen. Only one cantata—No. 16, *Du Friedensfürst, Herr Jesu Christ* (Thou Prince of Peace, Lord Jesus Christ)—is listed as having originated after 1740. In general, Bach now used old material. He also neglected his school teaching so much that in January, 1740, the council looked for an assistant to instruct the schoolboys in the theoretical subjects Bach no longer chose to teach.[11]

Despite the irritations, interferences, and the unsympathetic milieu of colleagues and even churchmen influenced by natural theology and the Enlightenment, Bach had brought his liturgical art work to completion. He had provided every detail of the Lutheran service with the proper music. Had his surroundings been more harmonious he would perhaps have evolved the chorale-cantata into a still higher form, and thus have completed a sixth series of cantatas. But from now on he would devote himself to the perfection of his musical science for its own sake and "for the glory of God," whom he now served within his private musical domain, for the purpose of instructive demonstration and as a spiritual and musical discipline.

He studied orthodox theology with more intensity now, for the one addition to his library made after 1736 was *Schola pietatis oder Übung der Gottseligkeit* by Johann Gerhard (1582-1637), one of the classics of Lutheran orthodoxy.[12] Gerhard had studied under Leonhard Hutter, whose catechism Bach had memorized in his school days. He also was an enthusiast for the earliest form of Pietism, then represented by Johann Arndt, with whom he was friendly. This association led to suspicions that his work bore a heretical tinge of mysticism, but in Bach's time he was cited as one of the best representatives of orthodox Lutheranism.[13] Gerhard aimed at proving that Lutheran evangelism is the true catholic church; and he found the true Christian principles in ancient writers such as Augustine, Anselm, Bernard, and Thomas á Kempis. The five volumes of *Schola pietatis* are representative of the trend of Bach's thought in his later years, which had not deviated one iota from his earlier orthodoxy, however slightly it leaned toward Pietism.

Gerhard's conception of the relation between philosophy and theology is diametrically opposed to that of Wolff and Gottsched, and others surrounding Bach. Gerhard said the science of philosophy had "neither the right to be an organ for religious insight or religious experience, nor to furnish means of proof for a specific dogma, nor to attack it on its own premises.[14] He does not categorize theology as antiphilosophical, only as hyperphilosophical inasmuch as its origin—meaning, of course, biblical revelation—is higher. If theology were set up against philosophy, Gerhard reasoned an insuperable dualism would invade the spiritual operations of the mind. (This is exactly the dilemma of the age of Beethoven.)

Gerhard along with Christoph Scheibler (1598-1653), another author found in Bach's library,[15] thus recognized an inner and mutual relation between the two faculties, and he favors the restoration of their co-efficacy, which Luther had distrusted. Both appeal to the church fathers, who made use of philosophy to support their faith, but as an auxiliary, if not a subservient organ of spiritual realization.

His acquisition of the *Schola pietatis* is an indication of Bach's fidelity to the revealed theology of the orthodox school—and some might say of his desire for an antidote against the independent, rationalistic philosophy that surrounded him in Leipzig. But it is more likely that he needed no such medicine. Scheibe's remark that Bach had not "investigated the forces of nature and reason" is to the point. There is no evidence that he tried to familiarize himself with the new deism, nor even with any tenet of natural philosophy. His acceptance of the Lutheran doctrine of original sin and the earning of grace through faith was so complete that any part of natural philosophy must have seemed entirely irrelevant to him.

After his victory over his employers he withdrew himself, as much as his office allowed—and quite a little beyond that—from his superiors, "these strange folk with little care for music in them," as he had long ago observed. Perhaps he became detached from the church. Perhaps he withdrew into a more private form of religion suggested by his reading of Johann Gerhard. Bach expressed a certain contempt for his own surroundings at the Thomas Church, it is true; this does not mean that he digressed from the Lutheran church as the embodiment of truth.

25

MUSICAL DISCIPLINE: AN ACT OF WORSHIP

THE last ten years of Bach's life were by no means years of human or spiritual loneliness. His Lutheran theology enriched his inner life with joyful confidence in the promise of grace. In contrast, Beethoven vacillated among various philosophies—Catholicism, a bit of oriental mysticism, and a romanticized deism of Schiller and Kant—ultimately experiencing true spiritual revelation, strikingly evident in his last piano sonatas and quartets, as well as in his *Missa Solemnis* and *Ninth Symphony*. Beethoven's religious revelations were of a more individual character, born from personal tragedy. The note of spiritual struggle is never absent in either his compositions or his writings; he suffered from an agonizing feeling of isolation caused by the loss of his hearing and by his unfulfilled craving for human affections. Bach's philosophy, on the other hand, was the steady rock of faith throughout his life, and he fully enjoyed the satisfaction of human relationships; tragedy was no precondition for his religious experience.

Bach had all the blessings of a good life, the fulfillment of human desires, and the recognition of his talents in his last years. At home he was surrounded by his family, his faithful Anna Magdalena and five of his children, plus his cousin Johann Elias Bach,[1] a man in his thirties who acted as tutor to the young children and as Bach's secretary. (The letters of Elias, a divinity student at Leipzig University, give glimpses of the mutually devoted Bach family.)

During this period Bach traveled frequently to perform organ concerts, usually as part of the inauguration of a new or newly renovated organ. In August, 1746, he visited the city of Zschortau, where he was invited to examine the new organ built by Johann Scheibe. A month later he went to Naumburg where Zacharias Hildebrandt of Leipzig had built a new organ.[2] He also traveled to Dresden for the ceremony of his royal appointment and to visit Count Keyserling. (These absences from his duties at the Thomas School probably vexed the officious council, but by this time these gentlemen seem to have resigned themselves to the stubborn independence of their "incorrigible" cantor.)

Bach's home was often cheered by visitors, for as Emanuel wrote in his short autobiography: "It hardly ever occurred that a master of music would pass through Leipzig without making the acquaintance of my father and letting himself be heard by him." These visits may have been interrupted intermittently when the military campaigns of Frederick the Great curtailed travel. Since in those days battles were localized and of short duration, however, travel was not completely suspended as it has been in recent wars.

In 1741 Bach went to Berlin to visit his son Emanuel, who had just become the court accompanist to the Prussian king. His stay was cut short when Johann Elias wrote urging him to return as soon as possible for Anna Magdalena, in the early stages of pregnancy, was in critical condition from hemorrhaging. Fortunately she recovered, and half a year later bore her last child, Regina Susanna, who lived until 1809.

A Private Performance for the King

In May, 1747, Bach again visited Berlin. This time his two devoted sons, Carl Philipp Emanuel and Friedemann, proudly presented their famous and adored father to Frederick the Great. Historians differ considerably on the circumstances under which Bach was introduced to the king. Forkel, who relied upon the report of Bach's son Friedemann, relates that Bach was repeatedly and urgently invited by the royal amateur musician—Frederick was a flutist of considerable ability. When at last Bach traveled north, accompanied by Friedemann, and announced himself, the King, impatient to hear the famed master Philipp Emanuel had often bragged of, did not give him time to change from his dirty traveling clothes into his black cantor's garb, but immediately led the weary traveler to his new fortepianos.

Authorities Spitta and Terry suspect that Friedemann embellished his tale a bit. The commonly accepted version relates that Bach had gone to Berlin not to seek more fame, but to meet his daughter-in-law and his first grandchild, born in 1745. When the king heard that Bach was in the vicinity, he summoned him to Potsdam, giving up the customary daily concert in which he himself participated, and led Bach from room to room to try out the new fortepianos that Silbermann had built. This account is verified by a report of May 11, 1747, in the *Spenerische Zeitung*.[3] According to this and all further evidence Bach improvised on all the instruments and then asked His Majesty to submit a theme for the improvisation of a fugue. Frederick gave him a rather long theme[4] which Bach immediately developed "in the most learned and interesting manner"[5] without the slightest preparation. The king then asked Bach to improvise a fugue in six voices on the same theme. According to Forkel, Bach explained that "not every theme is suited for such full-voiced treatment" and chose a theme of his own for this six-voiced improvisation. The *Spenerische Zeitung* reports that he complied with the king's request on the next day, when His Majesty took him to see the organs in Potsdam.

Upon his return to Leipzig, Bach composed an entire set of ten canons, one sonata in four movements, and two ricercars on the "royal theme." The second ricercar is a six-voiced fugue thus fulfilling in a more complete and polished form his extemporaneous execution of Frederick's request. When Bach published this *Musikalische Opfer* (Musical Offering), with the music printed by Johann Georg Schubler of Zella St. Blasii near Suhl, in Thuringia, he humbly stated in his dedicatory preface to the king that he had "noticed very soon that, for lack of necessary preparation, the execution did not succeed as well as such an excellent theme required."

The ricercars and canons bear Latin titles and inscriptions that echo an age long vanished. A quaint and rather cryptic acrostic on the word *ricercar* precedes one of these compositions:

> *Regis*
> *Iussu*
> *Cantio*
> *Et*
> *Reliqua*
> *Canonica*
> *Arte*
> *Resoluta*[6]

To the *Canon a 2 per Augmentationem, Contrario Motu* (two-part canon in augmentation and contrary motion) he adds: "*Notulis Cre-*

scendibus crescat Fortuna Regis" (As the notes grow, so may the King's fortunes). In the next canon, which modulates in successively ascending keys, he writes *"Ascendenteque Modulatione ascendat Gloria Regis"* (And as the modulation rises, so may the King's glory). It has been observed that for an artist the purpose and perpetual exercise of creation grows out of simply his pleasure in this exercise. This is always true in part, but even now that Bach had stopped writing for the liturgy, he continued to believe that the purpose of music was the glory of God, and that all other endeavors were but the idle jingling of Satan. In Protestant theology the glory of God meant more than singing His praise, and Bach, believing that his musical creations came from God and that he was only an earthly agent, accepted the divine source of all his music, whatever the occasion for writing it had been. God's glory, indeed the very quality of divinity, is embodied in His own creation.[7]

A Spiritual Sacrifice

The works of Bach's last eight years lead the thoughtful student and the sensitive listener into greater depths of spirituality than any of his earlier works. But a certain esoteric character also marks these compositions. The works were not written for the liturgical service, were not accompanied with lyrics to suggest a particular religious thought, in general did not specify what instruments were to be used for their performance. These qualities combined with the extraordinary predominance of contrapuntal intricacies—canons, puzzle canons, mirror fugues —lead many to categorize the works of his last years as studies in the musical theory and pedagogy. And indeed the display of skill for its own sake forms an undeniable aspect of this period's art. But this aspect is only one, and not the essential one, in his last works. From the time Bach gave up writing for the church he submitted himself to a rigorous discipline, and for a twofold reason: besides his desire to sharpen his acuteness in contrapuntal perception and quick insight into all possible moves of the intervals and their harmonic combinations the metaphysics of Werckmeister, Kepler, and their Pythagorean mysticism had taught him that this very discipline dealt with fundamental, primary elements of the divine spirit. The infinite possibilities of intervallic combinations within the movement from dissonance to consonance *was* the creativity of the divine spirit. "Anyone could do as well, if only he work as hard as I have," he told his students.

Musical discipline now became a spiritual sacrifice—an act of worship. By this means his personal creativity found identity with the highest creativity. The assiduous exercise of contrapuntal problems took on the sanctity of a religious exercise, and so completely did he devote himself to it that his skill indeed resembled the performance of miracles. For who had ever heard of a human creature spontaneously improvising a six-voiced fugue on a theme submitted to him only a few moments earlier? No wonder connoisseurs stood in awe for such transcendental skill, and no wonder that most of his pupils regarded Bach as something of a saint. It was said that one of his pupils, Johann Christian Kittel (1732-1809), kept hanging over his harpsichord a picture of Bach, covered with a curtain that was removed only at special occasions. No one was to behold the master's face except in an attitude of special reverence.[8]

The extant works of the years 1742-1750 consist of the *Goldberg Variations;* the second volume to the *Well-Tempered Clavier;* a prelude and fugue for organ; one cantata (perhaps composed at an earlier period); some canonic variations upon the chorale *"Vom Himmel Hoch da Komm' Ich Her";* a canon for the Society of Musical Sciences; another for J. G. Fulde; the *Musical Offering* for Frederick the Great; six chorales taken from various vocal movements in his cantatas and transcribed for the organ (printed by Schübler); 18 chorales in various styles; a canon in seven parts probably dedicated to the Thuringian organist Johann Schmidt in Talla; and *The Art of the Fugue,* a collection of 14 fugues and 5 canons.

Four major compositions of this period—the *Goldberg Variations* (1742), the *Musical Offering* (1747), the canonic variations on the chorale (1746-47), and *The Art of the Fugue* (1749-50)—were composed on one theme or one song only. The 30 individual pieces of the *Goldberg Variations,* including nine canons, have the same bass, and are thus forced to follow its modulations. Such treatment is particularly demanding when canons are superimposed upon a given bass. The royal theme is variously set in the *Musical Offering* as canons, ricercars, and a sonata in four movements are all made of the royal theme; the five canonic variations also are on the short hymn *Vom Himmel Hoch.* The entire *Art of the Fugue,* which comprises 18 compositions, four of which are canons, was written on one short fugal subject. From this one theme a dozen countersubjects were derived. Both the theme and its countersubjects appear in inversions, rhythmic variations, and even in the form of a hochetus.[9] In total there are 133 metamorphoses of the short fugal subject and 17 countersubjects.

Canons

No less than 33 canons of widely varying technique are found in Bach's last works, and he must have written innumerable others as trial and preparation. Canons appeared often in earlier works, but now he made an intensive study of them. Formerly his canons were made on short phrases of hymns, often rhythmically modified to make strict imitation possible. As we have seen, these canons had symbolical implications. In the canons of his last years he submits himself to infinitely more binding restrictions, demanding much more discipline than needed for fugue writing.

In a canon in unison the second voice sings or plays the same notes as the first, but enters either immediately after the first note of the leader (the *dux*) or later, depending on the possibilities of the counterpoint. In a puzzle canon the singer or instrumentalist has to discover that place of entrance himself, as well as the fitting interval for the companion chant (the *comes*), a task that may indeed be puzzling. (The puzzle canon that the learned society of Mr. Mizler received from Bach was never solved by any of its members. Now several solutions are extant.)[10] In a canon in the second above or below the *dux*, the melody is duplicated a second higher than in the leader. Similarly a canon can be built on a fifth or seventh or other suitable interval. Usually when the answer is given in different intervals, rather than in unison or octave, it does not duplicate the intervals exactly as they appear in the leading voice, for if it did so, it would play in a different key from the *dux*, and we would have a piece in two simultaneous keys. The half-steps and whole steps of the scale consequently have to be those of the key of the *dux*. In the *canone in moto contrario* every interval of the melody moves in the opposite direction of that in the *dux*, while the given bass imposes its usual restriction upon the harmony. Other types of canons include the crab canon and canon in four parts.

In the *Goldberg Variations* Bach composed canons answering in all intervals—a second, a third, a fourth, and so on. The writing of these demanded even more rigorous discipline, since the canons have to harmonize not only with each other but also with the bass. This bass may at times show some ornamental modification, but it never deviates from its basic harmonic and modulatory scheme throughout the variations.

In the five canonic variations on the hymn *"Vom Himmel Hoch da Komm' Ich Her"* the self-imposed restrictions are tightened. The *cantus firmus* of the chorale is always present in the first four variations, while the canons play against it, first in unison, then with the answer in the lower fifth, always making melodic allusions to the original melody. Then a canon in the upper seventh appears between the two lowest voices, plus a free melody in the alto and the chorale melody in slow notes in the soprano, thus binding all other voices to obey its course of harmonic demand. In the fourth variation the soprano duplicates the entire tenor in twice its tempo, while the *cantus firmus* is heard slowly in the bass, and a free voice is added in the alto. In the fifth variation the alto sings the original chorale melody, while the tenor intones it a measure later, inverted, and a sixth lower. Then the two sing the entire chorale again in canon, but this time a third apart, the alto singing the inversion and the tenor the original. Now the bass and the tenor take up the inverted canon, the tenor answering in the upper second, while two free voices are added to the ensemble. All this time the bass has played a free accompaniment. Next an inverted canon in the ninth appears between the outer voices. All four phrases of this Christmas hymn have thus been faithfully and consistently presented in inverted canons and in four different intervals. As a conclusion Bach has fitted all four simultaneously in diminution (twice its tempo) as well as in inversion.

In his *Musical Offering* 10 of the 13 compositions present canons on the royal theme—in two voices, with the royal theme as obligato. In the fifth canon of *Musical Offering*, however, Bach lets the second voice play in g minor, while the leader plays in c minor. This bitonality is then corrected by a third voice, a rhythmically varied and somewhat ornamented version of the royal theme. This theme then dominates the tonality and leads the harmony away from any bitonal chaos. The royal theme itself appears in several succeeding sections, modulating from c minor, through d, e, f sharp, g sharp, b flat, back to c minor. Each time it acts as the stabilizer of the bitonality. Number 8 is a mirror canon with the answer in the inversion. The next is a crab canon (*canon cancrizan*), a device as old as the science of counterpoint. Here the second voice plays the first one backwards, the last and the first notes beginning and ending simultaneously. This type of canon does not require as much skill as it may seem,[11] and since the ear cannot spontaneously detect and follow it, it is a sort of music for the eye. Bach wrote only one.

A four-part canon is generally written on such simple material that no particular difficulties arise. But in the *Musical Offering* Bach wrote one on the royal theme, which had to be ornamented in such a way as to make this difficult feat possible. It displays an unprecedented skill that can have been acquired only by faithful perseverance.

Many have judged the canon technique to be an idle game, like working a jigsaw puzzle. Indeed it is, except when endowed with disciplinary, artistic, and spiritual purpose. For Bach, the constant exercise of fitting and adjusting all possible positions resulted in a miraculous command over contrapuntal technique and sensitivity to the infinite harmonic possibilities of every note. He thus acquired the greatest freedom under the severest restrictions. This assiduous discipline enabled him to express depths of spiritual experience never sounded before or after, depths that suggest individual religious revelation.

This sacred purpose was lost during the era of the Enlightenment and its resulting style of *Empfindsamkeit*.[12] In Hamburg, Bach's son Carl Philipp Emanuel, who was temporarily influenced by the English Enlightenment, told the music historian Charles Burney that he regarded canons as "dry and despicable pieces of pedantry, that anyone might make who would sacrifice his time to them."[13] Even though he later recanted his derogatory opinion of polyphony, the statement is typical of the enlightened composers.[14]

The Art of the Fugue

In *The Art of the Fugue* the self-imposed discipline seems to have relaxed to the point that Bach seems to surrender himself to the ecstacy[15] of musico-religious revelation that was the reward for all these preparatory disciplines The "ground of being and meaning" seems to have been revealed to Bach in the cognitive form of musical creation. The idea that the nature of music was associated with Pythagorean concepts of mathematical proportions, which described the cause and ground of the existing world, had been deeply ingrained into Bach's mind by his reading of Kircher and Werckmeister. Even if Bach was no longer knowingly influenced by these Pythagorean-Keplerian notions, he always believed in music as a source and instrument of revelation.[16]

Bach gave no directions whatever for the performance of *The Art of the Fugue:* no tempo markings, no dynamics, and no suggestion of instruments to be used. He was occupied in his last years with musical substance only, not with its presentation. And musical substance here applies only basic, primary elements of music. Bach conceived most of his music, and particularly this work, independent of the expressive demands and limitations of particular instruments. (However, in the *Musical Offering* he did assign its sonata to the traverse flute which Frederick the Great played, a violin, and the unspecified continuo, which would have been played on one of Frederick's pianofortes by Carl Philipp Emanuel. Elsewhere in the work his only suggestions are for violins in two of the canons.)

Our manner of absorbing music is entirely different from that of Bach's time when the connoisseur admired mainly craftsmanship. Our romantically conditioned esthetics expect emotional reaction. We need an imaginative interpretation. A mere reading on a rather neutral instrument like the Silbermann fortepiano, or on an inexpressive harpsichord, or an organ without much registration, does not satisfy us. The work reaches us best with modern orchestration of modest size—and a modest and truly reverential attitude. Nevertheless, it is no coincidence that this, and all the works of Bach's last eight years, can be played on keyboard instruments, with or without pedal boards. This fact should not lead to the conclusion that Bach wrote *The Art of the Fugue* only for the harpsichord; as we have said he did not write *for* an instrument. But with the exception of one pedal point and the mirror fugues (which would require two keyboards), no stretches of more than an octave are ever required of either hand. Consequently if he had so desired, Bach could have played the work on one keyboard alone, without the use of a pedal board, although it seems most improbable since he owned three of them.

Bach never finished *The Art of the Fugue*, for death overtook him. The last part, *Contrapunctus XIV*, is broken off in the 239th measure. In the autograph is found a little note by Carl Philipp Emanuel Bach, saying: "During the writing of this fugue, where the name BACH in the countersubject is introduced, the author had died." The theme using the notes representing B (German for b flat), A, C, and H (German usage for B natural), appears like a musical signature in the last fugue of his life, technically the most perfect and as an art work the most profoundly significant of his mystic faith.

Bach had taken steps toward its publication before he completed the work. The finished parts were engraved by an unknown craftsman, perhaps one of his own sons.[17] On the back of Bach's manuscript of the last and uncompleted fugue, corrections of the engraving in the master's handwriting, appear. Carl Philipp Emanuel published the work posthumously.

The Persevering Spirit of an Era

During the composition of this great monument of contrapuntal art Bach's health was breaking down. For some time his eyesight had been failing, gradually dimmed by cataracts. This approaching blindness was much aggravated by a paralytic stroke that he suffered in May, 1749.[18] At that time the end appeared to be near. The Saxon prime minister, Count von Brühl, had been informed of the impending death of the Thomas cantor, and with indecent haste he arranged the formal examination for Bach's successor. Barely a month after Bach's stroke "the examination for the future post of cantor at St. Thomas was delivered with greatest applause by Herr Johann Gottlob Harrer, *Capell Director* of His Excellence Secret Council and Prime Minister von Brühl."[19]

But Bach not only recovered and lived for more than a year more, but once more rallied his fighting spirit in the defense of the sacred art of music against the aggression of enlightened academicians. This time he took up the cause of one of his favorite pupils, Johann Friedrich Doles, who for five years had been spreading the teachings of his revered master as cantor at the *Gymnasium* of Freiburg in Saxony. Then a new rector, Johann Gottlieb Biedermann, launched an attack upon music which, like Ernesti, he considered a dangerous hindrance to academic learning.

The controversy began after a musical festival on the anniversary of the Peace of Westphalia, for which Doles composed, rehearsed, and directed the music to a Singspiel, a musical play. The successful performance was repeated several times, and the profit to this enterprise amounted to 1,500 Thaler. Apparently half of this slipped into Biedermann's pocket, for "he gave account of only half the amount."[20] When he offered Doles only 30 Thaler for his work, the proud musician declined such a niggardly offer, saying that he was content with his success. As these transactions became known, Biedermann sought to avenge his injured reputation with a pamphlet, *De Vita Musica*.[21] With distorted quotations and unscholarly interpretations of Plautus, Horace,

Cato, and others, and by historical examples such as the disreputable Caligula and Nero, this essay attempts to prove that music has a detrimental effect upon human character. Although he admits that music itself must not be damned, he believes it leads men who practice the art into dissolute lives. He warns students not to become one of "Jubal's brood,'" an oblique attack on the biblical inventor of music.

His rancorous pamphlet brought forth an immediate hail of reprisals. Johann Mattheson of Hamburg wrote no less than four pamphlets in answer to *Vita Musica*. The literary commotion soon reached the ears of Bach, and painfully aware of the problem of a music-hating rector, he too wanted to protect his pupil. Unable to take up arms himself, due to ill health, he commissioned the organist and pianoforte maker Cristoph Gottlieb Schröter (1699-1782) to write a rebuttal to Biedermann's essay. Schröter exposed Biedermann's lack of scholarship and understanding of the art of music. He expressed the hope that schoolmasters in the future would guard themselves against stooping to such base utterances.

Schröter attempted to prove that any enemy of music is necessarily "a godless blasphemer." He quoted examples of similar controversies that shook the hallowed position of music in the life of the German *Gymnasia* and churches. Bach too recognized this growing danger. About this time he set an old cantata, *"Oh holder Tag, erwünschte Zeit"* (O Blessed Day, Wished-for Time), to a new text which reads in part: "Alas, beloved muse of harmony, sweet as thy music is to many ears, yet art thou sad and standest pensive there; many there be who scorn thy charms. . . . But calm thyself, fair muse; thy glory is not dead, nor altogether banished and despised."

Bach wrote to the cantor of Frankenhausen, G. F. Einicke, that Schröter's thesis was quite to his taste *(nach meinem goût)* and that he would have it published. "Should any more refutations follow, as I presume they will, I don't doubt that the author's *Dreckohr* will be cleaned and made more fit to listen to music." The word *Dreckohr*, meaning filthy ear, is a pun on the word *director*, *rector*, to wit, Biedermann.

At that time Bach's secular cantata, *"Phöbus und Pan,"* written 18 years before, was again performed, probably by Michael Schmidt, a student in Leipzig since March 12, 1749. Bach grasped the opportunity to take a dig at both Biedermann and Ernesti by changing a few lines. In the last recitative, the original text reads:

> And now, Apollo, strike the lyre again
> For nought is sweeter than thy soothing strain.

This he now altered to:

> Now strike the lyre with redoubled power,
> Storm like Hortensius, like Orbilius' roar.

and in another place to:

> Storm like Birolius, like Hortensius roar.

The implications were obvious to the learned world: Orbilius is the schoolmaster in Horace, and Birolius represents the name of Biedermann by way of an anagram, Birolius—Orbilius; Hortensius was a rival of Cicero. Since Ernesti was the famous editor of Hortensius, the learned world of Leipzig could also identify this well-known music-hater.[22]

A few months before Bach's death Schröter's article appeared in print, but with some harmless alterations,[23] a new title, an extension of a quotation from a writing by Mizler, and a notable improvement of the punctuation and the paraphrasing. Schröter took offense to all these changes. Although the tenor of the article had not suffered in the least, his literary vanity seemed hurt. He accused Bach as the culprit, and asked Einicke to write Bach about it. Bach protested his innocence, and suggested that the printer was guilty. Schröter persisted, angrily accusing Bach, in another letter to Einicke, of evading the issue. The changed title indeed has the ring of Bach's trend of thought: "Christian Judgment of the Programmatis, edited by Mr. Biedermann, etc." The improved paraphrasing and punctuation, however, are not typical of Bach's old-fashioned style, and Bach would hardly have quoted Mizler to support his own ideas.

Bach was spared further annoyance with trifling human vanities, for another paralytic stroke brought him to the portals of eternity. Six months before Bach's death a renowned oculist, the Chevalier John Taylor, had passed through Leipzig on his way from London to Vienna and had treated the master. The confusions and inaccuracies of the account of his visit to Bach in his memoirs are glaring. He tells his reader that Bach was 88 years old and the teacher of Handel. Although he claims to have diagnosed Bach's eyesight as beyond repair because of his previous paralytic stroke, he has just said in a preceding sentence that the celebrated master at Leipzig "received his sight by my hands."[24] Carl Philipp Emanuel Bach, in his father's obituary, puts the blame of Bach's decline upon the famous oculist, for he says: "Not only could he no longer use his eyes, but his whole system, which was otherwise thoroughly healthy, was completely overthrown by the operation and by the addition of harmful medicaments and other things."[25]

It is painful to contemplate that in his last days, when his art reached the loftiest heights of spiritualization, the divine light of this genius should have been clouded by the shadows of human strife, like the petty battle with Schröter, but the artist's stronger and predominant mood of serenity was very little disturbed, as evidenced by the *Art of the Fugue* and the last chorales.

Last Work: Testimony to a Life of Faith

The last half year of his life Bach continued working at his *Art of the Fugue* and at a revision of a set of chorale-preludes intended for publication. Constantly struggling with his ever weakening physique and his failing eyes, he managed to write out 15 of his chorale-preludes "in his own strong handwriting." Only an artist convinced that his art was a form of communication with the infinite could have continued working with such unrelenting passion. The Necrology states that he had hoped to have his sight restored by the operation because he desired "to be of further service to God."

By July, 1750, Bach must have known that the end was near. He called his beloved daughter Elisabeth, "Lissgen," who had recently married, to his side. Soon her husband, Bach's pupil Johann Christoph Altnikol, also came and took the last dictations from the now completely blind composer. Three chorale-preludes came down to us in Altnikol's handwriting. Two were revisions of earlier works: "Jesus Christ Our Savior" and "Come God, Creator, Holy Spirit," a Lutheran version of the ancient, ecstatic Ambrosian hymn *Veni Creatore*.

The third proved to be Bach's last musical utterance. Like *The Art of the Fugue*, it was never completed. He had used the melody of this hymn, *"Wenn Wir in Höchsten Nöthen seyn"* (Whene'er We are in Highest Need), once before, when leaving Weimar, but now Bach chose new words to express his present state of mind. In place of the original lyrics which were filled with thoughts of doubt and finite preoccupations,[26] he selected the first and last verses of a 15-stanza hymn by Justinius Genesius.

> Before Thy throne now I tread
> Oh God, and do I humbly pray:
> Do not turn Thy merciful countenance
> from me, grievous sinner.

> Grant me a blissful end,
> Awake me at the day of the Last Judgment
> Lord, that I may behold Thee eternally.
> Amen, Amen, hear and adjudge me.[27]

The entire poem is a supplication of a dying mortal, commending his soul to God's judgment in the full and humble Lutheran faith in Christ's promise of grace. Some of its verses resound with theological overtones that reveal deeper philosophical insight than most hymns. When the poet says "Thou hast, Father, made me in Thy likeness: In Thee I live, create and soar; Perish I must without Thee," and "God, Holy Spirit, Thou highest force, Whose grace creates everything in me," he goes beyond the obvious biblical mythology. A lifelong study of theology, the neo-Platonic philosophy of Werckmeister, the Pythagorean music philosophy of Werckmeister, Kircher, and Kepler, and most of all the spiritual dedication to the discipline of his art had brought Bach to a profound realization of the essential nature of being. But this metaphysical realization did not take the form of intellectualized philosophical concepts that might have challenged his simple faith or the Lutheran dogma. On the contrary, his philosophical readings supported and made more firm his biblical faith, as his new treatment of the last chorale reflects.

In the earlier Weimar composition the melody was freely ornamented in lyrical expression of tender personal and sorrowful feelings; thus transformed by ornamentation in the lyrical Italian style the melody alone carried the purpose of the composition. But in his last chorale, at one with the metaphysical heights of *The Art of the Fugue*, the completely blind composer dictated another contrapuntal web of divine logic to the original, unadorned melody. The three accompanying voices intertwine in inverted and diminished *stretti* (in simple chorale-motet style) to the calm chant above. We are reminded at once of Luther's description of contrapuntal music as singing and dancing angels hovering around the throne of God.

But this musico-metaphysical vision was broken off in the middle, as Bach was stricken unconscious by a final stroke of apoplexy. After ten days of fever, at 8:45 P.M., July 28, 1750, he "departed gently and blissfully," as recorded in the formal language of Necrology.

Epilogue

MUSIC FOR THE SPIRIT LIVING
IN A CHANGING WORLD

THREE days later the composer was buried. There was no special service. It cannot even be proven that he was honored with the customary procession of the entire school, led by a crossbearer.[1] He was given no memorial of any sort, not even a stone. A tablet on the wall of St. John's Church indicated only the approximate location of the grave, a careless procedure that caused great difficulties when 150 years later his remains were exhumed.

The Church lost no time in replacing their troublesome cantor. One day after Bach's death, even before his interment, the council held a confidential meeting[2] to decide on the appointment of a new cantor. Among the six applicants was Bach's son Carl Philipp Emanuel, who had put in his application long before his father's death. Other famous musicians on the list included Karl Heinrich Graun of Merseburg, and Johann Ludwig Krebs, esteemed by Johann Sebastian Bach as his outstanding pupil; but all had to yield to the irresistible pressure of the infamous Count Brühl, all-powerful prime minister to August II. A year earlier he had pressed for appointment of his own private musician, Gottlob Harrer. Mayor Stieglitz reminded his fellow councilmen that "the school needs a cantor and not a Capellmeister, although he also must understand music."[3] Subsequently Harrer was chosen unanimously.

This decision evidently was kept secret for some time, because 11 days later (August 9) Count Brühl wrote another letter to the council recommending his protégé. He suggests in circuitous phraseology that

Harrer will satisfy the modern taste better than the ponderous predecessor, whose art was regarded by more recent generations as turgid
and laborious, to quote Scheibe. He praises Harrer whom "I had sent
to Italy at my own expense, not only to learn composition thoroughly,
but also to acquaint himself with the brilliant taste of today."[4] Count
Brühl, in a shrewd estimate of the council, assured them that they
would have no trouble with Harrer, "since he is furthermore a quiet
and well-behaved man."[5]

Anna Magdalena's lot was sad indeed. Since her husband had died
intestate and without funds to insure her maintenance, she was forced
to sell his estate. According to law she inherited one-third while the
remainder was distributed among the nine children. Only three of
them were living in the parental house, but soon Johann Christian, age
15 and destined to be known as the London Bach, was put under the
care of his brother in Berlin for his education. The widow thus had two
daughters to provide for, Caroline, 13, and Regina Susanna, only 8
years old. The estate—comprising a little cash, 19 musical instruments,
some silver, tin, copper, and brassware, household furniture, a few
clothes, and Bach's library of theological works—brought in 1,122
Thaler and 16 groschen.[6] Although the inventory gives the impression
of a prosperous, if not affluent family, the unlucky widow had to appeal
to the almighty council for the traditional right to live in the cantor's
home for six months after his death. Even so, she was forced to sell
some of her husband's manuscripts to augment her income, and she
spent her last lonely days ignominiously in an almshouse.

To all appearances the art of the great master sank into oblivion.
Contemporary celebrities like Telemann and the members of the Mizler
Society wrote some eulogistic rhymes about Bach's unequalled skill
at the keyboard and in his art of counterpoint, and a few newspapers
mentioned his death with respectful regret, but the general public of the
eighteenth century did not realize his greatness as a composer. At that
time music rarely appeared in print, and only a few of Bach's works
were printed during his lifetime. Of these even fewer copies were cir-
culated, and then only among connoisseurs, an esoteric group of pupils
and sons of the master. It was not until the turn of the century,
when the publishing business began to flourish and music was available to a wider public, that Bach was rediscovered. At the time of his

death only those who had actually heard him play in church or recital could appreciate this great skill.

It is hard for us in the twentieth century to excuse those many persons close to Bach who survived him but did little to preserve his musical creations. Even his sons and devoted pupils neglected the simple task of collecting and saving manuscripts of their master. Poor devoted Anna Magdalena was forced to sell pieces of her husband's work in order to survive. Bach's successor found the library of the Thomas School too cramped and so disposed of the "old style" cantatas that the master had carefully filed there, each neatly marked with its title and designated place in the liturgical year. The manuscripts were still useful as paper, and some of these masterpieces of all time found their way into meat and butter shops, where they were used as wrapping paper. Others ended up outside in orchards, smeared with tar and bound around fruit trees as protection against insects. One copy of the *Well-Tempered Clavier* was found in the Danube. Three Passions have disappeared, Spitta believes, because Bach's son Friedemann sold them for cash when in later years he held no position.[7]

In the light of these astonishing instances of apparently gross neglect of valuable art, we must remember that eighteenth-century man conceived of music solely in terms of its function. And this function—to which Bach was deeply committed—was serving God and His church. Music was not worshipped for its own sake but regarded as an integral part of religious ceremony. Music was written to be played and sung, not to be stored away in a museum or library. When music was not longer used, there was no need to keep manuscripts of it. The nineteenth century revered art for art's sake, the twentieth century is concerned with the historical view, but the eighteenth century viewed music as a medium and incitement to the knowledge of its own motivation. Music was a means to the penetration of the absolute, to the exalting awareness of the spirit. Music was not self-sufficient, even for Bach who devoted his life to it; music was a branch of science. For that reason, and because belief in the Absolute and music's relationship to it, not historical importance, was the primary concern, the need for museums and means of perpetuating music was not understood.

In 1829, when Mendelssohn performed the *St. Matthew Passion* for the first time since its composition a hundred years before, he had received his copy of it from his teacher Carl Friedrich Zelter, who had bought the score as wrapping paper sold at an auction of a cheese store. Zelter was an old man when he taught Mendelssohn. He had inherited the Bach tradition from several of Bach's pupils: Agricola, Kirnberger, his teacher, and Johann Friedrich Fasch. He became director of the Berlin *Singakademie* and is remembered today mainly for his correspondence with Goethe. He was born only eight years after Bach's death. Although a great enthusiast of Bach's immortal music, he was a son of the Enlightenment and found the religious texts of the German chorales offensive, and did not wholeheartedly admire Bach's daring and gripping harmonies. Mendelssohn, who was more sensitive to the musical and religious mind of Bach, had to purge the score of Zelter's alterations and refinements of the original.

Mendelssohn had been converted to the Lutheran faith as a young man. He was brought up in a cultured Jewish family. His religious decision was guided by the philosophy of his grandfather and that of his idealistic contemporaries, including Hegel, whose lectures he attended. His performance of the Passion penetrated deeply the emotions of the German public. It gave the impetus to a growing interest in the study of Bach's music, and to new insight and evaluation of his religious intent. Hegel, the transcendental idealist among philosophers, was present at this memorable performance. Keenly aware of history, he saw this revival as both the end of the Enlightenment and a truer estimate of Bach's Protestant genius.

Nevertheless Mendelssohn's performance would have given offense to musicological critics of today, for he was less interested in the purity of Bach's style of performance than in the intensity of its spiritual and esthetic reawakening. Mendelssohn's audiences understood music only in the idioms of their own immediate past heritage. He used massive choruses, a large orchestra scored like his own symphonies, and full-throated singers, male and female, accompanied by the pianoforte, singing with altered phrasing. He drastically reduced the length of the work. If it had been performed with the modest and meagre setting of the score and the tiny chorus of half-grown boys that was at Bach's own disposal, the work would probably never have been successfully revived.

Today we have much more historical knowledge of the original and authentic style of performance of Bach's works than Mendelssohn had when he decided to perform the Passion. But still, consistent performances in "pure style" are extremely rare. And it is questionable whether they will ever be possible—or desirable. The true rebirth of Bach's art does not depend upon stylistic purity alone. Above all it needs the inspiration of its original motivation. It is clear that we are not living in an age of faith; Bach's world does not blend easily with our own. To know Bach's music as he intended it to be heard means to know what shaped his intellectual life, what theology formed the basis for his deep faith, in short, to truly know Bach's music we must try to comprehend the spiritual forces that inspired it. Whether our world is moving toward such renewed awareness of the metaphysical essence of Bach's religion is an unanswered question. May Bach's music help us to find the way if this is our destiny.

NOTES

The following abbreviations have been used in the Notes and Bibliography:

BG: Johann Sebastian Bach. *Johann Sebastian Bach's Werke,* ed. Bach-Gesellschaft. 47 vols. Leipzig, 1851-1899 and 1926. (Vols. 1-46 reprinted: Ann Arbor, Michigan, 1947)

BR: Hans T. David and Arthur Mendel. *The Bach Reader, A Life of Johann Sebastian Bach in Letters and Documents.* New York, 1945.

DTÖ: *Denkmäler der Tonkunst in Österreich,* ed. G. Adler. Vienna, 1894—.

DTB: *Denkmäler der Tonkunst in Bagern,* ed. A. Sandberger. Leipzig, Cologne and Augsburg, later Augsberg, 1900-1938. (Zweite Folge of *DdT*)

DdT: *Denkmäler deutscher Tonkunst,* ed. R. Liliencron. 65 vols. Leipzig, 1892-1931.

Full citations for references in the Notes are given in the Bibliography.

1. Early Years (1684-1703)

1. See Schmeider, *Thematisches-systematisches Verzeichnis,* p. 461.
2. Terry, *Bach, A Biography,* p. 293.
3. Paulsen, I, 31.
4. Monroe, p. 457.
5. Monroe, p. 484.
6. Monroe, p. 495.
7. Monroe, p. 487.
8. Comenius' *Didactus Magna,* as quoted in Paulsen, I, 465.
9. Compare the "Allemande" and "Courante" of Bach's first *French Suite* with Pachelbel's *Suite in E Minor,* and Bach's *A Minor Fugue, BG,* III, 334, to Pachelbel's *A Minor Fugue.* See Spitta, *Bach,* I, 644.
10. Compare Bach's *E Major Fugue* (*Well Tempered Clavier* II) with Froberger's *Phrygian Fugue.*
11. Forkel, *Allgemeine Geschichte der Musik.*
12. Paulsen, 375.
13. During the Reformation years this text was a favorite for its moral

lessons and its edifying admonitions to justice, honesty, and wisdom. Phocylides was one of the few authors of pagan literature who was tolerated by Protestant schoolmen, since his ideas on the immortality of the soul, and even of the resurrection of the body, singled him out as an exceptionally religious mind, though a pagan. Some lines of his poems are almost identical with passages in the Old Testament, a fact that must have elated the pious schoolmasters, even as it later aroused the suspicion of modern researchers. In Bach's time scholars thought Phocylides to be a contemporary of Pythagoras, and a poet named Phocylides actually lived during the sixth century B.C.; the "Preceptive Poem," however, is now accepted as the composition of a Christian Jew who lived in Alexandria during the first half of the first century A.D. See Rudloff.

14. Spitta, *Bach*, I, 187.

15. Thomas. Curiously, C. S. Terry, who uses Thomas as his source, does not mention the history text of Buno either.

16. Terry, *Bach, A Biography*, p. 30.

17. "pestis scholae, scandalum eccleciae, et carcinoma civitatis." Terry, *Bach, A Biography*, p. 26.

18. Spitta, *Bach*, I, 188.

19. Terry, *Bach, A Biography*, p. 28.

20. Terry, *Bach, A Biography*, p. 36.

21. See Junghans, p. 6.

2. Theology in the Classroom

1. Gass, p. 4.

2. Bainton, *Here I Stand*, p. 137.

3. Luther, *Von der Freiheit eines Christenmenschen*.

4. See Zielinski.

5. "cum lacte quasi materno primo elementa purioris doctrinae Christianae imbiberit." "Leonhard Hutter," in *Allgemeine Deutsche Biographie*, pp. 476-79.

6. Gass, pp. 255, 257.

7. Gass, p. 155.

8. Edition by Wilhelm Hertz, Libr. Besser.

9. Hutter, *Compendium*, p. 73.

10. *Ibid.*, p. 101.

11. *Ibid.*, p. 102.

12. Nebel, X, 329. For examples of his anti-Calvinism see especially pp. 279-83 of the Hertz edition of *Compendium*.

3. A Lutheran Sense of History

1. Barnes, p. 126.

2. Thomas.

3. Two eminent scholars, André Pirro and Charles Sanford Terry, based their description of Bach's school education upon the discoveries of Dr.

Thomas. But Terry, in *Bach, A Biography*, does not mention Buno, or the subject of history.

4. The Catalogue of the British Museum shows that the *Historia Universalis* was issued in 1672, 1692, 1700, and 1705. The University of Illinois kindly lent me their copies of the editions of 1672 and 1700.

5. "Eine kurtze summarische Abbildung Der merkwürdigsten Geist-und Weltlichen Historien von Anfang der Welt bis auf das Jahr 1671. In annehmlichen Bildern deutlich und kürtzlich also fügestellet/ dass sowol Alte/ als junge Leute/ auch diejenige/ so der Lateinische Sprache nicht gar kündig/ leichtlich fassen und im Gedächtnisz behalten können."

6. Preuss, p. 128.

7. See Bernstein, pp. 282 ff. For instance, the following passage from *Flavius Josephus against Apion* is very close to later accounts of the Arian and Athanasian controversies of 325 A.D.: "He (Moses) represented God as unbegotten and immutable through all eternity . . . unknown to us as to his essence." Whiston, *Josephus Works*, III, Book II, 3, #17, p. 591. Even Whiston, Josephus' orthodox translator and commentator of the early nineteenth century, is slightly suspicious of the genuineness of these words, which to him "seem" to show a regard to higher interpretations and improvements of Moses' laws, derived from Jesus Christ." (III, p. 591) Although the passage about Jesus Christ began to be regarded with skepticism as early as the sixteenth century, it took about 300 years before its authenticity was generally rejected. (Bernstein, p. 286) It is safe to assume that Bach, if he knew anything at all about these disputes, regarded the adversaries of the disputed passage as rank heretics.

8. *Wars of the Jews* in Whiston, *Josephus Works*, Book V, Chap. V, p. 456.

9. *Ibid.*, pp. 420-72.

10. Luke 21:5, 6, 10, 20, 22, 23, 24. Matthew 23:34; 24, 1 ff. Mark 13:2.

11. Daniel 9:26, 27.

12. Whiston, *Josephus Works*, III, Book II, 3, #17, p. 592.

13. Although Gesner edited anthologies of several classical writers, he did not include Josephus. This was for linguistic reasons. Josephus himself admits that it was "a difficult thing to translate our history into a foreign and to us unaccustomed language." (Preface to *Antiquities*, p. 60). He wrote in Aramaic, and the Greek that Gesner found in Josephus was of inferior quality.

14. See Fellerer, 123.

15. Terry, *Bach, A Biography*, p. 203.

16. See Eitner, "Johann Gottfried Walther," p. 165. Also Gehrmann, 468. See also chapter 12 of this book.

4. Music in the Schools

1. Plato, "The Republic," in *The Dialogues of Plato*, II, 108.

2. "Zum göttlichen Wort und Wahrheit/ macht das Herz bereit/ Solch ein Eliseus bekannt/ Da er den Geist durch harfen fand." *Luthers Schriften*, p. 375.

3. "Der schönsten und herrlichsten Gaben Gottes eine ist die Musica. Der ist der Satan sehr feind. Damit man viele Anfechtungen und böse Gedanken vertreibet; der Teufel erharret irh nicht." ("Tischreden") *Ibid.*, XV, 425.

4. Paulsen, I, 19.

5. Capitlaria anno 802. Monum. Germ. Hist. Leg. i, p. 106, as quoted in Schünemann, *Geschichte der Schulmusik*, p. 65.

6. Isidori Episcopi, Gerbert Scriptoris, I, 20, cap. III as quoted in Schünemann, *Geschichte der Schulmusik*, p. 65.

7. Migne Patrologia CI, 853, as quoted by Schünemann, *Geschichte der Schulmusik*, p. 6, and by Paulsen, I, 15.

8. Luther, "Tischreden," in *Luthers Schriften*, pp. 425-34. "Wer die Musicam verachtet . . . mit denen bin ich nicht zufrieden."

9. "Ein Schulmeister muss singen können, sonst seh' ich ihn nicht an." *Luthers Schriften*, p. 426.

10. Quoted from Schünemann, *Geschichte der Schulmusik*, p. 83.

11. *Ibid.*, p. 93.

12. Vorbaum, I, 6.

13. Spitta, *Bach*, I, 187.

14. Junghans.

15. Junghans, p. 4.

16. Preussner, p. 442.

17. Brieger Schulordnung 1581, in Schünemann, *Geschichte der Schulmusik*, p. 87.

18. Junghans, p. 9.

19. Junghans, pp. 8-12.

20. Preussner, pp. 414, 445.

21. Forkel, *Allgemeine Geschichte der Musik*, II, 65.

22. Junghans.

23. Junghans counted 102 numbers in the catalogue of church compositions, plus 190 anonymous works.

24. Montanus had a printing firm with Neuber in Nurnberg. *Thesaurus Musicus* contained work in eight, seven, six, five, and four voices, by Arcadelt, Clemens, Dietrich, Ducis, Lasso, Maillard, Scandelli, Phinot, Prenner, and Depres. Montanus died in 1563, and was replaced by Gerlach. From 1567, Neuber worked alone.

25. Georg Rhau composed a Mass for the occasion of Luther's debate with Eck. Luther wrote a preface to Rhau's *Neue deutsche Gesänge*.

26. Terry, *Bach, A Biography*, p. 45.

27. Jean Tinctoris wrote the oldest musical lexicon, *Terminorum musicae diffinitorium* (Naples, 1475).

28. Ambros, III, 65.

29. Preussner, p. 424.

30. Schering, *Bach und das Musikleben Leipzigs*, II, 64.

31. *Ibid.*, p. 39.

32. *Ibid.*, p. 47.

33. Terry, *Bach, A Biography*, p. 36.

5. *The Education of an Organist*

1. Böhm, *Samtliche Werke*; also, *DdT*, Vol. 45. Compare with *BG*, XXXVIII, 101, p. 43; 85, p. 257; 17, p. 242.

2. Preface to Böhm, *Samtliche Werke*.

3. The Gregorian modes were replaced very gradually by the major and minor tonality. The change was achieved more quickly in France than in Italy.

4. See Chapter 8.

5. *BG*, XXXVIII, 3, p. 243.

6. Sonata in A minor (*BG*, XLII, 29) after the Sonata I of *Hortus Musicus* (pp. 1-18); Sonata in C Major (*BG*, XLII, 42) after Sonata XI of *Hortus Musicus* (pp. 32-38).

7. Leti, *Histoire de la Maison serenissime de Brunswick* (1687), p. 327, as quoted by de Beaucaire, p. 104, and by Pirro, *L'Esthétique de Bach*, p. 423.

8. Horric de Beaucaire, p. 163.

9. Wolffheim, p. 427: "Im Jahre 1700 wird die Truppe aufgelöst; Bach hat also keine Oper Mehr in Celle gehört."

10. Horric de Beaucaire, p. 163.

11. Büttner.

12. Also see the transcriptions of portions of Lully's operas as keyboard pieces by d'Anglebert.

13. The organist Friedrich Wilhelm Ulrich was engaged in 1699 at a yearly salary of 12 Reichsthaler. Wolffheim, p. 429.

14. Terry, *Bach, A Biography*, p. 51.

15. Wolffheim, p. 428. Louis Gaudon was engaged in 1698.

16. See André Raison, "Livre d'orgue," Vol. 2 of *Archives des maîtres de l'orgue*. . . .

17. *BR*, p. 310, and Chapter 10, p. 186.

18. *BR*, pp. 215-24.

6. *Beginning of a Musical Career (1703-1706)*

1. "Figuralorganist" means an organist capable of improvising variations on chorales, and of reading figured basses; also one capable of producing concerted music.

2. *BR*, p. 150.

3. Terry, *Bach, A Biography*, p. 56.

4. Spitta, *Bach*, I, 220.

5. A small size violin, used for high parts, tuned C, g, c, a, or b flat, f, c, g.

6. A five-stringed large viola, tuned d, g, d', g', c".

7. A harpsichord with gut strings.

8. A Thaler: 75 Groschen; a Florin: 21 Groschen. In 1914 a German Mark was worth 24 American cents.

9. Weissgerber.

10. Spitta, *Bach*, I, 226.

11. *Ibid.,* 228.

12. *Ibid.,* 226.

13. Weissgerber.

14. Kluge's *Etymologisches Wörterbuch der deutschen Sprache.*

15. *Ibid.*

16. See Schmieder, *Thematisch-systematisches Verzeichnis,* p. 437.

17. A harpsichord with the usual two keyboards and an additional set of large keys, similar to the organ pedals, to be played with the feet.

7. Bach and Buxtehude

1. Curt Sachs, in his *World History of the Dance,* p. 373, dates the importation of the "new dance" about 1640. It came into Spain from Central America, and at that time was feared as a dangerous moral influence, like the saraband. The passacaglia was derived and indistinguishable from the chaconne, which was not much older and was also regarded as the "most passionate and unbridled of all dances."

2. Compare Buxtehude's Passacaglia, Peters ed., No. 4449, p. 59, measures 3 and 5, to Bach's *Passacaglia in C Minor* (BG, XV, 289), meas. 10-25; Buxtehude's meas. 8-17 to Bach's 26-33; Buxtehude's 33-45 to Bach's 33-41; Buxtehude's 62-69 to Bach's 130-38; Buxtehude's 66 to Bach's 82-99.

3. Peters 4449, p. 28.

4. Peters 243, p. 20. BG, XV, 92.

5. *Fugue in D Major, DTB,* IV, p. 43.

6. Spitta, I, 316; see also BR, p. 51.

7. Terry, *Bach, A Biography,* p. 70.

8. BR, p. 52.

9. Pirro, *Bach,* p. 37, refers to them as "soudains caprices d'accompagnement."

10. Bitter, I, 75, "dass bissher gar nicht musiciret worden." "Musiciret" implies the combination of choral and instrumental music.

11. *Ibid.,* 76, in the *Protokol.*

12. *Ibid.,* 77, in the *Protokol.*

13. Spitta, *Bach,* I, 327.

14. Bitter, I, 77.

15. Forkel, as quoted in BR, p. 302.

16. Spitta, *Bach,* I, 335.

8. Ornamentation

1. Girolamo dalla Casa, *Il vero modo di diminuir* (1584). Riccardo Rognoni, *Passagi per potersi essercitare nel diminuire* (1592). Giovanni Luca Conforto, Giovanni Battista Bovicelli, Giovanni Bassano, Lodovico Zacconi, Ganassi del Fontega also wrote on the subject. There are excerpts from these authors in H. Goldschmidt, *Vokalen Ornamentik,* and Kuhn, VII (1902).

2. See Kuhn, p. 70.

3. Printz, *Satyrischer Componist,* Cap. XII.

4. Dannreuther, I, 162.

5. Printz, *Satyrischer Componist*, Theil II, p. 49, par. 18.

6. Goldschmidt, *Vokalen Ornamentik*, p. 58.

7. See examples from the works of Diruta, Andrea Gabrieli, etc.

8. Printz, *Satyrischer Componist*.

9. *BG*, XLII, 29, 42.

10. Reincken's *Hortus Musicus*.

11. As quoted in Goldschmidt, *Vokalen Ornamentik*, p. 229. The work from which he quotes is *Regole, Passagi di Musica* (1593).

12. The first ornament is categorized thus by most theorists because of the repeated beats of *g* and *f*. Johann Andreas Herbst gives examples of several exclamations (the third ornament in the Palestrina example), each expressing a particular emotion. (See Allerup, who gives musical illustrations of the *exclamatio languida*, the *exclamatio effectuosa*, the *exclamatio viva*, and *piu viva* (quoted from Eitner in Dannreuther, I, 83).

13. *BR*, p. 238.

14. *Ibid.*, p. 246.

15. In *Essay on the True Art of Playing Keyboard Instruments*, Carl Philipp Emanuel Bach relates that "Embellishments may be divided into two groups: in the first are those which are indicated by conventional signs or a few small notes; in the second are those which lack signs and consist of many short notes" (p. 80, par. 6). Referring to the latter he says: "they are too variable to classify. Further, in keyboard music they are usually written out."

16. "Clavier-Büchlein vor Wilhelm Friedemann Bach, angefangen in Cöthen den 22 Januar A. Dom. 1720." *BG*, XLV, 213.

17. Aldrich, *Ornamentation in Bach's Organ Works*, pp. 1-2.

18. Nohl, p. 59. C. P. E. Bach, *Essay*, pp. 5, 12, 17, 18, 42, 85.

19. C. P. E. Bach, *Essay*, p. 85, par. 26.

20. *BR*, p. 310.

21. The symbol for mordant in Couperin's text is ↓, a sort of downward arrow. It is called *pince*. Bach used the sign ⋏⋏ for the same ornament, and called it mordent.

9. The Organ

1. See Gerbert von Hornau, III, 329.

2. The *Krummhorn* "was a slender cylindrical oboe ending in a curve that was reminiscent of the folk instrument with an ox horn." It was the oldest European instrument fitted with a wind cap and since the organ stop for *Krummhorn* is first mentioned in 1489, on a Dresden organ, the instrument itself must have been in existence before this time. The *Rauschpfeiff* belongs to a German family of oboes, *Rauschpfeiffen*, with narrow bores. *Schreyari* were "loud, shrill, double-reed instruments with a tapering bore and a reed-concealing cap." See Sachs, *The History of Musical Instruments*, pp. 320-23.

3. Gurlitt, p. 12.

4. In his annotations to Adlung, *Musica Mechanica Organoedi*, edition of 1768. Also see *BR*, p. 258.

5. *BR*, p. 236.

6. Already in 1610 the pedals of St. Martin's in Cassel had a powerful array of stops: Principal 32 feet, Octave 16 feet, Subbass 16 feet, Bourdon 8 feet, Rauschpfeiff 4, 2, ⅔. Trombone 16 feet, Trumpet 8 feet, and Cornet 2 feet. See Dufourcq, p. 145.

7. See note 2 for descriptions of *Rauschpfeiff* and *Krummhorn*.

8. "[I]n European artmusic, the rough horn of an animal was replaced by a wooden or ivory tube. This became the curved Cornet . . . or *Krummer Zink*." See Sachs, *The History of Musical Instruments*, p. 325, for a drawing.

9. *BR*, p. 314.

10. Praetorius, *Syntagma Musicum*, II. Johann Mattheson's edition of Niedt's *Handleitung zur Variation* gives over 60 different organ specifications. Niedt, *Musikalische Handleitung, Variationen des General-Basses*. Adlung, *Musica Mechanica Organoedi*.

11. Dufourcq, p. 119.

12. Adlung, *Musica Mechanica Organoedi*, I, 211.

13. *BR*, p. 258.

14. Praetorius, *Syntagma Musicum*, II, 99.

15. *Musica Enchiriadis*, attributed to Hucbald (840-930). See Reese, pp. 125, 254. The chanting in these parallel intervals then was considered as "sounding agreeably together." Whether this medieval art derives its name "organum," meaning instrument, from the organ is doubtful.

16. The new function of the mixtures, however, was not scientifically understood until the time of Gottfried Silbermann (1683-1753) and his school which included his brother Andreas of Strassburg and his pupil Zacharias Hildebrand. It was the epoch in which Jean Philippe Rameau (1683-1764) also took his departure from the scientific knowledge of the partials or overtones to construct his new theory of harmony. As we have seen from Adlung's criticism, Silbermann reduced the mixtures more than anyone had done before him. Whether Bach was in sympathy with this conception is impossible to ascertain by documented evidence; but considering that Adlung's editor Agricola was Bach's pupil, and in view of Adlung's veneration for Bach, apparent throughout his book, we may assume that Adlung's taste is a faithful reflection of Bach's.

17. *BR*, p. 290.

10. Bach in Mühlhausen: Encounter with Pietism

1. In an augmented and corrected edition of his father's book on the subject, a work written under the influence of Pietism. See Pirro, *Bach*, p. 45.

2. These passages were chosen from II Samuel 19:35 and 37; V Moses 33:25, I Moses 21:22; Psalms 74:16, 17, and 19; besides allusions to Deut. 33:25; Gen. 21:22; among others. A stanza from Johann Heermann's "O Gott, du Frommer Gott" was used to an anonymous melody. These various

quotations were woven together with a few lines of Eilmar. For full English text see Terry, *Bach's Cantata Texts*, p. 519.

3. Jordan, *Chronik der Stadt Mühlhausen*.

4. According to the custom of music publishing that prevailed throughout the eighteenth century, only the vocal and orchestral parts were printed—not the full score; the first printed editions of Haydn's symphonies follow the same tradition.

5. Its specifications can be found in Adlung's *Musica Mechanica Organoedi*.

6. Democratic inasmuch as the city council and the mayor were elected and rotated.

7. Spitta, *Bach*, I, 363; Pirro, *Bach*, p. 45.

8. The dates of the editions are taken from Terry, *Bach, A Biography*.

9. *Pia Desideria*, p. 18.

10. *Allgemeine Deutsche Biographie*, VII, 233-35.

11. *Encyclopedia Britannica* (11th edition), XXI, 593-94.

12. "Prediger sind Saugammen der Gemeinde, sollen gesunde, süsse Milch geben, so müssen sie zuvor selbst die Speise des göttlichen Wort schmecken, kauen, dauen, und ins Leben wandeln." *Allgemeine Deutsche Biographie*, XXII, 555-56.

13. Yale University graciously lent me this book through the interlibrary loan system. This collection is based on a Leipzig printing of 1498, which is the one Luther probably read. Tauler wrote between 1300 and 1361. His original text (ed. Leopold Naumann, Berlin, 1833) is in old low German (*niederdeutsch*) which in the eighteenth century was read by few, and with difficulty. The present edition of 1720 is a translation with considerable freedom, compared with the low German text, but without any apparent paraphrasing or reinterpretation.

14. Bainton, *Here I Stand*, p. 133.

15. Ed. of 1720, p. 664.

16. Clark.

17. Clark, p. 49.

18. Preface to the edition of 1720.

19. Pirro, *Bach*, pp. 43-44. Ahle, in the work mentioned by Pirro quotes Spener, Dannhauer, and Muscovius in their condemnation of figural music for church use. Dannhauer (1603-1666), the teacher of Spener, wrote *Christosophia* (1638), *Mysterio sophia* (1646), and *Hodosophia* (1649, re-edited by Spener in 1713), besides a *Katechismusmilch* in 10 volumes. Muscovius (1635-1695) wrote a work entitled *Bestrafter Missbrauch der Kirchenmusik und Kirchhofe* (Punished Misuse of the Church Music and Cemeteries) Lauban, 1694. See Eitner, *Quellen Lexicon*, VII, 124.

20. *BR*, p. 74.

21. Tholuck, p. 22. "Wie Luther, so will auch Spener uber die Moralität dieser Dinge mehr *secundum personam* als *secundum rem* geurtheilt wissen. Auf einem fortgeschritteneren Standpunkte stehen Francke, Lange, Anton,

Breithaupt." (regarding card games, dancing, smoking, comedies, ballgames, and so forth.)

22. Composing in Roman times was a matter of collecting and adjusting existing melodies to new words. Sometimes a slight change in the melody became necessary for this adjustment. This is the way Saint Gregory "composed" the Gregorian chant.

23. See Wolfrum.

24. Ed. of 1720, p. 657.

25. "wohl-zu-fassende Kirchen Music."

26. Bitter, p. 90.

27. Bitter, p. 89. He mentioned this twice. Once he says, "Wenn ich auch stets den Endzweck, nemlich eine regulirte Kirchen Music im Gottes Ehren," then again, "und Erhaltung meines endzweckes wessen des Wohl zufassenden Kirchen Music."

28. *BG*, XL, 57.

11. The Weimar Years (1708-1717)

1. *BR*, p. 69. C. S. Terry calls him Groom of the Apartments.

2. Terry, *Bach, A Biography*, p. 93; "get board money" *(BR)*.

3. See the preface to the toccatas in D major, d minor, e minor, g minor, and G major in *BG*, XXXVI, pp. xx, xxvi, xxxi–xxxii, xxxv, xxxvii–xxxviii.

4. Nos. 4514 and 4515 available in the Peters edition.

5. A ricercar is a multi-thematic, fugue-like composition that grew out of the motet, and gradually evolved into a monothematic fugue.

6. See Schmieder, *Thematisch-systhematisches Verzeichnis*.

7. See Schmieder, *Ibid.*, No. 18, p. 22; No. 21, p. 26; No. 61, p. 79; No. 71, p. 94; No. 131, p. 176.

8. *Ibid.* Schmieder thinks that No. 31 was revised in 1731 and No. 59 perhaps composed in 1723 (p. 631).

9. *BR*, p. 231.

10. This hypothesis was probably based upon doubtful statements by Lorenz Mizler, a vain, untalented, rather unreliable musicologist who was a pupil of Bach in Leipzig for three years. The theoretical speculations that, according to Mizler, did not interest Bach were most certainly his own, and not those of the preceding generation that fascinated Bach and Walther. Thus, neither the assumption of a cooling friendship nor that of Bach's aversion to musical speculation are well founded. See von Brodde, *Walther.*

11. *Ibid.*, p. 6.

12. Wette, *Historische Nachrichten*. Three letters have been preserved—by Drese, Kuhnau, and Johann Christoph Schmidt, *Oberkapellmeister* at the Dresden court in 1717—in which they praise Walther's book on composition.

13. Gehrmann, 468.

14. Robert Eitner, in his *Quellen Lexicon*, informs us that the MS is in the *Hochschule für Musik* in Berlin. When I tried to obtain a microfilm of it, I received the sad news from the librarian of the *Hochschule* that it is now

counted among the war losses which the library suffered in 1945. An extensive description of the work by Gehrmann appeared in the *Vierteljahrschrift für Musikwissenschaft* (see Bibliography). See also an article by Eitner in *Monatshefte für Musikgeschichte*, p. 165.

15. See Gehrmann and von Brodde, *Walther*.

16. Burney, II, 272.

12. Musical Speculation: Kircher and Werckmeister

1. His erudition and experimentation included every imaginable field of inquiry. Until recently a tourist could visit a small museum, *Museo Kirchiriani*, in Rome, where his numerous instruments for experimentation were on exhibit: microscopes, telescopes, magic lanterns, nautical instruments, maps, globes, skeletons, and monsters of all sorts—all witness to his multifarious interests. The exhibits included many musical instruments, and on the walls one could see a great variety of magical signs. A description of the contents of the Kircher Museum can be found in Julius Schlosser.

2. Meyer, p. 104.

3. In 1708 Walther still counted Kircher among the great musicologists of all time. *Musikalische Handleitung* by Friedrich Erhard Niedt, from which Bach and his students copied rules and maxims, praised Kircher highly. Werckmeister respectfully quotes Kircher, and another of Bach's mentors, Caspar Printz writes that Kircher is "so famous that there is no need to mention him further," in his *Historische Beschreibung der edelen Sing- und Kling-Kunst*.

4. Junghans.

5. Walther considers the derivation offered by Cyriacus Snegasius (1546-1597), a preacher and cantor in Friedrichsroda, related by marriage to Luther. Snegasius, in his *Isagoges Musicales*, gives the Greek *Mousa*, muse, or Apioumosthai, to investigate, as the derivation of the word music.

6. Printz, *Historische Beschreibung der edelen Sing- und Kling-Kunst.*

7. *BR*, p. 276.

8. In *Musikalisches Lexicon*, p. 648.

9. Serauky, *Andreas Werckmeister*, p. 122.

10. Goldschmidt, *Musikästetik des 18 ten Jahrhunderts*, thinks that Werckmeister also was acquainted with Leibniz' doctrine of perfection, but I have never found any reference to Leibniz in any of Werckmeister's works.

11. *D. A. Steffani, Abtes von Lepzig des Heil. Apostolischen Stuhls Protonotarii Send-Schreiben* . . . , edited by Andreas Werckmeister, pp. 39, 40.

12. Expressed in proportion: $531441/524288$, or 24 cents, a cent being a 1200th part of an octave, or a 100th part of a semi-tone in our present-day tempered scale.

13. Jacob Faber Stapulensis, Henricus Glarianus, and Franchinus. *Hypomnemata Musica*, p. 26.

14. "kann . . . in Fall der Noth ein gantz Comma in dre Schwebung ertragen/ ein Tertza minor noch mehr. Aber eine Octave gar nichts, Eine Quinte ¼ auch wol ½ vom Comma." *Ibid.*, p. 28.

15. *Ibid.*, p. 30.

16. *Ibid.*

17. Die nothwendigete Anmerkungen und Regeln. . . .

18. *Erweitert und verbesserte Orgel-Probe.* . . .

19. *Hypomnemata Musica*, p. 36.

20. *Mysterio Cosmographica* and his *Harmonia Mundi.*

21. *Musikalische Paradoxal Discourse*, Capitel 2.

22. *Harmonologia Musica*, Foreword.

23. *Der Edlen Musik-kunst Würde*, p. 21. Chaps. 1 and 4; also see *Paradoxal Discourse.*

24. *Ibid.*

25. "Böse Leute achten die Musik nicht viel." *Der Edlen Musik-kunst Würde.*

26. Foreword to *Harmonologia Musica.*

27. "und weil der Mundud Ectypus eine Idea des Architypui sey / und daraus fliesse / dass solche Harmonie in Gott selber auch sey." Contents, 2.

28. Werckmeister, *Der Edlen Musik-kunst Würde*, Chap. VII. item: Cap. X.

29. *Ibid.*, Chap. X.

13. Bach in Köthen (1717-1723)

1. Bitter, p. 107.

2. Terry, *Bach, A Biography*, p. 101.

3. Spitta, *Bach*, I, 514.

4. His *Musikalischer Quacksalber* (Musical Quack) describes the absurd craze in Germany for Italian singers and the attempt of many Germans to pose as Italians. His writings resemble Caspar Printz so much that *Satyrischer Componist* is believed actually to have been written by Kuhnau.

5. Bitter relates that the King of Saxony sent Bach a present of 100 Louis d'Or, which, however, failed to reach him, as the servant entrusted with its delivery absconded with the money. Terry does not mention this incident.

6. Terry, *Bach, A Biography*, p. 113.

7. *Ibid.*, p. 114. See also BR, p. 75, for an excerpt from The Court Secretary's Report which relates the story of Bach's arrest, confinement, and "unfavorable discharge."

8. Spitta, *Bach*, II, 3.

9. Smend, *Bach in Köthen.*

10. Seibel.

11. Heinichen, *Generalbassschule*, p. 3.

12. *Ibid.*, p. 7.

13. Aurelius Augustinus, *Musik*, Vol. 23.

14. *Musicalische Handleitung.*

15. "Was soll man nun mit solchen alten barbarischen Canon-Meistern machen? Ich meistenteils lache darüber, und wenn sie auch gleich aus Bosheit in ihre Hosen canonieren, so sind es ihre eigene, und verlangt nicht solche ihnen abzudisputieren."

16. See Chapter 9.
17. Terry, *Bach, A Biography*, p. 127.
18. *Ibid.*, p. 128.
19. *Ibid.*, p. 129.
20. Spitta, *Bach*, II, 10.
21. Now in the Royal Library of Berlin.
22. Terry, *Bach, A Biography*, p. 139.
23. The theme, which has been preserved by Mattheson, was a rather long one for extemporaneous use;

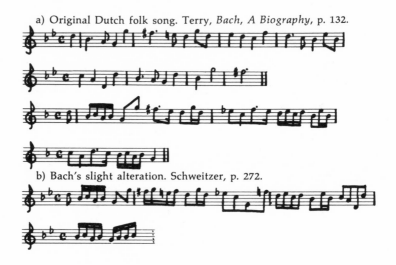

a) Original Dutch folk song. Terry, *Bach, A Biography*, p. 132.

b) Bach's slight alteration. Schweitzer, p. 272.

24. Mattheson, *Der musikalische Patriot*, p. 316, quoted in Spitta, *Bach*, II, 20.
25. The theme may be found in Johann Mattheson's *Grosse Generalbass-Schule* (Great School of Thoroughbass). See Schweitzer, *J. S. Bach*, I, 272.
26. Bach composed an ode for this memorable celebration but it has unfortunately been lost. Terry, *Bach, A Biography*, p. 138. Also see Bunge, p. 30.
27. Smend, *Bach in Köthen*, p. 28.
28. Translation by Terry, *Bach, A Biography*, p. 138.
29. "Bist du bei mir,/ Geh ich mit Freuden / zum Sterben und zu meiner Ruh' / Ach, wie vergnügt wäre so mein Ende, / es drückten deine schönen Hände / Mir die getreuen Augen zu."

14. Worldly Music of the Spirit

1. See Schmieder, *Thematisch-systematisch Verzeichnis*, p. 651.
2. Smend, *Bach in Köthen*.
3/4. Bunge, pp. 14-47.

5. Kirnberger, *Die kunst des reinen Satzes in der Musik. . . .*

6. By means of these instruments organists could keep in practice, when they did not have sufficient time to spend at the organ. The possession of these pedal harpsichords also explains the fact that Bach could display his phenomenal technique in the *G Minor Fugue,* as he played it for Reincken, despite the fact that he did not have access to any organ in Köthen. Three such instruments are included in the inventory of instruments Bach left at his death.

7. *BG,* XIIa, 27, No. 52.

8. *BG,* XXV, 105, No. 174.

9. *BG,* XXVII, 48.

10. *BG,* V, 1.

11. *BG,* VII, 173.

12. *BG,* XXVII, xx.

13. *BG,* XXX, 125.

14. *BG,* XVII, 142.

15. *BG,* XXXII, 99.

16. See Wilhelm Rust, *BG,* XVII, Preface.

17. *BG,* XXXII, 169.

18. *BG,* XVII, 45.

19. *BG,* XXIV, 276.

20. *BG,* XXIV, 249.

21. *BG,* IX, 252.

22. Cantatas 211, 212.

23. C. S. Terry's overly free translation gives it a polish and polite language out of keeping with the rustic original.

24. *BG,* XXXV, 73, Cantata No. 173.

15. *Compositions for the Keyboard*

1. *BG,* XXXVI, 118.

2. *BR,* p. 329.

3. *BG,* XLIII (2), 37.

4. *BG,* III, 263.

5. Spitta mistakenly calls this work a passacaglia for the reason that the entire work is composed on an ever recurring bass. A passacaglia bass, however, never consists of two sentences (also called periods), but of only four or eight bars, while this air has two long and repeated sentences, each of 16 measures. Handel has a set of variations also called "Passacaglia." This work is not a passacaglia either.

6. "Auffrichtige Anleitung, Wormit denen Liebhebern des Clavieres, besonders aber denen Lehrbegierigen, eine deutliche Art gezeiget wird, nicht alleine (1) mit 2 Stimmen eine spielen zu lernen, sondern auch bey weiteren *progressen* (2) mit dreyen *obligaten Partien* richtig und wohl zu verfahren, anbey auch zugleich gute *inventiones* nicht alleine zu bekommen, sondern auch selbige wohl durchzuführen, am allermeisten aber eine *cantabile* Art im Spielen zu erlangen, und darneben einen starcken Vorgeschmack von der

Composition zu überkommen. [Verfertiges von Joh. Seb. Bach, Hochf. Anhalt-Cöthenischen Capellmeister. Anno Christi 1723.]"

7. See *BG*, XLV, 213.

8. Schmieder suggests that two toccatas may have been composed either during the Köthen period or in Bach's last years in Weimar, but I am inclined to accept the latter suggestion. See *Thematische-systematisch Verzeichnis*, p. 562.

9. See above, p. xxx.

10. Ehmann.

11. Ehmann, p. 180.

12. Schering, *Bach und das Musikleben Leipzigs*.

13/14. See the prefaces to vols. II and XXXVI of *BG*.

15. After about 1765 *Klavier* referred specifically to the clavichord, while a harpsichord was called a *Flügel* (wing) because of its wing-like shape. Germans generally called it a clavicymbal or cembalo.

16. *BG*, III, xiv.

17. *BR*, p. 311.

18. Adlung, *Musica Mechanica Organoedi*, II, 158. Adlung in this complete description of *Pedalklaviere* tells us that the instruments sounded the strings either by tangents or plectra. The dip of the pedal was so regulated that the violence of the players' feet would not break the strings (p. 161). The pedals had three separate sets of strings, tuned at 16, 8, and 4 feet pitch. A set of pedals could be acquired in Bach's time for the incredibly low sum of three or four dollars (p. 160). Today Mr. John Chalis of Detroit asks $2,000 for such a set of pedals.

19. Schering, *Bach und das Musikleben Leipzigs*, p. 47. Schering, *Bachs Leipziger Kirchenmusik*, pp. 51, 61, 71, 76. Mendel, 339.

20. See *BG*, XLIV (2), 4, 9, and 10. For the manuscript of his 18 *choralvorspiele* he wrote out a pedal part on a third staff (see *BG*, XLIV, 140, 141).

21. Adlung, *Anleitung zur Musikalischen Gelahrtheit*, p. 554, says "sometimes one finds a sixteen-foot string on it, which consists of a spun eight-foot string." Sachs, in his *History of Musical Instruments*, p. 377, says that no English, Flemish, French, Italian, or Spanish harpsichords ever had a sixteen-foot stop, and that it occurred exclusively in *a few* German harpsichords of the eighteenth century.

22. *BG*, III, xiv. Schweitzer even suggests that the *Passacaglia* was originally written for pedal harpsichord. C. F. Becker states that "several of the chorale preludes in this collection are calculated for this instrument." The *Hochschule für Musick* in Berlin has a harpsichord that was believed to have belonged to Bach, but Georg Kinsky has cast serious doubt upon the authenticity of this instrument. See "Zur Echtheitsfrage der Berliner Bach-Flügels," p. 128.

23. *BR*, p. 329.

24. See Agricola's addenda to Adlung's *Musica Mechanica Organoedi* of 1768, II, 124.

25. Forkel says that Bach "liked best to play on the clavichord; the harpsi-

chord, though certainly susceptible to a very great variety of expression, had not soul enough for him."

26. Where the hammer of a pianoforte after its stroke falls back and is held down by the back check, the tangent of a clavichord remains clinging to the string. It creates the desired pitch depending on where it strikes the string, in the manner of the fingers of a violinist. The short end of the string is damped by a felt strip, while the long end emits its modest vibrations.

27. Cristofori called his innovation *gravicembalo col pian e forte.* This instrument has as yet no pedals, nor any stops for registration. Instead of quills or plectra it had little hammers with leather heads, producing an agreeable tone, less metallic and clanging than the harpsichord, but not as full and round as our pianofortes with their felt hammers. Two of these instruments still exist, one of which is at the Metropolitan Museum of New York. The author had the pleasure of playing on it through the kind permission of the curator Mr. Winternitz. Despite its age—and an unfortunate restoration by the Steinway Piano Company, who furnished the instrument with small felt hammers—its sensitivity to the slightest shades of loud or soft were still apparent.

28. This word, *tractaments*, may mean treatment, *Behandlung;* that is, manner of playing, hence also, the action.

29. Adlung, *Musica Mechanica Organoedi*, II, 116.

30. *Essay*, p. 112; p. 36.

31. Adlung, *Musica Mechanica Organoedi*, II, 124.

32. I am indebted to Mr. Curt Sachs for this information.

33. A hemiola occurs when the rhythm of six is divided in three times two, alternating with the division in two times three.

34. At the opening of the fugue it may seem as if the accent of the theme falls upon the first quarter note, that is upon the third strong beat (the piece is in four fourths, *alla breve,* as in musical illustration a) below, giving the usual accentual connotation to the bar line. As the fugue progresses, however, we see the second eighth note appearing as the first note after the bar line (see example b). This distribution and seeming distortion of the normal accents takes place especially in the numerous *stretti.*

16. *Call to Leipzig*

1. At that time Erdmann was stationed in Danzig as agent for the Russian Emperor. (Spitta, *Bach*, II, 253). The schoolmates had kept up an occasional correspondence. Bach mentioned having received a letter from Erdmann four years before he wrote this letter on October 28, 1730: "Es werden nunmehr fast 4 Jahre verfloszen seyn, da E. Hochwohlgeb. auf mein an Ihnen abgelaszenes mit einer gütigen Antwort mich beglückten." (Bitter, IV, 126) They had seen each other once since school days, in Weimar shortly before Bach left for Köthen. (Terry, *Bach, A Biography*, p. 204)

2. See *BG*, XLIV, Facsimile No. 9.

3. (Leipzig, 1684). Mr. Terry lists two editions of this book: part one of 1706, the other of 1710. I have read the copy of 1684, lent to me by the Theological Seminary of St. Louis. Mr. Terry's dates are only hypothetical as no dates were noted in the original inventory; they are obviously derived from extant copies and catalogues.

4. "wenn mich dann entsinne, dasz Ihren Wegen meiner Fatalitäten einige Nachricht zu geben . . ."

5. Richter, *"Die Wahl Bachs zum Kantor der Thomasschule,"* 63.

6. Terry, *Bach, A Biography*, p. 127.

7. DdT, Vols. 51/52, edited by Fr. Noack.

8. DdT, Vols. 29/30, edited by Arnold Schering (1938).

9. Although no compositions of his have survived, history has at least bequeathed us an amusing menu of a banquet at which Rolle, Bach, and Kuhnau gorged themselves on *"böffalemote"* (*boeuf à la mode*) and some 15 other dishes. This dinner took place in Halle, where in 1716 the three organists had been invited to inspect the new organ at the Liebfrauenkirche (see above, p. 141).

10. Bitter, IV, 108.

11. Bitter, IV, 109.

12. *BR*, p. 89.

13. Spitta, *Bach*, II, 185.

14. Richter, *"Die Wahl Bachs zum Kantor der Thomasschule,"* 67.

15. Arnold Schering tells us that there was a clause in the instructions for organists in which it is recommended that an hourglass be used to check the length of their playing. (*Bachs Leipziger Kirchenmusik*, p. 242)

16. *BR*, p. 92.

17. See Chapter 4.

18. Schering, *Bachs Leipziger Kirchenmusik*, II, 50.

19. *Ibid.*, 29. Schering believes that only 12 boys sang and that there were four reserves plus the *praefect*, making the total of 17 that B. F. Richter suggests.

20. *Ibid.*, 101.

21. Terry, *Bach, A Biography*, p. 169. E. E. Hochw. Raths der Stadt Leipzig Ordnung der Schule zu S. Thomae.

22. Schering, *Bachs Leipziger Kirchenmusik*, III.

23. Bach's inventory at his death lists 19 instruments. To this list should be added three pedal claviers claimed by his son Christian.

24. Schering, *Bachs Leipziger Kirchenmusik*, III, 5.

17. Fulfillment of Lutheran Reform

1. Bitter, I, 90. "Wenn ich auch stats den Endzweck, nemlich eine regulirte Kirchenmusik zu Gottes Ehren . . . aufführen mögen . . .", as stated in Bach's resignation from his post at St. Blasius in Mühlhausen.

2. Terry, *Cantata Texts*, p. 36.

3. *Ibid.*, p. 20; and Schering, *Bachs Leipziger Kirchenmusik*, II, 5.

4. Schering, *Bachs Leipziger Kirchenmusik*. Blume, *Evangelische Kirchen-musik*, p. 103.

5. Before the Reformation similar songs were whimsically called *Kirleisen*, a pun meaning Kyrie tunes.

6. Luther, *Von der Ordnung des Gottesdienstes in der Gemeinde*, as quoted by Philipp Wolfrum, p. 60.

7. See Orel, *Die Katholische Kirchenmusik von 1600 bis 1750*, in Adler, pp. 528-32.

8. Mary's Annunciation (1); Easter (4, 15, 31, 66, 108, 6, 145, 143, and 158); Circumcision (16, 41, 171, and 190); Michaelis (19, 130, and 149); Christmas: first feast (40, 63, 91, and 142), second feast (57 and 121), and third feast (64, 133, and 151); Three Kings (65); Pentecost: first day (34, 59, 74, and 172), second day (68, 173, and 174), and third day (175 and 184); Reformation Festival (79 and 80); Feast of Christ's Appearance (123); and Trinitatis (129 and 176).

9. "*Gott, wie dein Name, so ist auch dein Ruhm*" (No. 171, BG, XXXV) became the *Patrem omnipotentem* of the *Credo*. *Weinen, Klagen, Sorgen,* from the cantata by that name (No. 12, *BG*, 2) became the *Crucifixus*. "*Wir Danken Dir, Gott*" (No. 29, BG, V) became *Gratias agimus* and *Dona Nobis*. The first section of the cantata "*Schauet doch und sehet*" (No. 46, BG, X).

10. Spitta, *Bach*, III, 40.

11. *Ibid.*, 42.

12. BG, VIII, 3.

13. Spitta, *Bach*, III, 35. Spitta bases this statement on the liturgical rules as given out by Vopelius (see above).

14. The *Kyrie* of the *G Major Mass* comes from Cantata 179, part 1; its *Gloria* from Cantata 79, part 1; its *Gratias* from Cantata 138, part 5; its *Domine Deus* from Cantata 79, part 3; its *Cum Sanctu Spiritu* from Cantata 17, part 1. For the other derivations see Schmeider, *Thematisch-systematisches Verzeichnis* and Neumann, p. 196. In total, 18 movements of the combined four masses prove to be derivations from cantatas. See also the prefaces to these works in BG, XI.

15. See Terry, *Cantata Texts*, pp. 33, 55, 63.

16. In the King James version the words are thus: 46: "And Mary said: My soul doth magnify the Lord, 47: And my spirit hath rejoiced in God my Saviour. 48: For he hath regarded the low estate of his handmaiden: for, behold, from henceforth all generations shall call me blessed. 49: For he that is mighty has done to me great things; and holy is his name. 50: And his mercy is on them that fear him from generation to generation. 51: He has shewed strength with his arm; he has scattered the proud in the imagination of their hearts. 52: He has put down the mighty from their seats, and has exalted them of low degree. 53: He hath filled the hungry with good things; and the rich he hath sent empty away. 54: He has hopen his servant Israel, in remembrance of his mercy; 55: As he spake to our fathers, and to his seed forever." In the canticle this is concluded by *Gloria Patri, gloria*

Filio, gloria et Spiritui sancto. Sicut erat in principio et nunc et semper et in saecula saeculorum.

17. See Terry, *Cantata Texts,* p. 66,

18. All three are found in the Bodenschatz collection, "Florilegium Portense," in 2 parts. Part i of the first (Leipzig, 1603). Part ii appeared in 1621. There is no score of the work.

19. Wilhelm Rust, in his preface to *BG,* XI, xviii, says that for the publication of the *Magnificat* he used two scores, one in E flat. However, he only published the one in D, and the two Chorales, the *Gloria,* and the unfinished *Virga Jesse,* that were sung antiphonally in between the movements of the *Magnificat.* Vol. XI, pp. 103-12.

20. The first chorale "Vom Himmel Hoch da komm' ich her" has the *cantus firmus* in the soprano and diminutions in the other voices. It was sung after *Exultavit.* The second, *Freut euch und jubiliret,* is a free contrapuntal setting of the chorale by that name. Both of these are in German, while the Gloria that follows is in Latin. The second chorale was sung after *Quia fecit.* The *Gloria* was sung after the *Fecit potentiam,* and the *Virga Jesse floruit* after the *Esuientes implevit.*

21. See also Cantata No. 147, written for the Blessed Virgin's Visitation, recitative, *BG,* XXX, 204, and the English to the same text by Terry, *Cantata Texts,* p. 357, no. 2.

18. The Chorale

1. Luther, *Luther's Werke,* L, 368-74.

2. See Köstlin, p. 306.

3. In 1524 Luther wrote to Spalatin: "Es müssen Text und Noten, Weise und Geberde aus rechter Muttersprache und Stimmen kommen." (Wolfrum)

4. Bainton, *Here I Stand,* p. 346.

5. Terry, *Cantata Texts,* p. 13.

6. *Ibid.*

7. *Ibid.,* p. 12.

8. "*Allein Gott in der Höhe sei Ehr,*" *BG,* III, 199.

9. This scribbled memorandum has survived, and is reproduced by Terry, *Cantata Texts,* p. 32.

10. See Terry, *Bach's Chorales,* III, 21-22. Wilhelm Rust, in a preface to *BG,* XXV (2), pp. vii-ix, writes that Bach composed the *Little Organ Book* (*Orgelbüchlein*) in Köthen, and used the organ at the Lutheran Church there. He proves this thesis by the pitch of the pedal; only in this church was the pitch as high as the *Organ Book* reaches.

11. See Notes, Chapter 19.

12. Heinichen, *Neu erfundene . . . der General-Basses,* p. 24.

13. Kepler's *De Harmonice Mundi* (Augsburg, 1619), quoted from the *Encyclopedia Britannica* (11th edition), XV, 750.

14. See Chapter 17 for other Klavier works in this publication.

15. Composed in Dresden, 1625. See *BG,* XXXIX, 238.

16. Bainton, *Here I Stand,* p. 343.

17. "Kyrie, Gott Vater in Ewigkeit! Gross ist dein Barmherzigkeit, aller Ding ein Schöpfer und Regierer! Eleison!

"Christe aller Welt Trost! uns Sünder allein du hast erlöst; Jesus, Gottes Sohn! Unser Mittler bist du in dem höchsten Thron, zu dir schreien wir aus Herzensbegier! Eleison!

"Gott, hieliger Geist! Trost, Stärk' uns im Glauben allermeist, dass wir am letzten End' fröhlich abscheiden aus diesem Elend! Eleison!"

18. See Vaihinger, Jung, and Langer.

19. The Cantata

1. Spitta, *Bach*, II, 349.

2. Criticism of this relation between music and poetry was not lacking in Bach's time, nor in some of his biographers. The famous Hamburg master Mattheson—composer, opera director, singer, actor, harpsichordist, conductor, author, and critic—criticized Bach's cantata No. 21 *"Ich hatte viel Bekümmerniss"* (I Had Much Sorrow, No. 21) for repeating three times the word "Ich," over widely separated chords. This treatment, Mattheson felt, contradicted the sense of the text. Bach often composed entire staccato passages of several notes over a single syllable, as in Cantata No. 11, *"Lobet Gott in seinen Reichen"* (Praise God in His Realms), where the word *lobet* is cut up into *lo..o..o..o..obet* with staccato marks over the notes carrying the o's.

3. Quoted from Spitta, *Bach*, I, 473, and 479.

4. A term used by Bukofzer, p. 293.

5. *Johann Sebastian Bach*, I, 96.

6. Terry, *Cantata Texts*, p. 9; Schmieder, *Thematisch-systematisches Verzeichnis*, p. 65.

7. Smend, *Bach in Köthen*, p. 27.

8. *Die allerneueste Art höfflich und galant zu schreiben. . . .*

9. Spitta, *Bach*, 341.

10. A curious tax receipt has been preserved in which Bach acknowledges payment of Henrici of tax on three casks of beer. It is an insignificant little document, but it nevertheless throws a happy sidelight on the master's life. Certainly he was no pietistic teetotaler nor lacking in a sense of humor.

11. Göttingen, 1736.

12. Spitta, *Bach*, II, 348.

13. Terry, *Cantata Texts*, p. 12.

14. BG, II, 35. Recorded by The Cantata Singers and the Jacques Orchestra, London, FFRR.

15. Schering, *Bachs Leipziger Kirchenmusik*, II, 61; Mendel, 339.

16. Our bows today are about a third longer and the sticks are of concave construction, which enables them to tighten the hair whenever greater pressure is applied. With the convex stick the tension of the hair does not change as much when pressure is applied.

17. Often three or four wind instruments appear in the score. In our present-day conception of orchestral music we would say that such a combination of powerful wind instruments overbalances the total body of sound.

20. The Passions and Oratorios

1. Luther, *Deutsche Messe* (1526).

2. In 1538 this same motet Passion, composed exclusively in polyphonic style, appeared in a publication by George Rhau, where it was prefaced by Melanchthon.

3. From Brockes's autobiography, quoted in Willi Flemming, VI, 23.

4. *Jesus:*

> Das ist mein Blut im neuen Testament
> Das ich für euch und viele vergiessen
> Es wird dem/ es wird geniessen [partake or enjoy]
> Zu Tilgung seiner Sünden dienen.

Tochter Zion:

> Gott selbst/ die Brunnquell alles Guten
> Ein unerschöpflichs Gnaden-Meer
> Fängt für die Sünder an zu bluten
> Biss er vom allen Blute leer
> Und reicht aus diesen Gnaden-Fluten
> Uns selbst sein Blut zu trinken her.

Choral der Christlichen Kirche:

> Ach wie hungert mein Gemühte
> Menschenfreund/ nach deiner Güte!
> Ach! wie pfleg ich oft mit Thränen
> Mich nach dieser Kost zu sehnen!
> Ach wie pfleg et mich zu dürsten
> Nach dem trank des Lebens-Fürsten!
> Wünsche stets/ dass mein Gebeine
> Sich durch Gott/ mit Gott vereine.

5. See Terry, *Bach, A Biography*, p. 209. To judge from the text it had little music in it.

6. *Ibid.*, p. 196.

7. *Ibid.*, p. 180, for Picander's text with rhymed Evangelist. See also p. 194.

8. See Spitta, *Bach*, II, 537.

9. See Terry, *Bach, A Biography*, p. 218, with regard to the influence of Bach's friend Hasse in Dresden.

10. *Ibid.* Terry has reason to believe (from internal evidence) that the borrowing was in reverse order, that the Oratorio was composed first, but that the birthday cantatas were performed before the Oratorio.

11. If one accepts Terry's premise (in the above note) the *Christmas Oratorio* belongs in a category with the Passion and *Magnificat* as music written with one intent in mind.

21. Signs of Change

1. Bitter, IV, 140: *Verhandlung über die Aufführung der Passions Musik in der Nicolai-Kirche.* Excerpt: "Senat. Es solte der HEr Cantor auf EE.

Hochw. Raths Kosten, eine Nachricht, dass die Music in der Nicolai Kirche vor diesesmahl gehalten werden solte, drucken die Gelegenheit aufm Chor, so gut es sich thun liese, mit Zu Ziehung des Obervoigts machen und den Clav. Cymbel repariren lassen."

Johann Zachar. Trefurth, tit. jur.

2. Spitta quotes Scheibe as describing Görner as an inferior musician: "He can never set a pure line [of music], and the grossest blunders grace— or disgrace—every bar." As to his character: "completely possessed by conceit and rudeness. . . ." (*Bach*, II, 211)

3. See Bitter, IV, 137. "*Entfernet Euck, The heitern Sterne*," words by Christian Friederick Haupt.

4. See Richter, *Bach Jahrbuch* (1925), 5.

5. *Ibid.*, p. 9.

6. Terry, *Bach, A Biography*, p. 194 reads, "subject to the selection of being *convenient* with the Gospel. . . ." Spitta's English translation of 1951 (*Bach*, II, 232) reads "provided that the hymns chosen be in conformity with the gospels. . . ."

7. Bitter, II, 231.

8. Smend, *Bach in Köthen*, p. 209.

9. *Ibid.*, p. 78.

10. See Walther, *Musicalisches Lexicon*, and Terry, *Bach, A Biography*, p. 195.

11. Terry gives the complete list of their names in *Bach, A Biography*, p. 197. Other such lists appear in *Bach Jahrbuch* (1907), pp. 68-76.

12. Terry, *Bach, A Biography*, p. 174.

13. A protocol of the Council of June 6, 1730, tells: "3 Classen würden in einer stube informieret, diese stube sei auch das Coenaculum. Die cubicula wären auch schlecht beschaffen und schläfen in einem Bett zwei Kaben, . . ." in Bitter, II, 159.

14. Quotations are from the minutes of the meeting, which have been preserved.

15. Spitta, *Bach*, II, 245.

16. "Kurtzer, iedoch höchstnöthiger Entwurff einer wohlbestallten Kirchen Music; nebst einigen unvorgreifflichen Bedenken von dem Verfall derselben." (see Bitter, II, 145)

17. The complete text of the letter appears in *BR*, pp. 125-26; Spitta, II, 253-54.

18. Translations are by Gesner, Ernesti, Heyne, Voss, Jacobs, Dissen, Herder Schlegel, and Goethe.

19. Terry, *Bach, A Biography*, p. 172.

20. Bitter, II, 157.

21. Terry, *Bach, A Biography*, p. 212.

22. *Enlightenment Darkens Bach's Horizon*

1. His monadology did not appear until 1712, and was not translated into German until eight years later, after his death.

2. Wolff, *"Von Gott, der Welt und die Seele des Menschen,"* p. 126.

3. *Ibid.*, p. 127.

4. *Ibid.*, pp. 127, 128.

5. Troeltsch, *Gesammelte Schriften*, IV, 371.

23. *Wolffian Philosophy*

1. In Chapter 8 this article is discussed in connection with its information about ornaments.

2. See Spitta, *Bach*, III, 253.

3. See Chapter 8.

4. *BR*, p. 224.

5. Scheibe, p. 499.

6. When Leibniz was very young he was impressed with certain aspects of Kircher's thought. He even is believed to have tried to establish contact with Kircher. Lorenz Mizler, *Der Musikalische Staarstecher* (Leipzig, 1740), as quoted in Wöhlke, pp. 14, 40.

7. Gottsched: "A world is a general notion by which we comprehend the names of all things . . . because on account of the connection of the parts (of this world) one always has its cause in another, there consequently is truth in the world: namely one that originates in the law of sufficient cause, and that distinguishes it from the Land of Cocaine." Wolff, *Von Gott, der Welt, und die Seele des Menschen*, chap. 2, p. 17: "Through it [the law of sufficient cause] originates the distinction between Truth and Dreams, between the true world and the land of Cocaine." Mizler: "We wish to call all things that really exist with one word the world. And to acquire the knowledge of this world, as far as possible, is the task of philosophy." "Because there is only one truth, we must choose the least deceptive road to reach it; and that is the mathematical." Wolff: "And so it is clear that everything concerning understanding and reason [*Verstand und Vernunft*] can be explained by the soul's own power to form mental representations of the world [*die Weltvor zustellen*]; on the other hand, it is clear that nothing is contained in the body that surpasses the nature of a machine."

8. Chapter 1.

9. It comprises the first volume. The present English translation has published only the second volume, which contains the practical, contrapuntal instructions.

10. Bitter, III, 212.

11. Today there are extant 480 solutions. It is a triple canon in six voices.

12. See Wöhlke.

13. Falck, p. 9; Professor Jocher and Professor Ernesti: philosophy; D. Rudiger: Vernunftlehre; D. Kastner: Institutiones; D. Joachim: Pandkten und Institutiones; D. Dtiegelitz: Wechselrecht; Professor Haussen und Professor Richter: Mathematics.

14. See *Allgemeine Deutsche Biographie*, VI, 235-41.

15. Falck.

16. Spitta, *Bach*, III, 250.

17. It forms the last chapter of his *Versuch einer Critischen Dichtkunst*. . . .

18. *Ibid.*, p. 466.

19. *Ibid.*, p. 466.

20. *Ibid.*

21. *Ibid.*

22. *Ibid.*, p. 473.

24. *Conflict with an "Enlightened" Rector*

1. Terry, *Bach, A Biography*, p. 216.

2. Paulsen, II, 31-32.

3. A more detailed account may be read in Terry, *Bach, A Biography*, pp. 224 ff. and *Bach Jahrbuch* (1907), 70.

4. Terry, *Bach, A Biography*, p. 224.

5. *Ibid.*, p. 225. Chapter XIV, paragraph 4 of *Schulordnung* of 1723.

6. The entire letter appears in Bitter, IV, 181.

7. "Und durch Beschleunigung gebethenen Haupresolution . . . dieselben gesuchen dem Harrn Rector unverzüglich hierinnen Einhalt zu thun."

8. Terry, *Bach, A Biography*, p. 236.

9. Spitta, *Bach*, III, 11.

10. Terry, *Bach, A Biography*, p. 248; Spitta, *Bach*, II, 868 (German edition); *BR*, p. 162.

11. See *BR*, p. 166, for the reports on the candidates for this position.

12. 1736 is the date attributed by C. S. Terry to the edition of this work (*Bach, A Biography*, p. 275)

13. Actually Gerhard took special pains in this work to avoid any imputations of Pietism. See *Allgemeine Deutsche Biographie*, VIII, 767-71.

14. Gass, p. 207.

15. Scheibler. See Terry, *Bach, A Biography*, p. 273.

25. *Musical Discipline: An Act of Worship*

1. Grandson of Bach's uncle, Georg Christoph.

2. Terry, *Bach, A Biography*, p. 249.

3. David, *Bach's Musical Offering*, pp. 3-6.

4. Frederick wrote it out for Bach; according to Bach's own dedication of the *Musical Offering*, Frederick played it for him. Bitter, III, 215.

5. *Loc. cit.*

6. At the king's command the song and the remainder resolved with canonic art.

7. See Tillich, *Systematic Theology*, I, 264.

8. *Allgemeine Deutsche Biographie*, XVI, 45-46.

9. Hochetus (hochet) is a truncation of a melody into fragments. In the thirteenth and fourteenth centuries it appeared in alternate notes sung by different voices.

10. See note 11, Chapter 23.

11. In composing it one starts in the middle and works in both directions. To compose such a canon in more than one voice requires more skill. See example by Byrd in Prout, p. 238.

12. Willi Apel in *Harvard Dictionary of Music* describes *Empfindsamkeit* (*Empfindsamer Stil*) as a "denomination for the North German style of the second half of the eighteenth century represented by W. F. Bach, C. P. E. Bach Quantz, G. Benda, Reichardt, and others . . . who tried to arrive at an expression of 'true and natural' feelings. . . ."

13. Burney, II, 251.

14. Planemac, 586.

15. Ecstacy is used here in the sense in which Paul Tillich develops it: " 'Ecstacy' must be rescued from its distorted connotations and restored to a sober theological function. . . . Ecstasy (standing outside one's self) points to a state of mind which is extraordinary in the sense that the mind transcends its ordinary situation. Ecstasy is not a negation of reason. . . . This is the state mystics try to reach by ascetic and meditative activities. But mystics know that these activities are only preparations. . . . Ecstasy occurs only if the mind is grasped by the mystery, namely, by the ground of being and meaning." *Systematic Theology*, I, Ill.

16. Bach may actually have read Kircher as late as 1744.

17. Graeser, p. 6.

18. Terry, *Bach, A Biography*, pp. 262 and 263 about the conclusion to the history of this fact.

19. Riemer, p. 718. Terry, *Bach, A Biography*, p. 260, footnote 3.

20. Bitter, III, 229.

21. The complete title of his essay is: *De Vita Musica ex plaut.-Mostellar, Act. III, Sc. II Praefatus*, with an appendix: *Ad Orationes benevole auscultandas officiose invitat M. Jo Gottlieb Biedermann R. Freibergae* (Master Johann G. Biedermann, Rector of Freiberg, urges for kindly listening to this discourse).

22. Spitta, *Bach*, III, 258.

23. Both the original article and its alteration are in Bitter, III, 234-38.

24. Terry, *Bach, A Biography*, p. 263.

25. *BR*, p. 220.

26. Written in 1588 by Franz Eler: "Whene'er we are in highest need and do not know where to turn, and when we find neither aid nor council . . . then our only consolation is to implore Thee in common, The true God, for saving us from anxiety and distress."

27. *Leipziger Gesangbuch*; see W. Graeser, p. 81.

Vor Deinen Thron tret ich hiermit,
O Gott und dich demü tig bitt:
Wend dein genadig Angesicht
Von mir betrübtem Sünder nicht.

Ein Selig Ende mir bescher,
Am jüngsten Tag erwecke mich,
Herr, dass ich dich schau ewiglich:
Amen, Amen, erhöre mich!

26. *Epilogue: Music for the Spirit Living in a Changing World*

1. Bitter, III, 254.
2. ". . . in der Enge des Raths." *Ibid.*, 260.
3. *Ibid.*, 261.
4. *Ibid.*, 259.
5. *Ibid.*
6. Spitta calls Friedemann a dissolute fellow, but Falck proved that this damning judgment was based upon rumors spread abroad by Reichard and Rochlitz. See Falck, p. 7.
7. Bitter, III, 263.

BIBLIOGRAPHY

NOTE: Music publications are listed separately following the general bibliography.

Albert, Hermann. *Die Musikanschauung des Mittelalters und ihre Grundlagen.* Halle, 1905.

———. "Wort und Ton in der Musik des 18. Jahrhunderts," *Archiv für Musikwissenschaft,* Jg. V, No. 1 (January, 1923), 31-70.

Adam von Fulda. *Gradus ad Parnassum, oder Angührung . . . musikalischen Composition. . . .* Translated and edited by Lorenz Mizler. Leipzig, 1742.

Adler, Guido. *Handbuch der Musikgeschichte.* 2d ed. Berlin, 1929.

Adlung, Jacob. *Anleitung zu der musikalischen Gelahrtheit.* Erfurt, 1758.

———. *Musica Mechanica Organoedi* (1726), ed. J. L. Albrecht. With notes by J. F. Agricola. Berlin, 1768.

Agricola, Johann Friedrich. *See* Adlung, Jacob.

Aldrich, Putnam. "Bach's Technique of Transcription and Improvised Ornamentation," *The Musical Quarterly,* XXXV (January, 1949), 26-35.

———. *Ornamentation in J. S. Bach's Organ Works.* New York, 1950.

Allerup, Albert. *Die "Musica Practica" des Johannes Andreas Herbst und ihre entwicklungsgeschichtliche Bedeutung.* (Beitrag zur Geschichte der deutschen Schulmusik.) Kassel, 1931.

Ambros, August Wilhelm. *Geschichte der Musik.* 3rd ed. 5 vols. Leipzig, 1887-1909.

Arndt, Johann. *Sechs Bücher vom wahrem Christenthum necst dessen Paradiesgärtlein. Mit der Lebensbeschreibung des seligen Mannes nebst seinem Bildniss und 57 Sinnbildern.* 1606-1609.

Augustinus, Aurelius. *Musik.* Translated by Carl Johann Perl. *(Sammlung Wissenschaftlicher Abhandlung,* Vol. XXIII). Strassbourg, 1937.

Bach, Carl Philipp Emanuel. *Essay on the True Art of Playing Keyboard Instruments.* Translated and edited by W. J. Mitchell. New York, 1949.

———. "Selbstbiographie Carl Philipp Emanuel Bachs," in *Musikerbriefe,* ed. Karl Friedrich Ludwig Nohl. Leipzig, 1867.

Bainton, Roland Herbert. *The Age of the Reformation.* Princeton, New Jersey, 1956.

———. *Here I Stand; A Life of Martin Luther.* New York, 1950.

———. *The Reformation of the Sixteenth Century.* Boston, 1952.

Barnes, Harry Elmer. *A History of Historical Writing.* Norman, Oklahoma, 1937.

Beaulieu-Marconnay, Karl Olivier, Freiherr von. *Ernst August Herzog von Sachsen-Weimar Eisenach. 1688-1748.* Leipzig, 1872.

Bernstein, Leon. *Flavius Josephus, His Time and His Critics.* New York, 1938.

Bezold, Friedrich von. *Geschichte der deutschen Reformation.* Berlin, 1890.

Biedermann, Johann Gottlieb. *De Vita Musica.* Freiberg, 1750.

"Biedermann, Magister Johann Gottlieb," *Allgemeine Deutsche Biographie* (56 vols.; Leipzig, 1875-1912), II, 618-19.

Bitter, Karl Hermann. *Johann Sebastian Bach.* 2d ed. 2 vols. Berlin, 1881.

Blume, Friedrich. *Two Centuries of Bach.* Translated by Stanley Godman. New York, 1950.

⸻. *Die Evangelische Kirchenmusik.* Potsdam, 1931-1934.

Bojanowsky, Paul von. *Das Weimar Johann Sebastian Bachs.* Weimar, 1903.

Bonenberg, Johann. *See* Buno, Johann.

Borris-Zuckermann, Siegfried. *Kirnbergers Leben und Werk und seine Bedeutung für den Berliner Musikkreis um 1750.* Kassel, 1933.

Bovicelli, Giovanni Battista. *Regole, Passagi di Musica, Madrigali, e Motetti passeggiati.* Venice, 1594.

Brockes, Barthold Heinrich. *Der für die Sünden dieser Welt garmarterte und sterbende Jesus (1712). (Deutsche Literaturdenkmäler in Entwicklungsreihen,* Vol. 6.) Leipzig, 1933.

Brodde, Otto von. *Johann Crüger, Sein Weg und sein Werk.* Leipzig, 1936.

⸻. *Leben und Werke von Johann Gottfried Walther.* (Münsterische Beiträge zür Musikwissenschaft, Vol. 7.) Kassel, 1937.

Büttner, Horst. *Das Koncert in den Orchestersuiten G. Ph. Telemanns.* Wolfenbüttel and Berlin, 1935.

Bukofzer, Manfred F. *Music in the Baroque Era.* New York, 1947.

Bunge, Rudolph. "Johann Sebastian Bachs Kapelle zu Cöthen und deren nachgelassene Instrumente," *Bach Jahrbuch* (1905), 14-47.

Buno, Johann. *Historische Bilder, darinnen Idea Historiae Universalis, Eine kurze summarische Abbildung der fürnehmsten geist-und weltlichen Geschichte durch die vier Monarchien . . . von den ersten Zeiten der welt an biss auff das jetzige 1672te Jahr . . . in annehmlichen Bildern . . . deutlich für gestellet, . . .* Lüneburg, 1672.

⸻. *Philippi Cluuerii Introdutionis in universam geographiam, tam veterem quàm novam,* libri VI. . . . Amsterdam, 1697.

Burney, Charles. *The Present State of Music in Germany, the Netherlands, and United Provinces.* 2 vols. London, 1773.

Burtt, Edwin Arthur. *The Metaphysical Foundations of Modern Physical Science; A Historical and Critical Essay.* Rev. ed. Garden City, New York, 1932.

Cannon, Beekman C. *Johann Mattheson, Spectator in Music.* New Haven, 1947.

Carse, Adam. *The Orchestra in the Eighteenth Century.* Cambridge, England, 1940.

Cebes of Thebes. *Pinax.* Amsterdam, 1689.

Chrysander, Friedrich. *G. F. Händel.* 3 vols. (3rd vol. incomplete). Leipzig, 1858-67.

Clark, James Midgley. *The Great German Mystics. Eckhart, Tauler, and Suso.* Oxford, 1949.

Couperin, François. *L'art de toucher le Clavecin.* Translated into German by Anne Linde and English by Mevanwy Roberts. Leipzig, 1933.

——. "Dedications" and "Prefaces," in *Oeuvres Complètes de François Couperin,* ed. Maurice Cauchie (12 vols.; Paris, 1932-1933). Vol. II: "Mùsique de clavecin I," pp. 5-11; Vol. III: "Mùsique de clavecin II," pp. 3-8.

Curtius Rufus, Quintus. *The Life of Alexander the Great.* Translated by John C. Rolfe. Cambridge (Mass.), 1946.

Dalla Casa, Girolamo. *Il Vero Modo di Diminuir.* Venice, 1584.

Dampier, Sir William Cecil Dampier. *A History of Science and Its Relations with Philosophy and Religion.* Cambridge, England, 1929.

Dannreuther, Edward. *Musical Ornamentation.* 2d ed. 2 vols. London, 1924.

David, Hans T., and Arthur Mendel. *The Bach Reader, A Life of Johann Sebastian Bach in Letters and Documents.* New York, 1945.

Denifle, Heinrich Séuse. *Taulers Bekehrung. Kritisch untersucht.* Strasbourg, 1879.

Dolmetsch, Arnold. *The Interpretation of the Music of the XVII and XVIII Centuries.* New ed. London, 1944.

Dommer, Arrey von. *Handbuch der Musikgeschichte.* 3rd ed., re-edited by Arnold Schering. Leipzig, 1914.

Dufourcq, Norbert. *Jean-Sébastien Bach, le maître de l'orgue.* Paris, 1948.

Ehmann, Wilhelm. *Adam von Fulda als Vertreter der ersten deutschen Komponisten-Generation.* Berlin, 1936.

Eitner, Robert. *Biographisch-bibliographisches Quellen-Lexicon der Musiker und Musikgelehrten der christlichen Zeitrechnung bis zur Mitte des 19. Jahrhunderts.* 10 vols. Leipzig, 1900-1904.

——. "Johann Gottfried Walther," *Monatschefte für Musikgeschichte,* Jg. 4, No. 8 (1872), 165-68.

Erdmannsdörffer, Bernhard. *Deutsche Geschichte vom Westfälischen Frieden bis zum Regierungsantritt Friedrich's des Grossen, 1648-1740.* Berlin, 1892-1893.

"Ernesti, Johann August," *Allgemeine Deutsche Biographie* (56 vols.; Leipzig, 1875-1912), VI, 235-41.

Faber, Heinrich. *Compendiolum musicae pro incipientibus.* Braunschweig, 1548.

Falck, Martin. *Wilhelm Friedemann Bach, sein Leben und seine Werke.* Leipzig, 1913.

Fellerer, Karl Gustav. "J. S. Bachs Bearbeitung der 'Missa sine nomine' von Palestrina," *Bach Jahrbuch,* Jg. 24 (1927), 123-32.

Finck, Hermann. "Hermann Finck über die Kunst des Singens, 1556." Translated by R. Schlecht, with an introduction by R. Eitner. *Monatshefte für Musikgeschichte,* Jg. 9 (1879), No. 9, pp. 130-34; No. 10, pp. 135-41.

Fischer, Kuno. *Geschichte der neuern Philosophie.* 8 vols. (Vol. 1 is entitled

Vorlesungen über Geschichte der neueren Philosophie; Vol. 7 was not published; Vol. 8 is of the "Neue Gessammtausgabe.") Stuttgart, Mannheim, Heidelberg, 1852-1893.

Flade, Ernst. "The Organ Builder Gottfried Silbermann," *Organ Institute Quarterly,* IV, No. 4 (Autumn, 1954), 38-57.

Flemming, Willi. *Oratorium, Festspiel. (Deutsche Literatur; Sammlung litterarischer Kunst- und Kulturdenkmähler in Entwicklungsreihen,* Vol. 6.) Leipzig, 1933.

Forkel, Johann Nicolaus. *Allgemeine Geschichte der Musik.* 2 vols. Leipzig, 1788, 1801.

———. "On Johann Sebastian Bach's Life, Genius, and Works," translated by Mr. Stephenson (1808) in Hans T. David and Arthur Mendel, *The Bach Reader, A Life of Johann Sebastian Bach in Letters and Documents* (New York, 1945), pp. 293-356.

"Francke, August Wilhelm," *Allgemeine Deutsche Biographie* (56 vols.; Leipzig, 1875-1912), VII, 233-35.

Freyse, Conrad. *Eisenacher Documente um Sebastian Bach, im Auftrage der Neuen Bachgesellschaft.* Leipzig, 1933.

Gass, Wilhelm. *Geschichte der Protestantischen Dogmatik in ihrem Zusammenhange mit der Theologie überhaupt.* 4 vols. Berlin, 1854-1867.

Gehrmann, Hermann. "Johann Gottfried Walther als Theoretiker," *Vierteljahrsschrift für Musikwissenschaft,* VII (1891), 468-578.

Geiringer, Karl. *The Bach Family. Seven Generations of Creative Genius.* New York, 1954.

Gerbert, Martin, freiherr von Hornau. *Scriptores ecclesiastici de musica sacra potissimum. . . .* Saint Blasius, 1784.

"Gerhard, Johann," *Allgemeine Deutsche Biographie* (56 vols.; Leipzig, 1875-1912), VIII, 767-771.

Gerhard, Johann, ed. *Schola Pietatis, Das ist: Christliche und Heilsame Unterrichtung was für Ursachen einem jeden wahren Christen zur Gottseligkeit bewegen sollen . . . Nunmehro mit des seeligen . . . Authoris Evangelischem Weegweiser (verfertiget von D. Beern) . . . samt . . . Registern vermehret.* 2 parts. Nuremberg, 1719, 1718.

Gerhardt, Friedrich. *Geschichte der Stadt Weissenfels, a. S. mit neuen Beitragen zur Geschichte des Herzogtums Sachsen-Weissenfels.* Weissenfels a. S., 1907.

Goldschmidt, Hugo. *Die Lehre von der vokalen Ornamentik.* Charlottenburg, 1907.

———. *Die Musikästetik des 18. Jahrhunderts und ihre Beziehungen zu seinem Kunstschaffen.* Zürich, 1915.

Goodrich, Wallace. *The Organ in France.* Boston, 1917.

Gottsched, Johann Christoph. "Erste Gründe der gesammten Weltweisheit" (Leipzig, 1733-34), in *Das Weltbild der deutschen Aufklärung; philosophische Grundlagen und literarische Auswirkung: Leibniz, Wolff, Gottsched, Brockes, Haller,* ed. Fritz Brüggemann (Leipzig, 1930).

———. *Versuch einer critischen Dichtkunst, durchgehends mit den Exem-*

peln unsrer besten Dichter erläutert. Austatt einer Einleitung ist Horazens Dichtkunst übersetzt und mit Anmerkungen erläutert . . . 3d revised ed. Leipzig, 1742.

Graeser, Wolfgang. "Bachs 'Kunst der Fuge'," *Bach Jahrbuch,* Jg. 21 (1924), 1-104.

Gurlitt, Wilibald. *Die Wandlungen des Klangideals der Orgel im Lichte der Musikgeschichte.* Augsburg, 1926.

Hamel, Fred. *Johann Sebastian Bach.* Göttingen, 1951.

Harnack, Adolf von. *History of Dogma.* Translated from the 3rd German edition by Neil Buchanan. 7 vols. in 4. New York, 1961.

Hausswald, Gunther. *J. D. Heinichens Instrumental-Werke.* Leipzig, 1937.

Hegel, Georg Wilhelm Friedrich. *Geschichte der Philosophie.* Leiden, 1908.

Heinichen, Johann David. *Der General-Bass in der Composition.* Dresden, 1728.

————. *Neu erfundene und gründliche Anweisung . . . . . , zu vollkommener Erlernung des General-Basses.* Hamburg, 1711.

Henderson, Ernest Flagg. *A Short History of Germany.* 2d ed. 2 vols. New York, 1916, 1917.

Herbst, Johann Andreas. *Musica Poetica sive Compendium Melopoeticum, ...* Nuremberg, 1643.

————. *Musica Practica sive Instructio pro Symphoniacis, ...* Nuremberg, 1642.

Hertel, Richard. *Arnstadt un seine Umgebung.* Arnstadt, 1924.

Herz, Gerhard. *Johann Sebastian Bach im Zeitalter des Rationalismus und der Frühromantik.* Bern, Leipzig, 1936.

Horric de Beaucaire, Charles Prosper Maurice, comte. *A Mésalliance in the House of Brunswick,* from the French of Viscount Horric de Beaucaire. London, 1886.

Hunold, Christian Friedrich *(pseud.* Menantes). *Die allerneueste Art höflich und galant zu schreiben, oder auserlesene Briefe, in allen vorfallenden auch curiosen angelegenheiten, nützlich zu gebrauchen.* 4th ed. Hamburg, 1709-1710.

————. *Auserlesene und theils noch nie gedruckte Gedichte unterschiedener berühmten und geschickten Männer, zusammengetragen und nebst seinen eigenenen an das Licht gestellet von Menantes.* 3 vols. Halle, 1718-1720.

"Hutter, Leonhard," *Allgemeine Deutsche Biographie* (56 vols.; Leipzig, 1875-1912), XIII, 476-79.

Hutter, Leonhard. *Compendium Locorum Theologicorum. Addita Sunt Excerpta ex Jo. Wollebii et Ben. Picteti Compendiis.* With an introduction by A. Twesten. Berlin (Hertz), 1855.

————. *Compendium Locorum Theologicorum. Das ist kurtzer Begriff al ler Articulu Christlicher Glaube Latein, Itzo aber . . . in die teutsche Sprache übersetzt durch Leonhard Hüttern.* Wittenberg, 1610.

Jansen, Martin. "Bachs Zahlensymbolik, an seinen Passionen untersucht," *Bach Jahrbuch,* Jg. 34 (1937), 96-117.

Jeppeson, Knud. *Counterpoint.* Translated, with an introduction by Glen Haydon. New York, 1939.

Jordan, Reinhard. *Aus der Geschichte der Musik in Mühlhausen. (zur Geschichte der Stadt Mühlhausen in Thüringen,* Heft 8, No. 5) Mühlhausen, 1905.

————. *Chronik der Stadt Mülhausen in Thüringen,* 5 vols. Heinrichshofen, 1900-1906.

Josephus, Flavius. *The Works of Flavius Josephus with a life written by himself.* Translated by William Whiston. 3 vols. New York, 1902.

Jung, Carl Gustav. *Psychological Types; or The Psychology of Individuation.* Translated by H. Godwin Baynes. New York, 1923.

Junghans, W. *Johann Sebastian Bach als Schüler der Particularschule zu St. Michaelis in Lüneburg.* Lüneburg, 1870.

Kade, Otto. *Die ältere Passionskompositionen bis zum Jahre 1631.* Gütersloh, 1893.

Kinsky, Georg Ludwig. *Die Originalausgaben der Werke J. S. Bachs.* Wien, 1937.

————. "Zur Echtheitsfrage der Berliner Bach-Flügels," *Bach Jahrbuch,* Jg. 21 (1924), 128-38.

Kircher, Athanasius. *Musurgia universalis, sive Ars magna consoni et dissoni* (in x. libros digesta). Rome, 1650.

————. *Neue Hall-und Thon-kunst (oder Mechanische geheim-verbindung der kunst und Natur).* . . . Translated by Agatho Carione (*pseud.*). Nördlingen, 1684.

Kirnberger, Johann Philipp. *Gedanken über die verschiedene Lehrarten in der Komposition, als Vorbereitung zur Fugenkenntniss.* Berlin, 1782; reprinted in Vienna, 1793.

————. *Grundsätze des General-Basses als erste Linien zur Composition.* Berlin, 1781.

————. *Die kunst des reinen Satzes in der Musik.* . . . 2 vols. Berlin, 1771-1779.

"Kittel, Johann Christian," *Allgemeine Deutsche Biographie* (56 vols.; Leipzig, 1875-1912), XVI, 45-46.

Kleefeld, W. "Bach und Graupner," *Jahrbuch der Musikbibliothek Peters,* IV (1897).

Kloppenburg, W. C. M. "Een achtiende eeuwe Methode om Sonates uit de Mouw te schudden," *Mens en Melodie,* V (1950), 357-58.

Köstlin, Heinrich Adolf. "Luther als der Vater des evangelischen Kirchengesanges," *Sammlung musikalischer Vorträge,* III (1881), 34.

Kretschmar, Hermann. "Algemeines und Besonderes zur Affectenlehre," *Jahrbuch der Musikbibliothek Peters* (1911).

Kuhn, Max. *Die verzierungs-Kunst in der Gesangs-Musik des 16.-17. Jahrhunderts (1535-1650). (Publikationen der Internationalen Musikgesellschaft,* Vol. 7.) Leipzig, 1902.

Landowska, Wanda. "Bach und die französische Klaviermusik," *Bach Jahrbuch,* Jg. 7 (1910), 33-44.

Lang, Paul Henry. *Music in Western Civilization.* New York, 1941.

Langer, Susanne K. *Philosophy in New Key: A Study in the Symbolism of Reason, Rite, and Art.* Cambridge, 1942.

Latourette, Kenneth Scott. *Christianity in a Revolutionary Age; History of Christianity in the Nineteenth and Twentieth Centuries.* 3 vols. New York, 1959-1961.

Lavisse, Ernest. *Histoire de France depuis les origines jusqu'à la Revolution.* 9 vols. in 17. Paris, 1900-1911.

Lorbeer, Johann Christoph. *Lob der Edlen Musik.* Weimar, 1696.

Luther, Martin. *Martin Luther, Deutsche Messe 1526.* With a preface in facsimile edited by J. Wolf. Kassel, 1934.

———. *Luthers Schriften,* ed. Eugen Wolff. (*Deutsche National-Litteratur,* Vol. 15.) Stuttgart, 1891-1892. "Tischreden," pp. 425-34; "Von der Musika," pp. 425-26; "Frau Musica," pp. 375-76.

———. *D. Martin Luther's Werke; Kritische Gesammtausgabe . . . ,* ed. J. K. F. Knaake, G. Kawerau, E. Thiele and others. Weimar, 1883-1963". Von Ordnung Gottesdienst in der Gemeine (1523)," XII, 31; "Deutsche Messe und Ordnung Gottesdienst (1526),"' XIX, 44; "Lob und Preis der Himmelischen Kunst Musica," L, 368-74.

———. *Von der Freiheit eines Christenmenschen* (Wittenburg, 1520). (*Neudruche deutscher Literaturwerke,* No. 18, pp. 15-37.) Halle, 1879.

Marpurg, Friedrich Wilhelm. *Des kritische Musikus an der Spree erster Band.* Berlin, 1750.

Mattheson, Johann. *Behauptung der himmlischen Musik aus Gründen der Vernunft.* Hamburg, 1747.

———. *Grundlage einer Ehren-Pforte. . . .* Hamburg, 1740.

———. *Der neue Göttingsche . . . urtheilende Ephorus, . . . wegen der Kirchen-Musik.* Hamburg, 1727.

———. *Das neu-eröffnete Orchestre. . . .* Hamburg, 1713.

———. *Plus Ultra, Ein Stückwerck.* Hamburg, 1754-1755.

———. *Sieben Gespräche der Weisheit und Musik. . . .* Hamburg, 1751.

———. *Der vollkommene capellmeister.* Hamburg, 1739.

Menantes. *See* Hunold, Christian Friedrich.

Menck, Hans Friedrich. *Die Musik im Roman.* Heidelberg, 1872.

Mendel, Arthur. "On the Keyboard Accompaniments to Bach's Leipzig Church Music," *Musical Quarterly,* XXXVI (July, 1950), 339-62.

Meyer, Joachim. *Unvorgreiflich Gedanken über die neulich eingerissene theatralische Kirchenmusik und die darin bisher üblich geworden Cantaten.* Lemgo, 1726.

Meyer, Rudolf W. *Leibnitz and the Seventeenth-century Revolution.* Translated by J. P. Stern. Cambridge, England, 1952.

Miesner, Heinrich. "Ungedruckte Briefe von Philipp Emanuel Bach," *Zeitschrift für Musikwissenschaft,* Jg. 14, Heft 4 (January, 1932), 224-26.

Mizler, Lorenz. *Musikalische Starstecher. . . .* Leipzig, 1739-1740.

———. *Neu eröffnete musikalische Bibliothek, oder gründliche Nachricht nebst unparteiischem Urteil von musikalischen Schriften und Büchern.* 4 vols. Leipzig, 1739, 1743, 1752, 1754.

Mizler, Lorenz. *See* Adam von Fulda.

Monroe, Paul. *History of Education.* New York, 1933.

Moser, Hans Joachim. "Gesangstechnische Bemerkungen zu Johann Sebastian Bach," *Bach Jahrbuch*, Jg. XV (1918), 117-32.

"Müller, Heinrich," *Allgemeine Deutsche Biographie* (56 vols.; Leipzig, 1875-1912), XXII, 555-56.

Müller von Asow, Erich H. *Johann Sebastian Bach, Gesammelte Briefe.* Regensburg, 1938.

Nebel, Paul. "Leonhard Hutters Compendium," *Jahrbücher für das klassische Altertum*, Jg. 5, X, p. 329.

Neumann, Werner. *Handbuch der Kantaten Joh. Seb. Bachs.* Leipzig, 1947.

Neumeister, Erdmann. *See* Hunold, Christian Friedrich.

Neumeister, Erdmann. *Fortgestzte fünfffache Kirchen-Andachten in Drey neuen Jahrgängen auf alle Sonn- und Fest- auch Apostel-Trage. . . .* Hamburg, 1726.

Niedt, Friedrich Erhard. *Handleitung zur Variation. Wie man. . . . aus einem schlechten Gb. Praeludia, Ciaconen. . . . u. dgl. . . . Verfertigen könne*, verbessert. . . . u. mit. . . . Anm. u. einem Anh. v. mehr als 60 org. -Werken versehen durch J. Mattheson. Hamburg, 1721.

———. *Musikalische Handleitung. . . . Tl. 1*, handelt vom Gb. denselben schlechtweg zu spielen. Hamburg, 1700.

———. *Musikalisches A B C.* Hamburg, 1708.

———. *Mus. Handleitung Tl. III, Handelnd v. Contra-Punct, Canon, Motetten, choral, Recitativ-Stylo u. Cavaten*, op. posth. hrsg. v. J. Mattheson. Hamburg, 1717.

Orel, Alfred. "Die Katholische Kirchenmusik von 1600 bis 1750," in *Handbuch der Musikgeschichte*, ed. Guido Adler (2d ed.; Berlin, 1929), I, 507-36.

Paulsen, Friedrich. *Geschichte des gelehrten Unterrichts auf den deutschen Schulen und Universitäten vom Ausgang des Mittelalters bis zur Gegenwart, mit besonderer Rücksicht auf klassischen Unterricht.* 2 vols. Leipzig, 1896-1897.

Pfeiffer, August. *Anti-Calvinismus, oder Unterricht von der Reform.* Lubeck, 1729.

———. *Antimelancholicus, oder Melancholey-Vertreiber . . . Zum andermahl mit Fleiss revidiret.* 2 parts. Leipzig, 1684.

Pirro, André. *Dietrich Buxtehude.* Paris, 1913.

———. *L'Esthétique de J. S. Bach.* Paris, 1907.

———. *J. S. Bach.* Paris, 1906.

Plamenac, Dragan. "New Light on the Last Years of Carl Philipp Emanuel Bach," *Musical Quarterly*, XXXV (October, 1949), 565-87.

Plato. *The Dialogues of Plato.* Translated by Benjamin Jowett. 4 vols. New York, 1937.

Praetorius, Michael. *Syntagma musicum. . . . (1614-1619).* Facsimile edition, ed. by Wilibald Gurlitt. (Documenta Musicologica, Erste Reihe: Druck-schriften-Faksimiles, XXI, XIV, XV.) Kassel, 1949, 1958.

Preuss, Hans. *Bachs Bibliothek.* Leipzig, 1928.

Preussner, Eberhard. *Die Methodik im Schulgesang der evangelischen Latein-schulen des 17. Jahrhunderts.* (Ein Beitrag zur Geschichte des Schulge-sanges.) Berlin, 1924.

Printz, Wolfgang Caspar. *Historische Beschreibung der edelen Sing- und Klingkunst.* . . . Dresden, 1690.

―――. *Phrynis Mitilenaeus, oder Satyrischer Componist, welcher vermit-telst einer satyrischen Geschichte, die Fehler der ungelehrten . . . Com-ponisten höflich darstellet.* . . . Published in 3 parts: I, 1676; II, 1677; III, 1679. First complete edition: Dresden and Leipzig, 1696.

Prout, Ebenezer. *Double Counterpoint and Canon.* London, 1891.

Quantz, Johann Joachim. *Versuch einer Anweisung die Flöte traversiere zu spielen.* Berlin, 1752.

Rautenstrauch, Ernest Paul Johannes. *Die Kalandbrüderschaften das kul-turelle Vorbild der Sachsischen Kantoreien. Ein Beitrag zur Geschichte der kirchlichen Musikpflege in vor- und nachreformatorischer zeit.* Dresden, 1903.

Reese, Gustave. *Music in the Middle Ages.* New York, 1940.

Richter, Bernard Friedrich. "Johann Sebastian Bach und die Universität Leip-zig," *Monatschefte für Musikgeschichte,* Jg. 33, No. 7 (1901), 101-20.

―――. "Joh. Seb. Bach und die Universität zu Leipzig," *Bach Jahrbuch,* Jg. 22 (1925), 1-10.

―――. "Stadtpfeifer and Alumnen der Thomasschule in Leipzig zu Bachs Zeit," *Bach Jahrbuch,* Jg. 4 (1907), 32-78.

―――. "Die Wahl Johann Sebastian Bachs zum Kantor der Thomasschule i. J. 1723," *Bach Jahrbuch* (1905), 48-67.

Riemsdijk, J. C. M. van. "Jan Adam Reincken," *Tijdschrift der Vereeniging voor Nederlandsche Muziekgeschiedenis,* VI (1887), 151-58.

Rietschel, Georg. *Die Aufgabe der Orgel im Gottesdienst bis in das 18. Jahr-hundert.* Leipzig, 1892.

Robinson, James Harvey and Charles A. Beard. *The Development of Modern Europe; An Introduction to the Study of Current History.* New York, 1907-1908.

Rognoni, Riccardo. *Pasaggi per potersi essercitare nel diminuire terminata-mente con ogni sorte d'Instromenti et anco diversi pasaggi per la semplice voce humana.* Venice, 1592.

"Rome in the Absence of Pompey," *The Cambridge Ancient History,* ed. S. A. Cook, F. E. Adcock, M. P. Charlesworth (12 vols.; Cambridge, 1924-1939), IX, 475-505.

Rudloff, Johann Christian. *Geschichte des Lyceums zu Ohrdruf.* Arnstadt, 1845.

Rust, Wilhelm. *BG,* XVII, xiii-xxii.

Sachs, Curt. *The History of Musical Instruments.* New York, 1940.

————. *Sammlung alter Musik-instrumente bei der staatliche Hochschule für Musik zu Berlin.* Berlin, 1922.

————. *World History of the Dance.* New York, 1937.

Sannemann, Friedrich. *Die Musik als Unterrichtsgegenstand in den Evangelischen Lateinschulen des 16 Jahrhunderts. Ein Beitrag zur Geschichte des Schulgesanges.* Berlin, 1904.

Scheibe, Johann Adolph. *Abhandlung vom Ursprung und Alter der Musik insonderheit der Vokalmusik.* Altona and Flensburg, 1754.

————. *Der Critische Musikus.* 2d ed. Leipzig, 1745.

Scheibler, Christoph. *Geistliche Goldgrube nebst Trauer- Leichen- und Busspredigten.* 2 parts. Leipzig, 1727.

Schenker, Heinrich. *Ein Beitrag zur Ornamentik.* Vienna, 1903.

Schering, Arnold. "Bach und das Symbol," *Bach Jahrbuch,* Jg. 34 (1937), 83-95.

————. "Joh. Phil. Kirnberger als Herausgeber Bachscher Choräle," *Bach Jahrbuch,* Jg. 15 (1918), 141-50.

————. *Johann Sebastian Bach und das Musikleben Leipzigs im 18 ten Jahrhundert. (Musikgeschichte Leipzigs,* Vol. 3.) Leipzig, 1941.

————. *Johann Sebastian Bachs Leipziger Kirchenmusik. Studien und Wege zu ihrer Erkenntnis.* Leipzig, 1936 and 1954.

Schlosser, Friedrich Christoph. *History of the Eighteenth Century and of the Nineteenth till the Overthrow of the French Empire; With Particular Reference to Mental Cultivation and Progress.* Translated with a Preface by D. Davison. 8 vols. London, 1843-1852.

Schlosser, Julius. *Die Kunst- und Wunderkammern der Spätrenaissance; ein Beitrag zur Geschichte des Sammelwesens.* Leipzig, 1908.

Schmid, Ernst Fritz. *Carl Philipp Emanuel Bach und seine Kammermusik.* Kassel, 1931.

Schmieder, Wolfgang. "Johann Sebastian Bach als Briefschreiber," *Bach Jahrbuch,* Jg. 37 (1940-1948), 126-33.

————. *Thematisch-systematisches Verzeichnis der musikalischen Werke von J. S. Bach.* Leipzig, 1950.

Schröder, Otto. "Zur Biographie Johann Walters (1496-1570)," *Archiv für Musikforschung,* V (Leipzig, 1940), 12-16.

Schünemann, Georg. *Geschichte der Deutschen Schulmusik.* Leipzig, 1928.

————. "Geschichte des Dirigierens," in Hermann Kretzschmar, *Kleine Handbuch der Musikgeschichte nach Gattungen* X (Leipzig, 1913).

————. *Wilhelm Werkers Bach-Buch. (Zeitschrift für Musikwissenschaft,* Jg. 5, 1922-1923), 461-66.

Schweitzer, Albert. *J. S. Bach.* Translated by Ernest Newmann. 2 vols. London, 1911.

Seibel, Gustav Adolph. *Das Leben des Hofkomponist Johann David Heinichen.* Leipzig, 1913.

Serauky, Walter. "Andreas Werckmeister als Theoretiker," in *Festschrift Max Schneider zum 60. Geburtstag* (Halle, 1935), 118-25.

Sietz, Reinhold. "Friedrich Erhardt Niedt," *Das Musikleben,* V (January, 1952), 15-16.

Smend, Friedrich. *Bach in Köthen.* Berlin, 1951.

———. *Die evangelische Deutsche Messe bis zu Luthers Deutsche Messe.* Göttingen, 1896.

Sorge, Georg Andreas. *Gespräch zwischen einem Musiko Theoretico und einem Studio Musices.* Lobenstein, 1748.

Spener, Philipp Jakob. . . . *Pia Desideria,* ed. Kurt Aland. Berlin, 1955.

Spitta, Philipp. *Johann Sebastian Bach: His Work and Influence on the Music of Germany 1685-1750.* Translated by Clara Bel and J. A. Fuller-Maitland. 3 vols. in 2. New York, 1951.

———. "Der Tractat über den Generalbass und F. Niedt," *Musikgeschichtliche Aufsätze* (1894).

Sponsel, Johann Ulrich. *Orgelhistorie.* Nuremburg, 1771.

Sturm, Christoph Christian.

Tauler, Johann. . . . *Ausge wählte predigten Johann Taulers,* ed. Leopold Naumann. Berlin, 1933.

———. [*Predigten.*] *Sermon des groszgelarten in gnadé erlauchté doctoris Johannis Tauleri.* . . . Leipzig, 1498.

———. . . . *Predigten auff alle Sonn- und Feyertage durchs gantze Jahr, samt dessen ubrigen geistreichen Schriften, ingleichen auch D. Martin Luthers, Philipp Melanchthons, Johann Arnds und anderer gottseliger Lehrer zeugniese von solchen Predigten und Schriften.* . . . With a preface by Dr. Philipp Jacob Spener. Leipzig, 1720.

Teggart, Frederic John. *Theory of History.* New Haven, 1925.

Terry, Charles Sanford. *Bach, A Biography.* London, 1928.

———. *Bach's Chorales.* 3 vols. Cambridge, 1915-1921.

———. *Bach's Orchestra.* London, 1932.

———. *J. S. Bach's Cantata Texts, Sacred and Secular.* London, 1926. Tholuck, D. A. *Geschichte des Rationalismus.* Berlin and Halle, 1865.

Thomas, Friedrich August. *Einige Ergebnisse über Johann Sebastian Bachs Ohrdrufer Schulzeit aus der Matrikel des Lyceums geschopft.* Ohrdruf, 1900.

Tiersot, Julien. *Les Couperin.* Paris, 1926.

Tillich, Paul. *Systematic Theology.* Chicago, 1951.

Tovey, Donald Francis. *A Companion to "The Art of the Fugue" (Die Kunst der Fuge) [of] J. S. Bach.* London, 1931.

Troeltsch, Ernest. *Gesammelte Schriften.* 4 vols. Tübingen, 1922-1925.

———. "Leibnitz und die Anfaenge des Pietismus." Tübingen, 1925.

Türk, Daniel Gottlob. *Klavierschule, oder Anweisung zum Klavierspielen für Lehrer und Lernende.* . . . (Leipzig and Halle, 1789). Facsimile ed., edited by Erwin R. Jacobi. (Documenta Musicologica, Erste Reihe: Druckschriften-Faksimiles, XXIII.) Kassel, 1962.

Vaihinger, Hans. *The Philosophy of "As If": A System of the theoretical, practical, and religious fictions of Mankind.* Translated by C. K. Ogden. New York, 1924.

Vogel, August Hermann. *Christian Friedrich Hunold (Menantes). Sein Leben seine Werke.* . . . Lucka S.-A., 1897.

Vorbaum, Reinhold, ed. *Evangelische Schulordnungen.* 3 vols. Gütersloh, 1858-1864.

Walther, Johann Gottfried. *Musikalisches Lexicon oder musikalische Bibliothek* (1732). Facsimile reprint edited by Richard Schaal. (Documenta Musicologica, Erste Reihe: Druckschriften-Faksimiles, III). Kassel, 1953.

Wedgewood, James Ingall. *Dictionary of Organ Stops.* London, 1907.

Weissgerber Diakonus. *Johann Sebastian Bach in Arnstadt.* Arnstadt, 1904.

Werckmeister, Andreas. *Cribum musicum, oder Musicalisches sieb.* . . . Quedlinburg and Leipzig, 1700.

————. *D. A. Steffani, Abtes von Leipzig des Heil. Apostolischen Stuhls Protonotarii Send-Schreiben.* Quedlinburg, 1699.

————. *Der Edlen Music-kunst Würde, Gebrauch und Missbrauch.* Quedlinburg, 1691.

————. *Erweiterte und verbesserte Orgel-Probe.* . . . Quedlinburg, 1698.

————. *Harmonologia musica.* . . . Frankfurt and Leipzig, 1702.

————. *Hypomnemata Musica, oder mus. memorial* . . . *von der Composition und Temperatur.* Quedlinburg, 1697.

————. *Musicae mathematicae hodegus curiosus.* . . . 2d ed. Frankfurt and Leipzig, 1687.

————. *Musikalische Paradoxal-Discourse.* Quedlinburg, 1707.

————. *Musikalische Temperatur.* Frankfurt and Leipzig, 1686/87, 1691.

————. *Die nothwendigsten Anmerckungen und Regeln, wie der Bassus continuus.* . . . *könne tractiret werden.* 2d ed. Ascherleben, 1715.

————. *Organum gruningense redivivum;* . . . Quedlinburg and Ascherleber, 1705.

Wette, Gottfried Albin de. *Historische Nachrichten von der berühmten Residenz-Stadt Weimar.* . . . Weimar, 1737.

————. *Kurzgefasste Lebens Geschichte der Herzoge zu Sachsen welche vom Churfürst Johann Friedrich an, bis auf den Herzog Ernst August Constantin, zu Weimar regieret haben.* Weimar, 1770.

Windelband, Wilhelm. *Die Geschichte der neuren Philosophie in ihrem Zusammenhange mit der allgemeinen Cultur und den besonderen Wissenschaften.* . . . Leipzig, 1878.

————. *A History of Philosophy.* Reprinted from rev. ed. of 1901, translated by James H. Tufts. New York, 1958.

Wöhlke, Franz. *Lorenz Christoph Mizler, Ein Beitrag zur musikalischen Gelehrtengeschichte des 18 Jahrhunderts.* (Musik und Geistesgeschichte, no. 3.) Würzburg-Aumuehle, 1940.

Wolf, Abraham. *The History of Science, Technology, and Philosophy in the 18th Century.* 2d ed., revised by D. McKie. London, 1952.

Wolff, Christian Friedrich von, Baron. "Vernünftige Gedanken von Gott, der Welt und die Seele des Menschen auch alle Dingen überhaupt," *in Das Weltbild der deutschen aufklarung,* ed. Fritz Brüggemann (Leipzig, 1930), pp. 47-195.

————. *Vernünfftige Gedancken von Gott, der Welt, und der Seele des Menschen... Neue Auflage.* Halle, 1751.

Wolffheim, Werner. "Mitteilungen zur Geschichte der Hofmusik in Celle (1635-1706) und über Arnold M. Brunckhorst," in *Festschrift zum 90. Geburtstage Sr. Exz. des Wirklichen geheimen Rates Rochus Freiherrn von Liliencron....* (Leipzig, 1910), 421-39.

Wolfrum, Philipp. *Die Entstehung und erste Entwicklung des deutschen evangelischen Kirchenliedes in musikalischer Beziehung....* Leipzig, 1890.

Wolgast, Johannes. *Georg Böhm, ein Meister der Übergangszeit vom 17. zum 18. Jahrhundert.* Berlin, 1924.

Wustmann, Rudolf. *J. S. Bachs Kantatentexte.* Leipzig, 1913.

————. *Bis zur Mitte des 17. Jahrhunderts.* (*Musikgeschichte Leipzigs*, Vol. I). Leipzig and Berlin, 1909.

Ziegler, Marianne von. *Vermischte Schriften in Gebundener und Ungebundener Schreibart.* Göttingen, 1736.

Zielinski, Tadeusz. *Cicero im Wandel der Jahrhunderte.* Leipzig and Berlin, 1912.

Music Publications

d'Anglebert, J. H. *Pièces de Clavecin* (1689). "Publications de la Société française de Musicologie," ed. Marguerite Roesgen-Champion, Ser. I, Vol. 8. Paris, 1934.

Le Bègue, Nicolas. *Oeuvres complètes d'Orgue.* "Archives des Maîtres de l'Orgue des XVIe, XVIIe, et XVIIIe Siècles," ed. A. Guilmant, Introduction by A. Pirro, Vol. 9. Paris, 1909.

Bach, Johann Sebastian. *Johann Sebastian Bach's Werke*, ed. Bach-Gesellschaft. 47 vols. Leipzig, 1851-1899 and 1926. Vols. 1-46 reprinted in Ann Arbor, Michigan, 1947.

Böhm, Georg. *Samtliche Werke: Klavier- und Orgelwerke*, ed. Johannes Wolgast, 2 vols. (Leipzig, 1927-1932). Second revised edition by Gresa Wolgast. Wiesbaden, ca. 1952.

Buxtehude, Dietrich. *Ausgewählte Orgelwerke*, ed. Hermann Keller. 2 vols. Peters No. 4449. Leipzig, 1938.

————. *Dietrich Buxtehude: Abendmusiken und Kirchenkantaten.* DdT, XIV, ed. Max Seiffert. Leipzig, 1903.

————. *Dietrich Buxtehudes Instrumentalwerke: Sonaten für Violine, Gambe und Cembalo.* DdT, XI, ed. Carl Stiehl. Leipzig, 1903.

Couperin, François. *Oeuvres Complètes.* Paris, 1932-1933.

Fasch, Johann Friedrich. Concerto in F major for 2 oboes, 2 bassoons, 2 horns, strings and continuo, in *Gruppen-Konzerte der Bachzeit. Das Erbe deutscher Musik*, XI, ed. Karl Michael Komma, pp. 74-100. Wiesbaden, 1962.

————. (Selected chamber music), ed. Hugo Riemann. *Collegium Musicum.* Vols. 8-13. Leipzig, n.d.

————. "Sonata für zwei Oboen, Flöten oder Violinen, und Basso Continuo." Nagels Musik-Archiv, No. 56, ed. Ludwig Schäffler. Hannover, 1930.

Fischer, Johann Caspar Ferdinand. *Journal de Printemps* in *Orchestermusik des XVII. Jahrhunderts*. DdT, X, ed. Ernst von Werra, pp. 1-87. Leipzig, 1902.

――――. *Ariadne Musica* in *Deutsche Meister des 16. und 17. Jahrhunderts II. Liber Organi*, Vol. 7, ed. Ernst Kaller. Mainz, Schott (No. 2267), 1935.

Franck, Johann Wolfgang, Georg Böhm, and Peter Laurentius Wockenfuss. *Heinrich Elmenhorsts Geistlich Lieder*. DdT, XLV, ed. Joseph Kromotlicki and Wilhelm Krabbe. Leipzig, 1911.

Heinichen, Johann David. Concerto in C major for 4 flutes, strings, and continuo in *Gruppen-Konzerte der Bachzeit*. *Das Erbe deutscher Musik*, XI, ed. Karl Michael Komma, pp. 56-73. Wiesbaden, 1962.

Hurlebusch, Konrad Friedrich. Concerto for 2 oboes, bassoon, solo violin, and string orchestra in *Instrumentalkonzerte deutscher Meister*. DdT, xxix/xxx, ed. A. Schering, pp. 273-300. Leipzig, 1906.

Löwe, Johann Jakob. *Johann Jakob Löwe von Eisenach: Two Suites for String Orchestra and Basso Continuo*. Nagels Musik-Archiv, No. 67, ed. Albert Rodemann. Kassel, 1930.

Merulo, Claudio. *Toccate d'intavolatura d'organo. . . . Libro primo . . . 1598*, ed. Sandro Dalla Libera. Venice, Ricordi (No. 2626), 1958.

Muffat, Georg. *Florilegium I (1695)*, *Florilegium II (1698)*, DTÖ I/2 [vol. 2] and II/2 [vol. 4], ed. Heinrich Rietsch. Vienna, Artaria, 1894, 1895.

Muffat, Gottlieb. "Suite in B flat major," in *Early Keyboard Music*, ed. Louis Oesterle and Richard Aldrich. Vol. II, pp. 83-103. New York, Schirmer (No. 1560), 1904.

Raison, André. *Livre d'Orgue* in Guilmant: *Archives des Maîtres de L'Orgue des XVIᵉ, XVIIᵉ, et XVIIIᵉ Siècles*. Vol. 2. Paris, 1899.

Reincken, Jan Adam. *Hortus Musicus*, ed. J.C.V. van Riemsdijk. Maatschappij tot bevordering der Toonkunst, Vereeniging voor Nederlands Muziekgeschiedenis, Vol. XIII. Amsterdam and Leipzig, 1886.

Telemann, Georg Philipp. *Tafelmusik* (1733). DdT, LXI and LXII, ed. Max Seiffert. Leipzig, 1927.

――――. *Vierundzwanzig Oden* (1741). DdT, LVII, ed. Wilhelm Krabbe, pp. 1-28. Leipzig, 1917.

――――. "Concerto for violin and string orchestra, 2 flutes, 2 oboes, 2 trumpets, and timpani," in *Instrumentalkonzerte deutscher Meister*. DdT, XXIX/XXX, ed. Arnold Schering, pp. 103-95. Leipzig, 1906.

――――. "Concerto in D major for 3 trumpets, tympani, 2 oboes, strings, and continuo"; "Concerto in B flat major for 2 flutes, 2 oboes, violin, 2 violas, cello, contrabass and continuo," in *Gruppen-Konzerte der Bachzeit*. *Das Erbe deutscher Musik*, II, ed. Karl Michael Komma, pp. 3-25; 26-55. Wiesbaden, 1962.

INDEX

Abel, Carl Friedrich, 148
Abel, Christian Ferdinand, 148
accentuation, Bach's use of, 174-76
Adlung, Jakob, 93, 94, 172
Agricola, Johann Friedrich, quoted on Bach's organ, 92; on Silbermann, 94; on Bach and the pianoforte, 172
Ahle, Johann Georg, 77-78, 100
Albinoni, Tomaso, 118
Alcuin, 39
Altnikol, Johann Christoph, 285
Anglebert, Jean-Henri d', 85
Aria di Postilione, 67-68
Arndt, Johann, Pietism of, 105, 271; quoted on Tauler, 108; quoted on God, 111
Arnold, Johann Heinrich, 14
Arnstadt, Germany, 58-65, 74-78, 96
Art of the Fugue, 277, 280-82, 285-86
Augsberg Confession, 21
August II of Saxony, 22, 234
August III of Saxony, 262-63

B Minor Mass, 192-94, 262-64
Bach, Ambrosius (father), 8, 9
Bach, Anna Magdalena (wife), knowledge of French, 16; character and marriage, 151-52; notebook of, 162; musical education from husband, 164; Lutheranism of, 179; Leipzig life, 187; mentioned, 207; travels to Cassel, 244; bears last child, 274; sad lot as widow, 288, 289
Bach, Carl Philipp Emanuel (son), memories of Bach clan, 8; memoirs of, 55; and use of grace notes, 83; on father's use of ornamentation, 85-88; on father's registration, 93; on father's library, 122; on father's reaction to opera house, 128; schooling of, 144; as father's pupil, 151; on father's preference for clavichord, 170-71; comment on pianoforte, 173; and *B Minor Mass*, 194; mentioned, 209; on Mizler, 257; orthodoxy of, 258; presents father to Frederick the Great, 274; on canons, 280; note on father's death, 281; on father's last days, 284-85; applies for father's post as cantor, 287
Bach, Caroline. *See* Bach, Johanna Caroline
Bach, Christian. *See* Bach, Johann Christian
Bach, Elisabeth (daughter), 285
Bach, Emanuel. *See* Bach, Carl Philipp Emanuel
Bach, Friedemann. *See* Bach, Wilhelm Friedemann

Bach, Heinrich, 79
Bach, Johann Christian (son), 148, 258, 288
Bach, Johann Christoph (brother), 11, 14, 47
Bach, Johann Christoph (cousin), 9
Bach, Johann Christoph Friedrich (son), 215
Bach, Johann Elias (cousin), 273
Bach, Johann Ernst (cousin), 70, 78
Bach, Johann Gottfried Bernhard (son), 59, 144, 151
Bach, Johann Jacob (brother), 67
Bach, Johann Michael (father-in-law), 79
Bach, Johann Sebastian, modern man's emotional response to, 1-2, 5; Luther's influence on, 2-5; education centered in theology, 2-5; early years, 8-17; schooling at Eisenach *Gymnasium*, 9-10; orphaned, 11; musical training at Ohrdruf *Klosterschule*, 11-14; enters Knights' Academy in Lüneburg, 14-17; theological focus of education, 18-27; shares Lutheran death desire, 20; classical curriculum of, 20-24; reconciles spirit and matter: incorporates secular music into religious works, 26-27; historical understanding conditioned by Lutheranism, 28-37; indifference to integrity of past styles, 36; views on musical speculation, 36-37; musical education in school, 38-47; as chorister, 41; Italian singing methods' influence on, 45; study of other men's masterpieces, 47; education as organist, 48-55; organist Böhm's influence on, 48-50; exposure to French music at Celle court, 51-55; first job at Duke Johann Ernst's Weimar court, 59-60; organ as favorite instrument of, 62; as organist at Arnstadt, 62-66; immature compositions of Arnstadt period, 66-69; journeys to Lübeck to study with Buxtehude, 70-72; *Passacaglia* compared with Buxtehude's, 72-74; resigns from Arnstadt after court hearings, 74-78; becomes organist at *Mühlhausen*, 77-79; marriage to cousin Maria, 79; ornamentation of, 80-88; score of "A Mighty Fortress" compared with Buxtehude's, 80-81; Italian and French influences on, 81-88; genius as independent of any one national style, 87-88; powerful organ registration of, 92-93; preference in organs, 97; music as means to transcendental end, 99; musical creativity thwarted by Pietism in Mühlhausen, 100-12; city council commissions can-